BEST BOOK OF 2002 (Fiction), Southeast Booksellers Association

"*The Bridge* is about massive, indomitable human spirit and a powerful long-ing for freedom. Marlette writes with extraordinary grace, humor, and with such bursts of force that I was left in perfect wonder at the novel's close."

—Kaye Gibbons, author of *Ellen Foster*

"*The Bridge* is a remarkable book. I've long known that Doug Marlette sees his world more clearly than the rest of us. Now I know that he writes better about it too. What can I say? A novelist is born."

—Anne Rivers Siddons, author of *Nora, Nora*

"*The Bridge* is an exciting story about an amazing woman. . . . Guns are pulled, shots are fired, things happen."

—Linda Wertheimer, *All Things Considered*, National Public Radio

"Doug Marlette takes us deep into the heart of America, and deeper into the American heart. Marlette writes with acuity and intelligence, with broad hu-mor and a precise, loving attention to detail. His past and present not only lives and breathes, it lingers and it haunts your soul."

—Joe Klein, author of *Primary Colors*

"*The Bridge* [is] magic. . . . [Marlette] patch[es] together a quilt of life that is, in the end, so bright and beautiful that it is overwhelming."

—*Montgomery Advertiser*

"*The Bridge* [is] a great story—exuberant, proud, myth-challenging—and Mar-lette has a great, Dickensian time with the telling. . . . The plot is filled with clever foreshadowing and a series of physical conflicts that progress to a vio-lent denouement. . . . Pick and his Mama Lucy are complicated characters finding their ways to subtle truths. . . . *The Bridge* is a hugely ambitious novel. It encompasses history, myth, sexual politics, and family psychosis, and it takes some good satirical pokes at twenty-first-century life along the way. . . . Doug Marlette has done a novelistic good deed in digging up this buried and crucial piece of Southern history, and clearly he's had some fun doing it."

—Valerie Sayers, *Washington Post Book World*

Erica Berger

About the Author

DOUG MARLETTE is a Pulitzer Prize–winning
editorial cartoonist. He lives in North Carolina
with his wife and son. *The Bridge* is his first novel.

The
BRIDGE

DOUG MARLETTE

Perennial
An Imprint of HarperCollinsPublishers

A hardcover edition of this book was published in 2001 by HarperCollins Publishers.

THE BRIDGE. Copyright © 2001 by Doug Marlette. All rights reserved. Printed in the United States of America. No part of this book may be used or reproduced in any manner whatsoever without written permission except in the case of brief quotations embodied in critical articles and reviews. For information address HarperCollins Publishers Inc., 10 East 53rd Street, New York, NY 10022.

HarperCollins books may be purchased for educational, business, or sales promotional use. For information please write: Special Markets Department, HarperCollins Publishers Inc., 10 East 53rd Street, New York, NY 10022.

First Perennial edition published 2002.

Designed by Joseph Rutt

The Library of Congress has catalogued the hardcover edition as follows:
Marlette, Doug.
The bridge / Doug Marlette.—1st ed.
p. cm.
ISBN 0-06-018630-5
1. Grandmothers—Fiction. 2. Women in the labor movement—Fiction. 3. North Carolina—
Fiction. 4. Cartoonists—Fiction. I. Title.
PS3563.A6729 M35 2001
813'.54—dc21
2001016839

ISBN 0-06-050521-4 (pbk.)

02 03 04 05 06 ❖/RRD 10 9 8 7 6 5 4 3 2 1

How should we be able to forget those ancient myths that are at the beginning of all peoples, the myths about dragons that at the last moment turn into princesses; perhaps all the dragons of our lives are princesses who are only waiting to see us once beautiful and brave. Perhaps everything terrible is in its deepest being something helpless that wants help from us.
—*The Dragon-Princess*
Rainer Maria Rilke

PROLOGUE

Whenever I asked my father why his mother was such a piece of work he would answer, "Your grandmother's had a hard life." The implication was that she had not always been that way. But I knew only the Holy Terror version of my grandmother, the version I grew up with, the blue-haired ayatollah who dominated her family and frightened and humiliated me as a child, marking my impressionable young psyche indelibly, informing my relationships with women forever, and supplying me with radar, distant early warning, for Chernobyl Woman, the domineering female, and her secret sharer, the passive, gelded male.

"Put her away, Clayton." My grandmother's insistent tone scared me. "You've got to put Mary Alice away for her own good and for the sake of the boy. If you won't do it, I will."

Mama Lucy, as everyone in my small world called her, was sitting in our kitchen talking with my father. It was after midnight in late July 1959, and I was supposed to be asleep in my bedroom off the hallway, but I lay there wide awake, listening intently to their troubling conversation. Despite their hushed whispers and the low hum of the window fan, I could hear every word they were saying through the paper-thin walls of our modest ranch-style house in Delaney, North Carolina.

My father was weeping. "I can't, Mother."

"She's a danger to herself," she replied. I didn't know why my mother had been taken to Burlington this time, but she had been hospitalized for her "nerves" before, and whenever that happened my father would fetch his mother from her house not far from the hospital. She'd stay with us in Delaney forty miles away, cooking and cleaning and keeping an eye on me after school until my mother got well enough to come back to us.

"Now listen to me," Mama Lucy commanded. "You've got to be

strong, Clayton, and do what needs to be done. You've got to put her away!"

"I can't do it," he sobbed. "I can't."

At ten years old, I had never heard my father cry before. He was a World War II Marine Corps veteran and U.S. Marines didn't cry. But he did that night, and so did I. His voice caught as he choked back tears of frustration and despair in front of Mama Lucy in our tiny kitchen. "I can't send Mary Alice to that place, Mother. Don't ask me to do it. There's got to be more we can do."

I didn't know exactly what Mama Lucy meant by "put her away." It reminded me of when my dog got hit by a car and we took him to the vet, who explained as the dog whimpered and moaned that there was nothing he could do, that Laddie had to be put away. I cried and cried when my father and I left the vet's office without the collie pup who waited for me on the porch every afternoon and ran barking to greet me when he spied me walking down the street with my book bag after school, who frolicked with me on the lawn every day, and slept with me in my bed each night. My mother did her best to console me, but I didn't eat for a week after that, or speak to my father, and wailed, "I just want Laddie," whenever the subject of getting another dog was brought up.

Nor did I know where "that place" was, but I knew from my father's reaction that it was worse than the hospital in Burlington and farther away and there was something cruel and irrevocable about it, like death. And he couldn't face it.

I lay there awhile in the dark contemplating the unthinkable—that they would do the same thing with my mother that they had done with my dog. I got out of bed and moved through the shadowed hallway. I peeked around the corner, blinking into the smoky yellow light of the kitchen, and saw them sitting at the table: my father, his back to me, drinking a bottle of Pabst Blue Ribbon, chain-smoking Luckies and stubbing ashes into an ashtray overflowing with butts, and my grandmother sitting opposite him, her face in shadow as she hunched over a pot of butterbeans she was shelling for tomorrow's dinner. Her fingers nimbly snapped the pods and peeled back the hulls and dropped the beans into the pot, discarding the peels in a brown paper bag on the floor by her side. My father lit another cigarette with the silver lighter my mother had given him for Christmas. Suddenly Mama Lucy leaned into the light, clutched my father's arm, her jaw set and her face twisted with fierce intensity.

"Be a man, son," she urged. "She's been to every doctor, tried every drug. There's nothing you can do for her now. She belongs in an institution where they can take care of her and watch out for her. You and Pick can't help her none. She's beyond that now."

I brought the devotion of an only child to the question of what to do with the beautiful but troubled woman who was my mother, a devotion bordering on worship. Not only had she fed and clothed and loved me, but she had also championed me, defending the tender, softer, more vulnerable places in a boy's heart that are not always acknowledged in a hostile and indifferent world. For that I would always be grateful. She had nurtured my budding talent as an artist, always making sure I had plenty of paper and pencils and crayons around to draw whenever the urge struck. When I was four years old and only just starting to discover that I could squeeze pictures from my fingers, make my hand replicate with a pencil or chalk, however crudely, a rough facsimile of whatever my eye beheld, my mother, recognizing my talent, would take me for walks in the neighborhood and teach me to look more deeply at the shapes, contours, and lineaments of nature, to observe more attentively its textures and outlines and to see its colors more profoundly.

"What color is the sky, Pickard?" she would ask.

"Blue," I would answer.

"Look again. Can you see the yellow?" And I would look again and say, "No, it looks blue to me." Then she would point to a particular patch of sky and I would stare until my eyes beheld the heavens flecked with yellow and green and orange.

Then she would take me to the library and we would check out books on the French Impressionists and the Renaissance masters and she would show me how their colors were not flat and limited, one-dimensional like the Crayola crayons she bought me by the bushels, but were made up of many tints, hues, and shades. I don't know how this unschooled, untrained, overtly unartistic woman who, to my knowledge, didn't paint or even draw, learned to see like that, but I would always be grateful that she perceived in a simple stroll around Delaney—an unprepossessing town if there ever was one—the palettes of Monet, Cezanne, and Seurat or Winslow Homer. In doing so, my mother ignited my imagination and set free my own powers of perception forever.

In time I learned to answer her queries more adroitly.

"What color are the tree leaves, Pick?"

"Besides green, I see yellows and blues and oranges and pinks at the top where the light reflects from the sun. And the shadows are deep purples and reds." It became a joke between us. "What color is the apple, Pick?" "Blue, Mama." "And the banana?" "Violet and pink."

Of course, she made sure I had my own library card by the time I could write my name. And by passing on to me her own love of books and stories, she opened me up to a world beyond Delaney and the suffocating confines of our family. Her gentle encouragement ignited in me a passion for learning and stoked a curiosity about the wider world that would never be doused. She was my chief advocate and a tireless encourager of my gifts, and she countenanced no dissent from within or without the family. When a second-grade teacher recognized my artistic flair and suggested drawing lessons, my mother made my father drive me to art classes twenty miles away on his Saturdays off. When I saw a cartooning correspondence course advertised on a matchbook cover and sent away for the talent test, she talked my penurious father into paying for the mail-order lessons we couldn't afford and that I was probably too young to take. The previous summer, when I submitted drawings to my favorite artist at *Mad* magazine and received a standard rejection slip from a staffer who intercepted his mail, she wrote a ferocious letter of rebuke to the magazine's editor for allowing such a callous underling to dash the hopes of a nine-year-old boy.

Like many talented, intelligent women of her time and place with limited opportunities, my mother invested all in her only child. I became her agent, the one through whom she vicariously achieved her own unarticulated dreams and aspirations. My mother was my champion and I was hers. I would do anything to protect her as she would me, and I could not understand why that alone was not enough.

As I stood there in the dark listening to my father's plaintive pleas and protests I felt a knot in my chest and a hollowness in the pit of my stomach. Finally it began to sink in what Mama Lucy meant by putting my mother away. From time to time I had heard my father threaten Mama with Appalachian, the state psychiatric facility, but always in moments of frustration and despair, when the futility of trying to cajole and humor her out of her moods became too much for him. He would warn her that if she didn't stop crying he would have her committed to the "looney bin" in Asheville. I knew that was where they put crazy people and that my mother didn't want to go there. She'd had a taste of the trauma of such places during her short stays in the Burlington hospital's psychiatric unit and the look of panic in her eyes as he threatened told me she wanted no more of it. But I knew at the time, and I suspect so did my mother, that my father's threats were as transitory as smoke and that he could never send her away. I could not say the same for my grandmother's.

Though my father ultimately made the decision to commit my mother, I held Mama Lucy responsible. For it had all started that July night when I was ten years old, the night I learned to despise my grandmother. That was when I knew for sure that she was my mother's foe and therefore my enemy, too. I dreamed of the day we would receive a call saying Mama Lucy had died of a stroke or a heart attack, or was killed in a car wreck. We would all go to the funeral and weep and pray over her and tell stories about her life and lies about how we would miss her. When the call didn't come, I killed off my grandmother in my dreams.

I successfully avoided Mama Lucy and her snuff-stained kisses for most of my adult life. And if it had not been for my own public humiliation when my pride and temper sent me careening helplessly at mid-life back into the vortex of the family I was ashamed of and the region I had so desperately tried to escape, I never would have seen her again. It was not until I was stripped of my livelihood and left standing face-to-face with the woman I had spent a lifetime avoiding that I began putting together the stories of my family and the clues to our identity that had been for so long buried. And it was not until then that Mama Lucy, like Sophocles' monstrous sphinx—part woman, part beast, part bird of prey—challenging Oedipus on the road to Thebes, posed her own riddle to me, the answer to which, I had no way of knowing at the time, my life depended upon my figuring out.

PART I

DRAWING IN

A GIFT FOR
PISSING PEOPLE OFF

The cartoon showed a close-up of the pope wearing a button emblazoned with the words "No Women Priests." An arrow pointed from the inscription "Upon This Rock I Will Build My Church" to his forehead. Once I hit upon the idea, I drew it up quickly, faxed a copy to the Long Island office, sent the original to production by messenger, and forgot about it until it ran the next day in both the city and island editions of the *Sun*, as all my cartoons did. I knew it was a decent lick—not especially outrageous by my lights, but effective. After two decades drawing political cartoons it was pretty much second nature to me, and I could usually feel how they were going to land. And though I knew I'd drawn cartoons with more raw voltage, more reader irritation potential per square inch, I felt pretty good about this one.

It was a Pick Cantrell cartoon all right. It said what I wanted to say and nobody else would say it quite that way. I thought it would set off some tremors and rearrange the landscape a bit. Was it good for me? That's the only question any artist can ask himself about his work. The earth moved all right. But I didn't anticipate all the aftershocks.

As a political cartoonist, I have a gift for pissing people off. I receive hate mail on a regular basis, and sometimes death threats. The raw, visceral quality in my work comes naturally to me and has always surprised me. Sometimes it feels as if I'm merely a conduit, channeling somebody else's anger and attitude. My talent is like a pit bull on a very long leash, and each day when I take it out for a stroll I hold on for dear life.

In fact, there has always been something "non sequitur" about my drawings, as if their edge and meanness do not follow logically from me and my personality. "You don't *look* like your drawings," readers often comment upon first meeting me. "I always pictured you as short, dark, and bearded." My work seems angry, anarchistic, dangerous. But "sweet" was the word I most often heard used to describe me personally. On the surface I seem mild-mannered and easygoing. Physically, I am lanky, standing six-feet, two inches, blond, and blue-eyed, with the countenance of a child. Even now, as the crow's-feet impinge, and my hairline recedes, and my chins multiply, I appear open-faced, and harmless, like some Sunbelt Rotarian. I feel like an assassin. "Man, that was a mean cartoon," say readers. "Thank you," I reply. "You're just saying that."

Had I not come of age in the tumultuous sixties I probably would have wound up drawing a comic strip about cats. But the temper of those times set off something in me that sought expression in political cartoons. Bad times for the Republic are great times for satire.

I went to college on a football scholarship at a time when campuses across the nation were in upheaval over the war in Vietnam. Even a sleepy college town like Tallahassee was ablaze with insurrection when I arrived my freshman year at Florida State. Mass demonstrations, ROTC building takeovers, and bomb threats were nearly daily occurrences at the "Berkeley of the South." You could not pass through the student union without being accosted, harangued, and leafleted by partisans from SDS to Campus Crusade for Christ. After the dullness of my hometown, the volatility of campus life was thrilling, even more bracing than the drills and calisthenics I endured at afternoon practice.

Freshman year brought two catastrophic personal blows that would change my life in ways I had never dreamed. First, my mother died, just before my eighteenth birthday. Not long after, I injured my knee badly during a game. I would never be able to play football again. Whether or not these two events were connected I'll never know, but in some perverse way, they seemed serendipitous. My mother's death fueled my rage. And with the knee injury I lost my identity as an athlete, honed over the previous four years. I kept my scholarship, but with neither my mother nor football to anchor me I was bereft and directionless and immediately began looking beyond the classroom for an outlet for my numerous frustrations. Art became a way to hold on to the woman who had first encouraged my talents. I signed up for courses in still life and figure drawing and I soon started doodling caricatures of campus celebrities and prominent politicians in the margins of my notebooks and sketchpads. After a friend showed my satirical sketches to the editor of the student newspaper, the *Seminole*, I became the political cartoonist for the antiwar campus daily. I had found a home.

The newsroom, chock-full of bright, funny student radicals, was combustible. My work exploded. I drew three cartoons a week for the rest of my college days, and made a name for myself in the arena of opinion and ideas in a way my football exploits never had afforded me. My cartoons lampooned everyone from state legislators to the president of the university to the president of the United States. When Disney announced plans to build Disney World in the middle of Florida's orange groves, I drew a cartoon showing a Mickey Mouse in tourist getup asking impoverished migrant workers, "Which way to the Magic Kingdom?" It caught the attention of editors from the St. Petersburg and Miami newspapers, both of whom reprinted it and expressed interest in hiring me after graduation. I was on my way.

Six months out of college, after being lucky enough to draw a high number in the first draft lottery, thus obviating my need to choose between jail and Canada, and after a brief stint working night paste-up at the *St. Petersburg Tribune*, I landed a cartooning job at the *Charlotte Sentinel*, the biggest, most influential newspaper in North Carolina. My work immediately began making noise, attracting readers, hate mail, and reprints in national magazines. During my first year my antiwar, pro-amnesty, anti–death penalty cartoons created such a stir that Thomas Gallant, the man who owned the newspaper chain that owned our paper, and his brother, our absentee publisher Joseph Gallant, wanted me fired. They never ordered it directly, because it flew in the face of their much-vaunted reputations for non-interference in the editorial product of their newspapers. But the Gallants badgered my editors, who moved my drawings from the editorial to the op-ed page to distance the cartoons from the masthead of the paper.

My work catapulted me through the ranks of my profession and made my reputation as a *political* political cartoonist. During the seventies and eighties, my drawings got me in trouble with readers and occasionally with my own editors and publishers. And then in the late eighties I won the Pulitzer Prize for my cartoons on brown lung disease. They were part of a series the paper ran that exposed health hazards in the textile industry, and to my satisfaction and the satisfaction of the reporters who wrote the series, resulted in legislation that improved conditions in the workplace.

The Pulitzer could not have come at a better time. It was a first for my newspaper, and my bosses felt vindicated after all the heat they had taken for my work over the years, but secretly I saw it as my ticket to New York

City. For a variety of reasons, I had harbored a lifelong fantasy of living there. I was offered a job with the *Sun*. I had a wonderful wife, a beautiful two-year-old boy, a new job, and the Pulitzer Prize, and now we were moving to New York City, the Land of Oz.

The *Sun* was a successful Long Island newspaper owned by the *Boston News-American* newspaper chain. They were starting a New York City edition to compete with the other tabloids and the *Times* for a share of the huge market, and they needed a top cartoonist to stir the pot. My arrival was marked with great fanfare, with television commercials, rack cards, subway and commuter-train posters, and newspaper ads showing a photograph of a drawing pen with a wisp of smoke rising from the pen-point and my signature "Pick Cantrell" over it with the headline SEMI-AUTOMATIC ASSAULT WEAPON.

I arrived at the start of the new decade, just after the fall of the Berlin Wall and the end of world communism. New York City had just elected its first black mayor. George Bush was in the White House, Bill Clinton was still in Little Rock, and I was in the Big Apple. I had just turned forty-one years old and was running on all cylinders professionally, surfing the zeitgeist and having a ball. I should have checked my temper at the Mason-Dixon line.

My pope cartoon ran on a Friday in early August. The public reaction lit up the *Sun* switchboard like the night sky over Baghdad during the Persian Gulf War. Outraged readers bombarded the publisher, the editors, and me with howls of protest. "Sacrilege!" they screamed. "Blasphemy!" "I'm canceling my subscription!" "Fire Pick Cantrell!" My boss, editorial page editor Richard Kerfield, who had okayed the drawing for publication, called me at home Sunday night. "It's been a rough weekend and I have some bad news," he announced. "We're going to run an apology for the pope cartoon."

"Apologize?" I replied. "Why?"

"It was a mistake to run the drawing."

"How can expressing an opinion be a mistake?"

"You crossed the line. It was offensive to Catholics."

"What Catholics?" I fumed. "Catholic friends of mine liked it. They showed it to priests and nuns at a First Communion ceremony and they roared."

"The phone's been ringing off the hook. We can't get any work done. We've had a lot of negative reaction."

"It's August. People have nothing better to do than call the news-paper. You warned me yourself New Yorkers go bonkers in August."

"Look, you don't understand the history here," he said, alluding to my having worked for the *Sun* for only five and a half years. "The paper's relationship with the Catholic Church has always been rocky. This goes beyond the cartoon. Out here on the Island we're perceived as Jewish, secular and anti-Catholic. Your cartoon exacerbates a sensitive situation."

"What do you mean?"

"We made some mistakes in our coverage years ago. We didn't have a religion editor, and for a long time our news editor didn't take the religion beat seriously. He'd assign it to college interns and kids fresh out of journalism school, you know, late-sixties investigative types . . . secular Jews, agnostics, atheists. They resented covering what they considered church socials. Their attitudes showed in the stories. Maybe we were insensitive. It's been a sore point. The diocese complained, organized boycotts, had parishioners cancel subscriptions. And your cartoon played into it."

"Richard, my cartoon wasn't disrespectful," I said. "It's not disrespectful to satirize and criticize public figures. It's disrespectful not to. You secular humanists always get bullied by religious fanatics because they actually believe something and you don't. I'm sorry there's this history, but why should we take the rap because news-side showed poor editorial judgment in the past? You're just compounding the error."

"We're running the apology tomorrow. I just wanted you to know." Kerfield was retreating into his end-of-discussion, *fait accompli* posture — the last resort of the editor who's run out of arguments. I had to talk fast.

"Richard, it's a mistake. It'll demoralize the staff. If the *Sun* apologizes for cartoons we'll apologize for stories, too. The paper will look weak. The kooks and nuts will hammer us even more."

"That may be, but . . ."

Kerfield was the kind of guy who could make fog look flashy and ostentatious, but he seemed even more cautious and uptight than usual. "What's going on, Richard? I mean, I've had my share of disagreements with editors and publishers over the years, but an apology! This is a first."

"It's a first for all of us." He sighed.

"You don't think we should do it, do you?"

"Do what?"

"Apologize."

"It's my decision. We're running it."

"It's Garvis, isn't it? You took a lot of heat for running the cartoon and now you're falling on the grenade for the publisher, aren't you?" Kerfield may have had the backbone of a jellyfish but he possessed a Machiavellian survival instinct and a nose for the publisher's rectal regions.

"It's my decision, Pick. But if you want, you can write a dissenting view on the op-ed page. It's only fair to give you a chance to make your case. It's your call."

I tried to contain my anger. "Let me think about it."

The apology ran in the middle of the editorial page in Monday morning's paper.

MEMO TO READERS

On Friday, the *Sun* ran an editorial cartoon by Pick Cantrell, which, while conceived as critical comment on the recent papal declaration that women can never rise to the priesthood, was perceived by many readers as ridiculing the pope and the Roman Catholic Church. This was not the *Sun*'s intention. An editorial cartoonist's chief tools are symbols and imagery. With them, an artist telegraphs a message—pointed, funny, or both. It is unfortunate, and we regret, that any readers were given an unintended message in Friday's cartoon.

Cowards! I thought, sipping my coffee at the drawing board in my midtown office early that morning. The soft pink glow of summer smog-filtered dawn seeped through the bamboo slats of the shades on my window. The *Sun*'s Manhattan offices occupied a couple of floors in a landmark art deco building on Park Avenue. The newsroom on the other side of the glass panels of my corner office wouldn't come alive for another three hours, which was fine with me. I preferred working early in the morning, before the phones started ringing and all the other distractions took over. It was my best, most productive time for thinking. Or, as was the case this morning, brooding.

"This is New York, for Chrissakes," I muttered. I raised the blinds and gazed out the window at the surge of protoplasm spilling out of the Thirty-third Street subway station. "New Yorkers don't apologize for opinions. That's like a butcher fainting at the sight of blood." I dumped the rest of my coffee in the sink.

My wife, Cameron, had not wanted to move to Manhattan. She was a southern girl who loved our life in her native Charlotte and did not understand my New York obsession. Maybe I never should have left the South, I thought as I cleaned my sable-hair brush with soap and water in the sink. It was a consideration I had not allowed myself lately but one that I entertained almost daily the first year after we moved to the city. Walking down the street to buy bagels on weekend mornings exhausted me. The myriad assaults on the senses, the jackhammers, car alarms, ambulance sirens, screaming street crazies and homeless panhandlers in your face demanding money, the petty humiliations and relentless buffeting of one's vulnerabilities that the city routinely forces you to endure inspired a nostalgia for home in me that I never knew I possessed. The small-town southerner's natural curiosity and openness to experience is forced to shut down.

Talent as a currency is devalued in the city. Big fish from small ponds elsewhere are made mere minnows, to be swallowed up in the vast oceans of ambition, achievement, and narcissism that is Manhattan.

Shortly after we arrived in the city of my dreams, Cameron and I attended our first New York dinner party. Gathered in the parlor of the sumptuous brownstone were a number of our new neighbors—a world-famous heart surgeon, a legendary recluse novelist, a network anchor woman and her investment banker husband, a pop music mogul and his wife, and a celebrated artist.

After some obligatory small talk, Rita, the hostess, introduced me to the artist, who was famous for his *Time* magazine cover portraits and sketches for *The New Yorker*. He was a short, balding man with small, raisin-like eyes and the face of a ferret, and I had admired his work immensely. "They tell me you're a famous political cartoonist," he said.

"Do they?"

"I never heard of you," he said.

Typical of New York, the men were all witty and acerbic and the women elegant and flirtatious, except for the woman who later glared at me across the dinner table like a prosecutor at the Nuremberg trial as I conversed with our hostess about the neighborhood pre-school Wiley would be attending. My southern drawl seemed to unnerve her, to call to mind images of the gap-toothed banjo player from *Deliverance*. Every time I opened my mouth my IQ dropped below room temperature. Finally, in a vaguely British accent she asked, "I gather you're not from around here?"

"No, ma'am," I said. "How could you tell?"

My attempt at levity seemed only to annoy her and she quizzed me as though I were, indeed, a retarded child.

"Then where are you from exactly?"

"Charlotte, most recently," I said.

"Charlotte?" Her nose squinched, as if I had answered Kazakhstan.

"Yes, ma'am, but my people are from the North Carolina Piedmont. Alamance County, between Greensboro and Chapel Hill. Around Burlington, Graham, Saxapahaw, Mebane, Haw River, that area." I heard myself, like so many southerners with our overdeveloped sense of place, putting too fine a point on it, nailing down the locale with a kind of perverse specificity somehow motivated by an acute awareness of her infinite indifference.

"I don't see how anyone could possibly stand living down there with those people."

"Those people? You mean my kinfolks?"

"Surely your relatives are not . . ." She smirked at Rita. "Oh, you know . . ."

I felt my pulse quicken. "Actually, I don't."

"Well"—she quaffed her wine—"I'm certainly not going to explain."

"Have you ever been down South?" I asked.

"Once. I did a commercial shoot down there somewhere—"

"Felicity's a TV producer and filmmaker, Pick," Rita said, desperately trying to head off disaster. Cameron, sitting at the far end of the table, offered no help.

"Raleigh. That was it. Dreadful place . . . I could never live down there."

Our hostess smiled diplomatically and asked, "Why not? I hear it's lovely."

Felicity looked at me. "I couldn't take all the racists down there."

"Yes," I said. "It's awful. So unlike this garden of racial harmony y'all got up here—Howard Beach, Bensonhurst, Crown Heights—hell, New York's a goddamn paradise of brotherly love!"

"How about some more roast duck?" Rita chirped, trying to pull the conversation out of the nosedive it had taken. She was right to be concerned. There was something about New Yorkers like my dinner companion that brought out every ounce of redneck defiance, awakened every strand of unreconstructed Confederate DNA, every rebellious

"Fergit, Hell! Git Yore Heart in Dixie or Git Yore Ass Out!" impulse lying like a dormant virus in my bloodstream, and caused the years and decades to fall away and dropped me in a thicket dressed in a makeshift uniform of butternut and gray, squinting down the barrel of my squirrel gun at Chancellorsville.

"It's worse down there." Felicity was one of those spindly, fashion-conscious New York women, with an unerring instinct for self-caricature, whose choice of hairstyle and makeup only accentuated her most unflattering features. She had worked diligently to achieve a look that, as a man, I found grotesque and sexless, but as a cartoonist I greatly appreciated. Her skin had the pallor of an anemic vampire, and her hair was tucked so tightly into her ballerina bun that it appeared to be painted on. Her earrings and jewelry were gigantic, possibly serving as ballast, counterweights to keep her facelifts tightly in place. Her dangling hoop earrings were so large I was tempted to set them on fire and wait for small animals to leap through them.

"Besides," she continued, "southerners just sound so . . . ignorant. I just can't take anything they say seriously. I'm a Democrat, of course, but I must say I could barely bring myself to vote for Jimmy Carter because of that accent of his."

"Well, ma'am"—the chill in my voice could have frozen hummingbirds in mid-flight—"where I come from we call that bigotry."

Suddenly, all conversation ceased at the table. The servers froze like ice sculptures, as did Rita. All eyes, except Cameron's, focused on me.

"True," I continued, "some of my people *are* racists and bigots. What do you expect from poor millhands and farmers. They may be narrow-minded and provincial but at least they have an excuse—they were deprived. I meet New Yorkers like you who have every advantage, yet for all their privilege and erudition they're the most ignorant suckers I ever saw."

"Please pass the bread, Pick," said Cameron, her face flushing.

"Hold on, Cam," I said.

"Pass the bread, Pick!"

Rita scrambled for the bread basket, desperate to do something, anything to appease somebody.

But I wasn't finished. "Rule number one in New York: Don't look. You rush down the street with your eyes straight ahead, to keep the homeless and the wackos at bay. Self-preservation, sure, but y'all seem to live your entire lives that way, with blinders on. Down home, ignorance and provinciality is an affliction—here it's a choice!"

"Southerners," the heart surgeon sneered to the anchor woman seated beside him. "They can't stop fighting the Civil War."

"You mean the War of Northern Aggression, don't you, sir? Seems to me y'all're the ones who can't let it go."

"Us? Please." He cackled and searched the table for allies.

"You brought it up," I replied.

"Preposterous."

I drained my glass. The alcohol hit my bloodstream like a bomb. "I got one word for you, hoss." I leaned toward him and enunciated clearly. "Appomattox."

Rita, who had watched helplessly as the conviviality of her dinner party vanished looked close to a nervous breakdown. Reduced to desperate measures, she blurted, "Let's have coffee and dessert on the terrace!"

My inquisitor, who had retreated into silence during my soliloquy, fearful that she might be blamed for things getting out of hand, locked her teeth in a tight smile and said, "I hope I haven't offended you."

"Not at all," I lied, as the party moved outside. "But just out of curiosity, Felicity: Your accent. Where are you from originally?"

"South Africa," she said.

"You belong here, Pick!" Bob Garvis had commented in our first interview. "It's about time New York had a first-class political cartoonist like you. It's long overdue." His pitch was effective. The appeal to my ego worked better than dangling a wad of cash. For some strange reason New York City, the birthplace of political cartooning in this country, the home of Thomas Nast, the father of American editorial cartooning, the inventor of such enduring symbols as the Republican elephant, Democratic donkey, even our image of Santa Claus, the very same city where he had single-handedly brought down Boss Tweed and Tammany Hall with his *Harper's Weekly* drawings, had produced no other heavyweights of editorial cartooning in the modern era. New York was a satirist's dream, but the city of *Mad* magazine, *National Lampoon*, *Saturday Night Live*, Lenny Bruce, Don Imus, and Howard Stern had fired blanks when it came to graphic political commentary. The *New York Times* had no editorial cartoonist and never would. It was a control thing. The newspaper of record was too uptight. They would never allow strong political cartoons to dominate their carefully calibrated editorial pages. Meanwhile, the city's tabloids had played host only to minor league artists. So when the *Sun* called offering the opportunity to practice my craft in the Big Apple I leaped at the chance. "We're invading the city, Cantrell, and you're going to help lead the charge!" is how Garvis put it.

But something was wrong with the newspaper. I could feel it from the day I came on board. The generals in charge should have been Shermans but they were all McClellans—soft, uncertain, ambivalent, and unwilling to do what was necessary to win. Perhaps because the *Long Island Sun* had always been a wealthy suburban monopoly that dominated its market for fifty years and never had to compete before, management brought a cautious journalistic style to the task of running the city edition. In a big league battleground that required bold, innovative flair and aggressiveness, the "tabloid in a tutu," as our competition called us, just didn't have the killer instinct.

The New York staff and the Long Island editors who supervised them were constantly at odds. Long Island resented New York. New York felt muzzled. We got the money and attention. Long Island felt they were subsidizing our indulgence. Management called it creative tension. Those of us who had to deal with the pettiness, hostility, and editorial undermining called it stupid and self-destructive. At a party once in the Park Avenue newsroom I looked around at the astonishing talent assembled there to fight the battle of New York and voiced my concerns to Vic Hennessy, the dapper, bearded columnist sipping champagne next to me. "Yeah," he wearily agreed. "This is the only rag in town where the whole is less than the sum of its parts."

Gazing out the window at Norman Thomas High School across the street I considered the irony of a city that named buildings for radical socialists but apologized for opinions. I looked at my watch. It was already nine o'clock. My morning had passed and I didn't have an idea for the next day's cartoon. I needed to get moving but the apology had gotten to me. Cameron had warned me about this. When would I learn to roll with the punches? Then I read the apology again, retrieved the original of the cartoon from my file cabinet, and stared at it for a moment, and feverishly penned a response. It ran the following day on the op-ed page under the anemic headline CANTRELL DEFENDS CARTOON. Remarkably, Richard had agreed to run it as written.

It was a withering screed that vented all my frustrations with New

York, the *Sun*, and too many years of dealing with faint-hearted publishers. I let it all out, chastising my editors for their lack of fealty to the First Amendment, observing that I had been censored more in New York than I ever was in the Bible Belt, and, in a kamikaze blaze of righteous indignation, pointing out that the *Sun*'s lackluster support for women priests was hardly surprising since our masthead revealed few women in leadership positions.

Kerfield called from his car phone late that afternoon. "Garvis wants to see you in his office. I just talked to him and he's pretty upset."

"About the cartoon?"

"And what you wrote in the piece defending it." I could barely hear him through the static.

"Goddammit, Richard! You invited me to write a response and I did. Now you're telling me Garvis is pissed because I took him up on his offer?" I was being sent to the principal's office and I didn't like it. "Richard, I don't have anything to say to Garvis that I didn't say in the piece."

"Look, I'm losing my signal. I gotta be at a Foreign Relations Council meeting in the city. He wants to see you in his office at eleven o'clock tomorrow morning. Let me know how it goes."

"But Richard, it's our wedding anniversary. I promised Cameron I'd get off early and take her to a matinee and dinner. The sitter's lined up and everything. We've planned this for months. She'll never forgive me if I miss it."

"Pick, this is serious. Garvis is really pissed off. You could have been a little more circumspect."

"I didn't exactly sneak it into the paper."

"I told you it was a mistake. I never should have run it."

"Richard, you ran the cartoon because it was a damned good cartoon and you know it. You're covering for Garvis. He caved to the nuts and you're taking the heat!"

Silence.

"Your quote in the *Post* didn't help either, Pick."

I cringed. In the past few days the cartoon had gotten a lot of ink. The *New York Post*'s Page 6 had run an item about the controversy and so had *The Village Voice*. *Editor and Publisher*, the trade journal, ran a tease across the top of their front cover, SUN REGRETS CANTRELL CARTOON. I was quoted in the *Post* piece saying, "I don't mind kissing the publisher's ring, but I just wish he would take it out of his back pocket." I groaned when I saw that, wondering why I couldn't hold my tongue. Although I knew the reporter was a hack with zero sense of humor, I didn't think he would quote me. But there it was. I had embarrassed Garvis in print in a rival newspaper in the city where he was trying to be taken seriously.

"Can't we do it later in the week?" I asked.

"I'd get it over with if I were you."

I stared at a copy of the pope cartoon that ran with the Page 6 article that someone left on my drawing board. It stared back at me.

"May I help you?" Arlene Potts, Garvis's austere gatekeeper with the pinched smile was seated at her post behind her tidy desk outside his office. She had the appearance of a fortress in a Chanel dress—her interior castle well ordered. I knew she recognized me, as I did her, but she made me go through the motions anyway.

"I have an appointment with Bob at eleven," I said, looking at my watch.

"Yes, Mr. Garvis will be late," she said, returning to her computer keyboard. "He suggested you come back at twelve."

"But I have an appointment back in the city at two," I said.

"I don't know anything about that." She smiled tightly. "But he's in a meeting and said he would see you at twelve."

I could feel the lava rising in the pit of my stomach. This was a set-up. The old unilateral tango of the passive-aggressive manager. He was trying to get a rise out of me, to throw me off-balance, to validate the management view of me as a wild man, the crazy artist. Cameron had warned me that he'd drop the handkerchief to see if I'd pick it up. And I had promised her I wouldn't, that I'd try to keep it in the road. "You may sit here and wait if you wish," said Arlene, forcing a saccharine smile.

"I'll come back at twelve," I answered, heading for the elevator and the company cafeteria for some coffee and a chance to cool off.

"Nice piece," said a reporter I ran into getting off the elevator.

"You still working here?" asked an editor getting on.

High noon. When Arlene finally showed me in, Robert Garvis was sitting behind his famous desk. Without making eye contact he motioned me to sit on the sofa facing him while he scanned the papers on his desk.

The desk was the first thing you noticed when you entered his office and it was the largest one I had ever seen. Earlier in the century it was given to his esteemed predecessor, Harold Eisenburg, the founder and first publisher of the *Sun*, whose portrait hung on the wall behind the desk, by his friend President Franklin Delano Roosevelt, in gratitude for the paper's early support of New Deal policies. The antique mahogany desk with its ornate trim and intricate hand-carving looked out of place in the otherwise contemporary, chrome and plate-glass surroundings of the modern-day publisher's office, as out of place as the man sitting behind it.

Garvis, who began his career as a union-busting labor-relations lawyer for newspaper management in the *Boston News-American* chain, looked more like a tennis instructor than a newspaperman. He was a tanned, ruddy-complexioned midwesterner, a Gatsby gone-to-seed, with perfect teeth and a jawline that looked like the prow of one of the yachts he loved to sail on Long Island Sound. A bona fide WASP, tall and imposing, all bluster and certitude, he was a blunt instrument, seldom aware of how he was coming across, and intimidating to the short, Jewish men he liked to surround himself with. His self-assurance brooked no doubts from others or from himself. He was a Stepford executive, slick and polished and shiny, like the water-resistant polyurethane deck of his expensive sailboat. His blond hair was always trimmed and combed straight back, and he peered out at you from gecko eyes, set wide apart almost at his graying temples, the better to spot predators and other natural enemies sneaking up from behind.

"What makes you think you're equipped to comment on problems and issues of New York City?" he'd demanded during my second interview, when we were getting serious. "This is the greatest city in the world and the most complicated, subtle, and byzantine political scene in the nation—what makes you think you can handle it?" Clouds of smoke wafted in my direction from a cigar the size of a Poseidon missile. I gave him some verbal razzle-dazzle about the equally byzantine nature of southern politics and how New York in the nineties had replaced the Mississippi of the sixties as the nation's whipping boy, the repository of all our national problems—race, crime, drugs—only more vivid and caricatured. I told him I thought I'd feel right at home. I must admit I was tempted to turn down the job when he blew smoke in my face. But the opportunity to work in New York City was so compelling I ignored Garvis's bad manners and took him up on his offer. As long as he stayed out of the newsroom and off the editorial page, I didn't care who signed my check.

But that was five and a half years ago, when the *Sun* was one of the most successful newspapers in the country. Now we were losing ten million dollars a year with no end in sight. Corporate was scrutinizing our balance sheets. And Garvis, who was responsible, was now tense and unsure of himself. He wasn't smoking his cigar.

He looked up. "I don't know if this is working out."

"How so?" I asked.

"Your op-ed piece pissed me off!"

"Well, apologizing for my cartoon pissed me off."

"We never should have run the cartoon," he declared. "If I had been in the office that day I would have killed it."

"You would have been wrong."

"Well, we can agree to disagree about that." Garvis moved to the window that ran along the wall to my left. "This isn't about censorship, and it's not about kissing my ass, no matter what you told the *Post*."

"Bob, that was a joke. I didn't think the reporter would quote me."

"Richard dropped the ball on this one. And we let you have your say about it, and that's all well and good, even if there was shabby reporting on your part."

My adrenaline was pumping. He was trying to provoke me with insults. I had to watch it.

"Well, I apologize if there was shabby reporting in the piece. That's why I draw pictures for a living and am not a reporter. What exactly was inaccurate in what I wrote?"

"The part about the *Sun* being a boys' club. That was a lie!"

"I see."

"I bet you've heard from a lot of women in management setting you straight on that one."

"Actually I haven't." Surely he couldn't be that naïve about female executive gratitude for the boys' good works on their behalf. He wasn't that patriarchal.

"Well, you will!"

"I doubt it," I said, still trying to maintain an even tone.

"You have no idea how much this company has done to promote and include women!"

"Neither do they, from what I hear," I said.

"Cantrell, I just testified before Congress on sexual harassment guidelines for women in the workplace. I personally have fought for affirmative action for women in management."

I decided this was not the time to mention what I'd heard from some of the newsroom women—that they'd warn each other not to let Garvis catch them alone in the supply closet or pull them into the darkroom at company parties.

"You're right, Bob. But since you're being candid with me I owe you the same. I think you're a very smart man but you're profoundly misinformed about how women perceive their treatment here. Even, especially, female executives."

He flushed crimson and returned to his desk. "All right, Cantrell. Here's the bottom line. I'm seriously considering not renewing your contract. I'm not happy with your work."

"Funny, when you gave me your Publisher's Award last year you said I was the best-read item in the paper—that you heard more about my cartoons than any other feature. You said you valued my work immensely and that's why you were giving me the Publisher's Award. That's what it meant."

Garvis fell silent, betrayed by the testimony of his own words. But Bob Garvis had been a trial lawyer, and he knew how to recover when evidence was introduced that didn't suit his purposes. He simply dismissed it.

"Nobody argues you're not one of the best in the country or that you don't do quality work," he said, "but you don't do the kind of work that this paper can feel comfortable publishing."

"You knew the kind of work I did when you hired me."

"When we were moving into the city the paper needed a cartoonist who could hit homeruns for us. But there's a feeling around here that you're not worth the trouble. That you're not a team player. You don't fit in, Cantrell."

"Guilty as charged, sir. For a cartoonist, that's a job description. You want an accountant, not a political cartoonist."

"You think you're bigger than the newspaper. You shoot your mouth off in the press. You make us look bad with your bullshit."

"What bullshit is that, sir?"

"Saying the *Sun* was a boys' club. We deserve better than that! Buncha crap."

I couldn't resist. "Is that what you're gonna tell the jury when Mendez takes her case to trial?"

Garvis blanched. Luisita Mendez, a former assistant managing editor, left the paper earlier that year and filed sexual harassment charges against the former managing editor, who was kicked upstairs to become the Washington bureau chief. She was offered his old job if she dropped the suit, but she refused. The trial was pending, and it was a major potential embarrassment to *Sun* brass, who prided themselves on enlightened management. They were still trying to resolve it out of court. It was Garvis's baby, and Boston was watching closely to see how it would be resolved. I could see that Garvis was stunned that I knew the details of the case. He thought he had contained the story. Frankly, I was stunned that I'd brought it up, too, but I was seething. Luisita had been a reporter in Charlotte years ago and an old pal and confidante. I'd heard her complaints long before she filed suit. "How do you like my reporting now, Bob?" I asked.

Garvis stared at me with his lizard eyes. Then he spoke. "Okay, Cantrell, I've got a twelve-thirty lunch. I called you out here to inform you that if you want to continue your relationship with the *Sun* you're on probation, starting today."

"For what!"

"For insubordination. I don't want any more trouble from you. And as part of your probation, and as proof of your commitment to the paper, I want you in the office out here. You can draw on New York from here and it'll give you a better bead on Long Island issues."

"No way, Bob. Are you crazy? I never would have taken the job if I had to move to Long Island, and you know it. You hired me for the city. You wanted me to live in the city. That was your pitch. Remember? You said New York is a magnet, the vortex of civilization. You had me move up here, move my family up. Disrupt our lives. Now you want me to drive out here every day?"

"For the time being. If we renew, we'll put it in the contract."

I was reeling, trying to gather myself. "I can't ask my wife to move out here. She'll divorce me first."

"Lots of people commute."

"That's two hours out of the day. I can't afford all that time on a train or in a car."

"It's up to you. You commute for now and if we renew you move out here. It's part of the terms of your probation. I'm going to watch you closely, and if I get a sense of teamwork and a sincere effort to get along better with your colleagues we'll consider renewing your contract. But that will be up to me, Cantrell. Not you."

"That's no choice."

"I expect to see you in the editorial meetings every day starting next Monday at nine A.M. sharp."

I had expected a visit to the woodshed, but not this. I tried to regain my equilibrium. I knew whatever I did and said now would be for the record. Cameron would want me to swallow it. Count to ten. Sleep on it overnight. But I could feel the fury growing in my gut and I didn't know if I could resist.

"I'm late. You think about it. But when you leave this office, remember: you're on probation starting today." Garvis retrieved his suit jacket from the closet and turned to leave.

"That's not a probation, Garvis! That's a gelding!"

"Y'know, Cantrell"—Garvis slipped his arms into the Armani jacket, and tugged on his cuffs—"a lot of hotshots come through here who think they're bigger than the paper. Well, I've got news for you. This paper was here before you, and it'll be here long after you're gone. Nobody's bigger than the *Sun*."

"Does that include you, Bob?"

"What are you talking about?"

"You seem to be speaking for the paper like you're the *Sun*. I was just wondering if you included yourself in the hotshots who come through thinking they're bigger than the paper?"

"Of course I'm not the *Sun*! I'm a steward of the trust the owners placed in me."

"Well, I *am* the newspaper. I *am* the *Sun*."

He seemed stunned by my audacity. "What the hell are you talking about?"

"You heard me. Me and the reporters and writers and columnists, we are the newspaper. We're what sells this paper. Not the corporate suits who parade through these offices, like you, Bob. Bottom line: If I'm gone tomorrow readers will notice. You leave and nobody cares. There are maybe a handful of people in the country who do what I do. Guys like you are a dime a dozen."

"Fine. You don't want to work for me. No problem. We'll replace you."

"Oh, really? With whom?"

"I think you know him. He said he was a friend of yours. Steve Norris."

"You've been talking to Norris about my job behind my back?"

"Don't give me that shit—you talked to Fineman behind my back. We started looking at replacements the minute we read in *New York* magazine you were being wooed by Fineman."

"You can't believe everything you read in the media, Bob. Fineman woos everybody. He likes to seduce, but there's no follow-through. Besides, I wasn't interested. I could have told you I sent Fineman packing. Y'know, that's why you're getting your ass kicked in the city. You expect loyalty but you don't show it. And you don't compete. You assume you'd lose out to Fineman and you just try to save face and cover your ass. Dump me before I dump you."

My stomach was churning. Steve Norris was one of my oldest friends in the business. I'd run into him a month earlier at a cartoonists dinner and he asked me how things were going at the *Sun*. I described the paper's growing timidity, the usual cartoonists' complaint about dunderheaded editors. "Cretins!" he declared sympathetically as he poured another drink, encouraging me to open up. But I never suspected he was shooting for my job. I felt woozy over this news of his betrayal. I sat back down on the sofa.

"Steve's ready to take over," crowed Garvis, "if you don't think you can play by our rules."

"That son of a bitch," I muttered.

Garvis now circled for the kill.

"Yeah, that's some fraternity you belong to—editorial cartoonists. When word got out we might be looking to replace you, we had to beat 'em off with a club. They were delighted to stick it to you. And every one said he was a friend of yours. Hah! With friends like those . . . well, I rest my case."

Garvis started for the door, then stopped and sauntered back over to where I sat slumped on the couch staring at the floor. "Oh, another thing about this probation you're on, southern boy. I want you to run your ideas through Bolton from now on, so we can avoid situations like this pope mess in the future, understand?"

"Bolton? What for?" He knew I'd had some run-ins with Lawrence Bolton, Garvis's man in New York, over cartoons he didn't want to run even though Kerfield had approved them. Bolton was territorial, literalminded, and didn't like my accent. Or the fact that I made more money than he did.

"You do get along well with Bolton, don't you?" Garvis asked.

"I don't show ideas before I draw them. I never have."

"You don't want to be edited."

"It's not a matter of that, I—"

"It's not because he's black, is it, cracker?"

In our age of political correctness, of mandatory sensitivity, of well-scrubbed and well-policed public discourse, especially in the sanctimonious Northeast, I had noticed that for some reason Yankees like Garvis still freely and without inhibition used insulting epithets for white southerners like myself. Words like *cracker* and *redneck* flowed contemptuously from their lips with an impunity I found appalling, given the tenor of the times and the poverty, powerlessness, and marginalization of my people. Usually I wrote off such verbal tackiness to Yankee ignorance, lack of manners and breeding, cultural disadvantage, the all-too-human need to hate somebody. Usually I would just ignore it. Not this time.

Cracker ringing in my ears, I shot off the sofa and drove my fist into Garvis's jaw with a force that sent him flying over the corner of his desk and onto the floor. He lay there for a moment stunned, holding his jaw as I stood over him, my battered fist screaming in agony. Luckily, I draw with my left hand. He dabbed his bloody chin and gazed up at me in utter disbelief.

"That's it, Cantrell," he said. "You're fired!"

He must have thought that pronouncement settled matters between us, because when he pulled himself up and turned back to me to say something else he looked shocked as I kicked him in the balls. He dropped to his knees, cupping his groin and moaning. I circled around behind him and with the full force of my aging former quarterback's body shoved the desk across the floor of Bob Garvis's office.

"Jesus! Are you crazy! What the hell do you think you're doing?" He fumbled for the phone, which was now off the hook on the floor, and buzzed his secretary. "Arlene, call security," he ordered. Then to me, "You're ruined, Cantrell! You fucking redneck! You're crazy, you know that! You'll never work again!"

By the time Arlene arrived at Garvis's door it was too late. I had locked it from the inside and wedged the desk tightly under the doorknob. Nobody was coming through that door anytime soon.

"What's going on in there?" Arlene shrieked, pounding on the door. "Are you okay, Mr. Garvis?" Her keys were useless against the mass of the desk and there was no other way into the office.

Security likewise could do nothing for Garvis, except to lob threats through the door. "Let him go," they shouted, "or we'll call the police!"

The *Sun* was proud of its state-of-the-art security system, which they'd upgraded a few years earlier when a motorcycle gang had made death threats against some editors and reporters. Now the building was a fortress, with video monitors and consoles at every entrance, metal detectors and security guards policing every portal to make sure nobody without proper I.D. could get through. Every emergency was planned for, every contingency anticipated. Except one. They never imagined their editorial cartoonist would attack the publisher.

Now, with the barricade securely in place, I walked over to the glass trophy case on the far side of the room and sent it crashing to the floor. Garvis was on the phone again, holding his aching nuts and barking instructions to Arlene. "Call the police, goddammit! He's crazy! Call the fucking police!" I combed through the remains of the trophy case and picked out the biggest, most impressive cup, a silver chalice Garvis had won for the Northport Marina Open. Then I turned around and yelled at Garvis, who was cowering on the floor before me, "Okay, mother-fucker! Your ass is mine!"

Then I proceeded to beat the living shit out of the publisher of the *Sun* with his own yachting trophy.

By the time the police arrived, Garvis was bleeding from all his major orifices. I had broken his jaw, blackened an eye and opened a wound on his forehead that would surely require not only stitches but plastic surgery. His perfect teeth were in need of extensive bridgework. He would not be singing bass anytime soon in the Episcopal church choir.

Through the door I heard Kerfield urging me to give up and let Bob go. Somebody must have called a TV station because by the time the police arrived camera crews from the local Eyewitness News were setting up satellite dishes for live remotes in the *Sun* building parking lot. But before the tear gas could be dropped into the ventilation system or any gunplay could ensue, I unlocked the door and said, "All right, I'm done. I give up. Come on in."

I shoved the desk aside and collapsed on the sofa, exhausted, breathing heavily and drenched with sweat. Bob Garvis, bruised and bloody, lay sprawled under the portrait of Harold Eisenburg, yachting trophies scattered all around him. I watched his chest rise and fall, a puddle of blood forming on the Scotchgarded carpet just below his forehead, and I didn't resist when the police officers scurried over the desk, read me my rights, and snapped on the handcuffs.

2

MANHATTAN FAREWELL

The next morning after spending a long sleepless night in the Amityville jail I and six other scruffy miscreants were taken in serial handcuffs, chain-gang style, in a van to the Suffolk District Court, where we were turned over to the sheriff for arraignment. My attorney, Jeremy Weiss, was in the courtroom with the others when I arrived. Cameron was seated in a corner in the back. I had called Cameron from jail, and she had called Jeremy, a high-powered entertainment attorney, who was not a criminal lawyer but was the only lawyer I knew in New York. He had negotiated my contract with the *Sun*, and I was fairly certain that the only Long Island courts he ever graced were the ones at his house in the Hamptons, where he played tennis. I hoped he knew what to do.

The endorphin rush I had experienced during the assault, the sheer physical thrill I got from the release of animal fury, an ecstasy I had not felt since football, quickly gave way to deep depression and mortification over what I had done. As I sat there the cold gray austerity of the court-room, the perfect indifference of the law and the bleak prospects for my future permeated my spirit. The cases were called one at a time and the formal charges made by the prosecutor from the office of the DA—an imperious, wiry little man with a topiary beard named Mr. Morrison. I rose when my name was called, and with Jeremy, a tall, handsome former college basketball player looking dapper as always in his gray Hugo Boss suit, approached the bench alongside Morrison.

The judge directed the question at me. "Cantrell, the cartoonist? The *Sun*?"

"Yessir."

"Hmmph," he said, and I thought I detected a faint flicker of bemusement in his eyes. Judge Joseph P. Santorelli was a silver-haired, bearish man in his sixties, with heavy eyebrows and deep circles under his eyes. He studied the papers in front of him, then peered at me over the rims of his reading glasses. "And whom did you assault?"

"The *Sun* publisher, your honor," interjected the DA. "Robert Garvis."

The judge looked surprised. "Garvis? Bob Garvis?"

"Yessir," I answered.

He startled us all by laughing.

"Your honor, I see nothing funny about felony assault," protested Morrison.

Judge Santorelli ignored him. "Says here you roughed him up pretty good."

"Uh . . .Yessir." Perplexed, I glanced at Jeremy.

Santorelli continued. "I guess Garvis won't be participating in the golf tournament at the country club this weekend." He pounded the bench with his hand as if he'd just been told the latest hilarious lawyer joke.

"I object, your honor!" said Morrison.

"Shut up, counselor!" Judge Santorelli barked. Then, calmly perusing the documents before him, decorum restored to his demeanor and countenance as quickly as it had dissolved into merriment, he added, "This ain't a trial—this is an arraignment."

"Your honor, if I may—" Jeremy began, but Santorelli silenced him, and addressed me again directly.

"Why did you attack your publisher, son?"

"Something he said," I replied, looking down at the floor.

"Says here you broke his jaw."

"Assault with a deadly weapon, your honor," Morrison chimed in.

"I can read, counselor!" The judge glared at the DA and addressed me again. "Says you hit him with a yachting trophy."

"Yessir."

"I see." He studied the papers.

"This man is dangerous, your honor, and a menace. There's no telling what he might do next."

"I hear you, Mr. Morrison," the judge said. Then, fixing me with a look, he asked, "You're not gonna go tune up the same guy again are you, Mr. Cantrell?"

"No, sir."

"And you're not gonna run off to Venezuela?"

"No, sir."

"I believe you. No cash bail. Mr. Weiss, have your client sign this agreement saying if he flees before the court date we set he will pay the court ten thousand dollars."

The bailiff handed Jeremy a sheet of paper.

"Judge, aren't you going to send him to the facility?" asked Morrison.

"What for?" replied the judge impatiently.

"Sir, I highly recommend he be sent to the Pilgrim State Psychiatric facility for observation."

"C'mon, Morrison," said the judge. "He's an artist. He's supposed to be crazy." Judge Santorelli signaled the bailiff to call the next case.

I couldn't believe my good luck. Over the years every judge I had ever drawn for the occasional traffic ticket had been disastrous. For once when it counted, I hit the jackpot. As I sat down and Jeremy returned to his seat smiling, the judge added, "Oh, by the way Mr. Cantrell, I loved the pope cartoon. And I was an altar boy. Next case."

When we emerged from the courthouse, Cameron was standing in the parking lot beside our station wagon. She'd ridden out with Jeremy, who had dropped her off at the *Sun* to pick up the car. She looked tired and haggard though beautiful as always in her knit top and black jeans, her thick, luxuriant blond hair gathered in a loose braid.

Cameron hugged me, but said nothing as we got in the car, me in the passenger's seat. She asked directions but other than that remained mute as we made our way onto the L.I.E. heading west toward the city.

Cameron and I had been through a lot during our fifteen years together. When we first met she was a television news photographer for the CBS affiliate in Charlotte. Back then she wore overalls and cowboy boots, drove a Chevy truck, and lugged hundreds of pounds of camera equipment around, slung over her shoulders. She moved like a ballet dancer, a discipline she studied as a girl, and although she possessed the kind of slender, shapely legs that in heels and a miniskirt caused men to go weak in the knees, I never even saw her in a skirt for the first three years we dated. When we met she was a sexy tomboy, with a second-degree electrical engineering license and an unselfconscious femininity, as at home in a sports bar as in a bridal boutique. Definitely a guy's girl— beautiful, tough, independent, fearless. She had freelanced as a commercial film producer for several years after we got married until she got pregnant with Wiley and gave it all up to become a full-time mom. She had wanted to raise our son in the family-friendly atmosphere of Charlotte and had been reluctant to leave, but she had deferred to my dream and New York was home to her now. She had always been resilient and resourceful but I had no idea how she would handle this.

"You okay?" I finally asked.

"Shouldn't I be asking you that?" Her eyes were fixed on the highway.

"Honey, I'm sorry."

She spoke with the cold logic of a prosecuting attorney. "Why are you apologizing to me? Garvis is the one you beat up."

"He deserved it."

"Goddammit, Pick, he probably did, but did you have to be the one who administered it?"

We said nothing for a few more miles as we segued into the thickening morning traffic.

"Where's Wiley?" I asked to break the silence.

"At Sally's, playing with Sophie."

"Does he know?"

"That his father's a lunatic? No, I kept the television off and the newspapers out of sight since you called yesterday afternoon. He can't understand why he can't watch cartoons. But no, he hasn't heard. Yet."

"Good."

"He's going to find out, sooner or later, you know that. It'll be a little tricky telling him not to fight with friends on the playground at school from now on but—"

"You're angry."

"No," she replied. "I'm delighted you lost your job and we're stuck in New York City with no visible means of support. I've always wanted to be a welfare mom. In time when we're homeless we can live under the West Side Highway with the squatters."

I said nothing. After a couple of miles she spoke again. "Jesus, Pickard, what in the world were you thinking?"

"I don't know exactly. It was a whole series of things but when he called me a cracker I lost it."

She looked at me incredulously. "You beat up the publisher because he called you a cracker?"

"Among other things." I stared ahead, knowing how ridiculous it sounded.

"And you proved him right."

"You're taking it out of context," I said, my anger already beginning to build.

"What context? Name-calling?"

I looked across at her. "I said I was sorry."

"That's not good enough." Her eyes flashed with tears. She was fighting to hold back her anger. "Goddammit, Pickard!" she blurted finally, pounding the steering wheel with the heel of her hand. "How could you do this to us?"

I looked back at the road. "I wasn't doing it to you and Wiley," I answered. "I was doing it to Garvis. I didn't think—"

"That's right! You let your goddamned temper get the best of you and take us down the toilet. Dammit, I told you Garvis would try something like this. He was angling to get you back, Pick, for what you said in that piece. And he did. They thought when they hired you they could control you. They thought they could just buy some more prestige for their enterprise. But they underestimated the cost. You were too much for them. And when they tried to gloss over your differences, you didn't go along. Worse, you embarrassed them, showed them up for the yahoos they are. But you played right into their hands. You gave them the sword. He got rid of you without losing any real face. He got you out of their hair without revealing them for the assholes they really are. He wasn't counting on a broken jaw, but at least now he can tell his corporate overseers that you were a madman and there was nothing else they could do."

Cameron was getting to me, articulating my worst fears. "You weren't there," I snapped. "Garvis said I was on probation. And that we would have to move out to the Island. Are you up for that?"

She didn't answer.

"It's easy to Monday morning quarterback, but you weren't there!"

"I know that," she replied, "but I'm here and I have to deal with the consequences. When I heard what happened yesterday I thought about walking out, taking Wiley and moving out and just going to stay with my sister."

"I don't blame you."

"I didn't, because Wiley needs his father, even if he's a selfish maniac." She was close to tears. "A boy needs his father. I know that. I'm not stupid."

"Look, Cam," I pleaded, "we can live on the syndication income until I find a job."

"Jeremy said your syndicate is canceling your contract for breach. The arrest for felony assault is grounds."

"But Jeremy said we got lucky with the judge. He thinks he can get that reduced to a misdemeanor."

"The publicity scares the syndicate. You just gave them an excuse to bail."

"Shit." I saw the magnitude of my predicament refracted through the lens of my wife's eyes. "I'll get another job. I'm a good cartoonist, for god's sake. That still counts for something. Somebody will take a chance on me."

"You beat up a publisher. You think another one's going to want to be next?"

"I'll work in advertising. I've got a friend on Madison Avenue who's always said if I ever wanted to—"

"No, Pick. I'm making the call. You promised the next move was mine, remember? We're doing it my way. If we're going to be together then . . . I want to go home. We've done New York. This is no place to start over."

"I can't go back to Charlotte, you know that. Even if the *Sentinel* did take me back it would be too humiliating returning with my tail between my legs."

"Listen, I've been thinking, why don't I go back to work? You stay home with Wiley for a while. Just . . . till you sort things out. I was up all night thinking about this."

"Jesus. I just lost a position I worked toward all my life. I'm still trying to wrap my mind around that and you want me to consider quitting altogether?"

"Just for now. You've been under a lot of pressure. Hell, you've been at it for more than twenty years. You've been meeting deadlines since you were in college. Take a year off. Until this mess blows over. Let me worry about making a living for a change. Wiley's getting old enough to do without me all the time. And he would benefit from you in his life more."

"I don't know, Cam," I said. All my worrying and plotting had centered around finding another cartooning job. I had always worked as a cartoonist. My whole identity was wrapped up in that work. Meeting deadlines was like breathing to me. I didn't know what to think, or how to react.

"I had a long talk with Linda last night," Cameron continued. Linda DiCaprio was her best friend in Charlotte. They had worked together for years at the station. "The production company she's with now is opening an office in Chapel Hill. I know I haven't worked in ages, but she says the job's mine if I want it. The salary's not great, but it's something. We can go down right away and look for a place to live. I want

Wiley to know his relatives, his grandparents and cousins. Ever since we moved to the city we've talked about finding a summer place back home."

"But permanently? I never thought I'd go home again."

"We'll look in Raleigh–Durham–Chapel Hill. We can start a new life. Near family and friends. And it's beautiful down there. The Research Triangle is one of the most livable places in the country. Nice environment, less crime, slower pace, better quality of life than up here. Cost of living's a hell of a lot better, too. Good schools. Restaurants. Lots of culture with the universities close by. More Ph.D.s per capita than anywhere in the country. I've always loved that area."

"I don't know." It was so close to Delaney, and Burlington, the places I'd grown up and had tried so hard over the years to forget.

She forged on. "You can freelance. Stay home with Wiley while I go to work. Do some carpentry work if you have to."

I hadn't worked carpentry since college and I swore I'd never do it again.

"We've saved enough to live on for a while. My parents left me a little money—not much, but a little. We could invest it in a house instead of putting it away for Wiley's college. We'll scale down. You've always wanted to try other things—children's books, illustration, maybe even some writing—but never had the time. Now's your chance. You could even teach."

I stared at the traffic stopped in front of us at the tollbooths for the Midtown Tunnel.

Cameron pointed to her pocketbook on the floorboard by my feet. "There's a brown envelope from a real estate agent in Durham in there. Remember the pictures of that old house they sent me? The ones I showed you a year ago?" I retrieved the photographs of an old colonial Federal-style white clapboard house, run-down, but quite beautiful.

"We both loved it, remember?" Cameron continued, "but you said it looked and sounded like it needed too much work."

"I remember. So?" Looking at the photos, the fine lines and elegance of the old house leaped out at you, but upon closer inspection you could see where the photographer had done his best to disguise its deterioration.

"The agent called me a month ago, and said the couple who were going to buy it were transferred and the deal fell through. She wanted to show it to us the next time we're in the area. Look at it, Pick. What do you think?"

Cameron knew I was a sucker for old houses, just like she was. It was one of the pleasures we shared and one that first brought us together. On our first date when I picked her up at her old high-ceilinged pre-war apartment in Charlotte, I had repaired a loose molding in her dining room before we went out for dinner. She claims she fell in love with me right then and there watching me stand on the ladder, with my hammer taken from the toolbox I always carried in the trunk of my car. That little repair job was the beginning not only of our relationship but of a cease-less conversation between us about moldings, cornices, pediments and wainscoting, and old houses we'd love to own. There was something about such houses, especially the ones that needed a little work, that brought out a feeling in me of warmth, of empathy, almost a compas-sion, that you might ordinarily reserve for a cherished elderly relative or an irreplaceable family heirloom or an aging pet dog or cat. I am a walk-ing cliché, the embodiment of the joke about my boomer generation: What are the three strongest drives in a yuppie? The drives for food, sex, and restoring old houses.

I stared at the pictures and tried to imagine Cameron and Wiley and me on the porch and on the lawn and under the sprawling oaks.

"That's one of the more intriguing properties I've seen," said Cam, "at least as far as you can tell from the photographs and specs. But it needs a lot of work. Which is why it's so reasonable."

"Where is it located—Chapel Hill?"

"It's on the New Hope River in a little town called Eno near Chapel Hill. One of those old mill towns around there."

"Sure. It's not far from Burlington. I remember passing the signs on the highway when I was a kid."

"I called the agent and made an appointment to see it this weekend. I already made a reservation to fly down tomorrow to meet with Linda about the job and to look for a place to live. If I don't find anything I like we'll both look when we go to the family reunion on Labor Day."

"I can't go to any family reunion," I said. "Not now. Not after this."

"It's Mama Lucy's ninetieth birthday," Cam protested. "We're expected."

"All the more reason not to go."

"Your grandmother's not going to be with us much longer."

"Good."

"We already committed. We promised Wiley he could go see his cousins. Your father promised to take Wiley fishing. He'll be so disappointed if he can't. He's been talking about this for months."

"C'mon," I said. "You know my family. They'd just love it if I came dragging home unemployed, publicly humiliated like this. They've been waiting for me to screw up. You and Wiley go. Tell 'em I'm job hunting."

"Your dad called. He saw it on the news and read about it in the paper. All of your relatives are contacting him."

"This'll keep 'em buzzing for years."

By the time we reached the Upper West Side I was exhausted. Cameron had grasped the significance of my actions and the limitations of our options before I did, and while I was sulking in my jail cell she had seized the moment, and begun rearranging our lives.

"At least think about this, " Cameron said as she dropped me in front of our apartment before going to park the car. "I'm flying down this weekend. Come if you want—it's up to you."

I shut the car door and leaned through the open passenger side window. "I still think my best chance to resurrect my career is here in New York City. Not in the South."

As Cameron pulled away, a camera flashed and paparazzi poured out from behind the trash receptacles beneath the steps of a nearby brownstone. Then another swarm of photographers and TV cameras, larger and more predatory than the suburban crews that showed up at the paper, came running down the street toward me. These were the city tabloid pros who knew how to stake out a celebrity perp. They must have been keeping vigil up at the deli at the end of my block. "Pick! Pick!" they shouted, running toward me, cameras poised. "One shot, man!" "Yo, Pick, help us out!" "How'd it feel beating up Garvis?" "What are you going to do now, Pick?" "This way, Pick!" I sprinted up the steps, dodging mike-wielding reporters, and knocking cameras out of photographers' hands, disappeared through the front door.

"Daddy got in a fight, son," I said. "I got angry with my boss and hit him, and now I've lost my job. It was a big mistake. Those guys out there on the sidewalk are photographers who want to take my picture for the newspapers."

Reciting the unadorned facts of the events of the last twenty-four hours to my son over supper was excruciating. He sat there gazing at me with his milk mustache and half-eaten grilled cheese sandwich clutched in his hand, the abject stupidity of what I had done to myself and my family showing in the blank incomprehension on his face and the infinite forgiveness in his heart. I was mortified. I had always taken seriously my responsibilities as a parent. I knew that the most powerful force on the planet was the power of imitation. Monkey see, monkey do. I stopped smoking the day Wiley was born and had cut way back on my drinking. I didn't need Cameron to tell me I had let Wiley down.

Cameron and I sat there as our son finished his meal and digested what I had just told him. We waited for his reaction. He asked if I would have to go to jail and I told him I didn't think so. He asked to see the swollen knuckles on my hand where I punched Garvis and asked if they hurt. But mainly he just took it all in until finally he declared in the purest expression of little-boy bravado in the face of forces and events beyond his comprehension, "It's all right, Dad. You should sue 'em." It was all I could do not to burst into tears.

Friday morning, Wiley and I drove Cameron to La Guardia for the early flight to Raleigh-Durham. As I monitored the answering machine and my own moods that weekend, Wiley and I stayed inside watching videos and playing checkers. We left the apartment only to walk Flappy, the tiny white Maltese that Cam had given Wiley for his seventh birthday. The diminutive Flappy was hardly my idea of a dog, more like a starter-pet, a hairdo, whom I tolerated because she was our son's first and because Cameron was so taken with the little Q-tip. I didn't want to go out too much because I was still a bit paranoid about stakeouts, even though the media excitement had faded. I was actually more concerned with my own self-reproach and self-recrimination for what I had visited upon my family. By Saturday afternoon I was feeling claustrophobic and so was Wiley, so I promised to take him out to the park the next day. It would do us both good to get out. Besides, our time in New York was coming to a close and I wanted him to experience the city's pleasures as much as possible before we left. A profound sadness slipped over me as I watched Wiley and Flappy on what would probably be their last day in Central Park. I had been about Wiley's age when my mother was first hospitalized, when my life had been disrupted in a way almost as suddenly and irrevocably as his was about to be.

*   *   *

My mother didn't seem crazy to me when I was growing up. She just seemed sad. She was raised in Burlington, the oldest child of an emotionally distant mother and a brutish father, an itinerant electrician, who abandoned her and her brother and sister soon after she was diagnosed with polio. A series of operations left her with a stiff leg, and a limp and made it difficult for her to get around without her crutches—or a son she could lean on. Her lameness, and the unwanted stares and comments it attracted, made her feel humiliated. Because her mother had to work in a box factory to support the family after her daddy abandoned them, my mother was practically raised by her maternal grandmother, whom she adored. When her grandmother died at the age of eighty-nine my mother was devastated. I was seven at the time and I've always suspected that it was this loss that caused my mother's downward emotional slide. Sometimes when my father was away on business trips I would awaken in the middle of the night to my mother's sobbing. I would sit up in bed aware of a presence in the room and find her standing in the shadows just inside the doorway, weeping. I would sit with her for hours, listening, holding her hand, trying to talk her out of her black moods, explaining to her why life was worth living. "You're like me, Pick," she would say. "I can talk to you. You're just like me."

During the long absences that scarred my childhood, my father would take me to Burlington to visit my mother in the psychiatric wing on the eighth floor of Alamance General. I would sit in the lobby waiting room while he checked to make sure everything was all right, then we'd ride the elevator together and I would stand by the nurse's station while my father checked again before I was summoned to my mother's room. It was there in the hallways of the psychiatric unit that I first glimpsed the ravages of mental illness, intimations of what my mother would become. And all I could think at the time was that my mother didn't belong there in those corridors of madness among all those crazy people. She was being held captive against her will. Those first few visits so upset me that my father stopped taking me, even though my mother never stopped asking.

After the night I first heard Mama Lucy urging my father to "put her away," it would be several more years of turmoil in our family's war of attrition, our long sad seasons of battle with my mother's melancholia, of wrenching late-night conversations, of checking her in and out of the hospital in Burlington, of the failure of experimental psychotropic drugs, even the horrors of electroshock therapy with her returning home to us occasionally as a zombie, before my father relented and finally had my mother committed to Appalachian. That was the summer after I graduated from high school and I will never forget the day.

It was a long, miserable trip to Asheville on the hottest day of the summer. My mother had to sit in the backseat of our four-door Ford Fairlane where there was enough room for her to stretch out her stiff leg, just as she did on our short trips to Burlington or longer ones to Myrtle Beach on family vacations. I rode with her in the back, where I could hold her hands and keep her arms down so she wouldn't open the door and fling herself from the speeding car. She had tried that once on a trip to Burlington, but moved too slowly and my father stopped the car before she leaped out. She wept and screamed the entire four hours it took to drive from Delaney to Asheville. "How can you do this to me? How can you betray me like this, Pickard? I know your father doesn't love me anymore, but how can you send me to that place?" Tears streamed down her face and I turned to the window, trying to hold back the rivulets of sorrow already streaking my own. I didn't go inside the hospital. Instead, I waited in the car, unable to bear my mother's pleadings a moment longer. I had no way of knowing I would never see her again.

Cameron returned from her trip enchanted with her prospective new job, with the town of Eno, and with the house. "You're going to love it," she said. "Linda says Eno is the best-kept secret in the region. 'This quaint little old mill town is becoming the hottest, hippest place in the area to live.' It's still just enough off the radar to attract writers and artists and university professors."

"What about the house?" I asked.

"I put down the earnest money on it."

"You what!" I was flabbergasted. I thought she would check it out, then we'd look at it together, then decide. We had always made big decisions like that only after consulting each other.

"I know. I'm sorry." She sighed. "You should have seen it first, but we had to move fast. School begins right after Labor Day. And Linda wants me to start work right away. I had to go with my instinct. Oh, Pick, it's more than I had hoped for from the pictures. Much more. You're going to love this place. Trust me. And I got it for only two thirty. You can't buy a tenement in New York for that. Twelve acres. The land itself is worth that. And the house is a gem. It's even got a name—Oaklawn."

Cameron had it all figured out. Although the house was barely habitable we could live in one wing while we remodeled the rest of it. I would jump right into the renovation while Wiley started second grade and Cam began her new job producing and coordinating film shoots in the Triangle area for Oleander Productions. Cameron would work during the day in Oleander's Chapel Hill office, a fifteen-minute drive from Eno, and I would take Wiley to school, and work around the house. The renovation would take months, maybe a year or more. I could do most of the carpentry myself, but a lot of the more complicated jobs, those beyond my tools or talents like plumbing and electrical, would have to be contracted out. Still, I could handle all the key interior work— kitchen, bathrooms, and bedrooms—as well as external repairs, rotted cornerboards, porches, and the like.

"Oaklawn." Cameron gazed out the windows at the massive apartment building directly behind us, rolling the name off on her tongue like an incantation. "Imagine owning a house with a name."

"Maybe we could change its name to Peckerwood," I joked, but got nothing.

Cameron was way ahead of me. "But I want you to keep drawing," she said, placing a comforting hand on mine. "I mean it. Whatever you do during this period, take time to sketch."

"What, a scathing attack on property taxes in Eno? A whimsical look at plumbing costs in the Triangle area?"

"I don't know. Draw a portrait of me or Wiley. Some of the things you always used to talk about but never had time to do. Oils or watercolors, anything to keep your hand in."

"What if I don't want to keep my hand in?"

"C'mon, Pick—you know what I mean. It's not healthy to go cold turkey with something that's been part of your regimen, your lifeblood, for twenty years."

I couldn't think about drawing now. I'd wait and see what happened. I planned to throw myself into the renovation of Oaklawn. And prayed that because the move was so abrupt, the sheer magnitude of the renovation so absorbing, the details so endless and the transition so jarring, there would be little time to mope. Cam was sold, and my half-hearted protests weren't going to talk her out of it. Besides, we had decided to move and if we had to go back South, at least it wasn't going to be Charlotte, where I was known and would have to deal with that humiliation. I could start over in Eno, where the only people who knew me were my relatives—and I had successfully avoided them for most of my adult life.

3

REUNION

Tolstoy said, "Happy families are all alike; every unhappy family is unhappy in its own way." My family holds reunions.

It was a short drive, less than twenty miles, from Eno to my cousin Mack Cantrell's farm in rural Alamance County, where the Cantrell clan was holding one of its sporadic coagulations. We abandoned the frantic interstate after a few miles and took the more languorous scenic drive along the back roads and country highways familiar to me from childhood, through the piney woods and rolling pastureland of rural Eno and Alamance counties, out among the fields of cotton and tobacco, the acres of soybean and rows of corn, where the sight of weathered old railroad trestles, abandoned tarpaper shacks and ramshackle tobacco barns always stirred in me a sense of familiarity and belonging. And dread.

Heat shimmered off the highway pavement as we drove past the abandoned Cantrell homestead just outside Saxapahaw. My ancestors had dwelled here since the late eighteenth century in the same house where my grandfather was born in 1890. Once rich in land, the Cantrells were now dirt poor, and had been for generations. They coaxed out a living tilling the same stingy soil, until sooner or later they all either migrated to the towns to find work in the mills or stayed on the land and ended up buried beside the family homestead in the old Bethel Church cemetery.

Near the intersection of State Road 19 and the road to Snow Camp, I saw the cemetery looming up on the right and shivered, just as I had since childhood, at the sight of the old grave marker, planted in the shade of a gigantic spreading pecan tree, the legend on the tombstone where my great-grandfather is buried visible from the road, the family name CANTRELL glaring out at me as if it were cast in neon. From the time I was old enough to understand my ancestors were buried there that marker has been to me a warning and a summons, an intimation of my own mortality.

Two miles down the road was Mack Cantrell's farm. His grandfather was one of the few who stayed on the land when the others gave up. Mack raises Cantrell Sweet Potatoes and his wife, Mozelle, raises Cantrell Day Lilies, a more modest but realistic way of making a living from the parsimonious soil of Alamance County than the untrustworthy cotton or tobacco.

"I told your father a few weeks ago we'd come," said Cameron, "but with all the turmoil I imagine he thinks we're still in Manhattan."

"Let's keep it that way."

"Don't forget it's your grandmother's ninetieth birthday, Pick."

"She used to boycott reunions if my grandfather was invited."

"He's dead now. She'll be the center of attention. Don't worry. She'll show."

"That's what worries me."

"Gimme some sugar, Pick!" My blood froze whenever I heard those words on our ritual Sunday visits to Mama Lucy's when I was a child. She always greeted her grandchildren the same way—with extravagant hugs and kisses and with a pinch of Strong Dental snuff stuffed firmly in her cheek.

Back then, I didn't know what snuff was exactly, and I didn't want to know, but I knew it was nasty. My grandmother kept her stash in a shiny silver tin like a miniature treasure chest with a delicate filigree etched upon its lid. She kept the tin close at hand, along with her makeshift Coke bottle spittoon.

She would hoist the bottle to her lips and in a casual aside spit a hideous brown effluent into it. Then, turning back to me with a mischievous gleam in her eye and a yellowish-brown streak of saliva running down her chin, she would drawl, "Don't be bashful, now, Pickard Cantrell. C'mere and give me some sugar."

Panic-stricken, I would look to my mother and father for rescue only to see them standing there urging me forward and nodding their encouragement. I would turn back to Mama Lucy and catch my frightened visage reflected in her thick glass lenses. Then she would stoop toward me, arms extended, eyes closed, lips puckered. Not wanting to hurt her feelings or anger her but without a graceful exit, I would panic and run to my mother.

These are the scenes I see in super slo-mo: turning on my heels and breaking into a sprint but running through molasses. I glance over my shoulder and see Mama Lucy's arms reaching for me like octopus tentacles. She catches me on the run and clamps me to her ample bosom in one swift motion. I squeal in terror as she cackles maniacally and I smell the faint acrid sourness of processed tobacco on her breath. As she draws me to her I see traces of the fine brown powder edging the corners of her mouth, staining her teeth, streaking her lips and caking the wrinkles around the sides of her mouth. I arch my back, turn my head away, but there is nothing I can do. She administers a hammerlock, lifts my chin, and smooches me full on the lips. That is my first memory of my grandmother—familial affection wielded like a cudgel, an instrument of torture.

Mama Lucy lived in the "big house," and my granddaddy lived in the "little house" a few feet from her back door. When I was a child we would visit her every Sunday for family gatherings and then go out back and visit him. My grandparents never spoke to or acknowledged each other. They never divorced. I used to joke that they were staying together until the children were dead.

I envied my friends their Tweety Bird grannies, their Meemaws and Mamaws and Nanas, the sweet little old ladies who lived over the river and through the woods, who they adored and who adored them, and baked cookies for them and let them stay up late and slipped them nickels for ice cream when their parents weren't looking. Mama Lucy was not like that.

For one thing, none of my friends' grandmothers packed heat. Mama Lucy would pull her Smith and Wesson .38 Special out of her purse if you so much as looked at her sideways and she always brandished it recklessly, threatening neighbors and family with it, until the police finally confiscated it after she followed one of her daughters on a date to spy on her and her fiancé called the cops.

One day when I was very small and my daddy was at work, Mama Lucy burst into our kitchen in a fury looking for her youngest daughter, who was in her late teens at the time and had run away from home, as Lucy's girls did from time to time, especially when she was throwing one of her fits. The girl wasn't there but Lucy accused us of hiding her and pulled the gun on my mother. My mother faced her down and took it away from her and ordered her out of the house before she called the police. She told her it was exactly that kind of behavior that caused her daughters to run away and, though she wasn't there, if the girl did show up she would invite her to move in with us. Naturally, I sided with my mother.

From the time I could walk Mama Lucy put me and the swarms of her other visiting grandchildren to work on those Sabbath visits—shelling peas, shucking corn, picking tomatoes from her garden, trimming hedges and mowing her lawn. Whatever the task, it was never performed to her satisfaction. You always came up short. It wasn't personal. She had treated all her children this way, so why not her grandchildren? I was three and a half years old the first time I mowed her lawn. I could barely reach the handles of the push mower, or muster the strength to mow in anything but erratic, uneven rows. This displeased my grandmother mightily, for she prized neatness and prided herself on the fastidiousness of her lush green lawn.

"What's the matter with you, Pickard?" she'd yelled from the front porch, pointing to a patch of grass I in my wobbly trajectories had missed. "Cain't you do no better than that?" She turned on me, berating me and critiquing my mowing skills in front of everybody until I cried. Finally, my mother, who heard the ruckus from the kitchen, came to my rescue.

"What seems to be the problem?" she asked, eyeing her mother-in-law while trying to comfort me.

"He's mowing crooked," snapped Lucy. "What's wrong with that young'un? Ain't he never mowed a lawn before?"

"Well, no, actually, he hasn't," answered my mother. "We thought we'd wait 'til he's a little older before we asked him to do yardwork."

"You're spoilin' that child, Mary Alice," said Lucy, who never passed up a chance to criticize her daughter-in-law. "If he's big enough to play outside, he's big enough to work. And look at those spots he missed. He mows crooked."

"Probably because he's left-handed."

"What?"

"Pickard's left-handed. He favors one side because of it. He can't help it."

It was a novel defense and Mama Lucy didn't buy it, but I was grateful for my mother's effort on my behalf. It wasn't the first time she interceded between my grandmother and me and it wouldn't be the last.

My grandmother did not mellow with age. Over time she honed her natural gifts for pettiness and paranoia to an artform. She fought ceaselessly with neighbors even into her eighties—over property lines, trespassing pets, and personal slights and grievances, real and imagined. She spied on them and was spied upon. A master of manipulation, a black belt in passive aggression, she burdened her family with endless demands, temper tantrums, and rages, and confounded legions of physicians with phantom illnesses and ailments. When one specialist could not find evidence of the disease she claimed to have contracted, she demanded a second opinion and so he sent her to a shrink. She boasted that the world-famous psychiatrist from Duke University had never come across a case like hers and instead of charging her for his services offered to pay her to talk to him.

Mama Lucy was a case study, all right. A force of nature. Hurricane Lucy swept through the lives of her grown children, leaving destruction and chaos in her wake.

"Relax," Cameron said. "It'll be fine." We rode in silence down the last stretch of road, cutting through red clay embankments crested with pine and hardwoods before yielding to sprawling pastureland dotted with grazing cattle. The fields on the right belonged, as a sign on a fence informed us, to the producers of Cantrell sweet potatoes.

"Well, at least I got her a present," I said as we turned in at the red and yellow cluster of balloons tied to the fence at the entrance to their driveway.

"What do you mean? What present?"

"Just what she always wanted—a nationally recognized fuck-up for a grandson."

It was past noon when we pulled up the drive to Mack's farmhouse, and most of the family was already eating. The summer sun hung high in the cloudless sky and a gentle breeze rustled through the trees and buffed the edges off the early September heat—a perfect day for a homecoming picnic. The pungent aroma of freshly mown grass and newly baled hay faintly tinged with the scent of honeysuckle, wisteria and cow manure perfumed the air.

The piquant strains of old-time fiddle tunes and banjo riffs wafted on the breeze. Bluegrass is the unofficial soundtrack of Cantrell family reunions, and to my ear the Muzak of dysfunction. As we plodded up the winding driveway I saw a small coterie of cousins and in-laws with guitars, mandolins, fiddles, banjos and a stand-up bass, hammering out the high lonesome longings of "Little Maggie" among the hood ornaments and luggage racks of cars parked in a field alongside the drive. Hardcore bluegrass pickers by birthright, all of whom would rather pick than eat, they would remain out there all day while the rest of the clan hunkered down at picnic tables on top of the hill under a pair of green canvas canopies, no doubt rented from the funeral home in Saxapahaw.

The Cantrells are a fiercely modest clan, not given to ostentatious displays of personal wealth, material possessions, or hubris of any kind. Any and all forms of "showin' off," "puttin' on airs," or "gittin' above your raisin' " are generally frowned upon in my family, and whatever pride we might possess is religiously suppressed, except when it comes to our means of transportation. Any residual Cantrell strut and boast is channeled into the chrome and paint jobs or the horsepower per cubic inch under the hoods of our latest set of wheels. We Cantrells may not go far in the world, but we'll get there in style. No wonder a number of my relatives made their livings working on and around combustible engines—as garage mechanics, car dealers, auto parts specialists, service station attendants. Ambition in my family was gauged by whether you wanted to pump hi-test.

Close to two hundred of my kinfolks were already chowing down on steaming platters of fried chicken, country-style steak, honey baked ham, pork barbecue and Brunswick stew, field peas and corn, butterbeans, fried okra, corn on the cob, homegrown tomatoes, biscuits and gravy, persimmon pudding, pitchers of sweetened iced tea, and other traditional southern delicacies, a hearty cuisine frowned on by all the prim and skinny, but far less satisfied, nutritionists the world over for its toxic levels of grease, salt and cholesterol. Mama Lucy may have had a hellish temperament but she gardened and cooked like an angel. The same green thumb that produced the lawn she was so obsessed with also brought forth the sweetest corn, the most luscious strawberries, and red, ripe German Johnson tomatoes the size of softballs. When I was a boy it always seemed as if she made us wait an eternity before Sunday dinner was served, but when it finally appeared it was well worth the wait. Her biscuits were the lightest and fluffiest, and to this day the best I ever tasted, and her homegrown produce was world-class. She shared her recipes with nobody but her own daughters, and under her tutelage they all became fabulous cooks. She raised four beautiful daughters, my father's sisters, but with a lot less care and attention, some would say, than she gave her German Johnson tomatoes. But she left her mark on each of them in ways beyond their culinary skills. We Cantrells may have tasted our portion of defeat in life but we live by the unspoken credo that eating well is the best revenge.

Bible-believing Southern Baptists, my family also took the scriptural injunction to "Go forth and multiply" literally, so throngs of relatives show up at reunions, if for no other reason than because the food is good. Although my father and three of his sisters were the only ones of Mama Lucy's unlucky brood to survive into their dotage, they all had children and their children were now transforming the Cantrell gene pool from a puddle into a water park. A casual sweep of the grounds revealed legions of tow-headed, blue-eyed clones of my son frolicking on the lawn.

I recognized some of my aunts and cousins scurrying uphill and down like fire ants, between the farmhouse kitchen and the picnic tables, urgently toting their trays and platters of home-cooked delicacies. The older children chased after toddlers. Flappy joined the other dogs barking at cows in the pasture and harassing chickens strutting around the barnyard safely behind the wire fence.

My father and Tess were the first to greet us. Tess gushed, "What a nice surprise."

"Shame on you for not telling us you was comin'," my father said. "But you're just in time for dinner. We're already eatin'."

Cameron smiled and hugged them both. "Sorry we're late."

"Did you drive down from New York?" asked my father.

"No, just over from Eno."

"We just moved in this weekend," said Cameron, more tolerant and better able to deal with her stepmother-in-law's nosiness than I was.

"Cameron's going to work in Chapel Hill," I announced. "I'm going to stay home with Wiley and work on the house."

"Did you hear that, Clayton?" Tess gasped. "They bought a house in Eno."

My father was speechless.

"Surprise!" I said with a wan smile, adding, "It needs a lot of work."

"Why didn't you tell us?" he asked.

"It all happened so fast. We weren't keeping it from you," Cameron said. "We just had to move on it in time to get Wiley in school down here. Got caught up in all the details. Figured you'd find out soon enough."

Cameron was my one and only weapon in dealing with my family. My kinfolks might tolerate me, but they adored her. My marriage to

Cameron was the oil that smoothed my passage back into the family constellation. She was beautiful, warm, and friendly. She accepted and forgave my family's foibles more than she ever had her own, in part, I knew, because since her parents had died this *was* her family. She could spend days around my relatives without being driven crazy and vice versa.

"Well, good for you," said my father, tousling Wiley's hair. "Maybe we'll be able to get in more fishing now than we thought, huh, Wiley?"

It moved me to see my father take such an interest in my son. He showed Wiley the kind of open, unabashed affection that he had trouble showing me as a child. When I was Wiley's age my dad hadn't been much more than a boy himself and had not yet stumbled upon his natural gifts for fatherhood. Like many of his generation Clayton Cantrell escaped the textile mills by the grace of World War II. As a teenager he served as a Marine Corps medic on the blood-soaked beaches of Anzio and Salerno and southern France, dispensing morphine to the wounded and dying. As the eldest son of Lucille Barlow Cantrell he was used to hazardous duty. Tending the damaged came naturally to him, and that's probably why he married my mother. He felt at home among the casualties.

My mother, Mary Alice Lesser, was a shy, pretty, religious girl. He first laid eyes on her the night he came home from the war, when he stopped off at the Carolina Theatre in Burlington to greet his sister, who sold tickets in the box office alongside her. That night Mama Lucy welcomed him home with his first home-cooked meal in four years, then spoiled it by flying into one of her rages in the middle of the night and throwing him out of the house. My father never told her he had stopped off at the theater to see his sister and he claims he doesn't know why Lucy threw him out, but my grandmother was nothing if not intuitive, especially when it came to her family. I suspect she sensed that her firstborn son had met that night the woman he would marry. She knew that he was replacing her in his heart, and he paid for his betrayal with pre-emptive excommunication.

After the war my father spent his first year selling shoes and insurance and medical supplies before landing a job with the A.C. White department store in Burlington, where he worked his way up to district manager and was transferred to the chain's home office in the town of Delaney. He and my mother married and he moved his bride to Delaney to settle down and start a family.

My grandmother was not happy with his decision and refused to go to the wedding and forbade her children and husband from attending. The only one who showed up, the only one not intimidated by Mama Lucy, was my father's brother, Donly, whom everyone said I took after. He was the first in the family to go away to college. He even earned a master's, but soon thereafter contracted an incurable disease and died. Success in our family was a crime punishable by death.

Delaney sits near the top of the Piedmont crescent of mill villages that stretches in an arc from Danville, Virginia, down through the Appalachian foothills of North and South Carolina, Georgia and Alabama to Birmingham. By the time I was born in December 1948, the cotton mills were closing down in Delaney and the lumber industry was all that was left behind to support a workforce who could shop at White's and pay my daddy's salary. The once thriving downtown was a gallery of abandoned storefronts, seed and feeds, hardware stores and cafes. Next to the paper mill, stacks of freshly cut timber piled high on boxcars filled my nostrils with the pungent aroma of pine resin that hung thick in the air of Delaney, the defining smell of my youth. From the time I was sentient I ached to get out.

My dad, still a handsome man in his sixties, looked the same, harried and florid-faced though a little grayer and paunchier than the last time I saw him. Tess, as always, looked to me like the oldest anorexic in captivity. A nervous, compulsive woman, she moved with the quick, skittish movements of a trapped wren. Although I could hardly blame Tess for alienating my father and mother—they met and married after my mother died; he had been on his own for a while and needed a wife—I could never fully embrace her as a surrogate mom and she sensed it, which seemed only to fuel her frantic desire to please and be accepted and that, of course, made matters worse. Both of them seemed ill at ease and focused their attentions on Wiley. How much he had grown! My father shook hands and hugged me awkwardly and asked how the move down from New York had gone, but he said nothing about the incident.

In addition to the national coverage, my little dust-up had received full treatment in the local press. But my family was doggedly polite, and though they were choking with curiosity I knew they would not bring up the subject unless I did. They had glossed over far greater disasters and disgraces for decades, and it had always driven me crazy. Now I was grateful for their infinite capacity for denial and unsurpassed ability to avoid the obvious. Both my father and I were taken by surprise when Tess brought it up.

"Will the *Charlotte Sentinel* take you back?" she blurted as we made our way up the hill.

"No, ma'am," I said. "They have a cartoonist. They replaced me when I left Charlotte. And I'm not exactly employable right now. Even though the judge reduced the assault charge to a misdemeanor, I'm still on probation."

"I'm sure there'll be other jobs," Tess said. Her relentless optimism drove my father crazy. The two of them had settled into one of those perverse symbioses older married couples sometimes devolve into that seems centered around a mutual distaste and disapproval for whatever the other one utters.

"Actually, there aren't really that many jobs for editorial cartoonists," I explained. "Only two hundred or so in the entire country. And most of those are filled."

"Not much turnover, huh?" my father asked.

"That's right. Cartoonists tend to stay in one place until they die or retire. When a slot opens up, dozens swarm to fill it."

Dad said nothing as we strolled up the hill toward the others. My father and I were not especially close. A moody, insecure man, he'd always been threatened by my rapport with my mother. He was suspicious of my artistic talent, considering it exotic, somehow sissy and vaguely uppity, one more interest I shared with my mother from which he was excluded. My intelligence and early success in school was a reproach to his lack of education and my father was wary of my wit. He even greeted my nascent carpentry skills, an opportunity for male bonding if ever there was one, competitively, although he certainly considered it a more manly pursuit than drawing pictures. He seemed to give up on me early in my childhood, abandoning whatever dreams he had of filial rapport with an ideal son. He responded to my mother's illness and his disappointment in me by traveling more in his job, overseeing the stores in his district, which included North and South Carolina and Georgia, and was on the road, it seemed, more than he was at home. His lack of interest initially hurt my feelings but he rediscovered me as his son when I embraced football. My youth seemed divided into two halves: Before Football and After Football. During the first half I was my mother's son, and in the second my father's.

In grammar school I was a shy, skinny, marsupial-looking kid, all mouth and eyes, withdrawn, introverted, a mama's boy, who liked to read and draw. But, to the stunned surprise of everyone, in adolescence I blossomed into an athlete of some ability when, as a high school freshman, I found the game of football and my own innate physical gifts for it. The same eye-hand coordination that could replicate what I saw with pencil on paper in drawings could also make a football go where I wanted it to. The eidetic memory that enabled me to transform blank sheets of paper from nothing into something also allowed me to visualize pass trajectories. It helped me discipline my body to master the fundamentals of a new sport, to make myself move in imitation of what I imagined an athlete was supposed to look like, because I seemed to be able to see not just with my eyes, but with my entire body. But that was only part of it. I also brought another crucial ingredient to the task. "The boy likes to hit," said my coaches proudly, as I pummeled my way onto the high school varsity squad as a ninth-grade linebacker and was named to the 4A all-state team as a quarterback by the time I was a senior. I had a "golden arm" according to the newspaper headlines. As it turned out, that arm could not only draw a still life and hit a nail cleanly into a board, it also got me a Florida State University football scholarship, and made me only the second Cantrell ever to attend college.

Football was not only my ticket out of Delaney, it was how I anesthetized myself to the catastrophe that was befalling my family during my adolescence. My mother was in and out of the hospital more frequently as I entered high school and her struggles and her tension with my father at home provided a grim backdrop to my passage through the teenage years. I lost myself in the sweat and noise and grass stains and Friday night lights and marching bands and the sheer iridescent joy and challenge and validation of sport and physical achievement, and put on the sidelines of my life the crumbling ruins of my family. My emergence as a jock also put my artistic skills on the back burner but it opened the world up to me socially. If not for my talent as an athlete and my gifts later as an artist I'm sure I would have turned my inner turmoil upon myself.

In high school my father and I declared a truce. Football offered me an outlet for my rage and him an escape and an anchorage for his battered pride. As his home life deteriorated my gridiron accomplishments began to fill up his life. And as they did, Clayton Cantrell became my number-one booster, even as the gleam in my mother's eye for me had been reduced to a dull sheen and her interest in my athletic exploits became perfunctory. He attended all my games, even traveling with the small coterie of team parents to away games, where he would collect kudos in the stands for my performances and relief from dealing with my mother's moods. Although he didn't express it to me directly, the scholarship I earned to FSU made him proud. The day he read the recruitment letter from the university's head coach he cried, though he had no idea I was watching from the hallway.

"Well, look who's here!" It was my aunt Florence, emerging from the kitchen below. She was an overweight, moon-faced woman in her sixties, a faded former high school cheerleader (all of my father's sisters were good-looking and remained well-preserved past middle age), with a gregarious personality and misleading warmth that masked a wary and suspicious nature she had passed on to her sons. In her hand was a large plastic container of iced tea. "How you doin', sug'?" She hugged me with one arm while balancing the tea with the other. Sympathy oozed from every syllable. When it came to dealing with personal tragedy Florence was a virtuoso. She lost her first husband to colon cancer at a young age, raised two of the sorriest boys in the county who provided no end to heartache, and she was now on her own again since her second husband, Floyd, was killed the year before, when he was struck by lightning playing miniature golf at Myrtle Beach. Disaster stalked the Cantrell girls even on summer vacations.

"Pick's movin' back down here, Florence," said my father. Cameron had paired off with Tess while Wiley and his cousins foraged in an ice chest for canned sodas.

"He is? Well, I'll swan."

I relieved her of the pitcher.

She searched my eyes for signs of madness. "You doin' okay, hon'?"

"Fine, Flo," I said, changing the subject. "How's the boys?" Her sons, the Bailey brothers, Talbert and Jerry, though both now in their forties, were irregularly employed and occasionally incarcerated, and every so often, when they were between jobs and jail, would drift back home to live with their mama.

"Good as can be expected." She sighed. "Eatin' me out of house and home. That young'un of your'n, Wiley, is growin' like a weed. When y'all gonna let me baby-sit him?"

I looked around to see if Cameron had overheard her offer. Some parents would consider us lucky but both Cameron and I would sooner leave our son with the Manson family.

"We don't really get out much, Florence," I lied. "Not much need of sitters."

"Well, if you do, you just call me. I know my boys would just love to take 'im fishin'."

Sure, I thought. And use him for bait.

"Have you had anything to eat yet?" Florence asked. "I made some of my banana pudding. Don't you miss it now!" Southern mothers, like their Jewish counterparts, find the cure to all that ails you in massive quantities of food.

"Hey, peanut butter," my aunt Beth called from the kitchen. Beth was my father's youngest sister and was as thin as Florence was wide. As a teenager she had spent a lot of time at our house escaping Mama Lucy's wrath, and she never let me forget that peanut butter was my sole means of subsistence for the first eight years of my life. "What's this I hear about y'all movin' back down here?" Word was certainly spreading fast.

"They bought a house in Eno," my father confirmed.

"Mother was born in Eno." Lily entered the small circle forming around us and gave me a hug. Slim and attractive, with dark watchful eyes, Lily was the oldest living sister and the family historian. Questions about ancestral history were always directed to her. "Ask Lily" was the mantra.

"Really?" said Cameron. "Pick, you never told me your grandmother was born in Eno."

"I didn't know," I said. Estrangement had cut me off from the family archival memory.

"Your grandmother and granddaddy met and courted in the mills over there," Lily continued. "We all were born there—Clayton, Ruth Ann, Donly, Florence, me, and Beth."

"I was baptized in the New Hope River," added my father.

"No kidding," I said, feeling a slight tingle in my scalp. "The property we bought runs down to the banks of the New Hope."

"Yeah, your granddaddy was deputy sheriff over there during the depression," said my father. "Used to bust up moonshine stills out in the county. Sometimes he'd take me along with him."

"I knew there was a reason we bought that place," exclaimed Cameron.

"Yeah, because I'm out of a job and you found one," I said. "Don't go getting oogedy-boogedy on me now."

"Well, it's about time you came home," said Florence. "No matter what the reason."

"Florence, hush!" Lily said. She had monitored her sister's prodigal mouth since childhood.

We moved around the picnic tables, greeting relatives we hadn't seen in years. I felt wary, cautious, on edge. Cameron, in contrast, ingratiated herself effortlessly into the scene, bonding with the aunts and cousins and moms. Wiley, meanwhile, romped in the yard, oblivious to his old man's trial by kinfolk.

Once again I had underestimated this family. There were no averted gazes or downcast eyes, no furtive whispering behind my back. Cameron, Wiley, and I eased into the mix like biscuits in buttermilk. My personal setback, returning home crippled and thwarted, had restored the natural order of things. My family brought an easy grace and preternatural charm to coping with life's tribulations. Funerals, wakes, intensive care units—these were our natural habitats. Public humiliations and personal disasters—loss of jobs, spouses, businesses—were our métier. Their reaction was less schadenfreude, delight in my misfortune, than that of a sigh of relief and a sense of the Prodigal returning. Now that I had received my comeuppance, I could be received with a note of grace. I belonged now. I fit in. At last, I was a born-again Cantrell.

A commotion erupted at the other end of the canopy. Voices rose in anger, accusations flew. A middle-aged woman with a toddler on her hip slapped a younger woman seated on a bench in front of her, then tossed a glass of iced tea in her face, turned around, and stalked off.

"That's your cousin Wallace's wife," Lily whispered. "She and him split up and he brung his girlfriend to the reunion. We all told him not to do it, but you know Wallace. Headstrong just like his mama. He ain't been the same since he lost his job at the mill. That was his life."

"That was ten years ago," said my father.

Wallace hunkered over a beer and sulked in the corner of the canopy with his girlfriend.

"What happened?" I asked.

"The company that owned the Saxapahaw plant got sold off in one of them Wall Street leveraged buyouts," my father explained. "The new owners looked at their ledger sheets and shut down the factories that wasn't passin' muster. Saxapahaw musta been hurtin' their profit margins. Workin' the weave room was all Wallace knowed. He never found another niche for hisself."

" 'Cept in a bottle," said Lily. "He's mostly drunk the last ten years away. Clara put up with it for the sake of the kids. Then he took up with this girl half his age. The nerve of him bringin' her to the reunion!"

"Is Mama Lucy here?" I asked.

"She's in the kitchen with the girls, making iced tea," said Mack, hauling up another cooler from the house. A strapping, overalled bear of a man with a gentle, gregarious spirit as sweet as his prize sweet potatoes, Mack was my father's first cousin and the host of this get-together.

"By the way, Pickard," whispered Tess, "she doesn't know about . . ."

"About what?"

"About your getting fired," she stammered. My father glared at her.

"It's not exactly a state secret," I said.

"We just didn't want to upset her," said Tess. "At her age there's—"

"I'll tell her," I said.

My father led Tess away.

Mack handed me a beer. "I read about that set-to you had with your boss. None of the stories said why you hit him."

"He called me a cracker."

"Hell, Pick, if we ain't crackers, who the hell is? We define redneck for a generation."

"I guess I didn't like the way he said it."

"It's like 'nigger,' " Mack said. "Black folks can call each other that but nobody else can. Redneck, cracker, linthead, peckerwood, trailer trash— I can say it, but you can't. On behalf of peckerwoods everywhere I thank you for defending our honor."

"I heared he had to have plastic surgery."

I recognized the drawling voice immediately. Talbert Bailey, the infrequently employed roofer and ex-con, was Florence's eldest son, and a big meaty, red-faced former high school linebacker. He was seated at the end of the table, his plate heaped with food and blobs of potato salad dropped from his masticating maw onto the paper plate he was hunched over. He had always resented my artistic and athletic ability and, as usual, his social graces were as lacking as his table manners.

"Where'd you hear that, Talbert?" I asked.

Talbert grinned through another mouthful of potato salad. "Ever'body knows about it. Hell, you're famous." There was something brown, like a bit of potato skin, in his gap-toothed smile. Then I realized it was a plug of tobacco.

"I lost my temper," I replied. "A misunderstanding. You know how the papers exaggerate."

Talbert's brother, Jerry, wandered up grinning. "That's not what I read, cousin." He was a shorter version of Talbert, but with no eyebrows and more teeth. "Sounded to me like you understood each other real good. Said you beat the shit out of him."

"Somebody less famous woulda got sent up for what you done, cuz." Talbert sneered. "You got special treatment."

Mack laughed nervously. "Good for you, Pick. I had some bosses I'd like to whup up on, too. But you had the balls to do it."

Talbert, aware that I had noticed the wad of tobacco in his mouth, offered me a plug of Red Man. I waved it off but Jerry took him up on it. "Now you gonna have to work for a livin', cuz. Instead of drawin' purty pictures."

"Hey, Wallace," Talbert yelled over his shoulder, "you can git Pick a job over at the Saxapahaw mill, cain'tcha? Oh, I forgot." Talbert grinned. "You're unemployed, too."

"Lay off, Talbert," Mack said sternly.

"Hey, I was just tryin' to do a little networkin' for my old cousin here—ain't that what they call it up in New York, Pickard?" He took a long pull on his beer.

"You're drunk," Mack said.

Talbert crushed his beer can in one meaty fist. "I reckon when you're a hotshot like Pick Cantrell you don't need no help from kinfolks!"

"What are you driving at, Talbert?" I challenged.

"I was just curious what it's like bein' famous, is all. I ain't never been famous."

"I don't know what you're talking about."

"Sure you do, Pickard. We all seen you on television—even if it was for gittin' your ass fired. You get a lot of pussy bein' famous? I bet you do—I bet you get a lot of stray quim, don'tcha, cuz?" I turned to leave. Talbert ratcheted up the decibels. "Must be fun havin' 'em make a fuss over you like that. Gittin' your picture on TV and all. And they kept mentionin' that big prize you won a few years back, too—the Pew-litzer. 'Course, they didn't mention your mama was crazier'n owl shit!"

Just as I whirled around to confront him a deep baritone boomed, "Shut up, Talbert!"

My cousin Buzz Rankin set his banjo on a bench without looking up, and removed the picks from his fingers one by one. Slowly, deliberately, he turned his lanky body to face the Bailey brothers.

"Who you talkin' to, Buzzy?" said Talbert.

"I'm talking to you, Talbert." Buzz was a handsome, easygoing man, with heavy eyebrows and a high forehead but he looked angry now. His blue-gray eyes turned cold and steely. "Who else around here is running his mouth with his brains turned off?"

The Bailey brothers edged closer together. "You better watch it, Buzz!" Jerry said.

"Don't make me whup your ass like I did when we were young'uns, Talbert," Buzz said. "You boys know I will. My girls ain't with me today so I ain't gotta set an example. It'd do me good to take a Time-Life set of whupass to you boys right now. Just for old time's sake."

"I ain't got no truck with you, Buzz," Talbert said.

"You do now. You owe Pick an apology."

"It's okay, Buzz," I said. "I can handle this."

"What're you takin' up for him for?" demanded Jerry.

"I ain't takin' up for nobody, Jerry. Pick can take care of himself."

"You suckin' up to him just 'cause he's famous, huh, Buzzy?" Talbert said.

"No, I just don't like you trashin' kinfolks at a family reunion. Now I want you to apologize to Pick, 'fore I rip you a new asshole and rearrange your digestive tract to where you don't know whether to piss or fart."

I turned to my cousin. "Really, Buzz, it's all right." Just then Talbert leaped up from the table. Everybody in the vicinity backed off, including Jerry. Buzz stood his ground. The two men stared at each other. Then something in Talbert's bloodshot eyes shut down and his scowl changed into a broad, shit-eating grin. "Shoot, Pick. You know I was just shittin' you. Buzz here cain't take a joke."

It was a calculated retreat, but it was hardly an end to the hostilities.

"Banana pudding!" called a voice from down the hill. "Y'all come get it!" Florence and Lily were carrying huge dessert trays in our direction. Talbert and Jerry dumped their empty plates in a trash barrel and everybody breathed a sigh of relief.

"I see Talbert hasn't changed much," I said, shaking Buzz's hand as the tables around us, now that the Bailey boys were gone, began filling up again.

"He's always had a hard-on for you, Pick, you know that."

Buzz, my aunt Ruth Ann's firstborn, was only a year older than me. His mother had committed suicide when he was sixteen and although they lived out of state he and I shared the "crazy mother" bond. Ruth Ann's alcoholism and fragile emotional state rendered her helpless as a parent, so Buzz and his brothers and sisters had grown up in a series of foster homes and finally an orphanage. I had always admired him for making the most of the shitty hand life had dealt him. He had spent his teenage years raising hell and riding motorcycles. After impregnating a girl at the orphanage he dropped out of school so he could marry her. He worked at first as a day laborer, then as a cowboy raising horses, and finally went back to college at night and became a parole officer for wayward youngsters. When his wife ran off with a Baptist preacher, he raised his three children by himself. Buzz was a loving but demanding father. He wouldn't allow a TV in the house and while the kids were growing up he read books to them every night. His children, Mark, Laurel, and Violet, were devoted to their daddy and their studies. All were college grads with good jobs or were earning advanced degrees.

"Well, I'm just glad to see you're here," I said.

"I wasn't gonna come," he replied. "My little girl had an intramural volleyball game. She said I could skip it. She's a little embarrassed because I'm the only parent who comes to all her games."

"Violet's gonna get her master's at Carolina in special ed, Pick," said Mack. "If her old man ever lets her have her own life."

"Well, I'm glad you skipped her game, Buzz," I said.

Although Buzz did not share my estrangement from the family, he'd always seemed to understand it. And although he cherished his mother's kinfolk and clung to them like life rafts, he wasn't blind. At the last reunion I attended, before we moved to New York, he had surprised me by commenting on the chilly reception I received from the family before it had even registered on me.

"It's the Southern Disease. They're punishing you for winning the Pulitzer."

"I guess I do get the feeling I should be ashamed of myself." I'd laughed, inwardly cringing to think that he'd noticed that the chilly reception had hurt my feelings.

"Look," he'd said, cracking open a can of Miller High Life, "it's been like this since the first ape stood upright. The rest of them were probably a-hootin' and a-hollerin' and tryin' to pull him back down on all fours. Make him feel ashamed for darin' to lift his nose in the air instead of sniffin' shit along with the rest of 'em. Truth is, nobody likes it when somebody else breaks with the herd. It pressures the rest to do the same, and that's risky."

"It's only human, I suppose."

"Maybe, but we southerners got the franchise. Sherman torched us, but we developed a taste for ashes on our own. We took the role of the vanquished and victimized, made losing virtuous. We can't help it. We're southerners. The call of the trailer park. We eat it up, from child-hood, like barbecue and grits."

Now, five years later, Buzz's words were coming back to haunt me. Now I was returning home in disgrace. I was acting out the Southern Disease. Committing Bubbacide. Kudzu kamikaze. Cracker hari kari. When I was younger and trying to pull myself out of the swamps of ritual self-abnegation, my family's addiction to and intoxication with defeat drove me crazy. Now that I had crashed and burned the planets were aligned, and all was right with the world.

"Where's Mama Lucy?" Mack asked.

"Leave her alone," said Lily. "She's in the kitchen with the girls, teachin' 'em how to make iced tea. She'll be along directly."

"Yeah," said Lily's husband. Uncle Byron was a short stocky man with a garrulous manner and cheerful demeanor. "If we're gonna cut the birthday cake somebody oughta start lightin' the candles. It's gonna take a while."

"Is Mama Lucy still living in the old mill house in Burlington?" I asked.

"She won't leave it," my father said. "Sits there all day watchin' her stories."

"Stories?"

"Soaps," Mack whispered. Our family always lowered our voices when talking about Lucy, as though if we didn't she would swoop down on us out of the sky like the Wicked Witch of the West. Even in old age Mama Lucy dominated the family.

"When she's not watching soaps, she sleeps. Stays up half the night and sleeps most of the morning," said Mack.

"Like a vampire," I mumbled.

Cameron, who'd been listening from the sidelines, shot me a glance.

"And fights with the neighbors," Buzz added.

"How's her health now?" Cam asked.

"Who knows?" Lily said. "She's complained about it for forty years and she's still going strong."

"You know the boy who cried wolf?" Buzz laughed. "She's the grandma who cried cancer."

"Hush, now." Lily punched his shoulder and glanced back at the house.

"The girls are always carting her off to the doctor for one damned thing or another."

"She's lonely," Cameron said.

"We got her a pet bird—a cockatiel," Mack said.

"Petey," Buzz said. "She loves that bird more than she does her own children. She lavishes it with affection and showers it with invective and abuse."

"Every time I visit her that bird's on her shoulder, like she's Long John Silver or somethin'," said Uncle Byron. "Now she wants to take 'im with her on her doctor appointments."

Mack slid down the bench to make room for Byron. "Bird flies all over the damn house. Sits on her shoulder while she cooks and does housework. She talks to 'im constantly. She sits 'im down on a newspaper outside his cage, then dares 'im to set foot off the paper. If he does she chases 'im around the house whackin' 'im with one of them wax paper tubes. Near 'bout kills 'im."

"Broke his wing one time," said Byron.

"I'm surprised she ain't killed 'im," added Mack.

"I'm surprised he hasn't committed suicide," I said, ignoring Cameron's glare and reaching for the pitcher of tea.

"Not funny," said Mack.

"When he goes," I said, "better check the coroner's report."

"Don't be mean," said Cameron.

"No wonder you're a cartoonist." Buzz laughed. "This family's Loony Tunes."

"You don't like Mama Lucy much, do you, Pick?" Talbert said. He and Jerry had been skulking around the periphery of the conversation, bristling at the stories about their grandmother.

"Talbert, she's not exactly a Norman Rockwell figure."

"She's still your grandma. You oughta show more respect."

"I respect her," I said, "especially when she's pointing a thirty-eight at me."

Our innocent yarn-spinning had turned to indictments of Mama Lucy and as usual I was playing the Chief Prosecutor. It annoyed me that no one else dared to speak honestly about the burden her eccentricities placed on the family, and that when I did it made everyone so uncomfortable.

"Relax, Pick," Buzz said. "The sheriff took the gun away from her years ago. Or was that her car?"

"Better come on and eat," Lily shouted from the buffet table—it's gonna get cold."

"We already ate," Byron protested.

"Well, they's plenty more. Pick, let me fix you a plate, hon'. Everybody's gotta eat before we bring out the birthday cake."

Talbert grabbed another beer from the cooler. He popped the top and pointed down the hill at a big green Mercury Grand Marquis coming up the driveway. "Hey, who's that?" Behind the wheel was a well-dressed middle-aged black woman wearing a floppy white hat. Another person was slumped low in the passenger seat and the backseat was crowded with kids.

"Anybody y'all know?" said Florence, walking up to the table with a basket of hot biscuits.

"Looks to me like they got the wrong reunion," said Mack.

"They ain't none of your'n, are they, Pick? You always was a nigger-lover," said Talbert.

Florence slapped Talbert's bald head. He whined, "Ouch, Mama!" like a five-year-old.

Buzz and I walked down to greet the new arrivals. The people in the car stared warily at us as we approached.

Buzz leaned toward the driver's window and asked politely, "Can we help y'all?"

"Is this where Miz Cantrell be stayin'?" asked the woman behind the wheel. The little shriveled woman sitting across from her stared straight ahead. She looked like a tiny gray sparrow, her charcoal black eyes sunk deep in her leathery skin. Three young children gazed at us from the backseat.

"Which Miz Cantrell? We got a few of 'em today. It's a family reunion," explained Buzz.

"Miz Lucille Cantrell? She be havin' a birthday today. I got a cake fo' her." The woman driving the car handed me a foil-wrapped tin through the window. "Aunt Bessie wanted to drop it off."

"Well, aren't you sweet," said Buzz. "She's ninety today."

"I figured she was gittin' on up there. Bessie said it was 'bout that." She patted the older woman's hand who still just stared straight ahead.

"Would you like to come up and say hello? Mama Lucy's in the kitchen."

"Nawsir. That's fine. Aunt Bessie can't git around too good on her own. I would have left her home but she wanted to come along. Would you give Miz Cantrell the cake and tell her it's from Bessie Thurwell? They knew each other in the old days."

"Bessie Thurwell. I sure will," Buzz said. "I'll run get Lucy, if you like. It's no trouble."

"No." She started the engine. "Don't bother. We better be gittin' on. Just tell her Bessie Thurwell say 'Happy Birthday.' "

"Thank you for dropping by, Miss . . . ?"

"Brown," said the woman behind the wheel. "Odessa Brown. Bessie's my aunt."

I stooped down and thanked the little old woman through the window, but she didn't look at me. Buzz and I waved to the children peering at us through the back window as the car completed a tight turn in the driveway, pulled onto the highway, and disappeared down the road. We returned to the festivities. Lily took the cake and placed it on the dessert table among the other cakes and pies.

"Who was that?" asked Cameron.

"An old friend of Mama Lucy's," I said. "We'll have to ask her."

"I didn't know Lucy had any colored friends," said Mack.

"I didn't know she had *any* friends," I said.

Buzz joined the musicians who were tuning up their instruments to play again. He had picked banjo for as long as I could remember. In his spare time he and his band, the Tate Mountain Boys, played county fairs and fiddler's conventions up and down the East Coast. I found the buffet table, and loaded my plate with food—peas and corn, fried okra, and barbecue—then sat down at a picnic table near the band set-up so I could listen to the music more closely. I was swigging iced tea and gnawing on corn on the cob and listening to breakneck versions of "Little Maggie," "Salty Dog" and "Fox on the Run" when I caught out of the corner of my eye the aunts leading a small figure up the hill to the canopy.

Mama Lucy was clutching Lily and Florence by the arms, studying the terrain with downcast eyes. Every so often they paused so Mama Lucy could rest and regain her strength or survey great-grandchildren swarming at her feet. The matriarch's appearance acted on the crowd assembled around the band like an electromagnet on iron filings. There was a slight ripple, a tremor, then as she drew closer, people began to peel off, racing to retrieve drinks or food in a frantic effort to attend to her needs.

She was headed for the far tents when, to my horror, Lily and Florence changed her course and led her to my table. Florence cleared a space and retrieved a plate of vegetables and biscuits and iced tea they'd prepared for her.

Beth arrived with the foil-wrapped tin. "Look, Mother, somebody brung you a coconut layer cake." Mama Lucy's ancient eyes lit up when Beth removed the foil and revealed the fluffy white icing.

"A Bessie Thurwell, a colored woman." When Mama Lucy heard the name she became agitated, and started scanning the crowd around her. "Where is she?" she asked. "Is Bessie here?"

"No ma'am," Beth said. "She just dropped it off. Who is she, Mother?"

Mama Lucy stared at the cake, oblivious to her daughter's inquiries. She sighed and said softly, "Well, I declare."

She still had not noticed me, so I took the initiative. "Hey, Mama Lucy. How ya doin'?" She swiveled toward me squinting to bring me into focus.

"Whooo! Lookeheah! Aaooh! Pick, young'un, is that you? Lawwd, where you been, boy? Come over here and hug my neck! How long has it been?"

"Ages," I said, moving around the table to hug her. It always surprised me how diminutive this woman was, who loomed so large in my memory and imagination. When I released her she clasped my hands in hers and looked up at me. "I'm mad at you," she said solemnly.

This was vintage Lucy. Greet you enthusiastically and affectionately, then put you on the defensive by going on the attack. "What did I do?" I replied.

"You ain't come to see me."

I recalled the Sunday family excursions to Burlington when I was a kid and how if we visited our other relatives without paying homage to Mama Lucy first, there was always hell to pay.

"I've been in New York," I said. "I haven't seen anybody."

"That young'un of your'n is the only great-grandchild of mine I don't know."

"It's not his fault we moved to another state."

"I thought you was livin' over in Charlotte."

"No, ma'am. We moved to New York City."

"New York City! Hmmph!" She jabbed her peas and corn with her fork. "I wouldn't put a crick in my neck to look up at them tall buildin's!"

I returned to my seat across the table from her, and sipped my iced tea. "How have you been, Mama Lucy?" I said, taking a stab at conversation. "How's your garden?"

"I ain't talkin' to you, Pickard," she said. "You didn't come to see me the last time you was here."

"Well, you didn't visit me when I was here, either, Mama Lucy, so I guess we're even." My grandmother had skipped the last reunion I attended when she learned that my grandfather's brother might show up.

She studied me for a beat, looking for signs of insolence. I kept my expression deadpan, inscrutable. Two could play this game.

"You've put on some pounds, ain'tcha?" she said, taking the offensive.

"I'm afraid so." I hitched my pants to conceal my paunch.

"Good. You needed some fattenin' up. You was always a scrawny little thing. Florence says you lost your job." Lucy's abrupt segues were legendary, and were designed to throw you off balance. So much for keeping things from Mama Lucy so as not to upset her.

"Not exactly," I explained. "I was arrested for beating up the publisher."

"I swan, Pick, you're just like the old man." She clucked dismissively. "Your granddaddy never could stay in one place, either. Always changin' jobs."

God, she pissed me off. "I worked at the *Sun* five and a half years, Mama Lucy. I worked for the *Charlotte Sentinel* almost twenty. That isn't exactly itinerant."

"He had a temper too," she said.

My father returned to the table with Mama Lucy's iced tea and said, "Mother, Pick's moving back. He and Cameron bought a place in Eno, where we used to live."

She gave me a searching look. "Is that right?"

"Yes, ma'am."

Lily said, "He's gonna fix it up and Cameron's going back to work." Cam, who was now sitting with Wiley at a nearby table, looked up to see Lucy's reaction.

"She's got no business workin'. She should stay at home with that young'un." Cam flinched and turned back to Wiley.

"I'm staying with Wiley," I said.

Lily, feeling guilty that she'd lobbed the floater that Lucy placed deep into Cameron's court, asked, "What can you tell them about Eno, Mother?"

"Lived there all my early life," Mama Lucy answered. "Worked in the mill there. That's where I met the old man." The "old man," as she called him, was my grandfather, her husband of sixty-odd years, who had died in the early eighties. "Back then we *had* to work. We'd-a give anything to stay at home with our young'uns. Not like these girls today."

Cameron excused herself from the table, ostensibly to fetch her camcorder from the car, but really I knew because if she didn't she would have throttled my grandmother. It revealed a chink in Cam's ability to shrug off my family. I had to admit I felt a measure of satisfaction that I wasn't the only one feeling murderous impulses toward Lucy.

"I was born there, too," my father said in an attempt to change the subject. "I was just telling Pick—"

"That's right," Mama Lucy said to me. "That's where your daddy was born. All six of 'em. Clayton, Ruth Ann, Donly, Florence, Lily, and Beth. That's where . . ." There was a catch in her voice. "That's where little Sara, the one born between Donly and Florence, died of the whooping cough." She sniffed and used her napkin for a Kleenex.

Lily said, "Mother, have you seen Aunt Jenny? She drove all the way over from Siler City."

"Jenny is here?"

"That's her sitting in her wheelchair under the pecan tree." This was a ploy not only to distract Lucy but to occupy her so the girls could set up the birthday cake under the canopies.

Lily led her off toward the pecan tree and when she was out of earshot I turned to my father and said, "Daddy, I didn't know you had a little sister who died of the whooping cough."

"Oh, yeah. Mother lost her in infancy."

"No wonder she's crazy," I said. "It would kill me to lose a child."

"We buried my baby sister in a tiny little coffin. Child's casket. No bigger than this." He held out his hands about a foot and a half apart. "Carved mahogany. It won first place at the county fair." His eyes lit up at the memory of that tiny casket, reminding me of the strange delight my family took in personal tragedy, how we carried our grief with a perverse pride. Our coffins were always of blue-ribbon quality.

"That was back during the depression when y'all lived in Eno, won't it, Clayton?" asked my uncle Byron. "Lucy went through some rough times over there."

"Oh, yeah. That's where we lived when Mama got stabbed."

"What?" I wasn't sure I heard correctly.

"I remember when she was in the hospital we stayed with Grandma Barlow."

"Stabbed? Who stabbed her?" My father had dropped this piece of information as if he were describing the weather. Images of Saturday night honky-tonk warfare and blood feuds flooded my brain.

"She was bayonetted by a National Guardsman during a mill strike. I must have been about Wiley's age at the time. We was living in Eno like I said. Mother was in the hospital for a week or so. We stayed with Grandma Barlow. There'd been some trouble in the mills around here."

"Daddy," I said, aghast, "why didn't you ever tell me that before?" I imagined my grandmother as some depression-era Norma Rae, a left-wing martyr to the labor movement I couldn't square with the self-absorbed, snuff-dipping hypochondriac I grew up with. As far as I knew, Mama Lucy was apolitical. And if she had any politics they were those of a small-town, conservative Southern Baptist, not that of some cracker Emma Goldman or redneck Mother Jones. And when I imagined the stabbing scene I automatically sympathized with the guardsman. I pictured her harassing him like she had me when I mowed her lawn. If I'd had a bayonet I would have used it on her.

"How come nobody's ever talked about this?" I asked.

"*Union* was a dirty word around here, and still is . . . Always will be," Mack said from the next table.

"I reckon folks wanted to forget what happened," added Byron.

"They were afraid, still are," Mack concurred.

"Afraid of what?" I asked.

"Union talk. Where it'll get you."

"Come on—this is the nineties," I said. "That must have been sixty years ago."

"Smile for the camera!" interrupted a cheerful female voice. It was Cameron with her camcorder. "Come on, Mama Lucy, smile for us. Say 'cheese'!"

Lucy was making her way back over to the picnic area, holding on to Lily and Beth for support. But when she saw my wife with the camcorder she went into a routine we'd witnessed many times before. At first she shooed Cam away, protesting and fretting over her appearance, covering her face with her hands, complaining she had worn no makeup, tugging at strands of her hair and acting coy. But then, like a young girl teasing a suitor, she slowly inched out of her shell, both withdrawing and blossoming under the tutelage of the camera lens. Cameron played her like a matador working a bull. The longer she ignored Lucy's protests, the more Lucy transformed from a shrinking violet into a blushing chorine, then into a blazing diva. We all watched mesmerized by her performance. Buzz whispered to me, "I'm ready for my close-up, Mr. DeMille!"

When Mama Lucy finally got within range, the bluegrass band struck up a rousing version of "Happy Birthday" and we all sang along. Lucy wept and we led her to the cake, ablaze with ninety candles. The smaller great-grandchildren gathered around to help her blow them out.

"Make a wish, Mama Lucy! Make a wish!" they all squealed. She paused dramatically, gathered up her strength and blew. She snuffed all ninety and the tent erupted in applause.

Cameron captured it all on videotape. Lucy was led to a lawn chair where she could rest and hold court. As she passed I hugged her and Cameron asked, "What'd you wish for, Mama Lucy?"

She answered without missing a beat. "I wish Pick would come mow my lawn."

4

THE RUINATION OF
THE MAIDEN PINKS

We left the reunion exhausted and emotionally spent. The sun was sinking in the salmon-pink sky as we turned off Highway 70 onto Cheshire Street, the main approach into Eno. As we crossed the New Hope River bridge the white cupola of the old brick courthouse rose above the treetops, its western face catching the last fugitive rays of twilight as the clock struck eight, its gentle chimes underscoring the quaint nostalgia of the town's picturesque setting, like something out of a Frank Capra movie.

The moving van from New York had arrived the day after we closed on the house, and we had spent the weekend unpacking boxes, unloading furniture, and trying to get settled in before the reunion. Oaklawn was everything Cameron had said it was, but I had not allowed myself to really take it in during the move and now we were restarting our lives in an unfamiliar house in a strange little town I knew nothing about.

Cam seemed to believe all the hype about Eno being the next great place to be in the Southeast, but as far as I was concerned this little mill town might as well have been the other side of the moon. And she knew me well enough to know that after a long, harrowing day with my relatives I could be irritable and subject to dips in mood and spirit. The moment was fragile. But she also knew how much I could be affected not only by the purely visual but by the simple eloquence of the wordless affectionate gesture.

As we turned off Bennehan Street into the driveway alongside the weathered sign that read OAKLAWN, CIRCA 1833 she leaned over and with a maestro's sense of timing, kissed me on the cheek and whispered, "Welcome home, Pick."

It worked. I melted, and for the first time in days I let my defenses down. We passed the ruins of brick pillar lampposts and a rusted wrought-iron gate, and eased our way up the weed-infested dirt and gravel drive in the lengthening shadows of evening. The rambling two-and-a-half-story white frame house, with the sagging wraparound porches, soaring gables, and slate roof rose up out of the weeds and wisteria like a fading memory. Sitting as it did in stately isolation upon a hilltop in the middle of town, less than two hundred yards behind the county courthouse in the square, the house itself was hidden from view by a thick wall of lush green cedars and hemlocks standing sentry along the street, creating a natural privacy screen. The main house reigned magisterially over a vast sprawling acreage of desiccated lawn and grand and ancient hardwoods, particularly giant oaks, for which the property was named. Outbuildings cluttered the grounds behind the house like ducklings gathered around a mother mallard. A summer kitchen, an ice house, a smoke house, a latticed, wisteria-covered woodshed, they all seemed to spill randomly over the back lawn, which rolled down in a terraced descent until it disappeared into a thicket of hardwoods along the perimeter, hiding from view the banks of the New Hope River, whose serpentine path defined the rear property line.

The grounds were overgrown with weeds, dandelions, wisteria, and kudzu and were in severe need of landscaping. But it didn't take much to imagine what they would look like pruned and trimmed and mown. We were too far inland for Spanish moss but the leaves on the trees, even at twilight, hung heavily over the lawn with a humid languor, and the effect of the foliage's weight exuded a kind of low-country sultriness.

The house itself was imposing, but its beauty seemed unassuming, guileless, washing over the senses like a reverie of lost southern gentility, of what once was and would be no more. Yet this was no Tara. There was nothing of the neo-classical grandeur celebrated so wantonly in the architecture of the Deep South. This house was Upper South, essence of Old Catawba, from the tips of its eaves to the bottom of its foundations ("that vale of humility between those two mountains of conceit" as the saying went, distinguishing the Tarheel State from neighboring Virginia and South Carolina) and it showed a modesty and restraint and lack of pretense in its structure reflecting the spirit of the state motto, "Esse Quam Videri": To Be Rather Than to Seem. An exquisite product of the Federal period in the Colonial style, it stood proud but practical, dignified, yet unpretentious. The restraint and modesty of the Scots-Presbyterians who settled here in the rolling wooded terrain of the Piedmont, which reminded them of their beloved homeland, was evident in the understated elegance of all of its lines and details. These were not extravagant men who erected such structures. They built well, but in a manner that bespoke substance and plenty, not opulence.

Left unattended for years, the house itself had deteriorated considerably. The boxwoods around the porches and along the front of the house were ravaged. The slate roof had lost some tiles; the steps off the front and side porches were rotten and needed repair; the white paint was peeling; and on the east side the exterior surfaces were almost completely denuded, turned gray from the weather and the harsh daily poundings of too many August suns. Still, despite all, the house gave the impression of sturdiness. Even after decades of neglect its natural charm and loveliness shone through like the features of a bereaved beauty through a widow's veil.

We parked the car and Wiley and Flappy frolicked on the lawn as fireflies lifted up out of the grass. Cameron and I unpacked the assorted dishes and casseroles my aunts had insisted we take home.

Cameron closed the tailgate. "Are you squinting?" She had caught me. I always squint when I look at an old house I'm interested in, just as I do when assessing a drawing I'm working on. By squinting your eyes you eliminate detail, get the overall impression and gloss over nonessentials. With a drawing you can see its impact, how it will hold up after it is reduced and reprinted at different sizes in various newspapers. With a house it eliminates all the worrisome surface defects that may overwhelm your first impression. The amount of cosmetic work a house like Oaklawn needed was daunting but I had learned long ago to ask myself one question: Is the house still proud? Is it holding its shape? Has it got good bones? The corner boards were rotting. The rake board and shingle mold needed replacing. Many of the windowsills, the bottoms of doors, porch columns and porch boards were bad. But when you squint those flaws disappear and the spirit of the place shines through. A bad roof, corner board, porch column, any one of those can be replaced with a phone call. I try to see what will be there after those first few calls are made. Cameron caught me squinting my commitment to our new house for the very first time.

Mornings at Oaklawn were a delight. The sun broke through the canopy of trees in sheets and pillars like light through a rose window in some Gothic cathedral. We awoke to a symphony of birdsong: sparrows, wrens, whippoorwills, mourning doves, crows, and bluejays greeting the dawn. Over breakfast we saw through the kitchen window flashes of blazing scarlet as cardinals flitted from bush to tree. Squirrels scampered up and down the tree trunks, leaped from limb to limb, branch to branch, chattering in a manic frenzy.

I had cleared a path through our woods to the schoolyard that abutted our property so Wiley could walk through the meadow to school instead of taking the longer, busier route along the streets. Our morning walks to school felt like idyllic strolls through an enchanted forest, something out of the Brothers Grimm.

One morning Wiley and I were walking along the path, he in his khaki shorts, blue striped T-shirt and red Nikes, with his bright maroon knapsack full of schoolbooks on his back. In my black jeans and black T-shirt with a day-old growth of stubble, I looked like I was on my way to knock off a 7-Eleven. Flappy, resembling a miniature cotton-candy Dumbo in the high grass, strained at her leash, tripping over the huge flapping ears for which she was named. Suddenly she started yapping in her high-pitched yelps and before we knew it a huge yellow Labrador bounded out of the bushes excitedly wiggling her interest in a fellow canine. I jerked the leash, reflexively gathering the Maltese up in my arms while the Lab pranced around us. A voice shouted "No, Ginger! No! C'mere, girl!" and a pink-faced man in overalls and a red-and-blue flannel shirt and gray clerical collar raced up to us. Clutched in his arms was a set of unwieldy bagpipes.

"Sorry," he said. "Is your dog all right? Ginger's still a puppy and a bit rambunctious. She got away from me when I was rummaging in the backseat."

"She's fine," I said. "Just a little spooked. Don't worry about it!" I handed Flappy to Wiley, who eyed the big Lab warily as the man slipped a leash onto its collar.

"So you're the bagpiper?" I said. We had heard him playing in the distance in the mornings the weekend we moved in.

"I'm afraid so." He grinned sheepishly. There was nothing pious or ministerial about him. He was medium height and slightly built with thick brown hair, graying at the temples, with a warm, winning smile and the serious gray eyes of a scholar.

"You must be our new neighbor," he said. "I'm Russ Draper. Rector of St. Stephen's." He pointed to the lovely brick edifice of the Episcopal church sitting with dignity atop a hill beyond the meadow next door to the school. "I hope my playing hasn't disturbed you."

"No, it's lovely," I said.

"I used to practice in the basement of the rectory, but my wife banished me from the house. Made me bring it over here to the graveyard behind the church where I wouldn't disturb anyone but the dead. We heard somebody bought Oaklawn but I didn't know you had already moved in. I know you're pretty secluded but if I'd realized you were there already I would have asked permission."

"No, feel free. Your music helps us feel at home here."

"Where are you folks from?"

"New York City," I said. "But originally from North Carolina. I grew up in Delaney, but my father was born here in Eno. I just learned my grandparents worked in the mills here."

"I'm sorry—what did you say your name was?"

"I didn't. My fault. It's Pick Cantrell. And this is my son, Wiley."

Reverend Draper extended his hand. "Nice to meet you, Wiley. I have a boy about your age—Malcolm. We'll have to get you two together. Although you'll probably run into him at school."

"And the loudmouthed Maltese is Flappy," I said.

"Cantrell? The cartoonist?" he asked, stroking Flappy's ears.

"Afraid so."

"You don't say!" He beamed. "I'm an admirer of your work. I used to be at St. Matthew's in Charlotte. Used your cartoons in my sermons. So Pick Cantrell, what brings you back south?"

"Just needed a change of venue. I had a little trouble at my last paper."

"So I heard. Well, we're delighted to have you here. Have you explored the town yet? Quite a bit of history here."

"We just arrived last Friday."

"Well, let me know if you want a tour. I'm a big fan of this place and a bit of a history drone. St. Stephen's is the oldest Episcopal parish in the state. I guess you haven't been to the West End yet where your grandparents worked in the mills."

"No, but I'd like to see it." Though I hadn't mentioned it to Cam, I was fascinated by my family's revelations at the reunion—especially Mama Lucy's being bayoneted.

"I walk Ginger two or three times a week along the river and up on New Hope mountain where the old mill village was. You're welcome to come along. It's quite beautiful up there with the mountain laurel blossoming along the river trail."

"I'd like that," I said. "But I better get this guy to school right now. His mother will kill me if he's tardy."

"Say, there's a party coming up at Ruffin Strudwick's for his new book."

"Strudwick the writer lives here?"

"Eno's own. Everyone in town will be there. You and your wife should come. It'll be a good introduction to the place. I'll tell Ruffin. He'll be delighted to hear somebody bought Oaklawn. And another celebrity to boot."

"Tarnished, I'm afraid," I said, waving and turning toward the school-yard with entourage in tow.

"It's still a big deal in Eno," shouted the reverend. "Shoot, in Eno we give parades in your honor if you can read and write."

It seemed as though we had just installed the line and plugged in the wall jacks when the phone started ringing. "Pick, when you gonna come mow my lawn?" Mama Lucy would start right in, without identifying herself. "Where are you, Pick? That grass is gittin' overgrowed." She'd gotten our number from my father, and Cameron was none too pleased about it. Even though Mama Lucy was family, and being close to family had been one of her reasons for moving to Eno, she considered Mama Lucy's entreaties an assault on the barricades of our new life. She had never been a working mom before, and between the guilt she felt over being away from Wiley and the anger she felt at me for turning our lives upside down, she micromanaged me and my time. She insisted I treat my responsibilities as stay-at-home dad and house renovator as a full-time job and as a safeguard against depression; time spent with Mama Lucy was time away from my job. But when Buzz injured his knee jogging and had to go in for surgery, I agreed to help him out and mow Lucy's lawn. I hopped in the beat-up old Chevy pickup I had bought and drove to Mama Lucy's. I hoped it wouldn't take long. Though I had encountered my grandmother on occasion it had been at least twenty years since my last visit to her house and I set off without asking for directions, wanting to see if I could still find my way. Sure enough, it all came back to me. In Burlington, the visual cues, like bread crumbs, were all still there—the old abandoned Holt mill and its rusted water tower rising up beyond the Haw River, the blinking yellow traffic light at the bottom of the grade, where the road forks off to the right; the giant Pepsi-Cola sign still faded but visible on the side of the hardware store.

Little had changed, it seemed, in Mama Lucy's neighborhood. I cruised on automatic pilot to the second cross street beyond the water tower and drove past the church and descended the hill into a modest little neighborhood. There on the left, looking just as I recalled it, was the driveway.

Mama Lucy lived in a small white clapboard house with a simple gabled roof, faded green shutters, and a front porch swing. Originally, a mill house like all the others on the side streets near the Pioneer Plant, it had undergone a few modest additions and improvements in the fifty or so years since it was built owing to the skills and cheap labor provided by Mama Lucy's countless sons-in-law and grandchildren. Surrounding the house was a well-tended jungle of hydrangeas, crape myrtles, gardenias, sweet betsy, burgundy-leaved barberries, and white clematis. The clematis emitted a fragrance I would always associate with my grandmother and long languorous Sundays sitting on the front porch and in the side yard shelling peas and snapping beans and shucking corn. Out back Mama Lucy's garden was thriving just as it had when I was a boy.

Buzz had left the lawn mower and a gas can in the driveway. I cranked up the mower and started cutting the grass without announcing my arrival. If I alerted her she would hold me hostage and regale me with a litany of her ailments for at least an hour before I could get to work and I wanted to get home before Wiley got out of school. It was a warm morning and I worked up a good sweat mowing the lawn. I was just finishing the front when I saw Mama Lucy waving to me from the porch. She was saying something but I couldn't make it out. I mopped my brow with the sleeve of my T-shirt, switched the engine to idle and joined her on the front porch. Dressed in a bright orange floral print bathrobe, and bedroom slippers, and wearing curlers and a hair net, Mama Lucy looked as if she had just woken up, even though it was close to noon.

"Hey, Mama Lucy, you say something?"

"I was in the back and didn't know you was out here, Pick. Why didn't you let me know you was here?"

"I didn't want to disturb you."

"You watch out for my bulbs, y'hear."

"Bulbs?"

"Mind my tulips and peonies. I just planted 'em."

"Yes, ma'am."

"You missed a spot in the backyard," she said, indicating the back with her chin.

"I didn't miss it, Mama Lucy. I haven't gotten to it yet."

"Well, I seen you out there rushing through to git finished. Don't you rush now. Take your time and do it right. Buzz does a good job and you can, too."

"I'm not rushing, Mama Lucy." I could feel the old resentment starting to flare. For God's sake, Pick, I thought, she's ninety years old. Let it go.

"You got that mower on the right height settin'?" She pointed to the Sears Roebuck model idling by the road. "That grass you cut looks mighty high."

"It's set as low as it'll get. Any lower and golfers will mistake your front yard for a putting green."

"Well, just watch out for my stone walkway. That blade'll scrape the stone. Hurt the mower and the stone both."

"Yes, ma'am—I'm aware of that."

"That's Buzz's mower, y'know—he cain't afford to buy a new one."

Fuming, I returned to the yard. It had been a mistake not to stick my head in before I went to work. Now she was making me pay. Critiquing my every move. I was three years old again struggling with a lawnmower bigger than I was.

"And watch out for my daffodil bulbs!"

I pretended not to hear.

"Pick!" she demanded.

I revved up the motor.

"Pickard Cantrell! *Pick!*" I was startled that a woman of her size and age still had the ampage to to be heard over the roar of a lawn mower.

"*What!*" I shouted, easing back on the throttle and wheeling around to face her. Startled at the vehemence of my response, she added sweetly, "Don't you leave without lettin' me fix you some iced tea, now, y'hear."

I cranked up the mower and finished the front and side yards and kicked myself for letting her get to me. When I finished I killed the engine and wheeled the mower around back. All that was left to do was some weed work and the backyard, a narrow strip of ground between the house and her garden and a rectangle the size of a tennis court beyond.

"Pick, c'mere!" Lucy called from the back porch. She was squinting at the house next door. I trudged toward her, wiping my forehead with my sleeve.

"Shhh!" Lucy shushed me and ducked back into the shadow of the screen door. "Did she see you?"

"Who?"

"That old biddy next door. Did she see you workin' over here? Did she say anything to you?"

"No, ma'am."

"Well, she better not if she knows what's good for her."

"What's up, Mama Lucy?" I asked, trying to see what Lucy could see.

"Ol' lady Dawkins spies on me. Always stickin' her nose in my business. She tries to tell Buzz how to mow. I tol' her"—she covered her mouth with her hand, as she always did when she was about to curse or spit snuff—" 'If your bowels run off like your mouth does, you'da shit yourself to death years ago.' "

I chuckled. I had never heard Mama Lucy use that word before.

"Claims we got grass on her driveway," she continued. "And her with that walnut tree limb hangin' over into my backyard droppin' her walnuts all over and encouragin' squirrels to bury nuts in my garden. Walnuts kill plants. She's tryin' to kill my garden, Pick. And I know why, too. She's jealous of my strawberries. Throwed a whole mess o' watermelon rinds in my backyard. If she speaks to you, Pick, you come straight an' git me. An' if she tells you what to cut, don't you do it now, y'hear?"

Lucille Barlow Cantrell had been at war with her neighbors for as long as I could remember. Some of the battles ended in shouting matches, some in fisticuffs, others in court. Apparently in all the years I had been away the saga continued.

"Don't worry, Mama Lucy," I said, removing my shirt and scrutinizing the house next door for any sign of life. "If she speaks to me I'll ignore her."

"My, my," Lucy whistled, studying my bare sweaty chest "You sure turned out one fine-lookin' man, Pickard Cantrell."

Her comment caught me off guard and I suddenly felt ill-at-ease, desperate to put my shirt back on. "You were an ugly baby, I swear you were. Skin and bones and all mouth. That's why your mama was so overprotective of you. But I was sayin' to Florence after that reunion that I believe you turned out to be the best-lookin' of all the grandchildren. And you know I've had some good-lookin' young'uns."

"Well, thank you, ma'am," I mumbled. Until that moment I had never been complimented by my grandmother. For anything. And her doing so now felt creepy to me. I waited for the punch line.

She glanced furtively at Mrs. Dawkins's back window.

"I seen her lookin' out her kitchen window at you, Pickard. I swear that busybody'll be out here before you know it. Come on in. Take a break. The iced tea's about ready. And why don't you let me fix you a tomato sandwich? I growed 'em myself out back."

I declined the sandwich but accepted the iced tea. The heat and exercise had left me parched. The house smelled cool, musky, like sour milk and mildew, the smell of an old plastic shower curtain in a nursing home. It reminded me of my childhood. There was a moist feel to the place, as if it were constructed of wet cardboard. Even the window screens seemed to carry water, the floor tiles to be clammy, as if an afternoon thunder shower had just passed through the house. The occasional screeches of Lucy's pet cockatiel, Petey, from its perch in the kitchen, reinforced the house's jungle atmosphere.

"Pick, take your shoes off," Lucy shouted from the kitchen. "Don't you come traipsing mud on my carpet, son. I just vacuumed." After all these years the law was still the law. I glanced down at the brown brush-haired welcome mat. It looked like the same one I used to wipe my feet on as a child, and maybe it was. Back then my aunts were all fashion-conscious young women and their colorful feminine pumps and high heels—black, white, brown, yellow and red—littered the back porch floor as if a tornado had hit Imelda Marcos's closet. Female accoutrements—heels, makeup, nylons, undergarments, the smell of hair spray, perfume, and toiletries—were ubiquitous in Lucy's house and suffused it with an estrogen-charged atmosphere, beyond Lucy's powerful matriarchal undertow, that as a child I found overwhelming. As a carrier of the Y chromosome I felt like an intruder in this landscape, an alien on the planet of the doilies.

I slipped off my grass-stained sneakers and glanced out the window at the outbuilding not fifteen feet from the back door off the kitchen. My granddaddy had lived here while I was growing up. Not much more than a tool shed, it looked like the bastard dwarf offspring of the larger house my grandmother inhabited, but it was the abode of the only man in Lucy Barlow's life, and, by her lights, the source of much of her misery.

Dalton Earl Cantrell, my grandfather, was a tall, thin, handsome man with deep-set blue eyes, prominent cheekbones, and a high forehead crowned by a beautiful crop of white hair. Born in 1890 on a cotton and tobacco farm near Saxapahaw, his life encompassed much of the twentieth century. He was ten years old when Freud published his *Interpretation of Dreams*, thirteen when the Wright Brothers flew the first airplane on North Carolina's Outer Banks at Kitty Hawk, fifteen when Einstein introduced his theory of relativity, seventeen when Picasso painted *Les Demoiselles d'Avignon*, and eighteen when Henry Ford invented his Model T. He was already married for the first time and too old to serve in the army when World War I broke out. The first president he ever voted for was Woodrow Wilson and Franklin Delano Roosevelt got his vote four times. If he were running today he would vote for him again because, as he explained to me once, "He was the only president we ever had who cared anything about the poor man."

The man I knew was gentle and kind and soft-spoken, a man who loved to fish with cane poles in quiet ponds, to smoke Lucky Strike cigarettes, to whittle toy animals out of balsa wood and carve intricate walking sticks out of oak and pine, to cook giant vats of the best Brunswick stew I ever tasted, simmered all day over an open fire with all the ingredients ground fine by hand, and to go see his beloved Alamance Indians play the Durham Bulls in Carolina League baseball on warm summer nights. But to hear Lucy tell it, he was Beelzebub incarnate. And for all I knew he may have been quite a hellion in his younger days. There were rumors of drinking and womanizing but by the time I knew him those days were long gone. She lived in the big house and he lived in the small one and as far as she was concerned he deserved it. Before he died he moved into a cabin with a wood-burning stove on a small pond over in Saxapahaw, and lived out his last years alone. I never saw my grandparents communicate with each other directly during all that time. My aunts, by then middle-aged, complained about how embarrassing it was to ferry granddaddy, who was then too old to drive and barely able to walk, down to the Alamance county courthouse in Graham, to make his support payments to Lucy. The little house where my grandfather once lived was closed up now and used for storage.

The familiar low bong of the antique mantle clock in the family room tolled twelve o'clock. When I was a child I used to stand before it, marveling over the intricate machinery that caused its delicate hands to turn. I would watch Mama Lucy wind it with the copper key and long for the day I alone could set those hands in motion; but Mama Lucy, afraid that I would break it, never let me near it.

Lucy's house had always reminded me of a funeral parlor. One of my earliest memories—I was four years old at the time—was of seeing Uncle Donly's corpse in her living room. As was common in the South in those days, my uncle's body was laid out there in a coffin the night before the funeral for the family viewing and visitation. I remember my mother lifting me up to see Donly's body and to kiss him good-bye. The other memory I have of my uncle is of the warm summer evening when he walked me to the store, holding my hand the entire way there, and bought me a vanilla ice-cream cone. The next fall he returned to graduate school, where he contracted the disease that claimed his life. I will always associate that room with the dead Donly, the Cantrell everyone liked and admired, the smart, talented one. A garrulous, expansive spirit, he was the only one of Lucy's offspring who was not cowed or intimidated by her. All my life I was told that I took after him.

As I grew to manhood the loss of Donly Cantrell came to represent for me the death of hope in that family, the death of ambition and exuberance. After he died the furniture in Lucy's living room was covered with plastic and never used again. From that day on, we entered the house through the side door. A photograph of Donly, one of those hand-tinted black-and-white photos popular in the early fifties, sat on the coffee table in the family room. My uncle's handsome face looked—as it had in his coffin—pale, rouged and otherworldly, like some forgotten star of the silent screen.

The family room was the unofficial living room and Cantrell tribal gathering place. A faded floral-print sofa sat along the far wall under a framed print of da Vinci's *Last Supper* which hung next to a window draped with royal blue velvet curtains. Flanking the sofa on one end was a frayed royal blue overstuffed armchair out of a George Booth cartoon and on the other an electric heater the color of burnt copper. End-table lamps, equipped with forty-watt bulbs, provided the pale luminescence of dying fireflies. The television set opposite the sofa glowed more luminously, its muffled audio underscoring the emptiness of the room and providing a counterpoint to the ticking of the clock.

Lucy had argued and battled with my aunts and father in this very space. Once, on Christmas Eve, when I was eight, my father, fed up with my grandmother's seasonal shenanigans, her complaints and accusations and baiting of my mother, told Lucy off and drove us home before the holiday meal was served. Sitting in the backseat I witnessed his guilt and self-reproach for losing his temper and my mother's attempts to console him. Even though I was too young to understand what had caused the argument, I took quiet pride in him for standing up to Mama Lucy.

Staring at the gallery of family photos hanging along the wall by the kitchen door memories flooded over me like a gullywasher in a dry creekbed after a heavy summer rain. There was my father as a young man smiling shyly among a bevy of young laughing women, his sisters. There he was again in his Marine Corps uniform going off to World War II with his arm around Donly, also in uniform.

There were several photographs of the Cantrell clan, prominently displayed throughout the family room, shots of my dad and all his sisters, a few including Mama Lucy, but none of my grandfather. And none of my mother. That no Mary Alice Cantrell hagiography adorned Lucy's living room was not surprising. They were natural enemies. No matter how hard my mother had tried to make peace Mama Lucy considered her firstborn's marriage to Mary Alice a betrayal. Still, I looked for a photograph of my mother and father among the archives, perhaps a candid snapshot of them caught in the first flush of young love in the years before I was born. But Mama Lucy was a one-woman totalitarian regime and she purged her rivals with Stalinesque efficiency. My mother was now a non-person, her life and spirit erased from official Cantrell family memory. Nor were there photos of any of the spouses of Lucy's other children. Donly and Ruth Ann, her two children who had not survived adulthood, however, were memorialized in separate framed eight-by-tens. The survivors were all subsumed into the group shots. Fair or not, the only way one got loving attention in this family was to die.

One picture I could not identify. It looked like a depression-era portrait of one of those haunted figures from a Walker Evans photograph, a gaunt, handsome but rugged-looking man eyeing the camera suspiciously. He looked uncomfortable, as though wearing a necktie for the first and only time, and the wings of his collar bucked and flared, like he was trying to escape the confines of his ill-fitting suit. A pair of wire-rimmed glasses sat incongruously on the bridge of a nose that had obviously been broken, and more than once by the look of it. His hair was parted in the middle and one of his high-boned cheeks was disfigured by what looked like a scar. I lifted the frame from the wall for a closer look. I would not have guessed the man's identity had I not found written in cramped handwriting on the frame's lower-right corner the inscription *Davis Barlow, TWI, 1934.* Davis Barlow, my great uncle, was Lucy's brother. I wondered what TWI stood for.

"The tea'll take a minute to cool off," Lucy called from the kitchen. "Are you sure I cain't fix you a sandwich? I just picked fresh tomatoes from the garden."

I replaced the photo on the wall and answered back, "No, ma'am, I better finish up and get on back to the house." Something drew me up short. There, framed at the end of the wall near the corner of the room was a drawing of mine. It was a drawing of Jesus I had done when I was twelve years old. I had copied it from one of those standard religious portraits of Christ—the Aryan, blue-eyed Nazarene in profile, eyes lifted heavenward—found hanging on countless walls of homes and churches all across the South and decorating hand-held fans with tongue depressor grips and funeral home addresses emblazoned across the other side. I removed the drawing from the wall and studied it in the lamp's pale light. My mother had put me up to it, as some sort of peace offering to her mother-in-law at Mother's Day. The Prince of Peace iconography was more an expression of her piety than of either mine or Mama Lucy's. Still, it wasn't bad for a kid's drawing. In the corner of the pen-and-ink sketch were the words, "Happy Mother's Day, Mama Lucy," and the signature "Pick Cantrell" in the distinctive scrawl I had worked so hard to effect. One of the first things a young cartoonist does is develop his own signature and I struggled with mine throughout junior high. This version had a swooping upper-case *C* and the *T* was crossed in a slash, the *E* formed by three horizontal slashes, and the *L*'s resembled elongated check marks.

Lucy, entering, caught me studying the drawing. Petey sat on her shoulder calling, "Pretty bird! Pretty bird!"

"Pick, I want you to draw me another picture. That's the last one you ever done for me. Your daddy has one you drawed for the paper. I want one, too."

"Sure, but it may be a while. I've got a lot of work to do on our place before I can get back over here."

"I know you don't much like comin' over here. Seems like you been mad at me for as long as I can remember." She removed the bird from her shoulder and caressed it like an infant. Lucy had a way of coming at you from out of nowhere and she caught me flat-footed. As with most of her sins she considered herself faultless and the victim of unwarranted retributions. She truly didn't understand why I was stand-offish or why I held her treatment of my mother against her. But she was old and it was too late to get into that now.

"C'mon, Mama Lucy, that's not true." I held out my index finger and she handed Petey off to me.

"Yeah, it is. You never did like me much even when you was a baby. You used to squall whenever I picked you up."

"I did?" I was amazed at my precocious insight and that my antipathy was evident at such an early age, and remembered so many years later.

"Cain't hide who you are, Pickard." She turned back to the kitchen. "Don't break my clock now." She had caught me eyeing the copper key on the mantelpiece. "You're just like your granddaddy. That's why you cain't hold a job."

I bristled but she was already gone. I stared at the cockatiel perched on my forefinger, inspecting the bird's plumage and topfeathers that curved forward like a question mark. Petey cocked his head and gazed at me impassively. "Pretty bird," he said. "Pretty bird."

"Buzz'll be able to mow for you when the lawn gets too high again," I called to her. "Anyway, you probably only need another mowing or two before winter."

"I'm still gonna need somebody to help me clean out my attic," she parried.

"I'm sure Buzz won't mind."

"He cain't get up them steps with his bad knee and all." She returned and visited while the tea cooled. "I ain't been up there in years. Cain't get up them stairs like I used to, neither. Somebody's gonna have to help me clear it, though. The girls want me to have an attic sale. I know what they're up to. If I empty the attic, they think I'll go next. They'd like to set me out on the lawn and pawn me off, too."

"C'mon, Mama Lucy, that's not fair."

"Byron and Dace want to move me on out to Shady Grove, too. They won't rest 'til they put me in that old folks' home." She grabbed for her Coke bottle and spat. "Devil owed me a debt and paid me off in son-in-laws. Well, I ain't a-goin' and I told 'em so. I won't have nothin' to do with them places. Buncha old biddies a-gossipin' and carryin' on."

"The girls are just worried about you living here alone. They want what's best, is all."

"Well, they can just want! Florence says I can move in with her. But I don't want to. Why would I want to live with them sorry boys of hers?"

"She probably wants you to move in and straighten' 'em out." Petey paced up and down my forearm. The prickly feel of his claws on my flesh made me shiver.

"Where's that house you bought, Pick?" she asked, forgetting that I'd told her all about it at the reunion. "You live far from here?"

"Eno."

"Eno?" she repeated, her expression darkening. "Let me pour you some tea."

Lucy's ninety years seemed to have taken little toll on her mobility or energy. She moved into the kitchen in sudden tics and spurts, quickly, impulsively with the skittishness of a hyperactive child, as if her nerve endings were jump-started every few seconds by a sudden memory or spasm of obligation. "I'm makin' you a sandwich, too, whether you want one or not!"

"You worked in the mills over there, didn't you?" I asked loudly, uncertain if she could hear me. But for all her other ailments, her hearing, like her metabolism, seemed unimpaired.

"I started goin' with my daddy to the weave room when I was nine. He wouldn't let me work although I wanted to. Some of the others worked when they was that young."

"I guess that was before the child labor laws."

"That's right. In them days young'uns could work in the mill with their parents. Mine worked from six o'clock in the morning 'til six at night. The looms they put in—my mama and daddy helped break them in—were called Crompton looms. And they run ginghams, checkworks. It was a single-box loom. And there was a four-box loom. And there was a two-box loom. And they run different patterns. On the single-box they had to run plain material, like chambray."

She entered the room triumphantly, carrying a glass of iced tea that she offered me with a flourish. Lucy was proud of her iced tea and had every right to be. It was by far the best I had ever tasted and my early exposure to such extraordinary quality had made me a lifelong connoisseur of sweet tea, as it's called in the South, and a bit of a tea snob. She shared her recipe only with her daughters, but I had pried it from them years ago, although I had only hit-and-miss success replicating it myself. The secret had something to do with pouring the boiling water over the ice and rolling the lemons out and squeezing them and adding an ungodly amount of sugar—one cup per tea bag—all simultaneously, and mixing it all together while the tea was still boiling. The only tea that had come close to Mama Lucy's was my mother's and Lucy would always sulk when she heard anyone suggest such, but my daddy had learned that the quickest way to get Lucy to whip up a pitcher of her own was to start bragging on his wife's good iced tea. Lucy watched appreciatively as I sipped from the beaded glass, downing several swallows in long slow draughts, and continued her childhood reminiscence as Petey lifted off my finger, circled the room, and returned to Lucy's shoulder.

"One day the bossman come to me and he says, 'Lucy, don't you want to take a set of looms?' I says, 'You'll have to ask my daddy.' And Papa says, 'Why, she cain't weave. We never showed her nothin'. No, you cain't put her on a loom.' The bossman says, 'I been watchin' her helpin' y'all. She can run a set of looms.' Well, he just got me a little box, and give it to me to stand on to draw in the end on the loom I couldn't reach. So I had to stand on that little box and go behind the loom and tie the thread where it'd broke, and throw it up on the harness and come back and get on my box and draw it in."

"How long had your parents been working in Eno?"

"Quite a while. Papa give up sharecropping out in Alamance County to go to work there."

"So millwork was really a step up?"

"My mama used to say she liked to died and gone to heaven when they moved over there. They had electricity and runnin' water for the first time and she didn't have to tote buckets from the well no more."

Mama Lucy left again. When she returned, she handed me a plate with a thick, juicy tomato sandwich on it and ushered me back to the dining room table next to the empty birdcage. She sat down at the end of the table with her Coke bottle spittoon.

"It won't so bad, really," she offered in a manner that compensated for the brown deposit of Strong Dental in the corner of her mouth, a way of speaking, her snuff dialect I called it, in which she was fluent. It sounded like a speech impediment, but I had grown accustomed to it over the years. "Mill village life was like a family," she continued. "They took care of you. You knew everybody in that town and everybody knew you. Two hundred, two hundred fifty families. Neighbors always borrowin' from each other. An egg or a piece of fatback. Maybe a couple of Irish potatoes. We looked after one another. Not like today." Lucy's eyes sparkled as she warmed to the subject and her memories filled her up. "I remember lyin' in bed late at night when I was a girl, in the summertimes when the windows was up, smellin' the yarn mixed in with the wisteria and the honeysuckle, and starin' through the window screens up the hill to the factory lit up like a Christmas tree and listenin' to the roar of the looms. It was real soothin', would put you to sleep like the poundin' of waves on a beach. Like a lullaby."

I had never heard her talk about her girlhood or life in the mills before. I ate my sandwich and listened.

"My brothers and sisters worked all of them in Burlington—Pioneer, Needmore, and the Plaid mill, and this one down here." She waved her hand in the direction of the Holt plant on the river. "Virginia mills, Gibsonville, Swepsonville—I counted them up, there was about twelve or thirteen different cotton mills we all worked at one time or another."

"Including the one in Eno?"

"That's the only one I worked."

"That's where you and granddaddy met and courted, right? In Eno?" I was beginning to think maybe there was some pre-womb tug to our decision to move there.

"Oh, yeah . . . I just loved . . ." I thought I was about to hear the first declaration of affection for my grandfather any of us had ever heard. "I loved to spool," she continued. "And wind. I loved to work in the winding room. I didn't like weavin'. I've done everything in the mill except draw in, 'cause I never liked that. I always wanted to be on my feet. When I worked I didn't want to sit down." She went to check on something again in the kitchen, leaving me at the table with the bird on its perch in a cage with the door open, both of us free to contemplate the meanings of these new technical words from a mill life she took for granted—words like *spool* and *wind* and *draw in*.

"I never heard much about your life in the mill when I was growing up," I called after her. "At the reunion someone mentioned something about you getting stabbed by a National Guardsman."

I waited but she didn't respond. When she came back she seemed preoccupied, distracted.

"Pick, ain't you got some lawn to mow?" she asked.

"Were you hurt bad?"

Her face darkened. "That's water under the bridge. Ancient history." She gathered up my plate and napkin while I was in midbite.

"How come I never heard any of this before?"

"You never asked. Can I get you anything else to eat, Pickard?"

I had never seen Lucy avoid talking about any subject no matter how painful or embarrassing. I was intrigued, but not enough to prolong my visit. "No, thank you, ma'am. I gotta finish up and get on home before Wiley gets out of school."

"Well, I appreciate you mowin' my lawn. I know you didn't want to do it, but I appreciate it. And I'm gonna give you some biscuits to take with you before you go now."

I finished up the job in less than thirty minutes. The moment the mower went dead, Lucy was out on the porch again shouting instructions. "Don't forget to cut the weeds along the bushes. Buzz always trims the weeds."

"Yes, ma'am." Buzz had set a high standard. I finished up the weed work and was putting the mower in the back of the pickup to return to Buzz when Lucy called from the house, "I got some biscuits for you, Pick. Hold on."

I returned to the porch, wiping my face with my T-shirt. Now self-consciously I slipped it back on. She handed me a basket of fresh-baked biscuits loosely covered with tinfoil.

"Thank you, ma'am. We'll have these for supper with gravy and for breakfast with jelly."

"Does that wife of your'n cook biscuits for you?"

"She's working now, Mama Lucy. She doesn't have much time to cook." I could tell from her expression her disapproval hadn't wavered since the reunion.

"Well, she better learn how if she wants to hang on to a husband, that's all I can say."

"It didn't seem to help you much, did it?" The comment slipped out before I could catch myself.

She blanched and I turned toward the truck, biting my tongue. There was something about Lucy's pronouncements that made me want to puncture them, but it felt unseemly sniping at her while holding her gift from the oven.

"Thanks for the biscuits, Mama Lucy," I said. "I better get on back."

"I still need that attic cleaned out. I promised 'em I would let 'em have that yard sale. But I told 'em I had to clean out some of the junk up there first. They's some personal things I need to go through before I go sellin' it to strangers."

Damn, she's relentless, I thought. No wonder she had everybody jumping through hoops for her. It was easier to do her bidding than to withstand the assault. But no way was I coming back. Even if I was curious about that bayoneting.

I laughed. "Mama Lucy, I'm beginning to understand why you had so many kids. Cheap labor."

She looked at me blankly.

"Haven't you heard?" I teased. "Lincoln freed the slaves."

"Pick," she said, slowly scanning my handiwork. She pointed to the grass growing along the edge of her walkway, and looked at me disapprovingly. "Where's my pinks?"

"Your what?"

"My pinks. I told you to be careful with my bulbs and look what you done. I just planted a row of 'em out here by the walk."

"I'm sorry, Mama Lucy. I swear I didn't see any flowers planted along there."

"My maiden pinks is gone," she wailed. "You mowed down my pinks."

"But I didn't," I protested, not realizing that the bulbs she had planted had sprouts indistinguishable from wire grass, and that in my rush to finish, I had, indeed, defoliated her front yard. "I didn't see any."

"Look what you done, Pickard Cantrell! My bulbs for spring is ruined all because of you!"

5

THE MATING CALL OF
THE JUNIOR LEAGUER

"Be nice, Pick," said Cameron as we pulled up to the Strudwick estate's magnificent brick-columned entrance. "First impressions count, especially in a small town."

"I hate parties," I replied.

"It'll be good for you—for us." She checked her hair and makeup in the rearview mirror. "We can't be hermits forever. Besides, don't you want to meet the distinguished author?"

"Not really. I've met enough distinguished authors for one lifetime." If I was gun-shy about displaying my job loss and public humiliation in front of my family, the idea of parading it before a tribunal of highly accomplished and gainfully employed strangers at a book party did nothing for my spirits.

"You haven't met Eno's most famous resident, best-selling author and National Book Award finalist Ruffin Strudwick," Cameron teased in her best *All Things Considered* public radio voice. She adjusted her earrings before opening the car door. "He's just published his eagerly anticipated sexual bildungsroman, *Fallen Angels*, about his halcyon New York days in the late seventies before the AIDS epidemic struck. They say he was waiting until his parents died to come out with it, but they haven't cooperated so he published it anyway."

Her teasing didn't help.

"C'mon, Pick." She patted my hand and slid gracefully out the passenger side in her short cocktail dress. The parking attendant holding the door gazed appreciatively at her long tan legs. She grabbed my arm and guided me toward the entrance. "Everybody will be here. It'll be our big chance to meet and greet the Eno cognoscenti."

"Eno cognoscenti. Isn't that an oxymoron?"

Ruffin Strudwick's home—Sassafras, circa 1803—was one of Eno's most beautiful and historic houses. Featured in all the Chamber of Commerce literature, its colonial elegance was accented with Japanese lanterns hanging from trees and illuminating walkways like strings of incandescent pearls. From the street they looked like candles lighting up a gigantic birthday cake.

Since my visit to Mama Lucy's, I had settled into a routine at Oaklawn. When I wasn't working on the house or supervising contractors I spent my time exploring Eno—sometimes alone, sometimes accompanied by Russ Draper. Through my own exploration, supplemented by visits to the town library and literature from the Historic Eno Commission I picked up at the Chamber of Commerce, I was becoming, if only out of sheer boredom, fairly well-versed in the history of the town and its many storied homes.

Eno hemorrhaged history. It had once been a center of law, government, and commerce, and for a time after the American Revolution the provisional capital of the state. It may have lost much of its political and economic clout over the years, but it had forfeited none of its charm or pedigree and was one of the most self-conscious towns I had ever seen. Historic markers were as prevalent on the downtown streets as parking meters. The state's first paper mill was located here, says one. The ratification of the U.S. Constitution was debated on this site, declares another. A signer of the Declaration of Independence was buried here, a Whig candidate for vice president was born there, a governor lived in that house, a U.S. senator in another. And, according to my research, Strudwick's family had been one of the most prominent families in colonial North Carolina, and had provided the state with numerous governors, legislators, and senators, many of them born at Sassafras. Ruffin's namesake ancestor, Edgar Ruffin, was one of the early chief justices of the North Carolina Supreme Court. His law office still graced the grounds of Sassafras. The Strudwick and Ruffin family names adorned countless markers in the graveyard at St. Stephen's. But the Strudwick lineage had grown less illustrious since the Civil War, producing more accountants and overseers than jurists and statesmen. Ruffin, an only child and the latest scion of the Strudwick dynasty, was the sole remaining heir to their storied gene pool, and determined, it seemed, to single-handedly restore his family name to some of its former luster. Although, as fate decreed, he would also be bringing it to a screeching halt because, as Russ Draper put it, "Ruffin's queer as a football bat." Ruffin, however, had traded genetic for literary immortality. His breakthrough novel, a Civil War epic told from the viewpoint of a female Confederate spy who claimed to be Robert E. Lee's mistress, had created an uproar among Civil War scholars by suggesting that the relationship between Lee and Stonewall Jackson was latently homosexual. But it was taken seriously by the literary gatekeepers, and it established his commercial viability. His subsequent books, and sole progeny, regularly camped out on the best-seller lists.

"Welcome to Sassafras," said Ruffin Strudwick to the couple ahead of us. Cameron and I ascended the porch steps. "And you must be Pickard Cantrell." Our host gleamed. "I'm Ruffin Strudwick." I had to confess he cut a striking figure standing there in the foyer dressed in late-nineteenth-century garb—a velvet Edwardian three-quarter-length waistcoat, flared, purple pleated pants, a plaid woolen vest with a gold watch fob—punctuated by a pair of red high-top sneakers. He appeared to be about my age. His hair was bleached white and closely cropped in a style more frequently seen in Soho than rural North Carolina, and his ochre-colored topiary goatee and gold earring set off his hazel eyes. His angular face was flushed with alcohol and the giddy delight of the born party host and social director.

"Pleased to meet you, Ruffin." I smiled. "This is my wife, Cameron Cantrell."

"Gracious, girl. Aren't you a sight! You look fabulous!" He took Cameron by the hands, appraising her and twirling her around all in one motion. "And I wanted to be the most beautiful belle at the party. Pickard, you lucky thing."

"He is indeed." Russ emerged from the side porch, and pecked Cameron on the cheek. "So you two made it! Where's the lad?"

"He's at your house," Cam said. "We just dropped him off."

"I'm always the last to know." Russ sighed. "I've been on the golf course all day afflicting the comfortable."

"Can I get you something to drink, Cam?" I asked.

"White wine, please."

"The bar is in the back under the canopy," said Ruffin. "Pickard, I just want to say how pleased I am y'all have moved to our little Eno. I am such a big fan of your work. Or should I say *was*?"

"Back atcha." I forced a smile.

I left Cameron with Strudwick and threaded my way through the massive hallway that extended from the front of the house all the way to the rear, dividing it symmetrically down the middle, a classic Federal period floorplan. Black-tied waiters and waitresses carrying silver trays of hors d'oeuvres and canapes darted among the priceless antiques. A sideboard was stacked with hardback copies of Ruffin's *Fallen Angels*. Strudwick's comically haughty mug eyed me from the back of the dust jacket.

Moving through the mass of strangers, hoping not to be noticed I wondered again how I'd let Cameron talk me into coming. I stood in line at the bar on the sprawling terraced lawn. The sky was streaked with dark purple cirrus clouds backlit by the retreating sun. Behind us, stars began to wink overhead like tiny diamonds on a jewel thief's chamois. I turned back to the house and tried to imagine what it must have been like to inhabit such a home in the days before electric lights, gas ovens, and acetylene torch bug zappers. The house was not unlike Jefferson's Monticello in style and appearance. Strudwick, to his credit, had returned it to its former pristine elegance. I envied his meticulous attention to detail, not to mention his financial wherewithal to employ artisans who restored colonial brickwork and hand-carved mantelpieces with the care and know-how they deserved.

The party spilled out onto the lawn. Russ, drink in hand, emerged from the crowd with a woman in tow. "Pick Cantrell, I'd like you to meet Sandra Murphy." Gazing at me from behind tortoiseshell glasses was an attractive woman of indeterminate age with long, frizzy auburn hair, no makeup, clear porcelain skin, and large, startlingly blue eyes. Dressed in a green smock, heather gray leggings and clogs, with a purple backpack over her shoulder, Sandra looked vaguely familiar, bookish and slightly out of place among all the slinky cocktail dresses and expensive jewelry. She gave me a self-assured shake. "Sandy heads up the Southern Oral History Project at UNC–Chapel Hill," Russ explained. "She can tell you everything you need to know about the strikes."

"And more than you'd ever want to know," she added, smiling. "I already know Pick Cantrell and I'm a big admirer of his work. He wouldn't remember me but we went to school together in Delaney."

Slowly her features began to register.

"Sandy," I exclaimed. "Sandy Murphy! "Is that you?" I opened my arms and we hugged.

"It's been a long time. I'm surprised you remember me." She turned to Russ. "Pick was the star quarterback in high school and I was the class dweeb."

"You were not. You were the class intellect. The only one with brains in that school. I always admired you."

"Stop it. You didn't even know I was alive back then. You were eaten up with football and Cynthia Polson, the head cheerleader, as I recall."

"Yeah, I was a dumb jock all right, but I was a secret admirer of yours. I wanted to be Sandra Murphy when I grew up."

Sandra was a pretty, popular, and successful student at Delaney High who thrived in that adolescent milieu, cutting a wide swath through both the classroom and extracurricular activities. She was one of those golden achievers—yearbook, glee club, Girl's State, Governor's School— but she had always seemed restless to me, ambitious and driven more than most kids at that age. Although she had moved easily among the high school elite, the country club debutantes, her people were dirt poor and her father was the town drunk and she suffered for that. She seemed like one of the few of my classmates destined to get out of Delaney, and from afar I had identified with her drive and ambition, but I didn't know her well.

"Pick, I thought you'd traded in your pencils for a football helmet. Then you became a cartoonist!"

"I rediscovered it in college," I said, not wanting to get into my knee injury or my mother's death.

"I'm sorry about what happened at the *Sun*—losing your job and all."

"Thanks." I shrugged, surprised by her directness.

"Well, I hope it's not forever. Your work has been important to this region. When I taught middle school we used to cut your brown lung cartoons out and put them on the bulletin board in my current events classes."

Russ laughed. "Kind of makes you feel like one of those antiques Ruffin collects, huh, Pick?"

"I hope I haven't embarrassed you," she said. "But I mean it. We're all going to miss your work."

"Too bad you don't own a newspaper," I said, taking an hors d'oeuvres from the server. I was grateful for the interruption. Flattery that direct always made me squirm—even when I had a job and it didn't sound like a eulogy.

"Sandy's very passionate," Russ said, taking a crabcake canape from the tray.

"I remember," I said. "We had English lit together."

"Don't forget my grandfather died of brown lung, Russ," said Sandy, accepting a crabcake and napkin. "You'll have to forgive my fervor."

"We'll torture Pick over lunch someday soon," said Russ. "I'll hold him down, Sandy, and you shove compliments under his fingernails."

"I'll report you to Amnesty International," I replied.

"Sandy's working on a book on the southern cotton mill village culture," said Russ. "The strike you said your family was involved in is a big part of her research."

"Your family was in the uprising of 'thirty-four?" Sandy asked.

"If that's what it's called. It's all news to me. Tell me about it."

"There was a lot of labor unrest during the depression down here. In Gastonia in 1929, then all across the South in 'thirty-four after Roosevelt got elected, half a million textile workers went out on strike. Largest in U.S. labor history to that time. Closest we've ever come in this country to a revolution. The National Guard was called in to put it down. It was the first time southern cotton mill workers rose up en masse against the mill owners."

"What happened?" I asked, feeling ashamed that, despite having drawn cartoons about brown lung, I had only recently learned of this event.

"They lost," Sandy replied.

"This is a right-to-work state," said Russ. "You don't see much evidence of unions in the South nowadays, do you? Your wife's in the film business. Why do you think so much commercial work is shot around here, especially in Wilmington? No unions."

"Gastonia in 'twenty-nine and then the 'thirty-four uprising," Sandy continued. "That's when the decisive battles were fought down here. Pretty grim business altogether. Tragic. Bloody."

I told her about Mama Lucy being bayoneted.

"She was? Jesus! Did she live?"

"Oh, yeah," I replied. "Takes more than a bayonet to stop Mama Lucy. Happened in Burlington."

"That had to be September fourteenth, 1934, at the Plaid mill. Second week of the strike. A large crowd of workers clashed with National Guardsmen. Several were bayoneted and some were clubbed. There was another incident at the Pioneer plant that same day, though . . . Where did she work?"

"I don't know."

"What was your grandma's name?" asked Sandy.

"Lucille Cantrell. But her maiden name was Barlow."

Sandy looked at me as if I had said I was the illegitimate child of Elvis. "You're related to Lucy Barlow?"

"She's my father's mother."

"Davis Barlow's sister," Sandy said.

"Yeah."

"Davis Barlow was pretty prominent as a strike leader," Sandy said. "President of the Burlington local of the TWI, or Textile Workers International Union."

I recalled the initials on Dave's photograph in Lucy's living room.

"He was a major figure in the uprising. That's how I first heard about Lucy. And why I always thought of her as Lucy Barlow. He was charismatic, one of the most articulate spokesmen for the cause."

"Mama Lucy's brother?" The notion that my people, the Cantrells and Barlows, whom I had always thought of as so very conservative, and boring, dull as dust, could possibly have produced any colorful renegades and radicals of historical significance—and that my grandmother, Mama Lucy, with her hair curlers and Coke bottle spittoon, could be one of them—set my mind reeling.

"I guess it runs in the family," said Sandy. "I know more about Dave than about Lucy, but she was almost as famous back then. Quite a troublemaker."

"So Pick comes by it naturally." Russ winked at me.

"Maybe there's another Lucille Barlow," I said, still skeptical.

"I wanted to interview her for our book but we assumed she was dead. She must be in what—her late eighties by now?"

"Just turned ninety," I said. "What's the book again?"

"It's an oral history of mill village life in the Carolinas during the early part of the century. We've interviewed close to two hundred people who remember the way it was, but they're all dying out fast. A pivotal section will deal with the uprising of 'thirty-four, when it all started unraveling. Although it's harder to find anybody who'll talk about that."

"I've been helping Sandy find interview subjects," said Russ.

Sandy brightened. "Lucy Barlow, wow . . . Do you think she'd talk to me?"

"I don't know." I still couldn't believe we were talking about Mama Lucy.

"Getting to her would fill a huge hole in the book. Is she, uh . . . still lucid?"

"Clear as a bell. Too lucid."

"I'd love to meet her. We've interviewed a number of folks who remember the uprising. But nobody who was an active participant."

"Sure." I tried to imagine introducing a scholar like Sandy Murphy to Mama Lucy.

"Maybe Sandy could tell us about the uprising over lunch, Pick, and you could tell her about your grandmother."

"Or maybe Sandy could tell me about her," I said, smiling.

"Is this your first public outing since coming to town?" Sandy asked.

"I'm afraid I haven't been in the mood for socializing."

"Well, if you gotta party you might as well kick it off with one of Ruffin's do's," said Russ. "He's famous for his parties. Sort of a Gatsbyesque figure. He brings people together, then watches the sparks fly. There's a lot of firepower here today—politicians, academics, journalists, literati . . . ."

"Speaking of firepower." Sandy glanced across the patio. "The tall handsome man talking to the beautiful woman with her back to us, that's Roland Jameson, a WeltanCom executive. And I don't know who he's talking to."

"That's my wife. Who's probably still waiting for her drink."

"I'd go rescue her if I were you, Cantrell," said Russ. "Women swoon for Jameson. He makes their hearts go pitty-pat."

"He's married, isn't he?" asked Sandy.

"His wife's in the looney bin."

"My goodness, Russ." Sandy laughed. "For a rector you certainly have all the juicy dish."

"As a rector I try to keep the rectum out of my rectitude."

"I hear Jameson's loaded. We ought to try hitting him up for funding."

"Looks like he's enjoying his conversation with Cam." Russ winked, nudging me.

"My wife can handle herself," I answered.

"Oh, look," said Russ, pointing discreetly. "There's Nathan Price."

"Who?" I asked.

"The Dildo King. He owns Garden of Eden Enterprises," answered Sandy.

Russ said, "They make marital aides. You know, dildos. Penis enlargers. Adult videos. He started out as a photographer in New York, bought an alternative newspaper in the seventies, then started the business to take advantage of the so-called sexual revolution. They were in Chapel Hill for years. Then relocated in Eno when they outgrew their facilities. Biggest industry we got now. He's a good employer. Lots of folks work for him."

"He's certainly been generous to our project," Sandy said.

"Trying to buy respect. He married one of his models. Some say she was a porn star. But that could be gossip. She seems very nice. There's the producer from Tarheel Players sucking up to him now. Oops. She saw us. Now she's skulking away. Everybody wants his money but nobody wants to be seen talking to him. Every now and then some of the local Bible-thumpers picket the business. But he pays his taxes. Keeps a low profile. Don't see him out much at parties. He's a member of the Kiwanis and Rotary. Contributes to United Way. Does it just like the tobacco companies and defense contractors and other manufacturers of controversial products."

"Hey, his money's green," said Sandy. "I hear the Documentary Studies Center at Duke just got some Moonie money."

"Hmm," said Russ, "so that's why the new director asked me if I charged group rates for stadium weddings."

"Welcome back to the New South, Pick."

"If y'all will excuse me I better get Cam her drink." I made my way to Cameron, who introduced me to Roland.

The man's handshake was one of those bone-crunchers—more aggression than greeting.

"Welcome to the Triangle," he said, with a smile one part sincerity and one part dental whitener. Handsome in that tanned, too-perfect way, his eyes burned into you with ESTian fervor. His voice was deep, restrained, like a late night FM DJ.

"Roland is in charge of WeltanCom's marketing division," Cameron explained. "They're launching a new campaign involving TV ads and industrials. He asked me to come by and pitch Oleander."

"If your wife is as talented as she is lovely, we oughta be in business."

"She's the best." I smiled.

He handed Cameron his card. "Call me."

When we were alone she asked, "Are you okay?"

"Sure, why?"

"Strudwick's comment: 'Or should I say *was*.' What an asshole!"

"Forget it. He doesn't know what he said. Hey, I thought we were moving to a backward little town. This is like one of those power soirees in Manhattan."

"I know." Then excitedly, she said, "Pick, if I could land an account with WeltanCom Linda would wet her pants. They're a mammoth German digital multinational." Her eyes widened. "Oh, there's Lorraine. I want to thank her for the sitter."

"Pickard! Pickard Cantrell! There you are!" It was Ruffin Strudwick ushering an older couple toward me. "Pickard, I'd like you to meet my parents. Austin and Merlie Strudwick." Ruffin's father was a tall, thin, dissolute-looking man in a tan seersucker suit and white open-collared shirt over a dark blue dickey. His disproportionately large head gave him the appearance of a discarded lollipop. His features bordered on the grotesque—heavy-lidded pale blue eyes, bulbous red-veined nose, thick lips, a ravaged complexion, his face lined with wrinkles that looked branded in leather. His large gnarled hands engulfed mine and he looked away as we shook.

"Daddy used to be mayor of Eno," gushed Ruffin. "Back when I was just a whippersnapper and still disappointing him on a regular basis."

"Now, hush, punkin'!" Mrs. Strudwick poked her son's arm and batted her eyelashes at me. His father gazed around with a bored, stony expression. In contrast to her husband Mrs. Strudwick was outgoing, garrulous, with a deep husky voice and Merlot breath. She wore a white wool dress with fringe along the hem and cuffs and a red wool fringed cape, lots of gold bangles and brooches, reflecting light from a thousand candles, and big matching red earrings. Her makeup was thick, her eyeliner heavy, and her eyebrows applied with a surer hand than her lipstick was.

"Pickard is the political cartoonist who just got canned in New York, Mama," said Ruffin. "It was in all the papers. Y'all must have seen it on *Hard Copy*. He and his lovely wife just bought Oaklawn. Y'all make him feel at home."

"So you're the cartoonist," said Austin Strudwick, who had been eyeing me while Ruffin prattled on. "I remember your little cartoons. You gave my friend Senator Helms a hard time there for a while back in the eighties."

"He's a cartoon magnet." I knew Austin would have hated some of the savage cartoons I drew of the senator over the years—as a gallstone, a turkey, a hookworm and a condom. When he fought to squelch the

Martin Luther King holiday I drew him as a jester and suggested a national holiday honoring Senator Helms: April Fools' Day.

"Daddy's a big Republican, Pick. He may be the only one here. Don't talk politics. He raises money for the senator, much to my horror and shame." Ruffin disappeared into the crowd.

"I'll tell the senator you got fired," said Austin, hoisting his vodka collins to his lips. "Make his day."

Mrs. Strudwick's eyes lit up. "Look, Austin, there's the congressman." And grabbing his arm they moved on to flashier résumés.

The party was picking up steam and I took my drink to the edge of the patio to watch the swelling crowd. The patio area grew denser and more boisterous as the lines at the bar backed up with elegant revelers. The men, all tanned and casually attired, tieless and jacketed, exuded boredom, while their women seemed ready to play. A woman stumbled on one of the patio's slate slabs. She secured her shoe and moved on. I knelt down to see if the slate had been dislodged. The stone's surface was uneven. There seemed to be words carved in it. I shifted so I could read what it said. SARAH BEASLEY, D. 1857, one stone read. EZEKIAL CROWTHER, B. 1842, D. 1879, SMALLPOX, read another. The last, ANNIE LAURA GASKINS. There was no date. All of the slate in that part of the patio seemed individually embossed, some with simple epitaphs.

"Isn't that the tackiest thing you ever saw?" Sandy Murphy said, nursing her glass of Pellegrino. "They're headstones. From graves in the old Eno slave cemetery."

I stood up. "You're kidding."

"I wish. Years ago when Ruffin's parents still lived here and were putting in this patio, Austin, who was mayor then, got wind that the cemetery over in the West End had fallen into disrepair and was going to be incorporated into the historic district. Austin knew about the crumbling headstones, so late one night he went over there and stole some of them for his patio. Slate and marble, cheap and available. Those are the names of slaves you were reading." She pointed at the stones. "See. JOE TURNIPSEED, B. 1836 D. 1859, WILLIE SNOW, B. 1816 D. 1857. Later poor whites who couldn't afford anything else were buried there too." Around us Gucci, Prada, and Manolo Blahnik footwear trod across the gravestones of the people who had served the people who built houses like Sassafras and Oaklawn.

"Austin's a mess." Sandy sighed. "The meanest man in the county. And the greediest. As a cartoonist you must appreciate him. He looks like his policies. When he was mayor he tried to sell New Hope Mountain to developers. When the town wouldn't let him, he moved out to the retirement community in a fit of pique. There's a mean streak that runs through that family. Austin's father was superintendent of the mill back in the bad old days when your grandmother worked there."

"So his people were the boss of my people?"

"I'm afraid so."

"Figures. What's the deal with Ruffin and him?"

"They were estranged for years, as you can imagine. A right-wing Republican politician with a gay artiste for a son. Ruffin's first book, *Tyrannus Rex*, was a scathing indictment of his father. Accused him of everything but cannibalism."

"They seem to get along now."

"Ruffin got famous. Cynics say Austin saw the handwriting on the wall. Cashed in on his son's fame. Depressing how celebrity absolves anything. He decided it was in his interest to let bygones be bygones. Now he attends book signings with his son and autographs copies of *Tyrannus Rex*."

We were shouting over the din of the crowd. The party had grown louder as the guests grew more lubricated. I felt a hand on my shoulder, and turned to find Russ standing behind me with a man he introduced as Franklin Webb.

"Franklin represents the sensible side of Strudwick's illustrious family," Russ said.

Webb was a tall, thin pleasant-faced man in his mid-thirties, with a bemused expression on his face and an abstracted, aristocratic air about him. "I hear you moved into Oaklawn," he said. "I'm delighted you're fixing it up. Our family used to live there in the early part of the century. My grandfather used to take me there when I was growing up. We'd sit under the oak trees—it was deserted then—and he'd tell me stories. He said it was haunted."

"Seen any ghosts, Pick?" Russ asked.

"No, but heard some strange noises in the attic at night." I laughed. "Thought they were squirrels, though."

"Probably the ghosts of the Regulators," said Russ.

"You've heard the Regulator story, right Pick?" asked Sandy. "Rebels defeated by Governor Tryon's militia at Alamance Creek in 1771 were brought back to Eno to be tried and hung in front of their friends and family."

Franklin stirred the ice in his glass with his finger. "Hung on one of the oaks on your property and buried in a mass grave somewhere down by the river."

Goosebumps rose on my arms. "Funny, the Realtor never mentioned the house was haunted."

"Listen, when my family lived there it was haunted worse by the living." Franklin Webb moved to join his wife, who was summoning him.

"Who is he?" I asked Russ.

"Another prominent Enoan. Except his family had real power, unlike the Strudwicks, who just had the reputation. The Webbs ran this town for generations. They owned the mill. Now he's faded gentry, another Raleigh lawyer."

It was time for another drink. Standing in line, I caught a glimpse of Cameron laughing with a group of people I didn't know. Her eyes sparkled, and her smile was radiant. Her long blond hair was styled in a french twist atop her slender neck. Good for her, I thought. Cameron was more social than I was and took to parties like a bee to honey. I teased her that her epitaph would be, "The Lord Called and Cameron Could Go." Our abrupt relocation, although her idea, had cut her off from our friends in New York and forced her to start over on new terrain. In addition to the stress of beginning a new job, she also had a son who needed to be situated in school and a house and husband both in need of restoration and rehabilitation. For her, dressing up and socializing, trying out her new professional persona in a fresh social milieu was bracing for her, like breathing pure oxygen. For me it was more like mustard gas.

I ordered a bourbon on the rocks. Someone behind me said, "I hear the cartoonist who got shafted for beating up his publisher is here." Another voice said, "Good god, Ruffin will invite anyone to add color to his parties."

I grabbed my drink and melted into the crowd. One of the advantages of cartoon celebrity is that you can remain anonymous. Your work gets the attention, not your face. I wandered beyond the well-tended gardens and terraces, away from the lights and noise of the party. A soft breeze carrying the early autumn aroma of burning leaves mixed with the faint floral scents from the Strudwick greenhouse and gardens, creating a heady redolence that perfumed the night.

"Hi!" a voice said behind me. "You're not being very sociable out here all by yourself."

Turning I saw a woman wearing a wide-brimmed straw hat and matching sandals walking toward me, drink in hand. Her slinky black dress hung to her ankles and was slit above the knees on both sides. Slender and attractive, she moved with a supple feline grace, lithe and purposeful. Her voice was low and husky.

"I was just looking at the property," I replied, not really wanting to engage. When she drew close I saw that she was really quite lovely, with large green eyes and cheekbones prominent enough to reflect the moonlight. Her long red hair hung in waves to her shoulders. An unlit cigarette teetered between her slender manicured fingers. Her nails were the color of blood.

"Beautiful, isn't it?" she said, searching her purse for a light. "Quite a spread here."

"Yeah," I said. "Something else."

"He inherited it, y'know. Lucky genes." She found her lighter and handed it to me. Her fingers brushed my wrist as I lit her cigarette.

"I'm Pick Cantrell."

She exhaled, fanned the air, and dropped the lighter into her purse. "I know," she said. She offered me her hand. "I'm Lisa Price." Her bones were small and delicate, like a bird's. "You bought the old Oaklawn place. We looked at it when we moved here from Chapel Hill. Decided we'd best build out in the country. Didn't think Eno was ready for the Dildo King to occupy one of its historic gems."

"Oh. You're . . ."

"The Dildo Queen. That's me."

"I'm sorry," I said, embarrassed, but not exactly sure why.

"Don't be." She smiled. "I'm used to it. It has its compensations."

"How did you know we bought Oaklawn?"

"I didn't. But when Ruffin told me who you were, I put two and two together."

"Oh."

"Anyway, I saw you heading out here and decided to join you. It's getting to where you can't even light up outside without offending somebody. Our host, for instance."

"Ruffin?"

"He's fanatic about it. Won't let you smoke in his house, near his house, his guests, his plants, his sky. He's a bit anal, if you haven't noticed."

"We just met."

She smiled. "I mean, he winks at his boyfriends launching gerbils up their assholes but he goes ballistic about a little smoke on his curtains. Go figure."

Something in my expression must have registered with her because Lisa Price quickly apologized. "Listen to my mouth. I don't even know you and I'm already getting graphic. No wonder the Junior League won't invite me to afternoon tea."

"No, it's just . . . one rarely finds such wicked badinage in Eno. Maybe the East Village."

"Nathan says I'm too direct, that I have no internal editor."

"Well, if that's anything like an external editor, you're not missing much."

"So Pick Cantrell, what brought you here to Eno?" she asked.

I told her about my blowup in New York—like everybody else, she'd heard about it on the news—and a bit about the move and then she asked, "Can't you go to work somewhere else; or under a pseudonym or something?"

"I don't think so. My style is too recognizable."

"Maybe you could sell ideas to other cartoonists."

"No. Good cartoonists like to come up with their own. Anyway, it doesn't matter. I'm restoring the house. Thanks for your concern, though."

"What a waste of talent."

"Hey, you haven't seen my Sheetrock."

"No, but when they showed your stuff on television I recognized it immediately. You're good. What a shame. Mmm. I know how it feels to lose your vocation."

"Oh?"

"I wanted to be an actress. I know, just like the millions of other girls, you're thinking. But I was serious. Went to the Royal Academy of Dramatic Arts in London, then moved to New York and started auditioning, did some modeling for a while to make ends meet, then met Nathan and got sidetracked. He was a photographer at the time. Believe me, I know what it's like to be kept from doing what you love. At least you had it taken from you. I took it from myself."

"So did I."

We both fell silent. Lisa stubbed out her cigarette on the trunk of an elm tree.

"Hey, look at that!" she said, pointing above the treetops.

A huge bird soared above the pines circling over the banks of the New Hope River. For a time it floated there, riding the air currents lifting from the still-warm earth. Then it plummeted into the trees and out of sight.

"What was it?" I asked.

"The white hawk," Lisa said. "Redtail actually, an albino. Or so they say. We sometimes see him from our house, a couple of miles from here. But I think he nests around here somewhere. I've seen him before at Sassafras. Look"—she shot a hand skyward—"there he is again."

In the near distance the giant raptor pumped his wings, climbing into the sky, where he began his glide. His contours appeared silhouetted against the moon's silvery luminescence as he drifted overhead, patrolling his aerial domain.

"I can watch him floating on the thermals forever," said Lisa dreamily.

We both gazed at the beauty and singularity of this majestic creature. "I thought owls were the only nocturnal raptors."

"It's still light enough to hunt, I suppose."

"He seems lonely," I said.

"You sound like you can identify," Lisa replied. I could sense her eyes on me. I suddenly felt self-conscious and uncomfortable with the intimacy of her comment.

"Takes one to know one, I guess."

"I'm sorry," she said. "I shouldn't complain. I made my choices. But as you might imagine, the Junior League isn't exactly putting the rush on the Dildo King's wife."

We stared at the moon and the empty hawkless sky.

"You know the mating call?" I said to break the awkward silence.

"Pardon me?"

"The mating call of the Junior Leaguer."

"What's that?"

I called out in a boozy, drawling falsetto, "I'm so druuunk!"

Lisa nearly spit out her drink. When she recovered, she said, "That's a riot. I've got to tell Nathan."

"Pickard. Pickard Cantrell," a voice boomed through the darkness. It was Ruffin Strudwick again. I had the feeling he was stalking me.

"I better go," said Lisa. "Nice meeting you, Pickard. Thanks for the pep talk."

"Forget the Junior League," I said. "You're too good for them."

She smiled and started away. After a few steps, she turned back and said, "You're a nice man, Pick Cantrell."

Ruffin caught me by the arm and pulled me back toward the lights and crowd. "What are you doing up here flirting with the Dildo Queen? Not that I blame you." Ruffin, I realized as he dragged me off to meet yet another guest, was several sheets to the wind by now. He approached someone standing with his back to us on the edge of the crowd. "Allow me to introduce the illustrious Anthony Weeks," Ruffin declared as his friend turned to face us. I was already extending my hand before the name registered.

"A little blast from the past, am I right?" Strudwick's bloodshot gaze bounced between us like a malevolent Ping-Pong ball.

Tony Weeks was pencil thin, pale and effete, with a high forehead and close-cropped thinning blond hair, and watery, colorless eyes. Self-consciously trendy, he wore a black leather biker jacket over a black T-shirt and black jeans. He seemed edgy and uncomfortable.

Weeks had despised me from the moment we met years earlier when he was a new columnist in the newsroom of the *Sentinel*. I had met hook-worms with better personalities. Resentment seemed his natural state and word from staffers after I left was that he hated me with an irrational obsession and had even suggested to my former editor that they not buy my cartoons from my syndicate as retribution for my abandoning the *Sentinel* for another newspaper. Predictably, after I'd beaten up Garvis, Weeks had penned a column that claimed that I was a disgrace to journalism and that my Pulitzer Prize should be rescinded and suggested that I should be barred from ever working again.

Strudwick must have been aware of Tony's antipathy toward me, hence his pleasure in introducing us.

"Oh, yes, Pick Cantrell," Tony said, sipping his wine spritzer with a forced casualness, as if he had only just now recognized who I was. "Someone said you had moved back here. I suppose you heard about the column I wrote about you after your dismissal."

"You wrote a column about him?" Strudwick inquired disingenuously, looking at me. "Did you see it, Pickard?"

"No," I replied, "but I heard about it."

"What on earth did it say?" Strudwick asked.

Weeks gathered himself up as though he was performing in a spelling bee. "I said that Pick Cantrell should be barred from the profession. I said his work had grown tiresome. Clichéd. I said his New York work was not what it had been at the *Sentinel*. And never was."

"Ouch!" said Strudwick looking at me for my reaction.

I munched an ice cube. Swallowed. "He's right."

Strudwick and Weeks looked disappointed by my reaction.

"Right about what?" asked Strudwick.

"What he wrote. That I should be punished for what I did. It was inexcusable." My contrition had thrown them off. "As far as my work not being what it used to be"—I rattled the ice cubes in my glass—"I agree."

"That's very, uh, brave of you to admit that Tony was right," Strudwick said.

My smile was weary. "Even a stopped clock is right twice a day. Weeks would have knocked my dick in the creek no matter what I'd done or what my work was like. He's a critic. He can't help himself." I turned to Weeks. "But while we're on the subject, I've got a question for you, Tony. What have you ever created?"

He looked at me blankly.

"Have you ever written a play or a poem? Painted a painting? Have you ever made up anything from scratch?"

"Is this some sort of rhetorical question, Cantrell?"

"No, it's a straight-up question. I want to know. I'm curious."

"That's not fair, Pick," said Strudwick.

"No, I didn't think so," I said, looking Tony in the eye. "To be an artist you have to have an open heart. You don't have an open heart, do you, Weeks?"

"I do too!" he protested.

"No, you don't. That's why you're a journalist."

"Good journalism can be creative," Weeks declared.

"That's right, Pickard," Ruffin said. "Tony's written some very well crafted columns. The piece he did on my last book was excellent. He has a distinctive voice."

"It's as pretentious as that ear-bob of his, and you know it," I said. "Just because he blew smoke up your ass doesn't mean you have to defend him. Art is about surprise, a fresh way of looking at the world. Tony Weeks never surprises. He is as predictable as shower curtain mold."

"At least I have a job," Weeks hissed. I ignored him, because the bourbon was working its magic now, and I was warming to my topic.

"Have you ever gone out on the high wire, Tony?" I asked. "Or do you just criticize the ones who do? You're like the umpire at a tennis match perched above the court. 'Ooooh,' you squeal, 'that was out of bounds! Ooooh, you stepped over the line!' You never get down on the court, do you? Never put yourself even the slightest bit at risk. You're a coward, Tony."

"You're just jealous because I have a job and you don't."

"You don't have a job, Tony, you have a problem." A crowd was beginning to gather around us. I saw Russ and Sandy tuning in from the fringe. Ruffin, noticing, suddenly seemed uncomfortable with the scene he had wrought. "Why don't you tell Ruffin about Chicago, Tony? Tell him how you lost your job at the *Post* and ended up at the *Sentinel*."

Weeks looked stricken, as if I had slugged him in the solar plexus and driven the wind out of him. "I don't know what you're talking about."

"Sure you do, Tony. I can fill Ruffin in if you want. It seems Tony here, when he was in Chicago and just starting out, wrote one of his now-patented scathing reviews of a local production of *Oliver!*"

"Who told you this? Where did you get your information?" demanded Weeks with a look of panic in his eyes.

"It was a classic Tony Weeks thumbs down," I continued, ignoring him, "a real scorched earth pan, excoriating the costumes, sets, directors, actors—for their lack of talent and for sullying an esteemed classic of the musical theatre. He salted the earth when he was finished so nothing would grow there ever again."

"Sounds like he was just doing his job," said Strudwick. "What's wrong with that?"

"It was children's theatre, Ruffin. He singled out the kid who played the Artful Dodger, said he had the worst voice he'd ever heard, and even suggested that the kid never be allowed on stage again."

"It was my responsibility to uphold standards," Weeks protested. "How were they ever to learn if I didn't? The director asked me to take the show and my job seriously, even if they *were* only children."

"The kid was ten years old, Tony!" I said, then turned to Ruffin so I wouldn't have to look at Weeks's face anymore. "Anyway, the kid's sorry excuse for a mother read the review to the boy, who was devastated. Later he climbed up in the closet, grabbed his father's gun, and blew his brains out. His mother heard the shot from the other room while she was reading Mr. Weeks's sterling prose to the kid's brother and sister."

"She had no business letting the children read that!" Weeks countered.

"That review was for the adults who organized the production. She was totally irresponsible reading that."

"Naturally, there was a lot of controversy and a lot of upset parents and his editors were embarrassed because they were caught with their pants down and should have flagged it but didn't notice he was dumping on a children's production. So they ended up suggesting Mr. Weeks seek other employment. That's how he landed at the *Charlotte Sentinel*. Lucky us, huh, Tony?"

"The child was unstable," he spluttered. "And the father was a fool for keeping a loaded gun in the house. The paper should have backed me up. I stand by that review. I owed it to the kids to treat them as stringently as adults. It's the critic's duty to uphold standards no matter the age of the artists. The paper behaved deplorably."

"I give you a thumbs down for your performance, Tony," I replied. "Zero on a scale of one to ten. Here's your blurb: 'Craven. Cowardly. Bullying. Immoral.'—Pickard Cantrell, critic-at-large."

I grabbed Tony Weeks by his lapels and pulled him close. "So tell me, Tony," I said. "How does it feel to be reviewed?" Then I released him, downed the last of my drink, and headed for the bar.

I was fuming. I had been set up by our host. I ordered another bourbon, aching to leave but unwilling to let Weeks or Strudwick think they had had anything to do with it.

I polished off the drink. Cameron stood at the edge of the patio with Strudwick. Both of them were looking in my direction. Cameron's face was a mask of disapproval and disappointment. What was he telling her? I walked over and Strudwick scurried away.

"I'm going home," I said. "Are you ready?"

"I'm not going anywhere with you. What was *that* all about?"

"Nothing. I think we should pick up Wiley."

"Wiley's spending the night at the Drapers. They'll drop him off in the morning."

"Fine," I said. "I'm leaving."

"Well, I'm not. I was having fun until your little run-in with Tony Weeks."

"I didn't have a run-in."

"A frank exchange of views then. Ruffin says you were rather rude."

"He's lucky I didn't cold-cock him."

"Oh, that's lovely, Pick. He's here to do a profile on Roland Jameson. Thanks for the help with the WeltanCom account."

"You ready to go?"

"I'll ride with Russ, thank you very much." She started toward the bar.

"Here." I slapped the car keys into her palm. "I'm walking."

I beat myself up all the way home. I didn't know who I was angrier at—Cameron, Tony Weeks, Ruffin Strudwick, or myself. Had I, as Cameron suggested, crossed the line with Weeks? I thought I'd shown admirable restraint. But maybe I was out of line. I couldn't tell anymore. What was it about Tony Weeks that set me off? Why did Cameron take Ruffin's word over mine? She was going to be hard to live with tomorrow, that was for sure.

The walk to Oaklawn was only a mile or so. The night had turned cool and leaves fell like rain from the trees and scattered on the wind. Clouds moved across the sky in fast motion and the full moon overhead illuminated the grounds of Oaklawn as if it were daytime. Katydids and peepers blared loudly, drowning out the sounds of distant traffic. As I turned the corner into our driveway, I noticed in the pale halo of the streetlight at the foot of the drive, a set of tire skidmarks stretching from the drive out onto the street. Winking in the moonlit grass and on the pavement and spilling out of a brown paper bag onto the edge of the driveway below the sign reading OAKLAWN, CIRCA 1833, was a shattered bottle that looked as though it had been thrown from a passing vehicle upon the brick pillar of our entranceway. A label among the shards and fragments identified the vintage as Mad Dog 20/20. It was horrid, rotgut stuff, drunk by winos and by those either too cheap or too desperate to care. I had a pretty good idea who had thrown it.

6

DEAR PRESIDENT ROOSEVELT

Inside the house, I poured myself another bourbon and sat down in front of the downstairs television set, where I promptly fell asleep. Cameron didn't wake me when she returned from the party and when I arose on Sunday morning I found a note written in her hand informing me that she and Wiley had gone to church and afterward would be in Chapel Hill running errands. She was giving me a wide berth. Clearly, she didn't want to discuss what had happened at the party and frankly I was relieved. But her silence was ominous.

For Cameron, the Strudwick party had represented a debut of sorts and I had ruined it for her. Now she would be known among all her new friends and neighbors as Cameron Cantrell, that delightful and beautiful new woman in town who was married to the drunken asshole, Pick Cantrell. To a tough, independent competitor like Cameron, playing the role of victim was an excruciating fate. The last thing in the world she wanted was to be seen as the noble, long-suffering wife.

Cameron and Wiley returned that afternoon. I was working on the side porch. Cameron virtually ignored me during lunch and studiously avoided mentioning anything about my behavior at the party. An arctic chill had seeped into her voice. I could not muster the courage to offer an apology. Nuclear winter had arrived early at Oaklawn.

I was out on the porch hammering furiously, engrossed in my work as I had been all week when my grandmother called with an urgent news-flash. "Petey got out!" she cried. "Petey's flew away!"

"Calm down, Mama Lucy," I said. "Tell me what happened."

"Petey got out, Buzz!" she wailed. *Buzz?* She was confusing me with my cousin. "I was shakin' out the dust mop and the screen door was open and Petey flew out. You gotta come git' him, Buzz. He's settin' on a limb up in that walnut tree."

"This isn't Buzz, Mama Lucy. This is Pick. You dialed the wrong number." But this only seemed to confuse and upset her more.

"Where's Buzz? He's gotta come git Petey! Is that you, Pick?"

"Yes, ma'am. Slow down."

"Pick! Pick! I thought you was Buzz!" She gasped, embarrassed but undeterred. "Petey flew away! You gotta come get him. Petey got out!" Between her sobs and gulps for air I could hardly understand her.

"If he's gone, Mama Lucy, what can I do?"

"Lord a-mercy, now, he's settin' out there on the telephone wire. Somebody's gotta come git 'im!"

She'd lost it. If she believed I was coming over there to climb a telephone pole she was crazier than I thought. I considered calling Buzz but I knew he was still laid up with his knee and wouldn't be able to help. I really didn't have time to go over to her place, but I was afraid she would have a stroke if I didn't do something. It would be easier to drive over there myself than to find somebody else to help her. Even if I couldn't retrieve the bird, I could try to calm her down. She sounded dangerously unhinged. I imagined her in the front yard climbing the telephone pole in her bathrobe and slippers. If she hurt herself trying to catch that bird I'd never hear the end of it. I looked at my watch. It was just after lunch and if I was going to pick up Wiley when he got out of school I didn't have much time.

When I arrived half an hour later, Mama Lucy was standing in her yard staring up at the telephone line running from her house to the pole on the street. She was dressed in blue sweats and her hands were shading her eyes from the sun. The cinnamon-colored cockatiel was perched jauntily up on the wire. Mama Lucy coaxed and cajoled him from below. "Pretty bird!" she called. "Pretty bird!" Then she would whistle and call sweetly up to him, "C'mon down, Petey. Come to Mama Lucy!"

When I got out of the car and shut the door Petey spooked and flew out over the street in a wide arc, then circled back and landed on the roof of the house. Perched there on the eaves of one of the dormer windows, whistling merrily, he cawed, "Pretty bird! Pretty bird!"

Mama Lucy rushed over and pulled me by my jacket sleeve toward the backyard. "Come on, Pick. He's up there on the roof and I got a ladder in the shed you can climb up and git him off with."

"Hold on," I said. "Let's try to coax him down first."

"I been out here all mornin' sweet-talkin' him." She put an index finger to her lips, shushing me. "He ain't comin' down by hisself. We gotta git to 'im without scarin' 'im off." Why she was whispering as if the bird could overhear us was beyond me, but I wasn't about to challenge her.

"Have you tried bird food?" I whispered.

"I tried ever'thing. I even brought him a jelly biscuit, his favorite, but he just sits there ignorin' it. I ain't sure he can see it from up there. His eyesight ain't so good. It's gotta be right in front of him. If you could climb up there, Pick, and git close enough with this biscuit in your hand he'll hop on your finger to eat. That's how Buzz got him the last time."

"This has happened before?"

"Oh, yeah. Petey's got out once or twice and flew back in the door behind me when I give up and went back inside. But I already tried that—'tendin like I was goin' back inside. He ain't goin' for it. Last time Buzz got to 'im on the roof with the biscuit. 'Course, Buzz's got a way with animals."

I removed my jacket and handed it to Lucy. "Where's the ladder?"

"Don't forgit this," Lucy said, wrapping the jelly biscuit in the napkin and slipping it into my shirt pocket. I retrieved the ladder and set it up in the back of the big house where the hydrangeas didn't block access. I climbed up and made my way in a crouch across the gray shingled roof, moving slowly, deliberately, so as not to startle Petey, who was still sitting on the dormer's peak whistling occasionally and repeating, "Pretty bird." When I got to the front of the roof I ducked down behind the dormer and inched my way around the side until I was crouched beside the bird. He seemed oblivious to my stealthy approach from behind. I reached into my pocket for the jelly biscuit that was already leaking grape stains onto my shirt. Just as I unwrapped it and turned to engage the bird my foot shifted a few inches and rasped across the rough sur-faced shingle. Luckily I didn't tumble off the roof but Petey, startled by the sound, bolted from his perch and flew in a beeline across the yard and into the walnut tree's dark branches. Crouched there on Mama Lucy's roof I felt abandoned and ridiculous, like some redneck gargoyle.

"Now he's in ol' lady Dawkins's walnut tree." Lucy scowled into the dense foliage, oblivious to my plight. "Can you see him, Pick? I cain't see him, but I know he's up there. Climb up there and git 'im."

"I don't think I can," I said. After nearly breaking my neck climbing down the ladder, I joined her under the tree, where we searched the leaf-covered limbs for the elusive cockatiel. "The lowest limb is twelve feet from the ground and it's only an eight-foot ladder," I reasoned. "It's not tall enough."

"It'll reach to the top of the garage. When you git up there you can step onto that limb."

I squinted up into the walnut tree's branches to make sure there was a quarry up there to justify the pursuit. After much straining and moving around for better angles I finally spotted the bird sitting on one of the uppermost branches, imperiously perusing the scene below like an Incan god. To my disappointment, there was a large limb hanging just close enough to the garage roof to serve as a way onto the tree.

"Okay. I'll go over and ask Mrs. Dawkins if she minds me climbing her tree."

Mama Lucy grabbed my arm and shushed me. "No, Pick. She won't let you if you ask. She'll raise Cain." She looked around furtively, checking Mrs. Dawkins's kitchen window. "She ain't there in the kitchen. She's watchin' her stories on TV. Just climb up there real quick and I'll keep a lookout."

"I don't know, Mama Lucy."

"Move quick. You'll be down before she knows it. Hurry, before he flies away."

Unable to muster the will to argue, I fetched the ladder and propped it on the side of the garage, out of sight of Mrs. Dawkins's prying eyes. I scurried up the ladder, jelly biscuit in hand, crossed the roof and eased myself onto the large tree limb. Looking down on Lucy my perch seemed much higher than it had from the ground.

"Hurry," Mama Lucy urged.

"I am." As a boy I was a compulsive tree climber and had climbed this old walnut tree many times with the help of my father, who had boosted me up to that high first branch. But that was decades ago when I was fearless and about a hundred pounds lighter and a hell of a lot more flexible. Thankfully, the branches were sturdy and grew fairly close together. I shimmied my way up the tree, keeping my eye on Petey. The cockatiel sat close to the trunk on a branch near the very top of the tree eyeing me as I got closer and the branches got thinner and farther apart. Finally, I pulled myself to within an arm's length of the bird, and situated myself so I could maneuver. I gingerly removed the biscuit from my pocket and held the treat out to Petey. The bird seemed unimpressed. The limb beneath me groaned. Petey lifted off. I lurched forward, dropping the biscuit, and clutched the thick trunk for dear life. Meanwhile,

Petey circled the yard again, then in one final aerial maneuver, glided directly to Mama Lucy's outstretched hand.

I was sitting there like a fool with my thumb up my butt, praying I wouldn't drop to my death and watching the reunion of Mama Lucy and her precious Petey, when I heard a car door slam and the squawk and static of a police radio. Glancing down, I spied two cops heading for me across the lawn. Ol' lady Dawkins, it seemed, had detected a stranger in her walnut tree, panicked, and called 911 and was now peering out her kitchen window and eagerly awaiting the arrest of the perp who had violated her property's airspace. Meanwhile, Mama Lucy had disappeared into the house with Petey.

I stared down at the officers from my perch, thinking, *just what I need, an arrest for trespassing when I'm already on probation*. From the safety of the back porch Mama Lucy shouted threats at the officers and promised to have them arrested for trespassing. My descent took a good ten minutes, and when I finally dropped the last few feet to the lawn, I sheepishly tried to explain to the officers what I was doing in the next-door neighbor's walnut tree. Luckily, the Burlington Police Department already knew about the ongoing battle between Mama Lucy and Mrs. Dawkins. This wasn't the first time they had been called to arrest one woman or the other or innocent bystanders like me. They were fairly good humored about it, but they issued me a warning to satisfy Mrs. Dawkins and asked me not to climb her tree anymore. I assured them I would not.

When I went inside to check on Petey and to bid Mama Lucy farewell, the trouble-making cockatiel was already back in his cage nibbling on his jelly biscuit and Lucy was in the family room watching television. Game show music blared in the background. Parched from my brush with death and drenched with sweat, I foraged in the refrigerator for something to drink before I hit the road. Standing in the cool solace of the refrigerator door pouring a glass of iced tea, I heard Mama Lucy mumbling in the living room.

"Trespassin'," she muttered. "I ain't payin' no fine and you better not neither, Pickard Cantrell. As many times as that woman's trespassed over here with them walnuts fallin' in my garden."

Entering the living room, I was shocked to find Lucy leaning forward squinting intently through the lens of a magnifying glass at the television set across the room. I knew her eyesight was fading but I had no idea it had come to this. Even though she wore glasses, I always assumed she had X-ray vision and eyes in the back of her head. But now, watching her strain at Bob Barker through a lens the size of a Moon Pie, I realized that this was the only way she could make out what was happening on the screen, which, besides chasing after fugitive cockatiels, was her only known form of diversion. I watched for a while as she moved the lens away from her face, then drew it closer in order to correct and compensate for cuts and camera angles.

"Well, I better be going, Mama Lucy," I said, trying to take in stride the image of my grandmother looking like some demented Sherlock Holmes in drag, straining to deduce a clue from the electronic incomprehensibility of a Zenith television set. Like so much about my grandmother, the image and effect were both sad and comic.

"When you gonna mow that lawn again, Pick?" she asked. Her jubilation over recovering her cherished cockatiel was gone; we were back to business as usual. "It needs one more mowin' before the frost hits." I nearly choked on my iced tea. After complaining about the job I had done a couple of weeks ago, she was trying to put me back to work.

"You don't want me out there mowing down your pinks again, do you, Mama Lucy?" I asked, trying to hide my dismay.

"Well, that's the truth," she answered. "You flat out ruined my pinks. And you didn't finish weedin' the curb the last time, neither. I had to git down and do it myself after you left."

This was too much. I had to clear out of here before I strangled her.

"If Buzz cain't mow I guess I'll have to git somebody else. I'd let Talbert or Jerry do it before I let you back out there." A cataract-covered eye the size of a small Frisbee blinked at me through the magnifying glass. "But maybe I'll let you haul down stuff from the attic. Cain't do too much damage that way."

Bristling, I headed for the door. "Don't worry, Mama Lucy," I said. "Buzz is on the road to recovery and will be back soon to take over and do it right."

"You sound like your mama," she said.

"What docs that mean?" I demanded, wheeling around.

"She talked that way to me when I got on her nerves."

"What way?"

"Pouty. Peevish. Mary Alice never did like me. From the time Clayton married her your mama hated me."

We were on dangerous ground now. The subject of my mother was not one I cared to discuss with Mama Lucy. In an instant all the tiptoeing around old resentments and injuries, the pretending and pretense that had characterized my encounters with her since coming to Eno had been stripped away and the ancient wound laid bare.

"My mother didn't hate anybody," I said.

"She hated me and I knew it."

"She didn't hate you. She should have, but she didn't. That was her problem. She was too much the good Christian girl to hate you. She was too busy understanding everybody—even enemies like you. She felt sorry for you. She had every right to hate you the way you treated her But, no, she saved all her hate and aggression for herself. You're one of the lucky ones. You learned how to turn it onto others. That's why she's dead and you're still around."

My outburst stunned Mama Lucy as much as it did me.

"What way?" she demanded. "I treated her fine."

"You never approved of her marrying Daddy, and you know it."

"That's a lie," she said.

"No, it's not. You forbade the family to go to their wedding. Your firstborn's wedding. Even Granddaddy wouldn't defy you. Only Uncle Donly went. He was the only one with gumption enough to stand up to you."

"They could have gone. I never stopped 'em."

"And there'd have been hell to pay. You steamrolled your family and you tried to steamroll my mother. You criticized everything she ever did. Just like you do me!"

For whatever reason something primitive and ugly was erupting from the deepest part of myself. All my plans to discuss the mill strike and politely request an interview for Sandy dissolved in this nuclear meltdown. I may have taken Lucy by surprise, but I knew she wouldn't roll over. I could feel her back stiffen and the dry kindling in her belly ignite. Even as I spoke I saw her eyes burning and her bile rising. The old Lucy, Queen of Mean, Princess Warrior, defending her long-cherished assumptions and rationalizations and deep-seated beliefs about herself, roared to life like a lioness defending her brood.

"What do you know about it?" she spat. "You was just a baby. You was always too sensitive for your own good. Just like her. I told Clayton she was spoiling you rotten!"

I flashed on a long-ago scene with my grandmother that had occurred when I was a teenager. It happened a few days after my father and I had driven my mother to Asheville to commit her to Appalachian State Hospital. I was eighteen years old and was working carpentry in the afternoons to earn money for school and my mother was in a mental hospital and my father was back at work again. In the mornings I worked out at the Y to get in shape for football practice, which was due to start shortly in Tallahassee, just before freshman orientation. Returning home late one morning I found Mama Lucy's car parked in our driveway.

She was checking in on us as she often did during my mother's absences but our conversation took a nosedive when she told me that I was responsible for my mother's illness and that if I had any decency I would not burden my parents with college costs but would drop out of school and go to work and pay them back for my room and board and for bringing me up for all those years. I told her she didn't know what she was talking about, that there were no college costs, that I had earned a football scholarship and that if she ever read the papers or attended any of my games she might have noticed that. She said she didn't care if my education was free, I had no business going off to school with my mother in the hospital and my father all alone and that I should get a job at the lumberyard in Delaney until my mother was better. By then I considered Mama Lucy certifiable and I told her as much. Unaccustomed to such insubordination from her grandchildren, she blew up at me and stormed out the back door. I let her bluster and fulminate at my ingratitude and insolence for a good five minutes, then I smiled sweetly, told her to "Have a nice day," and shut the door in her face. Now, a quarter century later, we were at it again.

"Your temper gets the best of you, Pickard," she said. "Always has. You was always a little too wound up. Unstable, like your mama. I reckon that's why you're outta work. Mary Alice was too emotional for her own good, too, and overly dependent from the start. If I didn't want Clayton gittin' mixed up with a crippled girl it was 'cause I loved him and wanted what was best for him."

"No," I said. "It was because you were jealous toward anybody who could claim his affections. You demanded absolute fealty from all your children, especially your older son. Still do. Anybody who would dare compete for his loyalties and interfere with his devotion to you was your enemy. You waged war on all your children's spouses. My mother didn't stand a chance against you."

"She was crazy as a bedbug."

"Maybe. The world made her crazy. People like you. But I'll tell you one thing: She had more maternal instinct in her little finger than you have in your entire body. As a mother you weren't worthy to hold her apron strings."

"At least I never went to the looney bin."

The dam had burst. There was no holding back. "Your house *was* a looney bin."

"You have to defend her. She's your mother," Lucy snapped. "And why wouldn't you? You was always a mama's boy. I told Clayton she was too soft on you."

"You mean she didn't beat me?"

"She should have taken a switch to you—taught you some respect!"

"They call that child abuse, Mama Lucy."

"She pampered you. That's why you was ruint by her. I told Clayton, but he wouldn't listen."

"Why would he take your advice? He was raised by you!"

"Don't you sass me, young man! I didn't put up with that from my children and I won't have it from my grandchildren either. I raised six young'uns and I reckon they turned out all right."

"Yeah, only one suicide," I replied. "Five out of six ain't bad."

She blanched at the words. Nobody in the family had ever mentioned Ruth Ann's suicide. I felt like a bully.

Tears welled in her eyes. "You don't know what you're talking about."

"Maybe I know too well."

"You are a mean man, Pickard Cantrell."

"Well, I come by it naturally."

"Nobody's ever talked to me that way."

"Nobody could get a word in edgewise."

"So cruel. So cruel." She was weeping openly now, her head buried in her hands.

I steeled myself against it. This was how she always won. "Well, you just leave my mother out of this."

She sobbed for a solid two minutes, while I stood there glowering, paralyzed by what had just transpired. Not knowing what I should do next, I waited for her to make the next move. Finally she looked at me and said, "Get out of my house!"

"Fine! I wish I'd never set foot in this place!"

"Get out!" she croaked. "And don't come back!"

I stormed out of the room, and burst through the screen door, nearly tearing it off its hinges and punching a hole in the screen in the process. My wrist was bleeding as I climbed into the truck. I heard a howl from the darkness of the house, "I'll mow the lawn myself!"

Navigating the back roads between Saxapahaw and Eno, I wrestled with my guilt and rage. My emotions careened wildly between impotent fury one minute and crushing remorse the next, as I tried to assess the situation and its ramifications. On top of the shame I felt for reaming out my ninety-year-old, ninety-pound grandmother I knew I had just made a huge blunder, a major tactical error within the family. But I was still pissed off at the old lady and didn't trust my temper enough to drive back and make amends. I might blow up again. As I drove around the back roads I lost track of time, and when I finally came to I realized I was late picking Wiley up from school.

When I arrived at Occaneechee Elementary School the last bus was pulling out and the playground was almost empty. Panic-stricken, I rushed down the narrow hallways to Wiley's homeroom. There his teacher told me that Wiley as usual had waited out front for me to arrive, but that when I didn't show up by 2:55 she had panicked herself and called Cameron at work. Cameron had told her to send Wiley to the Drapers across the street. She would pick him up at 5:00 when she got off work.

I drove to the Drapers, and after retrieving Wiley and apologizing profusely for my tardiness and the confusion, drove us both home. When Cameron returned that evening she was steaming. She and I had exchanged few words since the party and this didn't look as though it was going to be a meaningful dialogue.

"Where were you?" she demanded as we unloaded groceries from the station wagon. "Why did Wiley have to go home with Malcolm?"

"I'm sorry I was late," I mumbled.

"Sorry's not good enough, Pick. I never want Wiley to worry where his parents are. You've seen those kids who don't know from one minute to the next who's picking them up. You've seen the anxiety on their faces. I will not have Wiley feeling that way."

"C'mon, Cam, I was only a few minutes late."

"A few minutes is an eternity to a seven-year-old. We're lucky he could go home with Malcolm."

"It won't happen again."

Wiley came out onto the porch and punted his football onto the lawn. He raced after it, Flappy yapping at his heels. "Hey, Dad, you wanna play?"

"Not now, Wiley," I shouted back from the car. "You've got to eat and finish your homework before you can play ball." I carried the groceries inside.

"You were at your grandmother's again, weren't you?" Cameron asked.

"Yeah, so?"

"Helping her is more important than taking care of your own son, is that it?"

"Cam, that's not fair." Outside in the front yard Wiley was practicing his open field running against Flappy.

"Wiley," I shouted, "I told you to get in here right now!"

"What did you do this time—reseed her lawn?"

"You sound jealous."

"I *am* jealous. On behalf of our son. She's had her life. Wiley deserves our undivided attention. I feel guilty enough going off to work every day."

"I lost track of time."

"Yeah."

"Jesus, Cameron, what's the matter with you?"

"I'll tell you what's the matter! You nearly come to blows with some asshole at the Strudwick party. You can't control your temper that's already lost you your job. You humiliate me at the first social event we go to in the town we're trying to make a home in. What's the matter with me? What's the matter with you!"

"I told you I had to—"

"But not to stay all day!"

"I didn't stay all day!"

"Is the sign painted?"

The non-sequitur threw me. "What sign?"

"The *No Trespassing* sign I asked you to put up to keep out the god-damned nosy tourists who drive through whenever they feel like it. Remember? You said you'd pick one up at the hardware store."

"I—I haven't gotten to it yet."

"And you haven't finished the porch either, but Mama Lucy's going to win the Garden Club award for best lawn in Alamance County!"

"I wasn't mowing her lawn."

"Then what were you doing?"

"Petey got out," I blurted. Then, realizing how ridiculous my subsequent explanations would sound, I shut down.

"Oh, well, I'm glad it was serious."

"She was upset."

"Don't they have a fire department in Burlington for that sort of thing? Retrieving cats and birds from trees? Who are you, Dr. Doolittle?"

"She called here by mistake. What was I supposed to say? Screw you and your bird, old lady, I'm busy?"

"Yes. That's exactly what you should've told her."

"Easy for you to say."

"Apparently easier than it is for her faithful manservant, Pickard."

"You're out of line, Cam! You're irrational and I'm done discussing it."

"If you spent as much time on this house or helping Wiley with his homework as you have with that old bat—"

"Screw you, Cameron! I've been there twice. You're just pissed off 'cause she irritated you at the reunion."

"Watch your language," she said, closing the front door and looking to make sure Wiley was out of earshot. "Dammit, Pick, it infuriates me. You may be right, but there's something about the way she manipulates you and arranges to get help. If it's not you it's somebody else. Of course she called here by mistake. For her, you and your cousins are all interchangeable. As long as the work gets done. Yes, it irks me that she's taking time away from my child and my house, but what irks me even more is that you go along with it."

"It's not like that, Cam," I said, following her into the kitchen.

"I admit I was the one who wanted Wiley to know your family. But Mama Lucy's toxic. The stories you've told me—how she terrorized you and your mother. You used to blast your family for kowtowing to her! Now you're mowing her lawn like her own personal yard boy."

"I didn't mow the lawn!"

"Rescued her goddamned parakeet, then! Whatever! Hell, you've got every right to defoliate the lawn and burn down her house."

"I might as well have," I said.

Cam was readying another thrust and parry when her expression changed. "What do you mean?"

"We got in a fight. She started criticizing my mother and I blasted her. Made her cry. She threw me out of the house. I feel guilty as hell. That's why I was late."

Cameron stared at me as my words sank in. Then she shook her head.

"Oh, great. Now you're blowing up at her, too. That'll run through the family like shit through a goose. They'll chew on that for years. Congratulations, Pick!"

I couldn't win. "First you say I should burn her house down, then you criticize me for telling her off. Make up your mind, Cameron!"

Cameron jerked open the dishwasher and began jamming dishes into it. "I'm not saying she didn't deserve it, but Jesus Christ . . ."

Amazingly, I found myself coming to Lucy's defense. "She—she's got her own story, Cam. We both know that monsters don't spring full blown from Zeus's brow. She had a hard life, Cam—she's been through a lot."

Cam listened with cold-eyed impatience. "Your grandmother's ninety years old. She's had her life. Now it's our turn! And it's not gonna be about taking care of her." She slammed the pantry door. When she turned around Wiley was standing at the kitchen door with a frightened look on his face.

"Mom, what's the matter?" he asked.

"Nothing," Cameron said, shooting me a glance as she went over to hug him. "Your father and I had a disagreement."

"I heard you arguing again." His words drove a dagger of guilt into our hearts. Our exchanges over the last few days, though infrequent, had grown increasingly testy and apparently had not gone undetected.

"Your mom and I are loudmouths, bud, and argumentative. We can't help it. We both were born that way. Let's go out and pass the football."

"It's getting late, Pick," Cam said. "Wiley needs to eat and get his schoolwork done."

"Aww," Wiley complained.

"Your mom's right, big boy."

"C'mon, sweetie, no arguments," Cameron said, taking his hand. "I haven't seen you all day. Let me help you with your homework while your father puts water on for pasta. How would you like butter sauce tonight, huh?" She glanced at me, indicating the stove with her chin, and guided Wiley out of the kitchen and up the back stairway. Rummaging in the cabinet for a colander, I came across the liquor bottles we stored down there among the pots and pans. The temptation to pour myself a drink at that moment came over me so strong it scared me. I closed the cabinet and put on some water to boil. That night after we tucked Wiley in and I read him a story, Cam turned in early and I sat up watching an old movie on the downstairs television, but resisted an after-dinner glass of wine to put me to sleep. Later I let Flappy outside to do her business. Pale moonlight illuminated the side porch, and the green plastic gallon container of scraggly maiden pink bedding plants I had bought to replace the ones I had destroyed at Mama Lucy's.

The next morning I struggled to get out of bed. I was still reeling from the encounter with Lucy and I knew I needed to atone with Cameron for my recent screw-ups. I made coffee and brought Cameron a cup, placing it on the bathroom counter as she got dressed. My gesture was met with a distinctly chilly reception. I roused Wiley for school and made his breakfast. Cameron joined us at the table and we ate in silence. My wife believed in the expiation of sin.

Escorting Wiley to school I saw Russ standing on the creek bridge, squeezing an unfamiliar Irish dirge from his old battered pipes. The tune actually fit my mood better than the usual morning rendition of "Amazing Grace." After dropping Wiley off and apologizing again to his teacher for the previous day's mix-up after school, I stopped at the bridge to thank Russ for letting Wiley come home with Malcolm the day before.

"No problem, Pick." Russ grinned, ruddy-faced and out of breath from inflating the pipes. "By the way, I was walking Ginger along the New Hope down behind your property the other day. There's an old ice pit back there. It's overgrown now. But you might want to alert Wiley. Ginger almost took a tumble yesterday. A child could get hurt falling in and they'd have a heck of a time getting out."

"Jeez, that's all we need. Thanks for the warning."

"Sure. I was thinking about walking Ginger along those trails up the mill hill over in the West End. Wanna come?"

"I'd love to, but I've got to do some work on the house before the weather turns too cold. Maybe next time." I didn't want to tell him about my run-in with Mama Lucy and that the interview Sandy Murphy hoped for was not likely to happen.

"Well, let me know when you want to. By the way, why don't you give a talk at St. Stephen's about your family's connection to the 'thirty-four uprising. I'd sure love it if you'd fill that slot the Sunday after Halloween."

"I'll think about it," I said, caught off guard.

"Hey, would you look at that!" said Russ, pointing up in the air. High above us, circling in the sky, was the albino hawk.

"He's hunting woodchucks," Russ said. "Groundhogs. He can spot 'em from way up there. I wish I had eyesight like that. I can't even read my sermons without bifocals. Anyway, let me know if you want to come along with me and Ginger."

"I will." I watched the hawk make lazy circles overhead for a while as I headed back toward the woods and the path leading back to Oaklawn. Just before I slipped under the canopy of hardwoods the bird plummeted into the trees in the distance and disappeared from sight.

Buzz called and wanted to have lunch. I knew this was coming. The tom-toms had been beating overtime and word of my blowup with Mama Lucy had spread through the family like smallpox. Buzz had been dispatched to hear my side of the story, and, if possible, to broker a peace accord between the warring factions. We decided to meet at Mimi's on the square in Eno, across the street from the courthouse. The streets of downtown Eno are lined with small shops, antique stores, boutiques, and restaurants like Mimi's, where the rents are cheap and the pace is slow. Today you catch a whiff not of the cotton mill culture but of the leftover hippie counterculture, as artists and craftsmen, potters, chefs, and masseuses and other assorted granolas from the sixties who found their way to off-the-beaten-path communities like Eno in hopes of creating their own Woodstock nation now live and work and play, informed by a baby-boomer television sitcom idea of small town innocence and community—an acid flashback of Mayberry.

Mimi's is the town hot spot, a popular hangout where the locals, and the lawyers who descend on Eno to try cases at the county courthouse, gather to commune and ingest tofu burgers and vegetarian chili and swill herbal teas and listen to new age music and otherwise pretend they are not carnivores. The restaurant is run by a couple of sixties refugees so the service is glacially slow but the food is decent, if you're into sprouts. The wait staff sports nose jewelry, tattoos, and garish hair; for a place that prides itself on serving healthy cuisine they all look uniformly pasty, sickly, and stoned.

Buzz, still on crutches from his knee operation, was sitting on a bench out front, watching a parade of newsvans, with their aerial antennas and swiveling satellite dishes, jockey for position outside the Eno county courthouse. Later that day in an event that would be televised not only in the Triangle but also throughout the state, a jury would assemble to decide the fate of two men accused of robbing and beating half to death a gas station clerk on Cheshire Street. Before the trial began a team of Eno County police officers, many of whom bore a disturbing resemblance to Deputy Barney Fife, would escort the manacled prisoners from the jail, across Cheshire through the throng of video cameras and news personnel, to the old county courthouse. The proximity of these ritual proceedings to Oaklawn had evidently—and conveniently, it seemed to me—slipped the mind of the real estate broker who had shown Cameron the house. But since nothing untoward had ever occurred during these infrequent judicial and media events, and since Cameron and I had recently and on our own found so many other things to argue about, I filed away any misgivings I had to be discussed at some later time.

Buzz looked grim when I arrived. We went inside and placed our orders.

"I took Lucy to the doctor this morning," he said.

I filled my glass with sweet tea. "Don't tell me, I'm killing her."

"Naw, c'mon, Pick, you know I wouldn't try to play you like that, man. I just thought you'd want to know. She fell down and hurt herself. Bruised her hipbone. It's her eyesight. She thought she was sitting on a chair that wasn't there. Doctor says she was lucky she didn't break her back. He's keeping her in the hospital in Chapel Hill a couple of days. She's gotta stay off her feet for a while. But you know Lucy. She can barely see as it is and she won't let us move her into a home." Buzz moved to a table near the front window.

"What does that have to do with me?" I sat down across from him beneath the shelves of scented candles, preserves, and incense. I had expected the full-court-press guilt barrage from the family's designated messenger, so I was poised to play the hard-ass, even with my favorite cousin.

"Hey, man, it's me. You ain't gotta do that with me, Pick. I'm on your side. When I heard what you said to her I wanted to shake your hand. Did you really say five out of six ain't bad?"

Hearing my words repeated back to me made me want to cringe. "I'm afraid so."

"Whoooeeee! Man, you got balls the size of boulders! I wish I'd been there!"

"How's she doing?"

"She's invigorated. She loves having somebody to fight with. If it weren't for her falling down she'd probably still be dancing a jig. You've probably added ten years to her life."

"Swell." I groaned. "How's the family taking it?"

"Oh, you know, everybody's upset with you on her behalf. But they're scared of you, too. They know what you did to that publisher. Half of 'em want to string you up, the other half want to give you a medal."

"I was betting on excommunication."

"Aw, they ain't gonna do that. Don't you know blood's thicker'n water? 'Course, you ain't gonna get canonized anytime soon, neither, but hell, everybody knows Lucy's had that coming. Even Talbert and Jerry, who offered to come over here and whup your ass for her, admit she can be a tad trying sometimes."

"Talbert and Jerry? What's with them?"

"Dumb as a box of rocks. But mean. Scary. Especially Talbert. They were just trying to suck up to Lucy with their threats. Nobody takes 'em seriously. Everybody knows some of that should have been said to her years ago. Maybe she could have made some changes."

"Nobody changes, Buzz. Like Gertrude Stein said, 'They just get moreso.' Especially people like Lucy. People like her just blame everybody else. Besides, it's too late now for change even if she could."

"I like to believe it's never too late."

"You've got a sunnier view of life than me."

"I doubt it. I know you loved your mama, and it was a shame what happened to her, but remember—my mother was the suicide."

Buzz's mother, Ruth Ann, had died of an overdose of sleeping pills in her mid-forties. She was a great beauty. But she had what we now call low self-esteem and questionable judgment when it came to men, both of which led her to abuse an assortment of substances. I remember when Buzz was a little boy he would come visit my family. For him, being around a family as relatively stable as ours was at the time was as comforting as easing into a warm bath. He was intrigued by our life, all aspects of it, dinners, attending church on Sundays, being ordered to bathe at night. All the things I took for granted or resented and resisted, he delighted in. Only when I grew older and realized how bad his own home situation was did I fully grasp the poignancy of his enchantment with the routines and rituals of our life, however fragile it might have been itself, and he made sure when the time came that he provided his own children those same routines and rituals, the ones he first glimpsed and grew to love at our house.

"Y'know, Lucy was only seventeen when Mama was born," said Buzz. "When Mama turned eighteen Lucy was only thirty-five and still a good-lookin' woman. She and Mama used to go out jukin' together. They'd get all dolled up and go out honky tonkin' and all like they were girlfriends. Everybody thought they were sisters. I reckon Lucy wasn't much of a mother back then." Buzz studied the remains of his chili. "More like a sister really. Married so young, she was a baby having babies. I always suspected my mother's low opinion of herself had something to do with how young Lucy was when she had her."

"She probably didn't even want my daddy and your mama," I said.

Buzz stared out the window at the traffic on Cheshire Street. A news van with the WRAL logo emblazoned on its side panels maneuvered around a parked car and disappeared from view.

"Did I ever tell you about the time when I was about nine years old and we lived in Fayetteville with one of Mama's boyfriends? He was a bail bondsman down there, and by that time Mama wasn't working and she was stayin' at home mostly drinking and on her pills. We'd get gas at the service station down the street and Mama would always flirt with the boy who cleaned the windshields. I used to get so embarrassed. Then one afternoon I came home from school and found Mama in bed with the filling station attendant and I called the police and they came and arrested my mother. That's when the county moved against her and put us in foster homes. I reckon that was the beginning of the end for my mother. I always felt like it was my fault. For calling the police."

"Your mama probably drank because she thought Lucy's problems were her fault."

Buzz gave me a searching look. "I know this is none of my business, Pick, and you tell me if I'm out of line, but I always suspected your tension with Lucy had something to do with the way she treated sweet Mary Alice. We all loved your mama and I know it's hard to believe but so did Lucille in her way. These are big loaded issues and I probably should shut up but I know what it's like to lose a mother and to feel like the ones who should have done right by her didn't. What I'm trying to say, I guess, is, if I can forgive Lucy, so can you."

I shook my head. "This family is like living in a lunatic asylum. What should I do? Tell me what to do, I'll do it."

"Hell, I don't know. I don't give advice. My advice is not to ever give advice or to take it." Buzz dragged his spoon through his chili and said, "But if you're asking me what might smooth things over and get you back on track with the rest of the family I'd say just make a trip over and apologize."

"Why doesn't she apologize?"

"She can't. You know that. She's just one of those people. Lost in her righteousness. If anything's going to happen you're going to have to instigate it. You're going to have to step up. Be the mature one."

"She always counts on other people's maturity. But I'm not mature, not this time."

"She's not going to want to carry this out any longer," he continued. "She ain't got that much more time on God's green earth. She needs to be making amends, not settling scores."

"What do you mean?" I asked, searching Buzz's eyes.

"It's not just her hipbone. Or her eyesight. I talked to the doctor who examined her. He noticed shortness of breath. She had fluid in her lungs. Pain in her chest. Angina. He asked her how long her ankles had been swollen. She said she didn't know they were. Admitted having trouble getting up steps. And with her breathing. Doctor ran a chest X ray, found out she has a big heart. Doesn't understand how she's done as well as she has for so long."

"Damn!" The guilt was back, and stronger than ever.

"I know. You're surprised she even had a heart. He's keeping her in the hospital to get her on digitalis and diuretics. No more salt for Mama Lucy."

"The way she cooks, that alone's gonna kill her. How serious is it?"

"At her age, serious."

"How much longer has she got?"

"Not too long. A few months, maybe a year at most." Buzz let the news sink in. "I'll fill in the rest of the family later but I thought you'd want to know."

"Will she be okay on her own now?"

"Doctor thinks so. If she watches her diet. Everybody's going to insist now she be put in a nursing home, but Lucy'll fight 'em tooth and nail."

"So I guess I better apologize, huh?"

"Gesture is everything. If you feel comfortable with it. Even if you don't."

"She'll slam the door in my face."

"She ain't gonna have the strength to slam any doors. But I'll go with you. She won't slam the door on me. She owes me. She likes to act big with me, ordering me around and all. That's just her way. But underneath, she knows I look after her. And she's grateful."

"I can't do it, Buzz."

"Why not?"

"Because."

"Why?"

"Because"—I felt silly uttering it—"if I do, she wins."

"Pickard, son," said Buzz, smiling as he reached across the table and placed his hand on my shoulder, "you know as well as I do this ain't no contest."

We arrived unannounced the day after Mama Lucy was released from the hospital. I brought along the container of maiden pink bedding plants as a peace offering. Mama Lucy was slow answering the door because the doctor had advised her to use a walker. We heard her shouting that she was coming before she finally peered through the curtains, saw Buzz standing there, and opened the door. She was gripping her walker and was still in her bathrobe and curlers. When she saw me hanging back on the porch steps, she nearly fainted.

"Can we come in, Mama Lucy?" asked Buzz. "Pick and I have something to say."

"I ain't got nothin' to say to him," she muttered, looking away.

"Hear me out, Mama Lucy," I pleaded. "I'm sorry for what I said to you the other day."

"I don't want to talk about it."

"C'mon, give Pick a chance," Buzz said. "He drove all the way over here to talk to you."

"No."

I showed her the container of maiden pinks. "I mean it, Mama Lucy. I'm real sorry for what I said and I just wish you'd give me a chance to make it up to you."

"You hurt me, Pick. Sorry don't count."

"It was wrong what I said to you and I apologize. I've been under a lot of pressure lately, and I took it out on you. You didn't deserve that."

"You shouldn'ta said what you did about Ruth Ann."

"I know."

"That was cruel."

"Yes, ma'am, it was."

Buzz asked, "Haven't you ever said cruel things you didn't mean and would give the world to take back? Life's too short to waste on fussin' and fightin' with kinfolks, you oughta know that better'n anybody, Mama Lucy."

"In all my born days I ain't never had nobody talk to me like that."

"He's got a mouth on him," said Buzz. "All us Cantrells and Barlows do. He can thank you for that. Apple don't fall too far from the tree."

Now, hearing Buzz put it so bluntly it was my turn to cringe, but I saw Lucy glance at him, then at the pinks I was holding, and I thought I saw a hint of a smile tug at the corners of her mouth. Then she retreated back into her thoughts and hurt feelings. She looked small and frail, her features half-hidden in the shadows of the doorway. Then she squinted at me and Buzz and said, "Y'all eat anything yet?"

Minutes later we were sitting at the kitchen table devouring a hearty breakfast of scrambled eggs, sausage, gravy, and biscuits while Mama Lucy bustled around us cleaning and scrubbing and carrying on about the weather, her garden, her great-grandchildren, anything to dispell with language the bad feeling that had lingered since the last time I was here. The adventurous Petey was now incarcerated inside his cage, serving hard time for his wandering ways. Lucy finally sat down with us at the table and we ate biscuits and jelly and filled the room with small talk until Buzz looked at his watch and announced that he had an appointment with his orthopedist in Chapel Hill. I seized the opportunity to take my own leave, figuring the rapprochement was a success. I was heading to the door with Buzz when Lucy said, "Pick, I know you gotta get on home, but before you go would you just bring something down from the attic for me?"

My heart sank. "What's that?" Buzz grinned and waved to me, then gripped his crutches and limped out to his truck. Here we go again, I thought. But penance had to be paid and I might as well get it over with.

"It's a cedar chest my mama gave to me when I got married. It's full of old clothes and picture albums and newspaper clippings and papers and I don't know what all. It's up there. If you could move it down here and set it in the livin' room so's I can go through it? I could at least get started sortin' through that mess, like I promised the girls. It won't take a minute. I promise I cain't git up them steps no more and even if I could there's no light up there and it's too hot to set up there in the daytime."

There was no use arguing. Lucy followed me to the attic stairs and started issuing orders as I made my way up to the attic door. I unlatched the eye-hook and opened the door, stepped inside, and was hit by the heat, as if I were walking into a sauna. The tiny attic was dim even at midday. There were stacks of clothes and a lot of old furniture, lamp shades, a trunk or two and a chest of drawers. In the corner covered with an old quilt and stacks of clothes and blankets and ancient newspapers was the cedar chest.

"It should be over there near the window," Lucy called from the base of the stairs. "You see it?"

"Yes, ma'am. It's gonna be a bear to get down without some help, though. It'd be easier just to unload what's inside and bring down the contents."

"What?"

"Let me haul down some of this and you can start sorting. Then when Buzz heals up we'll come over together and move the chest down." Lucy, apparently satisfied with my solution, started clearing the kitchen table.

"We may need a dolly or something to move it later," I warned. When I was a child the chest had sat in the master bedroom at the foot of the four-poster bed. The grain of the polished wood, unchanged since then, was still a rich mixture of burnt umber and gold. The top latched shut in front, but luckily it had been left unlocked. I raised up the lid and found the chest full of old sweaters and vests and winter wear as well as assorted papers and boxes of photographs. I removed the garments and stacked them on the floor, then carried as many of the papers as I could lift down the steps and piled them on the kitchen table. I returned for more. Several trips later the chest was empty. I descended the stairs drenched with perspiration and carrying the last stack.

Lucy said, "Is that everything, Pickard? Don't leave a mess up there now, y'hear?"

I returned once more to police the attic and tried to lift the chest again now that it was empty. It was considerably lighter but I still knew I would never get it down the stairs alone. I scooped up some papers I had dropped on my way downstairs. As I stooped to pick up one last stack I noticed a sheaf of papers that had slipped down behind the chest and got caught between it and the attic wall. The prodigal file would have remained invisible had my last attempt to lift the chest not jarred it loose and scattered items onto the floor along the wall.

As I reached down I spotted a small brown book wedged among the papers. I picked it up and held it up to the window light to investigate. Its cover was frayed coffee-colored burlap, and was bare except for a small silhouette in the lower right-hand corner of a young man reading a book under a tree. The legend "Property of Eno Public Schools" was stamped on the inside cover with the name "Lucille Barlow" carefully inscribed in blue ink in the upper right-hand corner. It seemed to be a high school English literature text, a collection of stories with selections from Poe, Hugo, Twain, Dickens, and a number of other writers. As I flipped through the pages an envelope slipped between my fingers and fell to the floor. I picked it up and turned it over. The address was written in pencil in longhand across the front: *President Franklin D. Roosevelt, White House, 1600 Pennsylvania Avenue, Washington, D.C.* The small envelope, yellowed and soiled by time and the touch of hands, was unsealed. There was a piece of paper inside. The absence of a stamp or postal meter mark indicated that the envelope had never been mailed. Printed in the upper left-hand corner, in the same hand that had signed the textbook was the return address: "Lucille Barlow, Rte. 2, Eno, North Carolina."

I opened the envelope and removed the folded page. There, printed carefully in pencil in Lucy's beautiful hand on pulpy, yellow, blue-lined stationery, was the following note:

September 8, 1934

Dear President Roosevelt,

I know I wrote you before and I know you are busy but things down here are getting a lot worse. As you know, the strike started up a few days ago because people just couldn't take it anymore. Now everything's gotten out of hand.

I don't know where else to turn, Mr. Roosevelt. I believe you are a God-sent man and as far as I can see you are our only hope.

The words stopped halfway down the page. There were two more sheets of paper but nothing on them, as if the words had abandoned her halfway through.

I returned to the kitchen, where Lucy was cleaning up and handed her the envelope. "Mama Lucy, what's this?" She studied the envelope for a moment, then removed the letter.

"Lord," she said, "where did you find this?"

"In the attic. It fell out of this book."

She stared at the letter for a long while.

"You never finished it," I said. "What were you doing writing President Roosevelt? Why didn't you mail it?"

Suddenly her eyes filled up with tears. It was as if a flood of memories dammed up for ages had been unleashed. She inched her way slowly into the family room with the aid of her walker and collapsed on the sofa, burying her head in her hands. I had seen her weep many times over the years, and I was suspicious of her tears. I had seen her break down spontaneously over burnt toast, over the unfairness of a traffic ticket. She was so fluent with her remorse that for me the emotion had become trivialized. Still, I had witnessed moments of genuine bereavement as well. I had seen her weep for the loss of her son, for the suicide of her daughter, and when I cut her with my harsh words, but never like this. She wept with her whole body, every part of her being. She wept as if every molecule of her existence were wracked with an unfathomable sorrow, an inconsolable grief.

"I'm sorry. I didn't mean to upset you again." I took the letter from her hand.

"Pick! . . . Pick . . . Eno . . ." she gasped, between sobs. "Where you live . . . A terrible thing happened there! . . . Something terrible happened in Eno!"

After a time, the story flooded out.

PART II

LINTHEADS

7

MILL MOTHER'S LAMENT

Don't go, Dalton," Lucy pleaded as her husband stood on the front porch in the half-light of early morning, slipping his dark blue suit coat over his white shirt and faded burgundy suspenders. The gun in its holster peeked out from under the coat, the gun he seldom carried unless he was riding out into the countryside to surprise bootleggers, in his role as deputy sheriff of Eno County. "I woke up with a bad feelin' this mornin'," she said. "Like somethin's gonna happen. I couldn't sleep and that was before Sheriff Roberts come a-knockin'."

That morning, the sheriff had rapped on the door and warned Dalton of a possible confrontation at the Bellevue mill shift change at seven. He was needed at the plant to help keep order. That was that. Tall and lanky, Dalton Earl Cantrell was a man of few words and he especially didn't like explaining his duties to his wife. "I'm late," was all he said.

"Who's gonna feed the young'uns if somethin' happens to you?" demanded Lucy. "My paycheck ain't near enough."

Dalton adjusted his brown fedora. "I got to go, you know that. They expectin' trouble and want to be ready. I'm stoppin' at the courthouse. Sheriff says he's gonna deputize anybody owns a gun. Sheriff's a reasonable man. He'll keep things calm if them hotheads let 'im." He turned around at the bottom of the porch steps. "You just stay here with Bessie and the young'uns. And I mean it, Lucy, don't go down there at shift change. This is Gastonia all over. Sheriff says the governor might be sendin' more National Guard into Eno. That's how serious it is."

Lucy knew it was serious. The strikers had shut down the looms last Monday and the National Guard had been called in to keep them running. Those who weren't striking—Lucy included—worked for three days like that. And every day there'd been some incident. Machine guns had been set up at the main gate. Eno was like a time bomb set to go off. The tension was especially thick in the West End. Arguments broke out at the general store. Fights erupted in the pool hall. Like most places, the town was divided—half for and half against the union.

Lucy had read the articles in the Raleigh newspaper Dalton brought home from the courthouse. There had been labor strife for years all across the South, spontaneous combustions of frustration and rage that flared up among workers, like it had in Gastonia five years earlier. The Textile Workers International union had called this strike for better wages and conditions for millworkers nationwide, not only cotton and rayon hands in the Carolina Piedmont, Georgia and Alabama but silk workers in Philadelphia and New Jersey, woolen and worsted workers in Rhode Island and Massachusetts. Lucy didn't know anything about those places up north but she read how the strike started on Labor Day, the fourth of September, her birthday, and spread across the South like brushfire through pine needles. Nearly five hundred thousand cotton mill workers had shut down the looms from Gadsden, Alabama, to Knoxville, Tennessee, from Newnan, Georgia, to Honea Path, South Carolina. Mill town to mill town toppling like dominoes up through the North Carolina Piedmont, to places she did know, like Burlington and Eno. Boss men at the plant tried to play it down but Lucy could read and she knew the strikers at the Bellevue plant in Eno weren't alone. Her own brother Dave, who had worked in mills all over the area, was now working for the union.

Lucy was a spooler on the second shift and usually came home at night just after eleven o'clock to the house on Cornwallis Street not far from the one she grew up in on the hill. It hadn't been easy going to work this week with so many people she knew on the picket line. The shouts and the taunts of "Scab" and "Traitor" coming from folks she grew up with hurt her feelings, though she knew Annie Laura didn't call her that. It was worse weaving her way through the gauntlet in the afternoons than it was at night when she got off and the picket line was smaller and less vocal.

She wished she could stay home with her children, but Lucy, like many of the women, had to work to survive. Bessie, the colored help, came at six each morning to help around the house. After Lucy left for the mill, she'd watch the children until Dalton got home in the evenings, which was sometimes after six. Lucy, bone tired after a long shift in the weave room, still rose early to feed Dalton before he was due at the courthouse and the kids before they got off to school. This morning, however, there would be no time for breakfast.

"I mean it, Lucille. This could turn ugly," Dalton said. "Stay home with the young'uns where you belong." Lucy didn't know why he kept repeating himself, although if she thought about it she did too know. This trouble at the mill was just the kind of thing she would be right in the middle of. Though she continued to work, she was sympathetic to the strikers. She'd been listening to her brother Davis talk about what the union could do for working folks and most of her brothers and sisters had already joined the picket lines. But Lucy, with so many mouths to feed, couldn't afford to lose her job or to miss a paycheck even for a few days. And how would it look for the deputy sheriff's wife to be seen on the picket line? Dalton could lose his job.

She stood at the door watching Dalton's beat-up old '28 Chevy disappear down the street. He'd bought the car so he could take the job as deputy sheriff. A hundred dollars a month wages was good money but the car cost him four hundred. Then she turned to Bessie, who was frying up some fatback, and told her to watch the children while she ran out for a bit.

"Where you goin'?" asked Bessie.

Lucy slipped a sweater over her green cotton dress. It was early September, and the morning was unseasonably cool. The sky was soft and pink outside and you could tell it was going to be a clear beautiful day even though the fog hadn't lifted from the river bottoms yet.

"I got to warn Annie Laura," Lucy said. Her friend had been on the picket lines day and night since the strike began and had become a fixture at all the union meetings and rallies. Sometimes she led the strikers in song to keep up their spirits. Annie Laura filled Lucy in on the goings-on with the strike and Lucy told her what she heard inside the company.

"You heard what Mr. Dalton said, Miz Lucy," Bessie said. "They ain't nothin' for you over at that mill. Them flyin' squadrons just stirrin' up trouble."

The flying squadrons, swarms of union supporters and agitators from other mill towns, had arrived in Eno Monday night, honking their horns and urging workers to shut down the looms and join the strike. Bessie was annoyed with the flying squadrons because they had ruined her surprise. She had made Lucy a coconut layer cake for her birthday but Dalton had received word that the squadrons were on their way from Haw River and he returned to the mill to keep the peace. Annie Laura dropped by to say that she couldn't stay, the strike was coming, and the present she had been working on for Lucy wasn't finished yet. She was very excited and mysterious about it but said she wanted it to be just right for Lucy's twenty-ninth birthday. So with Dalton gone and Annie Laura running off to see about the strike and the children asleep, when Lucy finally got home it was just Lucy and Bessie and the cake. Lucy didn't mind but Bessie's irritation quickly turned to genuine fear.

"Don't you go off up there behind Mr. Cantrell's back," Bessie now scolded as Lucy opened the door.

"What do I want to go up there for?" Lucy said. "Don't I get enough of that place every day? I'm goin' to Annie Laura's. Somebody's got to warn her."

Lucy was annoyed with Bessie for taking Dalton's side, even though she knew it was out of concern. Lucy was a year or two older than Bessie and they had practically grown up together. Bessie Thurwell's mother, Onnie Lee, had worked for Lucy's mama and papa and her daddy worked on the loading dock at the mill. Coloreds weren't allowed to work inside the mills, only at the loading dock, and their women cooked and cleaned for millhands so the wives could work. But even with two paychecks, the Cantrells sometimes had to compensate Bessie with produce from the garden. All Lucy knew was that if the sheriff came by to fetch Dalton that early in the morning something mighty big was up. She kissed the kids and told them to mind Bessie until she returned.

"I'll be back before the young'uns leave for school," Lucy said as the screen door clapped shut behind her.

Annie's house was on the street behind them. To save time, Lucy cut through the backyards, and turned onto the street where Annie Laura lived. When she rounded the corner, she paused. A stack of furniture was piled on her friend's front yard. Annie Laura's brother-in-law was slumped in a chair with his head in his hands. His two girls sprawled on the porch with their heads in their mama's lap. They were all weeping.

"What happened, Carl?" Lucy asked.

Carl, looking like he hadn't slept a wink, said, "Sheriff Roberts and some company dicks come last night and cleared us out."

"Dalton Earl won't with 'em, was he?" Lucy asked.

"Naw, I s'pect Dalton wouldn't have no part in it. He's a good man. I think the sheriff was ashamed hisself. He wouldn't look me in the eye when he served the papers."

"But why? Why'd they do it?"

"Annie Laura," he said bitterly. "Said she's union and union cain't live in no company house. Ol' man Webb's orders. He's crackin' down." Carl slumped lower in the chair. "We got no place to go, Lucy. Union ain't gonna house us. No matter what Annie Laura thinks."

Lucy had heard the company was starting to move some of the strike leaders out of their homes but hoped the presence of Carl and his wife and kids would act as a buffer. She should have known better. Annie Laura was too visible. Not only did she lead the singing at the rallies, she was also one of the most articulate speakers in Eno. Folks were already comparing her to the martyred Ella May Wiggins, the mother of five, who had been murdered during the strike in Gastonia. Last spring Annie Laura had talked the Eno mill baseball team into letting her embroider the letters TWI on their uniforms above the Bellevue letters. Annie Laura wasn't married and had had a pretty rough time of it taking care of her younger brothers and sisters most of her life. But since all this union talk started with her a while back, Lucy had never seen her so happy, so alive. It was as though she had fallen in love, not with a man but an idea.

"Where is Annie Laura?"

"Over at the mill," Carl said, dragging a shirt sleeve over his dark, sunken eyes. "She's down at the shift change. Heard there was gonna be a fight. I wouldn't go over there if I was you, Lucy. You'll wind up like us. This is got out of hand. The governor's done called in more soldiers like it's a war."

Lucy ran down Hillsborough Street past the colored graveyard near the West End depot. From the hill, she saw a large crowd surging toward the factory. The area was already alive with activity, much more than usual for the shift change, as though it were high noon, rather than seven in the morning. She could make out Scott's General Store and the pool hall in the distance. Men congregated around it in clusters, talking and whispering with an air of tense expectancy.

She was walking down the street when a big yellow roadster turned the corner behind her and cruised past slowly, then pulled off into a drive about thirty yards ahead. Seconds later it turned around and came back in her direction. A wave of anxiety washed over her. The street was deserted. The driver flashed his headlights and pulled up next to her.

Spencer Webb, the mill owner's son, rolled down the window and peered out at her. "Lucy," he said, "is that you?"

Lucy's heart skipped a beat.

The last time she'd seen Spencer Webb was at Panther's Den when she told him she was getting married; she never thought she'd see him again. In the years that followed he kept turning up in her life at odd times and was always nice to her, and they picked up again like no time at all had passed.

"Spencer Webb, what are you doing here?"

"Wanted to get out this morning," he explained. "Keep an eye on things."

"I thought you moved up north."

"I did. I'm back down here until this mess blows over. My law practice will survive without me for a time. Are you going to work?"

"I'm on second shift now."

"Then I'd turn around and go home if I were you. Trouble's brewing." He glanced nervously down the road in the direction of the depot. "Too many hotheads. I've never seen my father this angry. Mother called me home so I could be with him until the strike's over. She thinks I can reason with Daddy. Balance what he's being told. I doubt it. I only irritate him. The governor wants him to let the National Guard handle this. Daddy hired the extra security. But these Yankee detectives he brought in are feeding him a bunch of baloney about our family being in danger from the union militants. My mother lost the baby a few weeks ago. He was only a couple of months old. Mother's devastated and Daddy's crazy with remorse."

"I'm so sorry," Lucy said. "I didn't know."

"Why would you? She's forty-eight. At my age I never expected to become an older brother again. It was a miracle the baby was born at all. Then the next thing you know, he's dead in the crib. Just one of those things. Daddy thinks the union's to blame."

Lucy was appalled. "You don't think they had anything to do with it, do you?" Even the most militant union people she knew were not capable of such things. Annie Laura herself said that if the union couldn't get what they wanted without violence, then they didn't want it.

"No," Spencer said. "I don't think they did it. But this strike doesn't help matters any."

"Your daddy's the one who started the stretch-out, Spencer," Lucy said fiercely. "Folks just cain't keep up with all the extra work they s'posed to do. And for less pay. And he's layin' lotsa folks off. And runnin' 'em outa their homes. This is all his doin'."

"I know, Lucy. I know." His expression was pained. "I'm sorry."

Lucy felt guilty. Spencer didn't deserve her rebuke. He had always been a good friend to her. "You know I'm sorry for what happened to your mama, Spencer," she said. "There's nothing worse in this world than losing a baby."

A few years ago, before Dalton got the deputy sheriff's job, Lucy had lost Sara, a baby girl, born between Donly and Florence, to the whooping cough. They were just scraping by and couldn't even afford a decent casket. A philanthropist donated a mahogany child's coffin, hand-carved with intricate filigree. Later she and Dalton were baffled and touched to learn that the woodwork had been awarded First Prize at the Eno county fair. Dalton claimed the donor was someone from the courthouse or church group, but Lucy suspected that it was Spencer Webb. She had never known for sure until today.

Spencer looked sad as he said, "How are you, Lucy? How are your children? Are they getting enough to eat?"

"Depends how long the strike lasts," she answered honestly. "At least Dalton's got a job. We get by."

"Listen to me," he said. "Don't go up there today."

Lucy detected a new urgency in his voice. "Why are you telling me this?"

"I just . . . don't like the feel of this. I worry about the welfare of our people, even if my father doesn't." He looked at her earnestly. "We appreciate you not joining the picket line."

"A lot of my friends and family are out there."

Out of the corner of her eye, Lucy saw a group of men march out of the Bluebird Café, onto the train tracks and head in the direction of the mill. "Oh, my goodness." Lucy, spotting her brother Davis at the front of the pack, said, "I better go," and set off in the direction of the depot.

"I'm worried about you," Spencer called after her. "Keep your family safe."

As Lucy closed on the men, she shouted, "Davis! . . . Davis!" Her brother waved his brown felt hat to signal that he'd heard her and started back in her direction.

"Hey, little girl," he said, hugging her and swinging her around. "Who was that I saw you talking to in the big yellow car?"

Lucy flushed. She didn't think he'd seen her. "Nobody . . ."

"You're a married lady, Lucy—with young'uns—and you still carry on like a single woman. Put that energy to better use and come on over to the picket line this morning. We're gonna let them know how we feel about scabs."

"I'm workin'. You callin' me a scab?"

"No, but you oughta be out here with us, like your friend Annie Laura. She sings like an angel. You and her can sing duets like y'all used to do in church. You oughta hear her sing 'The Ballad of Ella May Wiggins.' "

"I don't want to end up like Ella May Wiggins, havin' songs wrote about me. Annie Laura, neither. Have you seen her?"

"She's probably already up at the gate, where we oughta be now. Come on."

A wave of foreboding, stronger than the one she'd felt that morning, flooded over Lucy. Looking at Davis, so handsome and rugged and alive, she inexplicably burst into tears. "Dave. Don't go up there. You can stay at our house. I woke up with one of them feelings I had when Daddy died. Davis, somethin's gonna happen! I just know it!" She clutched at the lapels of his suit coat, but he pulled her hands away.

"Get ahold of yourself, girl. Go on home if you're scared. I gotta go. I'm picket captain. Folks're dependin' on me." A look appeared in Davis's eyes, a bright, wild gleam she sometimes saw at church in the eyes of the newly converted, the ecstatic and the saved. He was caught up in something bigger than himself and there was no reaching him. Annie Laura looked the same way when she talked about the union.

Just then a truckload of soldiers barreled down Hillsborough Street, crossed over the tracks, and headed for the mill. Then another and another. Their beds were packed with grim-faced young men staring out the back into the gray mist of morning.

Davis shouted to his companions up ahead. "See, boys, us on the mill hill ain't seen a shred of the democracy we was hearin' so much about in the Great War when we was gittin' shot at by the Huns and them boys there waren't old enough for knee britches. I didn't see none of them in the Argonne Forest back in 'seventeen. This strike's the closest thing to democracy they're ever gonna see and it's our duty to show 'em what it's all about." The men cheered at Davis's swashbuckling words. "The mill owners bring in their toy soldiers to keep democracy at bay."

Lucy marveled at her brother's fearlessness in the face of the guardsmen's bayonets and weapons. Lord God, that was her old nemesis Jake Satterfield staring at her from the back of the last truck! And Dalton's little brother, Bud, sitting across from him! She'd forgotten he was old enough to be in the guard now.

"Go home, boys! You don't belong here," shouted Davis at the last truckload of soldiers rumbling by. "Go on home or join us on the picket line!" More trucks arrived from the opposite direction and turned toward the mill. They were coming from Durham as well as Burlington. The tension in the air, already thick, thickened.

"What kind of trouble are they expectin'?" Lucy said. She knew the guard had been keeping open the Pioneer plant in Burlington, where her brothers Charlie and Vernell and her sisters Eunice and Icy worked, and there had been some disturbances there on the first day of the strike. And Lucy had heard stories about what happened in Gastonia at the Loray plant in 1929, how some said the National Guard had rioted. It scared her.

"C'mon, Davis. We better get on up there," called one of his cronies. "Just a few minutes 'til the whistle."

Lucy could feel the danger in the air, like some wild animal had been set loose in a crowd. She felt the hair on her arms and neck stand up. She thought about Dalton's warning and remembered what Spencer Webb had told her, and her premonition that morning burned like a hot coal in the pit of her stomach. She thought of Clayton, Ruth Ann, Donly and the babies and felt them calling for her. She wanted to race home, but first she had to make sure Annie Laura was all right. Maybe she could talk her into coming home with her. Especially now that everybody had seen the soldiers arriving in trucks. She crossed Hillsborough Street and the tracks to the road that led up to the mill. She followed along behind Davis and his crowd. A lot of people were moving toward the factory, people she worked with or went to church with, and not all of them were going to work. There were children accompanying their parents, holding their hands, apparently skipping school to join the action, heading up the steep grade toward the mill. Damn fools, Lucy thought.

The main building of Bellevue Mill, where she had worked for so many years, sat back from the road like a fortress on the hill, plain, rectangular, and unadorned, three stories of brick and mortar, austere and immutable with the severe and graceless institutional lines of a prison, or an orphanage or an insane asylum. Bracketed on one end by a single brick smokestack, fat and bulky like a turret on an ancient castle, and on the other by a dilapidated, rusted-out, tin water tower, the front of the building's brick facade was plaited with row upon row of tall, narrow, elongated arched windows, left open to let in the air but with windowpanes painted gray like the autumn sky, to keep out the direct sunlight that could fade and damage cloth and yarn. The entrance was located down at one end, set in the recesses of a windowless brick turret attached to the main facade. The entire building was surrounded with chain-link fence and barbed wire, and now a throng of angry picketers.

When Lucy arrived, the third shift was filing out of the front gate. The workers arriving for the first shift were greeted with taunts and jeers from the crowd now surrounding the mill. Platoons of National Guardsmen entered through the main gate, which was guarded by dozens of sinister-looking machine guns. A short red-faced platoon sergeant with angry eyes ordered some of his men to circle around to the opposite side of the mill. Others including Bud and Jake's unit were to follow him through the mill's front gate. Turning around, Lucy saw Sheriff Roberts leading a mob of armed civilians up the street. Dalton, carrying a rifle and walking along behind, wore a worried look on his face. He moved to the front of the line and ushered the men past the guard and through the front gate. Lucy's pulse quickened.

When the phalanx of newly deputized townsmen appeared, the crowd of picketers and sympathizers surrounding the mill erupted with boos and jeers. It looked like the sheriff had deputized anybody who could carry a gun; some of the boys were mighty young—no more than fourteen or fifteen years old, Lucy guessed. Lucy thought she heard someone shout Dalton's name as he ran by. The guard at the gate waved them through and they followed a group of guardsmen into the mill. Soon rifles began poking out of the second-story windows and within minutes there were guns sticking out of windows all up and down the front of the plant. To Lucy, the mill looked like a storybook castle, armed to the teeth. She scanned the windows for Dalton, but couldn't see him anywhere.

The flying squadrons and local union sympathizers were angry at the guardsmen. But Lucy reckoned it was better to have troops in the windows who were trained in handling crowd situations and knew how to show restraint, than trigger-happy amateurs and civilians.

The folks from the third shift didn't want trouble and had mostly gone home but those remaining were bunched together, exchanging angry words with the strikers. The crowd of flying squadrons and picketers grew. More cars pulled up as word spread through town that something was up at the mill. Outside, the atmosphere grew more charged and rowdy. As the crowd thickened outside, shouting matches and fights broke out between the third shifters and strikers who were shouting at them, "Scabs!" "Sorry sumbitches!" "Stay home!" Lucy searched the throng for familiar faces and for a moment thought she saw Annie Laura among the strikers, but then she disappeared into the crowd.

Outside the gate, picketers were holding up signs and chanting slogans. Davis moved among them shouting orders and leading chants. Many of the strikers carried sticks and clubs, but Lucy saw no guns.

Just when the ruckus had hit a fever pitch and the shouting and carrying on was getting out of hand, Lucy heard her brother Davis give an order. She couldn't quite make out what he said, but the effect was dramatic. The crowd, which had been rowdy and raucous during the shift change and when the deputies arrived, suddenly settled into a brooding quiet.

Guardsmen shouted at the strikers to go back home. "There's nothing for you here. Go back to your homes." Soon they, too, fell silent. A calm like the eye of a hurricane came over the entire gathering. Then Lucy heard a female voice, singular and pristine, rise up in song above the milling throng. The voice seemed to emanate from everywhere and nowhere, and Lucy recognized it as though it were her own. It was Annie Laura, and the song she was singing was "Mill Mother's Lament" by Ella May Wiggins.

We leave our homes in the morning
We kiss our children goodbye
While we slave for the bosses
Our children scream and cry

And when we draw our money
Our grocer's bills to pay
Not a cent to keep for clothing
Not a cent to lay away

Lucy moved closer. Near the front gate, the picket line parted and Davis removed his hat as Annie Laura emerged from the crowd, and linked arms with two of her fellow strikers. Her hair was down and she wore a plain brown dress with a white collar and a yellow-and-white polka-dot scarf and Lucy had never seen her looking prettier.

And on that very evening
Our little one will say
I need some shoes, dear mother
And so does sister May

Annie Laura's voice hung in the air haunting and crystalline, mesmerizing both the crowd and the guardsmen and deputies gathered in the mill's second-story windows. Lucy's eyes roamed the crowd. Out beyond the strikers and the onlookers, Spencer Webb's car moved slowly, deliberately down the road, as though it were part of a funeral procession.

Now it grieves the heart of a mother
You everyone must know
But we cannot buy for our children
Our wages are too low

Near the end of the building deputized men began passing picker sticks out the windows to supporters gathered below. Normally workers in the weave room used the two-foot long wooden sticks to throw the shuttle through the warp of the loom; for the edgy deputies they were effective truncheons. Then came broom handles, shortened for use as clubs. When the strikers saw what was happening they shouted with rage and converged on the window. The men inside struck at them with their clubs through the opening.

Then Lucy spotted Buck Shaver, another striker, heading for the window. He was a big man and moody and Lucy knew as much because Dalton had been required to arrest him a time or two at the pool hall and let him sleep off a drunk in the county jail. Buck's face was a picture of fury. A nonunion fellow was grabbing the picker sticks, and pulling them out the window. Buck Shaver punched the man on the back of the head. Then somebody hit Shaver. And another man busted his head with a picker stick and the big man toppled to the ground where he lay motionless in a spreading pool of blood. The scuffle acted on the crowd like a malevolent magnet: within seconds the entire human panorama—strikers and spectators, guardsmen and deputies; workers leaving with the shift change and those just arriving—shifted and surged, en masse, toward the corner of the factory. Screams, shouts, cries of protest merged into a roar. Fights broke out all over the yard. Then over the din Lucy heard the sharp crack of a gunshot.

She looked up at the row of windows on the second floor where she thought the shot had come from, and saw a line of rifles pointed at the crowd that was gathered in the area where the fight had broken out.

She heard someone inside yell, "They got guns!" Then the men at the windows started shooting. A series of pops like firecrackers and puffs of smoke rose from the windows. Another volley came seconds later. To Lucy, it looked like the building itself were spitting fire.

As the onlookers tried to flee, more fights broke out. Bodies dropped all over the yard. Some of the picketers panicked and charged the mill. Lucy looked for Annie Laura but her friend had melted into the confusion. She saw Davis sprinting toward a fallen striker, then lost him as tear gas canisters flew and her eyes stung and her vision blurred. She reached for the red bandanna in her dress pocket she used to wipe her children's noses. "Shoot, dammit!" somebody screamed in a high-pitched voice from inside a window behind the fence. "Stop them bastards!"

8

THE GREAT WHITE HAWK

Your grandmother's hallucinating," Cameron said that evening as I stir-fried some veggies for dinner and Cam flipped through the mail. "My grandma got senile toward the end, too."

"I don't know," I said. "It didn't sound like senility." That afternoon when Cam got home from work I told her everything—about my apology to my grandmother, the Roosevelt letter, and all I'd learned of Mama Lucy's incredible story. Cam was as surprised by the letter as I was, but she was skeptical, if not outright dismissive, when it came to the story of the shootings.

On that matter I, too, had my doubts. Maybe Mama Lucy *was* hallucinating. Maybe her heart problems had starved her brain of oxygen and driven her around the bend. Maybe she was making up yarns about herself as a means of getting attention. She had always been a great storyteller and had a reputation among the family for stretching the truth for effect. Or maybe her memory was playing tricks on her, selecting fragments from her past and present and stitching them together with fictions she'd read and movies she'd seen and perhaps scenes she'd only imagined.

"She sounded pretty convincing," I argued. "And it really upset her to talk about it."

"I'm sure it did. But then why hasn't anyone else in the family ever talked about this before?" Cameron asked. "Bad news moves through your family at the speed of light. How could nobody know about something so traumatic? If what she says is true, why is there no mention of it in the history books, no markers or memorials?"

"I don't know," I said. "I'll have to ask Sandy Murphy. She works for the Southern Oral History Project. She told me things at the party about Lucy nobody in my family ever talked about. She may know something."

"Don't you think she would have mentioned something that big that night?" She was losing patience with what she perceived as my credulity.

"Maybe she didn't know either. Maybe nothing was ever written about it because it's not the history of rich people. Winners write the histories, you know that. These were poor people, Cam, life's losers. They had no money, no influence, nothing. Nobody cares about people like that. I'm not saying what Mama Lucy told me is gospel, but it *is* possible something like that could have been overlooked or suppressed."

Even so, Cameron was right to question. I had wondered about the same things myself, but I hadn't pressed Mama Lucy at the time because our conversation had worn her out and she'd put an end to it before she could finish the story. Nevertheless, I was intrigued and wanted to hear more, but it would have to wait. I had neglected my duties around the house too much already.

I got up early the next morning and set to work on the side porch. In an effort to appease Cameron, I had made the porch my top priority. I had already replaced all the rotten wood and repaired the steps. All that was left was to sand the whole thing down and apply primer and two coats of paint. The job wouldn't dry for a day or two but that didn't matter; what did, was that Cameron notice my efforts and see the evidence of my progress. She wanted me to finish the entrance areas before frost set in so we could plant more boxwoods and perennials around the porch. If I stayed with it, I could probably finish the job by the time she got home. I scraped and primed and painted and worried about our marriage. The porch was not the only thing in need of repair.

Cam and I were drifting. All the recent upheaval—me losing my job, our moving to Eno, Cameron returning to work—had taken a toll on our marriage. With each passing day, the damage was becoming more noticeable. The guilt I felt over what I had done to Cameron and Wiley was enormous. But it wasn't enough. I was desperate for atonement. But Cam seemed neither willing nor able to grant it. So while my wife attempted to resurrect the career she had given up to raise our son, I threw myself into the task of renovating the house, not only because the house needed it, but also because doing so made me feel useful, and kept my despair at bay. Work was my salvation, and my penance. But even as my work made the house itself more livable, Cam and I grew farther apart. It almost seemed as though there was an inverse relationship between the state of our house and that of our marriage. The question that now hovered over every board I sanded or brick I laid was whether when I was finished the result of my handiwork would be a hearth and home or a spectacularly appointed sepulcher.

By noontime the October sun had risen high in the cloudless sky and it was hot enough for me to take off my shirt. A soft autumn breeze kept the blazing sun from becoming too uncomfortable while I worked. As I finished the first coat of gray paint on the porch floorboards and steps, I heard Flappy yapping inside the house. I glanced out at the side yard to see what was up. A voice called to me from the front porch.

"Hi, Pick. Remember me?"

A woman in dark glasses smiled from the porch across the boxwoods. She looked like she had stepped out of one of Cameron's catalogues, stylish in a navy skirt, form-fitting mustard-colored turtleneck, and tweed waist jacket with leather-lapels and high-heeled midi-boots. In her hand was a bag with a logo emblazoned on the side. I didn't recognize her until she removed her shades. Then I realized it was Lisa Price from the Strudwick party.

"Oh, hi," I said, grabbing my T-shirt.

"Don't dress on my account." Lisa laughed. Her smile flashed and glistened.

"I was on the way to a hair appointment and brought you and your wife a little housewarming gift from WellSpring," she said. "WellSpring is the Chapel Hill equivalent of Dean and DeLuca or Zabar's—yuppie culinary heaven. Is she here?"

"Cameron? No, she's at work."

"Oh, well, don't let me interrupt. Just tell me where the fridge is and I'll put it in there. I know you must be busy."

"No, actually, I was just going to take a break while this paint dries."

"Is that your pooch I hear barking?"

"That's Flappy, our vicious watchdog. She barks like crazy anytime somebody pulls up the driveway. She's harmless. I'd better let her out before she goes nuts. She needs to go out anyway."

We moved inside and I showed Lisa to the kitchen, offered her some lemonade, then dashed upstairs and changed my shirt. When I returned Lisa was gazing out the kitchen window.

"I love the view of the backyard. You should put in a pool," she said.

"You sound like my son, Wiley."

"Well, it's just lovely. You're doing a splendid job."

"It's coming along," I said, realizing too late that Cameron would kill me for allowing anybody in the house before it was ready to show. She was much more vigilant than I was about putting her best foot forward. In college when I did carpentry work during summers I got used to owners and real estate agents and all manner of people traipsing through the unfinished masterpiece. I probably had more of a tolerance for imperfection and ambiguity than my wife.

"I forgot you had so many outbuildings."

"Oh, yeah," I said. "More than we need."

"No such thing as too many. May I see them?" she asked. "I'm simply transfixed by outbuildings. That is, if you don't mind. I don't want to be a bother."

"Sure. Hold on." I grabbed a glass of lemonade and led her outside.

"These old outbuildings always remind me of little gifts around a Christmas tree."

"Ah, historic Eno," I said, leading the way to the summer kitchen. "We have so many we don't know what to do with all of them."

"I shouldn't be interrupting you. I know what it's like to restore a place. You feel like you'll never get done with all the distractions."

"No, I like showing off the history of this place. That's part of what we fell in love with. We couldn't believe how much this house just creaked and groaned with it."

"Well, I'm sure you will contribute to the fabled history of the house." She took my arm as we walked back through the grass. She wobbled on her heels. "I should have worn my hiking boots. I really didn't expect a tour. I was just stopping off on my way to the hairdresser."

We stopped at the brick structure off the back of the main house. "This is the summer kitchen. The slaves cooked the meals here in the old days. I guess the heat was too much in the summertime. And the owners didn't want the house to catch on fire."

"It's amazing to think that slaves once toiled on these grounds."

I opened the rickety door. Lisa glanced inside but didn't go in, deterred by the heat and dust and detritus of our move.

"I've got to get in there and clean it out," I said as we moved on. "Over there's the smokehouse and the ice house."

"Where do you work?"

"I've got a little shop for my work tools in the basement."

"No, your artist's studio."

"I don't really have one," I confessed.

"C'mon. Every artist has a studio."

"I'm sort of on sabbatical. I stored my drawing table and materials in the ice house. Someday if I ever go back to work I'll wire up the summer kitchen and work in there."

"What do you mean 'if'?"

"When."

"I would think so. This place is so visually stimulating. Just look around you. From every angle it's a landscape. I don't know how you can keep from it."

I smiled. "You sound like an artist."

"Not really. I told you I was an aspiring actress before I met Mr. Price. Now I smoke. Make smoke ring sculptures. Paint in the air. It's very Zen. It's there for the moment—then poof! It's gone."

"C'mon, check this out." I pushed open the door to the ice house. The windowless brick cellar was dark and dank. "How about this for a studio space?"

"Well, the light leaves something to be desired," Lisa observed as we eased down the brick steps into the musky interior, leaving the door open.

"I prefer that. I do my best work in the dark."

"I hate to admit this, Pick, but from the cartoons of yours I remember seeing, it's hard to tell. Are you liberal or conservative?"

"Neither. I think we should all wean ourselves of labels. Liberals think I'm conservative and conservatives think I'm liberal."

"Do you have any of your work handy that perhaps I could take a look at?"

"Not really."

"You don't want to show it?"

"No, it's not that, it's just . . ." A sudden feeling of vulnerability I had not experienced in years washed over me, a need to impress and a fear that my work might disappoint Lisa Price.

"Maybe some other time."

"No, I'll show you," I blurted, feeling ridiculous for my reluctance. "There's a portfolio of old cartoons out here somewhere." I retrieved a leather case from behind the door. Unzipping it, I sat down in my old swivel chair and began thumbing through some of the prints and originals. Lisa moved in behind me and watched over my shoulder.

"I can't believe you keep them out here!" Lisa said. "Aren't you afraid of what the weather will do to them?"

"You're right. It's a little damp out here. Maybe I should move them inside."

Lisa slipped closer as I laid the drawings on the table. "Oooh, wicked," she enthused. "Very funny. You are good."

Lisa's perfume was intoxicating in the confines of the tiny unventilated outbuilding. I wasn't sure if it was her scent or her compliments that were making me shy.

She squealed with delight. "These are delicious. How in the world did you think of that?"

"That was my job."

Lisa perused my work, punctuating the silence every so often with her rich throaty laugh. The more she liked the drawings, the more ill-at-ease I felt. Finally, she turned and put her hand on my shoulder. "Pick, do you ever draw anything besides cartoons? Portraits, landscapes, that sort of thing?"

"I used to. In college. Not much since I turned professional."

"Do you miss it?"

"Sometimes. I'd love to get back to it someday."

"You should. I know exactly what you should draw."

"What's that?"

"Me. I'd love a Pick Cantrell portrait of me to hang in our house."

"You don't want that, Lisa. I'm a cartoonist."

"What's the matter?" she teased. "You don't think you could catch my likeness?"

"I'm a caricaturist," I explained. "Caricaturists are assassins. We distort the flaws and blemishes."

My discomfort only seemed to embolden her. "Go ahead. Hit me with your best shot. I can take it. Besides, I'm beyond humiliation."

Then I found myself reciting a line I used in chalk talks or public speeches that usually worked to graciously deflect requests to instantly caricature the teacher or president of the group. "There's a saying in cartooning that the uglier you are, the easier you are to draw. As a political cartoonist I've been blessed with great subjects. That's why I can't draw you, Lisa. You're just too good-looking."

The minute I said this I realized my mistake. You didn't use the same line you used to deflect requests by Kiwanis Club members on an attractive woman.

"Do you think so?" She put down my drawings and turned her green eyes upon me with laser intensity.

Flappy's barking broke the spell. "Excuse me," I said, brushing past her as I headed out the ice house door. "I should have put the dog back inside." I was moving quickly toward the sound but something in the timbre of Flappy's bark caused me to pick up my pace. By the time I got to the summer kitchen I had broken into a run.

As I drew closer I thought I heard something new in her bark, a strangled terror and another sound I had never heard before, a heart-stopping screech. I hurdled shrubs and stacks of two-by-fours, piles of bricks and wheelbarrows as I raced past the summer kitchen, and rounded the corner of the house. My heart leaped to my throat when I saw what was causing the ruckus.

The mysterious albino hawk had swept down into our yard and was lifting Flappy off the ground in its powerful, gigantic claws, beating its wings fervently as the dog, which, though small, was twice the size of a groundhog, snapped and barked and yelped until she fell to the ground only to be caught up again as she tried to scamper away. Feathers and fur flew. I watched, temporarily paralyzed, as the mighty predator swooped down like an angel of death, grasping the poor pooch firmly in its powerful claws. It was lifting off the ground reaching a height of a few feet when once more the dog, snapping and biting, feces flying in pellets, wriggled free and dropped earthward. Undaunted, the bird attacked again as the terror-stricken Flappy scrambled toward the house. This time the bird caught her from behind, lifting off with a viselike grip that appeared to be welded to Flappy's back and throat. I scoured the driveway for something to throw at the bird, but rocks and sticks seemed puny, inadequate against the enormous raptor.

Then my gaze fell upon the football Wiley had left in the yard again overnight. I raced across the lawn, scooped up the waterlogged pigskin, and calling upon the all-state quarterback lying dormant in my muscles and sense memory, rifled the ball at the bird. My pass caught the great white hawk in the upper torso, with a muffled thump. Flappy dropped at least twenty feet to the ground, landing with a sickening thud in the grass as the hawk tumbled earthward before righting itself in midflight. But by then I had reached the whimpering Flappy and dived on top of her, covering her with my body as I kept my eyes peeled for another aerial assault. The great white hawk circled the yard once, then twice, then finally retreated, flapping its wings gimpily heavenward toward the solace of its aerie among the towering treetops of Oaklawn.

Flappy was hurt badly. Her stomach and throat were punctured and torn and she was matted with blood and whimpering pathetically. Lisa rushed up behind and shouted, "Wait! She may have broken bones. Get some towels for the bleeding. And a pillow. There's a vet not far from here. Put her in the station wagon. You can ride in back with her."

Lisa, already late for her appointment, dropped us at the veterinarian's. "Let me know if there's anything I can do," she said. I called Cam at work and by the time she arrived a half hour later the vet had examined Flappy. The prognosis was bleak: The lacerations were serious but treatable, but the fall had broken Flappy's pelvis. "I doubt she'll ever walk again," the vet said, "although I can't say for sure." He warned of the operation Flappy would need to reattach her femur to her pelvis with a pin and of the weeks of extraordinary attention she would require if she had any chance at recovery. If we wanted his advice, he recommended we put her to sleep.

"No," snapped Cameron, "we'll take her home after you do the surgery."

"Fine," the vet said skeptically. "It's your decision."

When he left the room to fetch painkillers, I whispered, "Cameron, are you sure? I know it's hard, but maybe we should listen to the doctor."

"No, dammit. I'll stay home from work and nurse her through this if I have to. If Flappy's going to die, it will only be after we've done all we can for her."

I knew there was no arguing with her. I had seen Cam's fierce commitment when she cared for her mother who had died of cancer shortly before we moved to New York. For months on end she had accompanied her to chemotherapy treatments, sat up with her night after night at the hospital, changed her soiled bedsheets and undergarments, and in the process made the hospice workers seem slack, insensitive, and inexperienced.

When I picked up Wiley from school and told him what happened he burst into tears. He cried again when he saw Flappy that afternoon at the vet's. By then, she'd already had the operation and her flank was shaved and the large metal staples securing the incision were all too visible. Her back legs were trussed up in a cast and she mewled in pain every time she was moved. I couldn't help thinking of my childhood dog, Laddie, and how devastated I'd been when he died. Now Wiley knew that same helplessness.

Flappy came home the next day. That night Cameron and I alternated turning her every couple of hours to relieve pressure to her hips, and between shifts the dog's pitiful moaning kept us awake. The next day we were both wasted from lack of sleep. Cam came home from work at lunch to check on the dog. Although, technically, Flappy belonged to Wiley, the dog was my wife's alter ego and Cameron was fiercely protective of her, suspicious even of the advice of vets, and she grew peevish and critical whenever I attended to her pet, as if I might hurt her again. When Cameron returned to work I turned the poor pooch and dispensed her medicine and took her outside to pee.

Flappy's mewling woke us at four the next morning. I stumbled through the darkness to the dog's makeshift pallet. As I groggily lifted the dog's hind legs, Cameron flipped on the lights, momentarily blinding me. Flappy, startled, snarled and nipped my hand.

"You're hurting her!" Cameron snapped, shouldering me aside to tend to the whimpering animal.

I rubbed my injured hand. "I'm sorry. I couldn't see."

"Just . . . leave her alone. I'll deal with it."

Angry and confused I retreated to the bathroom and rinsed my wound under the tap. When I returned Cameron was standing in the bedroom doorway cradling the dog in her arms.

"What's going on?" I asked.

"It's pointless for us both to be up all night," was all she said. Then she turned her back and disappeared through the door. That was the night Cameron moved out of our bedroom. At the time I had to admit I was grateful.

9

MILK OF AMNESIA

You're not going back over there again, are you?" Cameron demanded a few days later as she brushed out her hair at the bathroom sink. I was looking for Wiley's sneakers so I could get him dressed for school.

"Over where?" I answered, although I knew exactly where she meant.

"Burlington."

"Who said I was?"

"Your father. He called when you were in the shower. He wanted to know if you needed help with the renovation—"

"Curiosity's killing 'im!"

"—or whether you're still planning to go to Lucy's to clear out her attic." She had me. She grabbed a barette off the countertop and pinned up her hair. "When do you stop having to go back over there?"

"I don't *have* to go over there," I said. "I volunteered."

"What is this, guilt over your fight with her?"

"It's just until Buzz gets off his crutches. She wants me to move some stuff out of the attic. I don't mind." I was confused about how I really felt and it showed. I had never been interested in what Mama Lucy had to say before and now I was hanging on her every word. Seeking her out was disorienting, screwing up my internal gyroscope. Pretty soon Cameron and I were having the same fight we'd had before all over again, but this time she seemed to have lost her passion for it.

"Look, I just hate seeing you jump when she says jump, that's all. Falling into a pattern of coolie labor for her."

"You want me to be your coolie, is that it? You don't like the competition."

"Never mind." Cam grimaced, turning on her heel to return to the bathroom.

"She's dying, Cam," I shouted after her. "She's not going to be around much longer."

"What are you, her nurse now? You heard your aunts. She ought to be in a nursing home."

"She will be soon enough," I said. "C'mon, Cameron, I don't want to fight. I just want to ask her about the letter to FDR, that's all."

Cameron clearly did not share my enthusiasm for investigating my roots. It was as if I were burdening her with the details of a recurring dream or filling her in on the plot of a TV movie she didn't want to see. I put my arms around her but she tensed and turned her face away. I let go and went back to searching for Wiley's missing sneakers.

"It's manipulation, Pick," she called as I retrieved Wiley's shoes from under our bed. "Pure and simple." I headed down the stairs. Cameron shouted from the bathroom, "I mean it, Pickard. I don't want you going back over there!"

"Well, get used to it," I yelled back. " 'Cause I'm going." Our son was sitting at the kitchen table over his juice and melon, regarding me apprehensively. I dropped the sneakers to the floor at his feet and swept past him, shouting angrily back up to Cameron, "And you can drop Wiley off at school." Then I slammed out the side door, on my way to my truck and the ride back over to Burlington.

"Now, Pick, when you gon' draw me up a picture I can hang?" said Mama Lucy, setting down her magnifying glass and switching off the TV. "You said you would."

"I will, Mama Lucy, I promise." I pulled up a chair. "But about the incident. I've been thinking about it since we talked. Why exactly did you decide to go out on strike?"

"Well, I didn't at first. It won't until what happened in Eno and after that I joined up. A lot of folks didn't trust the union. Said it was outsiders stirring things up. Troublemakers comin' down from up north and all."

"Then why did you join?"

"We were fed up. Conditions just kept gittin' worse and worse. Union may have been outsiders, but they were treatin' us better than the bosses. It got so bad with the stretch-out there was nothin' else we could do. A body can only take so much."

I was not completely ignorant about the labor movement. I had been steeped in the philosophy and rhetoric of protest in college. The tactics, strategies, and goals of the sixties insurrections were direct descendants of the trade union movement. The brown lung series I worked on had mentioned the "stretch-out"—what workers in the twenties and thirties called the techniques of "scientific management" mill owners used to speed up production—efficiency experts were brought in to monitor output, clocks were put on machines, workers were made to double up and take on more jobs for the same pay.

"We was tendin' machines by the acre. Couldn't keep up. And wages just got lower and lower. We didn't have time to eat. Or we'd git behind meetin' our quotas. It was insultin'. We'd git so tired, Pick. I remember one time we was runnin' speed frames and a friend of mine, Euna Mae Sykes, had been up with her baby with the croup three nights in a row and even though she knew those flyers could snap off your finger like a twig or snatch your apron, she just got to noddin' off on the job, couldn't keep her head up and them flyers grabbed her hair and wouldn't let go until it ripped off her scalp. I never seen so much blood. She was screamin' but nobody could hear her over the looms it was so loud. We finally got her calmed down enough to get her in a car and to the hospital but she was back at work that afternoon all bandaged up. Didn't want to lose a half-day's wage. The blood won't even cleaned up off the floor yet. When the bandages come off we all chipped in so's she could buy herself a wig from a catalog."

"Good Lord."

"An' if the machines didn't git you the cotton dust did. Seemed like almost ever'body got the TB at one time or another. They got sent off to the sanitariums."

"What did Granddaddy think about the strike?"

"Pssh. The old man won't takin' sides for nobody. Dalton was only out for his own self. He and Davis had words about it many a time." She grabbed her walker and headed for the kitchen with me trailing behind. She was getting around better since her fall and seemed spryer than I remembered, more open and expansive. "Davis and Dalton didn't get along. Not from day one. Davis didn't want me to marry your granddaddy. Said he was too old for me, didn't have no business marryin' a girl my age."

The kitchen counter was laid out with biscuit fixings. "A quart of flour, shortnin' the size of a hen egg, and enough buttermilk to get it all wet," she explained as she went through this process religiously. Lucy turned her homemade biscuits out with the regularity of a commercial bakery. What she couldn't eat or give away she fed to the squirrels or put in her bird feeders. "Pick, would you hand me that rollin' pin a-settin' in that drawer there behind you?"

"How old was Granddaddy when you got married?" I asked, retrieving the utensil from the drawer, then hoisting myself up on the counter to watch her work.

"Thirty. I was fifteen. Just turned. Davis didn't want me quittin' school again, y'see. I quit after the fifth grade to go to work in the mills, you know, to help out like ever'body else. I was eleven years old then. Though, like I tole you, I went with Papa when I was younger. He was workin' in the weave room at the time. A-fixin' looms. Oh, yeah—we'd go and play there long before they put us on the payroll. I'd go after school and help my older sisters when I was nine. That's how I learned to spin. Daddy just couldn't support the family on a dollar and a quarter a day. So we all pitched in when we got old enough to work, me and my brothers and sisters. But Davis—he was the oldest, and I was his favorite—he said, 'Lucy, you're too smart to waste your life in the mills. You got to get an education.' And when he come back from the war he told Daddy he wanted to take my place in the mill so's I could go back to school. That's how I finished eighth grade. Davis. And Davis hated millwork. He didn't have to, neither. He had other opportunities. But he done it for me. He wanted me to go to high school but I got married instead. Davis was so mad. He never forgave the old man for that."

"How come Granddaddy didn't take sides in the strike?"

"I told you he was workin' for the sheriff at the time. He had family on the picket line, though. An' he used to talk union hisself before he quit the mills in 'twenty-nine. He worked every job in the cotton mill and could get work any time he wanted to. He knowed it inside out. Weavin', spinnin', cloth-doffin', drawin' in, fixin' the looms. Just restless, is all. Couldn't set still in one place. What do they call it today? Hyperactive? That was Dalton Earl." She laughed. "Put his family through hell. Run a grocery store for a while over in Greensboro. Worked for a car dealer in Mebane. Went to work as a surveyor for the railroads over in Gastonia in 'twenty-nine. After the trouble over there when he come back he wouldn't work in the mills no more. Went to work for the sheriff over there in Eno. But his brothers was mostly union." Her eyes glazed as if an unpleasant memory was impinging. " 'Course, there was the one, the youngest, Bud. He was in the guard. He was there when . . ." Her voice cracked. She turned her back to me, her head bowed. I was losing her again.

"Look, Mama Lucy, if you don't want to talk about what happened in Eno I won't bug you about it, but you never told me, why were you bayoneted?"

"Annie Laura," she whispered.

"Annie Laura? Your friend."

"She's the whole reason I got mixed up with the strike."

"C'mon, Lucy, we gon' be late gittin' back to the weave room," shouted the girl outside the kitchen window screen. "They gon' dock us." She was sitting on the tire swing hanging from the sycamore tree in the backyard, spinning like a top in her sunflower yellow dress, her blond braids flying, her bare feet dangling in the dirt and kicking up a cloud of dust. Lucy was sitting at the kitchen table, reading.

"C'mon, Miss Priss! You always got your nose stuck in a book! C'mon, we're late."

"I'm a-comin', Annie Laura," Lucy said, finishing her glass of milk and grabbing what was left of her molasses biscuit. "We got ten minutes. Hold your horses!"

When the noon whistle blew at the mill the two girls always ran home to Lucy's house for lunch. Most of the hands brought their lunch in paper bags and ate outside but Lucy's house was less than a mile from the mill and Lucy's mama and Onnie Lee, the colored help, with her little girl, Bessie, would cook a hot meal for them and they'd still have time to get back to work before the whistle blew or the boss man came through checking the shift.

Lucy's house sat on the hill just up the street behind the short row of storefronts, that, along with the railroad depot, constituted all there was of West Eno's commercial district. Across the railroad tracks and a half mile up the road was the Bellevue mill, not more than ten minutes walk from home.

"Well, you can be late, Miss Priss, but I'm goin' on ahead without you!" shouted Annie Laura. Lucy raced out the back door carrying the copy of *Treasure Island* Dave had given her, slamming the screen door and skipping down the steps into the shade of the backyard, but Annie Laura was already out on the dusty street running down to the railroad crossing. A freight train stopped on the tracks blocked their path to the mill. The train was so long you couldn't see where it started or ended. Usually, when the tracks were clear they could cross them right there at

Lucy's street and head directly toward the mill. With the train stopped, they had to go around.

Lucy detoured back down Occaneechee Street.

"Where you goin', girl?" shouted Annie Laura.

"To work," Lucy said, head down, reading as she walked. "Where do you think?" The shortest way around the train was to walk along Hillsborough Street until you came to the intersection of Old Bellevue Road that ran under the narrow overpass beneath the tracks, take a right and follow it all the way around as it curved back over to the mill. That was the long way, and it would add another ten minutes to their return trip, but it was safer.

"This way," called Annie Laura. "C'mon!"

Lucy, absorbed in her book, walked backward, lifting her eyes from the pages momentarily to look at her friend, who had climbed up the gravel embankment and was pointing at the tracks under a boxcar.

"No, ma'am," declared Lucy, turning around.

"You're gonna make us late," shouted Annie Laura.

"I don't care," Lucy shouted back. "Daddy'd take a hickory switch to me if he found out. I'm goin' around."

"C'mon," Annie Laura pleaded, "the train just got here. It ain't goin' nowhere anytime soon."

"You go ahead then."

"Scaredy-cat! I bet I beat you back. I'll race you."

Lucy was faster than Annie Laura and in races she always let her get a head start and still beat her, but that was at Eno grammar school before they dropped out to work. Lucy was thirteen years old, a smart, spirited, and strikingly pretty young girl with flashing brown eyes and hair the color of cured tobacco leaves. She had grown a lot over the summer, and her mama had to sew her some new clothes that fit. Annie Laura had teased her about filling out in a womanly way but Lucy just figured she was jealous because she didn't have any bosoms of her own yet. Lucy's mama made her two dresses but she wouldn't wear the blue one to work because of the way the men at the factory looked at her. The one she had on was plainer and not so clingy as the other one but still pretty.

Lucy turned around and watched as Annie Laura disappeared into the shadows under the boxcar. Lucy didn't want to go against her daddy, but she wasn't one to lose a race, either, even if it meant mussing up her new dress, so she stopped and looked both ways up and down the track, then scrambled up the gravel embankment and ducked underneath the car and scurried across the tracks like a crab until she came out the other side.

Annie Laura was standing there grinning. "I knew you couldn't skip a dare."

Having saved ten minutes, the two girls ambled casually up the dusty dirt road toward the mill, arm in arm. Suddenly behind them the train came to life and lurched on the tracks with a great creak and groan and the big wheels started moving and the whistle let out a loud piercing blast. Annie Laura and Lucy looked back at the space between the wheels where they had crawled through seconds earlier, filled with tons of rolling steel and grinding wheels and dust, and they both shivered. Then she and Annie Laura looked at each other, and laughed, and ran back up the hill to work.

"Tell me more," I said.

"Why?"

"Because it's interesting to me," I replied.

"Nothin' interestin' about it. Was hard work. Mornin' to night." She closed her eyes as if conjuring a tide of memories. "Twelve-hour days when I first started. Six to six. All the women there when I went to work were so much older." She smiled at the thought.

"Like who?"

"Miz Copeland, she and I was good workers. She worked with me on the spoolin' frame that combined the thread from ten to fifteen bobbins. It was simple enough to learn but problems come up when the thread broke and you had to tie off your broke ends with a knot. There'd be all four of us—there was two spoolers, one on each side. Miz Copeland was crazy about me 'cause her son liked me, Linwood Copeland. Later on she told me until he died he kept a picture of me down there in a trunk. I liked him, too. I'd be with him, too, but I didn't love nobody at that age to spend the rest of my life with. Anyway, the women, they'd say, 'Lucy, carry this note to that fellow up yonder in the spinning room and I'll give you a dip of snuff.' "

"You're kidding. Cameron has a fit if I give Wiley a Twinkie."

"What I remember is the noise. The loudness. You had to yell to be heard over the clacketa-clack of the machinery. No conversation to help break up the drudgery." She closed her eyes. "The smell of the yarn. The cotton dust floatin' in the air like tiny insects. Snuff spit out on the floor. That's where I learned to dip snuff. Nothin' else to do. Couldn't talk to nobody. Kept your mouth busy while you was workin'. Ever'body dipped snuff back then. I musta been ten year old first time I took a dip. My daddy taught me how."

"What did you do for fun?"

"Oh, when we was young'uns, before the war when the mill was run by a waterwheel and the water in the mill trace would get low due to drought, we'd go out on the river among the rocks and have a picnic and swim or just wade, git our feet wet 'til the water level built back up. Or I'd go down to Scott's store, y'know, we all went from the mill ever' day, got ice cream or made us a freezer of ice cream. You could work there at Bellevue, go out when you caught up your bobbin, and make ice cream, cut watermelon, have a party and go back in and go to work. They had a load of watermelon just brought in lyin' out in front of Scott's, y'know, and we'd go down there and just set and eat and spit the seeds and watch the trains go by. That's the way it was in the early days as long as you kept up your work. Or sometimes we'd take pictures with a Kodak camera. After work we'd listen to the radio in the evenin's. Go to the picture show. Sometimes there'd be fiddlin' and pickin' on the porches of some of the mill houses or on a Saturday night they'd move all the furniture out of one room and everybody would dance and clog. Seems like ever'body picked a banjer. Church socials and picnics. We had our fun."

It was Saturday and Lucy and Annie Laura were sitting on the bench out front of Khoury's Dry Goods on Cornwallis Street, practicing their duet for church the next day and watching the cars go by. Although they were both only thirteen years old they could pass for older, and were already considered the prettiest girls in Eno. Grown men would stare and ladies would smile just to look at their big bright shiny eyes and clear, smooth complexions, like they were a pair of rare orchids blossoming in tandem.

When they finished the last verse of "When the Roll Is Called Up Yonder" they were both surprised to hear the sound of clapping behind them. Lucy turned around and saw two boys standing inside the screen door. She knew one of them was Sam Khoury. He was a short, dark boy with jet-black hair, intelligent, sensitive brown eyes, and a Roman blade of a nose that gave him a hawk-like appearance just like his father who owned the dry-goods store. Sam worked the register when his father was away. Their family had moved to Eno a generation earlier from Pittsburgh. His father had been born in Lebanon and still spoke to his family in the Arabic tongue of his native Middle East. They kept to themselves mostly, but Mr. Khoury was well respected in the community as an honest, hardworking businessman even if they were Roman Catholic. She didn't know the other boy who worked at the post office counter in the back. When a customer arrived Sam retreated inside to tend the register but the other boy sauntered out and leaned against the railing and said, "Mighty hot today, ain't it?"

"Hot enough," answered Lucy, who had never been accused of being shy. Annie Laura punched her and giggled.

"After all that singin' you young ladies care for a Co-cola?"

"I reckon a dope would be all right about now, but we spent all our money on this candy." Lucy held up a length of twisted black licorice she was chewing on. The girls smiled at each other. The boy ducked inside and reappeared with two Coca-Colas. He handed one to Lucy, who received it grandly. "Why, thank you, sir." She smiled and batted her eyelashes. This boy was nice-looking.

"We can't afford that," said Annie Laura, looking alarmed.

"It's on the house," said the boy, bowing extravagantly as he handed Annie Laura the second cola.

"Well, wasn't that sweet of you," said Lucy, smiling at the young man. "My name's Lucy and this here is Annie Laura. What's yours?" She turned up the bottle and took a swig.

"Spencer Webb," he said. He winked at her and grinned big as you please with the most beautiful smile Lucy had ever seen.

"I liked to flirt," Lucy announced. "We didn't have nobody but the railroad men to flirt with 'cause walkin' down the railroads tracks they'd call out to us from the trains. Or toot their whistles. Oh, they was plenty of mill village boys interested in takin' me up to Panther's Den."

"Panther's Den?"

"Little place up on New Hope Mountain above the mill village. Kind of like a clearin' with a cave, you know, where the young people would go to court and spark. Lawd, it was beautiful up there, lookin' out over the river. Especially in springtime. Fields of blackberries an' mountain laurel everywhere you looked. We'd gather 'em up in baskets and take 'em back home with us. Me and Linwood Copeland was always slippin' off up there. Mama would send my sister Eunice to spy on me. Mama didn't want me datin' Linwood. She wanted me to go with Dalton Earl."

"Granddaddy."

"Uh-huh."

"You mean it was like a lover's lane?"

"Uh-huh. Except we didn't have no cars. We had to go by foot. Seemed like I was always sneakin' off up there. I had a lot of friends because I enjoyed bein' with whoever I was with and 'cause I loved to laugh. You didn't date like couples. You was always with other people in a group."

Notwithstanding her comment when I'd mowed her lawn shirtless, I had never really thought of my grandmother as a sexual creature before, but as she rolled her biscuit dough with arthritic hands and recalled her long-ago adolescence I saw the spark of girlish flirtation still alive in her eyes.

"This was before you met Granddaddy?" I asked.

"And after," she confessed. "Your grandaddy was jealous of ever'body. I declare he wouldn't let me go to church or go anywhere on my own. I didn't want to be with him. I'd pretend I didn't see him and start to running and he'd say, 'Where's the fire?' "

"But it sounds like he had reason to worry. You just said you two-timed him."

"That's none of your business," she said, placing the cut dough on a cookie sheet.

"These were mill boys?" I asked.

"And some from town. They might call us 'lintheads' behind our backs but they weren't too proud to flirt with us."

"Mill girls."

"That's right—West End girls. Of course, mill village boys were mighty jealous of who the girls courted. And they was mean, too. I remember one time . . ."

"Well, ain't that nice," drawled a menacing voice. Jake Satterfield, a big bruising mill village boy a couple of years older than the girls, and his running buddy, Bobby Joe Hullender, sidled up behind the boy who had fetched Lucy and Annie Laura their Cokes.

"Listen, slick," Jake said to the handsome boy. "These here are mill girls. You town boys don't mess with them. I don't care if you are a Webb. They ours."

"C'mon, Lucy." Annie Laura took Lucy by the arm, thanked the young man, and they both hustled down the sidewalk toward the West End without looking back. They had heard what Satterfield and his friends had done to Jessie Honeycutt when they caught her talking to a town boy. They ripped her dress and cut off a hank of her hair and beat up the boy. A few blocks later Lucy and Annie Laura looked back. Jake and Bobby Joe were about twenty yards behind them.

Lucy picked up a red clay dirt clog and flung it at the boys. The dirt clog struck Bobby Joe on the shoulder. Jake laughed. The girls hurried away.

"You better not let me catch y'all flirtin' with these town boys, y'hear?" shouted Jake. Lucy suspected that Jake had a crush on Annie Laura and somehow held Lucy responsible for Annie's lack of interest in him.

"Leave us alone, Jake," said Annie Laura. "Go on back to town."

"We're too young for you, Jake," added Lucy.

"Old enough to bleed, old enough to butcher," Jake drawled. The boys howled with laughter.

"Yeah," Lucy said. "My daddy's got an ol' sow about your age." They kept walking, afraid to look back. Suddenly the boys were beside them.

"C'mon, Lucy," said Jake, "lemme have a swaller of your Co-cola."

"That's a purty dress you wearin', Annie Laura," Bobby Joe said. "What y'all all dressed up for?"

"Leave us alone, Jake Satterfield," shouted Lucy, picking up her pace.

"I seen you flirtin' with them town boys, Lucy. I bet you'd-a let one a them have some of your dope."

"Jake," said Lucy sweetly, changing tactics but still not stopping. "You want some of my Co-cola?"

"I'd love some of your Co-cola, Lucy Barlow."

"You ain't afraid of germs?"

"I ain't afraid of your germs, Lucille."

"Here then," she said, offering him the bottle she had been shaking with her thumb in the lip. Fizzy brown soda spewed from the bottle with the force of a fire hydrant, drenching the boys.

"Run, Annie Laura, run." Lucy hurled the Coke bottle at Jake and they both took off, the two fastest girls in town, sprinting for the West End with the lumbering Jake Satterfield and Bobby Joe Hullender in furious pursuit. The girls approached the depot. The Southern Express 11:15 to Durham was sitting on the tracks taking on passengers for the short ride into the Bull City. Lucy spotted the conductor checking tickets and knew the train would be pulling out soon. They dashed past the cluster of passengers boarding. Not until they reached the freight cars behind the series of passenger cars did they glance back. Their pursuers were fast closing in on them, nearly bowling over everyone remaining in the depot.

Lucy looked at the length of the train, and then without hesitation pulled Annie up the steep gravel incline. They ducked under the freight car and scrambled across the tracks. By the time Jake and Bobby Joe reached the car they had disappeared from sight. The conductor shouted "all aboard." Lucy, watching from the safety of a kudzu bower in a ravine across the road, saw the trouser legs of the two boys pacing frantically, looking under the boxcars, trying to decide whether to risk following suit. The decision was made for them when the train whistle blew. The engine belched forth steam, stranding the boys in the summer heat with sticky soda syrup drying on their skin, clothes, and hair, frustrated, humiliated, and cursing the two girls, the Southern Railroad, and the Coca-Cola Bottling Company.

"Mama Lucy, it sounds to me like you were a hot ticket," I said, trying one of her freshly baked biscuits. "Quite the babe in your day."

"I turned some heads," she acknowledged. "They was some said I was the Belle of Eno. My sister Icy claimed she was. But she was always stuck on herself. Couldn't keep away from the mirror. But ever'body said I was the best lookin' of the Barlow girls. I reckon I was right fetchin'. Not as pretty as Annie Laura. She was the beauty. 'Course, after the accident the boys didn't come around as much."

"What accident?" I asked.

Like flicking a switch, her face darkened. "It won't too long after the run-in with Jake. And it was my fault, Pick. I was readin' a book."

"C'mon, Lucy. We late." Annie Laura was standing by the tracks where the train, standing idle, was blocking their way back to work. "I don't know why I eat lunch with you. You don't even talk to me. You're too busy readin' all the time."

"I'm sorry, Annie Laura." Lucy tucked *Little Women* under her arm and scrambled up the gravel embankment. "I was at the good part. It ain't personal."

"From now on I'm gonna eat with Euna Mae Sykes. At least she talks."

"She talks your ears off." Lucy looked up and down the length of the freight train but saw no sign of activity. With their recent success negotiating the occupied rails, Lucy had become bold and put her daddy's injunction out of her mind. "C'mon," she said, ducking under the boxcar and scuttling across the tracks to the other side.

"Not 'til you apologize!" Annie Laura shot back at her. Lucy slid down the gravel embankment and looked back at Annie Laura. Lucy could see the bottom of Annie's gingham dress. Her slender legs were stiff and straight like a statue, like nothing could make her move, and Lucy just knew she had her arms crossed and that look on her face when she got her feelings hurt.

"I said I'm sorry, Annie Laura."

"Louder."

"I'm sorry, Annie Laura." Lucy clambered up the gravel embankment. The last of the lunch break stragglers were returning to work. "C'mon, now you're gonna make us late."

"I didn't hear you," replied the voice from the other side.

Lucy put down her book, cupped her hands to her mouth, tilted her head back, and hollered, "I'm sorry!" But when she looked down Annie Laura was already peeking at her from beneath the boxcar and grinning just as big as you please.

Then, without warning, Lucy heard the gut-wrenching shudder as the freight train suddenly came to life and lurched forward. The shock of it knocked Lucy back down the embankment. A split second later, lying on her back on the ground, she heard the awful grinding of steel against something soft as the wheel caught Annie Laura's left leg below the knee.

"Annie Laura screamed and I screamed but the train whistle drowned us both out."

It took a lot out of Mama Lucy to tell me the story of how her best friend lost her leg. We had moved from the kitchen back into the living room, where she could sit down. She had finished the story slumped on the sofa, looking frail and gray, like a baby bird fallen out of its nest. With nothing to break the silence in the room but the steady tick-tock of the mantel clock, I began to feel the weight and burden of my own curiosity upon her, how the memories my questions dislodged were freighted with emotion and possibly too much for her. I shifted my focus to a topic I hoped wouldn't upset her.

"You never told me before, Mama Lucy," I said. "How exactly did you and granddaddy meet?"

"In the Bellevue mill." She sighed. "He had his eye on me when I was workin' in the windin' room. He was drawin' in. They made the best money, y'know. The draw-in hands made the pattern in the cloth. The way they drawed in the thread in the warp was the way it come out. Took a sharp eye and nimble fingers. Your granddaddy was good at it, that and weavin' too, on account of him being so tall and all. He didn't have to walk around the loom to fix any damage to a thread. He could just reach up and fix it."

"When he wasn't putting the moves on you," I said, trying to lift her spirits.

Lucy smiled. "He never tried to talk to me on break or when the shift changed. He just stared. I'd ignore him. Just made him more interested. But sure enough, we met in the old mill right over there in Eno where you live now. I caught him starin' at me in church a few times. He come up to me after church one Sunday mornin', introduced hisself. We went to the West End Baptist Church, you know. Daddy was a deacon there. Your granddaddy asked my daddy if he could walk home with us. Embarrassed me to death. I musta been fourteen. He was older than me. You know Dalton Earl was married before me. His wife died in the flu epidemic of 1918, not long before we met. Lost his wife, his sister and her husband all in the same night. It was like a plague. Ever'body lost somebody. Annie Laura lost a sister. They was stackin' bodies in the armory like cordwood. He got a lot of sympathy from the ladies in the church for that. And he played it to the hilt. I think my mama thought more of him than I did. I didn't want to go out with him."

"Why did you?"

"Box supper on the church grounds. All the girls who was old enough would fix a box supper and then at church they'd sell 'em, raise money for choir robes and the like. And the boys would bid on 'em and then go get the girl who fixed the dinner and they'd get to eat with her."

"And that's how you ended up with Grandaddy Dalton?"

"That's how."

Lucy was excited about the box supper at the church that night. At work Mrs. Copeland had told her how Linwood, working overtime in the weave room as a sweeper on the graveyard shift, had saved up for weeks to buy Lucy's box, which was fine with Lucy because she had been crazy about Linwood ever since they were young'uns. She remembered him before he even wore shoes, when he was barefoot and used to wait for her outside the church so he could walk home with her and how he had slipped his hand into hers when he was only eleven and she was nine, and how they walked along together hand in hand and he wouldn't say one word and neither would she, but her papa walking on ahead of them would glance back over his shoulders and see them and Lucy just knew he was laughing because she could see his shoulders shaking.

But now she was older, old enough for cooking box suppers and getting bid on by boys like Linwood, and yes, she was old enough to know she was still crazy about Linwood Copeland and he was crazy about her. So when she finished her shift that day she ran home and worked in the kitchen all afternoon preparing biscuits and country ham and pork chop sandwiches. The night before she'd stayed up late after her sisters Eunice and Icy went to bed, making banana pudding with the special whipped egg-white topping that her mama taught her how to make. If Linwood had worked that hard saving up his hard-earned money and was willing to spend it on her cooking, she was going to make sure he got his money's worth.

At church she and Annie Laura slid onto a bench near the front in the Fellowship Hall where all the girls sat while Preacher Sykes bid off the boxes. Annie Laura was a wreck because this was her first box supper and she didn't think anybody would bid on hers even though Lucy knew she was the best cook around next to Lucy. But to tell the truth there was many a time Lucy had watched the boys stare at Annie Laura's wooden leg instead of her creamy complexion and beautiful green eyes and she had seen how they backed away instead of talking to her and she had listened to them tease her and talk about it behind her back. Now that they were there and looking around the room at the shy and silly boys drifting in and out and slouching around the doorway Lucy was starting to feel guilty. She had been the one to encourage Annie Laura to give it a try. If none of those boys bid on her friend's box they'd hear about it the next day.

When the bidding got started, Annie Laura slumped down in her seat as if she was trying to disappear. The preacher reached for her offering to auction off, then, sensing the risk of hurt feelings, passed it over for the time being. Lucy was watching Linwood, who was sitting by the side windows with some of his friends from work. They were teasing him and slapping him on the back when the bidding got started. It seemed like everybody knew he was sweet on Lucy and that he was ready to bid on her box. She could watch boys forever, the way they horsed around and pretended they didn't care about anything in the world, but a few minutes later Annie Laura punched her and when she turned to see what she wanted, Annie Laura was cutting her eyes toward the door. There in the back was a tall good-looking man, older but lean and lank, with dark wavy hair, neatly parted and combed back, and piercing blue eyes, standing there staring at Lucy. She looked away. Dalton Earl Cantrell. What was he doing here? When Lucy looked back again he was still staring at her. By the time the preacher got to Lucy's box Linwood was ready and waiting. Before Preacher Sykes could lift it off the table Linwood piped up, "One dollar!" It was nearly a day's wage, and his buddies cheered. Suddenly Lucy heard a deep voice from the back of the room. "One dollar twenty-five cents." It was Mr. Cantrell. Lucy flushed. She looked at Linwood, who, panicking, glanced at Lucy and blurted, "One dollar fifty cents!"

Lucy just closed her eyes.

"One seventy-five!" said Cantrell.

"Two dollar!" said Linwood. Now his friends were egging him on.

"Two-fifty!" said Cantrell.

"Two seventy-five!" said Linwood, less certain but still full of bravado. But Lucy knew his heart wasn't in it because she knew he didn't have that kind of money. That was over two days' wages and his mother had told her proudly how he'd saved up one day's.

"Five dollars!" said Dalton Earl Cantrell with a tone of finality. Linwood couldn't compete with that. With a last glance at Lucy, he shrugged his shoulders dejectedly and turned away.

"Sold!" shouted the preacher.

When Mr. Cantrell came up front to pick up the box, Linwood was standing near Lucy, drawing himself up to his full height. Mr. Cantrell was six foot two and thirty years old. Linwood, barely seventeen and dressed in overalls, looked the boy he was next to the handsome, dapper Dalton Earl Cantrell. He was fit to be tied and paced back and forth, crossing to Lucy, cutting his eyes at her, and said, "Lucy, you better pay no attention to him, or I'll tell your mama."

Lucy said, "What are you talking about, Linwood?"

"Mr. Cantrell. He bought the box." Dalton Earl, oblivious to their conversation, inserted himself between Linwood and Lucy.

"Hello, Miss Barlow, remember me? It was a pleasure walking you home from church last week." He pointed his hat at Annie Laura. "And good evening to you, Miss Annie Laura Gaskins. I sure do enjoy the duets you two sing on Sundays." Lucy had heard Dalton Earl was a Methodist but he'd been coming to the Baptist Church lately.

"Would you like to take the box outside and eat out under the stars?" asked Dalton Earl.

"Why don't we just eat here on a table in the back when the bidding gits done?" Lucy countered. He didn't push, so they ended up there. They were soon joined by Annie Laura and Linwood, who had outbid Jake Satterfield and used all the money he'd saved up for Lucy's box supper doing it. Annie Laura was grateful for Linwood's gallantry. She could tell that Jake Satterfield had been emboldened in his pursuit of her since she'd lost her leg and it gave her the willies. She would rather suffer the humiliation of not being bid on at all than to sit with Jake Satterfield while he ate her cooking. Jake threatened Linwood with a licking after the party for outbidding him, but Linwood didn't care. He was too distracted by his own usurpation by Dalton Earl Cantrell.

It was quite a party. Mr. Cantrell barely said a thing, just commented every now and then on how good the food was, and passed the time staring out the window. Linwood glared at him and Annie Laura sat across from Linwood, not eating and watching him not eat. At one point Mr. Cantrell excused himself to have a word with Preacher Sykes outside and while he was gone Jake and his friend Bobby Joe slipped up on the silent table.

"Hey, Lucy," Jake said, "can I have a swaller of your Co-cola?" Before she could answer he grabbed it and took a long swig out of the bottle and set it back down on the table, daring Linwood or anybody else to do something about it. "Man, was I thirsty." He wiped his mouth with his sleeve as Bobby Joe laughed like a mangy hyena and they sauntered out into the night.

Nobody mentioned what Jake had done when Mr. Cantrell returned because he might try to do something about it and Lucy didn't want to feel beholden to him. She thought she had gotten rid of him when they finished eating and cleared the table and he went off to find a trash can. She had hardly spoken to him over supper and would only talk to Linwood. But the luckless Linwood Copeland, after the incident with Jake, had disappeared, humiliated beyond endurance not only by his defeat by Mr. Cantrell but by his own lack of action against the bully. He did manage to whisper to Lucy that he would be waiting for her outside.

But, lo and behold, Mr. Cantrell came up to her as she started through the door, took hold of her arm and said, "May I walk you home, Miss Barlow?"

Linwood was bug-eyed when they walked out the door together, but what could she do? Coming down the steps with Mr. Cantrell she saw her sister Eunice standing there with a friend.

"I'm gonna tell Mama," said Eunice.

Lucy didn't answer. She knew Eunice was jealous because Mr. Cantrell hadn't asked her to walk home or bought her box supper. So Linwood and Annie Laura trailed them back to Lucy's house and when they got there Lucy ran inside. Dalton Earl called out "Good night!"

Lucy didn't think she'd ever see him again.

She was wrong. He called on her twice after that. On his third visit they sat in the living room and her papa and mama sat out back on the porch where they sat when Eunice had callers. Eunice was on the living room settee pretending to read but listening to their every word. After a while Dalton Earl removed a picture of his first wife from his wallet and showed it to Lucy. She studied it. She was a beautiful woman, Lucy thought, although she looked old enough to be her mother. "You remind me of her, my late wife, Virginia," Dalton said.

"Oh," Lucy said. Then, not knowing what else to say, she added, "Thank you."

But she felt funny about it, uncomfortable and awkward, and she knew Eunice would report back to Mama. So Lucy jumped up and banged out a hymn on the piano she'd learned for choir. After a few minutes, Mr. Cantrell sat down beside her and said, "Lucy, will you marry me?"

It was all so sudden and awkward for a girl her age, confusing like a dream, and before she knew it Lucy heard herself say yes.

"And do you know what, Pick?" said Mama Lucy. "When I said yes, I swear I thought I was gittin' rid of him because he told me he was fixin' to go to work in Danville 'cause he had a job up there and he wanted an answer so he could get me an engagement ring. I knew all the older girls at the mill were crazy about him so I figured he's gonna find somebody up there and I'll get rid of him and I'll go ahead and say yes. And every time he'd try to get me to push the marriage up, I'd put him off. At first he'd come back to town, and he'd say, 'Lucy, I can't go to all this expense travelin' back and forth from Danville. You've got to set a date.' For months and months I kept puttin' him off, thinkin' he was gonna find somebody else."

"Surely you liked him some, though, didn't you, Mama Lucy? Or it wouldn't have gotten that far." It was odd and discomfiting hearing my grandmother renounce her romance with my grandfather so glibly. After all, he had been the father of her children, including my father, the *sine qua non* of my own existence. It felt like a personal betrayal somehow and I felt defensive on Granddaddy's behalf.

"I liked him," she answered without conviction. "I thought he was a fine man. Everybody else liked him. Mother was crazy about him. Y'know, she won't but eight years older than him. She knew Dalton and his first wife. Virginia ran the boarding house in the West End before she died. "

"So your mother pressured you to marry Granddaddy?"

"She wanted me to marry him because she thought he had a bankroll after Virginia died but he didn't have ten dollars in his pocket when we got married. But he let on like he had money. Dressed fancy and drove a fancy car. He was all show. None of the mill boys could compete with that."

Lucy was in the spool room checking her ends when Mr. Sumner came in. He scanned the room and his eyes lighted on her. She glanced down at her bobbin, hoping he'd go away. She didn't like the way the floor foreman looked at her and she generally tried to avoid him. He'd known her since she was nine years old and was a friend of her daddy's, which he was always reminding her of—that, and how much she looked like her mama when she was younger. But ever since she'd filled out he was always saying something about how she was dressed and making her feel uncomfortable. She was afraid he would call her into his office to discuss something in private like he did with some of the other girls. They all knew what he was up to in there. Annie Laura told her about the time he made her go over her weave while he sat next to her breathing in her ear and touching her hair and letting his hand graze her bosom and pretending it was an accident. She couldn't say nothing because her daddy was sick and out of work and she had younger brothers and sisters who counted on her paycheck. If she said anything she'd be laid off.

"You," he barked at Lucy. "Come with me."

She glanced at her coworkers, Mrs. Copeland and Ruby James and Annie Laura, and they looked back at her helplessly. Sumner took her into the hallway. "They's a letter here from the post office for you. Special delivery. You can fetch it out back. The Webb boy brung it. He wouldn't let me give it to you 'cause he said he'd get in trouble if he didn't give it to you hisself on account of it's a felony for anybody else to tamper with the U.S. Mail. Don't be long."

She'd turned to go when he grabbed her arm and pulled her back around. "Oh, and Lucy," he said, looking back over his shoulder to see if anybody was around, winking, and reaching up to brush her hair off her shoulder. "Let me know what you got in the mail and if there's anything in there for me."

"Yessir, Mr. Sumner," Lucy mumbled.

Lucy shuddered, feeling Sumner's gaze on her as she headed for the door. It was only a matter of time, she thought, before she got pulled into his office. When she got to the rear exit she caught her reflection in the windowpane. Her hair was in her eyes. She pulled it back and straightened her dress and pushed through the door to the loading dock.

"Hey there." It took a moment for Lucy's eyes to adjust to the bright sunlight, but when they did she saw the delivery boy, smiling just as big as you please, his bicycle lying beside him in the dirt and gravel by the loading dock. It had been a while since the day she and Spencer Webb first met and he bought her a Coke but she had seen him many times behind the post office counter since then. He had never again acted quite so bold as he did that first day but she knew he had asked about her.

"Miss Barlow?" He leaped onto the platform and pulled an envelope from his back pocket, beaming his big sassy grin. His smile was the first thing she had noticed about him. She had never seen anything like it. It was dazzling.

"I'm Lucy," she said shyly, not used to being called Miss Barlow. That's what her mama was called.

He stared at her, then studied the letter in his hand, and asked, "Do you know a Mister D.E. Cantrell?"

"Yeah." She knew right then and there that her fiancé, Dalton Earl, had written her a special delivery letter because he had gotten no answer from all the others he had sent to her by regular mail. He'd been up there in Virginia for weeks and it seemed like he wrote to her every other day. But she had not answered his letters and he was writing special delivery now to make sure she got it.

"Well," he said, "how would you like to hear from him?"

"I don't care."

"You don't?" He returned the letter to his back pocket and smiled at her flirtatiously. "You really don't want it?"

"I'm not crazy about it, to tell you the truth."

"Somebody must really think you're pretty special to send you a special delivery letter. It costs a whole lot more than regular mail."

"Well, if you got it give it to me."

He reached into his pocket and pulled out the envelope again. But when Lucy reached for it he pulled it away and held it behind his back and turned away like he was leaving. Then, just as quickly, he spun around and, bowing low like one of those old-timey actors she'd seen at the picture show, presented her the letter. Lucy plucked it from his hand and curtsied deeply like the one of those ladies in the same picture show. She slipped the envelope into her pocket without looking at it.

"Aren't you going to ask me how I knew you were here?" he asked.

"How did you know I was here?"

"I'm not really the mailman. I help out sometimes at the post office and I saw the letter addressed to you and asked if I could deliver it."

"How did you know it was me?"

"I've seen you and your friend in town before. The girl with one leg."

"Annie Laura."

"I see you and her at Khoury's dry goods store. We met once. I bought y'all a Coke."

Lucy shrugged, as if she didn't remember.

"After you left one day I asked Mr. Khoury, the postmaster, what your last name was. You remember? I'm Spencer Webb."

"Oh yeah, I forgot," she said coyly. "You're related to Mr. Webb owns the mill."

"That's my daddy. You won't hold it against me, will you?"

"I don't reckon. We cain't help who our mama and daddy are, now can we?"

"I don't guess so."

"Well, thank you for the special delivery, Mr. Webb."

"Call me Spencer."

"Thank you, Spencer. I better get back to my bobbin, before I get in trouble."

"Are you going to the pumpkin-carving out at Chicken Bridge on Friday?"

"Who wants to know?"

"Maybe I'll see you there."

"Do you go? I thought it was just for . . ." She blushed, uncertain how to deal with the awkward protocols of class.

"Daddy donates the pumpkins every year," Spencer said. "I help deliver 'em."

"When you ain't deliverin' the mail?"

"Right." Now it was his turn to blush.

She turned back toward the mill. "Who knows? Maybe I'll see you there."

"Good-bye, Lucy Barlow."

" 'Bye, Spencer Webb."

He mounted his bicycle and wobbled off down the hill, waving at her over his shoulder.

She headed back into work, her heart pounding, her stomach aflutter, dizzy with the pleasures of innocent flirtation and wanton desire, the flashing smile of Spencer Webb filling her thoughts, while she fingered the letter in her pocket, the letter that she knew she was going to have to answer, but would think about, as usual, only when she was good and ready.

"And that's how your granddaddy's letter brought me and Spencer Webb together, Pick. And that night at home I knowed I had to answer the special delivery, 'cause Dalton Earl would know I got it, and I sat down to write in the room on the table at the foot of the bed, and when I did, I swear if that writin' box didn't start a-movin'.' "

"The writing box?"

"Where I kept my writin' paper. You know, stationery. And I'm not lyin' to you, it started movin' and a-rattlin' just like somethin' was . . ."— she shook her head as though in defiance of the memory—"and I thought, y'know, we had a lot of rats, so I thought, 'Oh it's probably a rat in there.' And I picked the paper up right quick, y'know, and no rat. And I thought I'm just a-seein' things. And I started to writin' the letter again and when I started to write, all of a sudden the paper I had put back in started to come out of the box! It liked to scared me to death!"

Mama Lucy was well known in the family for her experiences with the occult and the supernatural. Her fluency in the metaphysical and occasional lapses into talk of the otherworldly would impinge suddenly and without warning on any conversation—dreams, visions, premonitions, clairvoyance, and all things extrasensory and, to my mind, florid, flaky, and hysterical were taken in stride.

"I don't know what it was," she continued. "But it was 'cause of what I was writin' in my letter. 'Cause I had said on there, 'I haven't got any letters from you.' He had no way of knowin' if I got 'em or not. I said to Dalton Earl, I said, 'I'm sorry but I hadn't gotten any letters.' See, I knew that he would know I got this special delivery and that's why I was answerin' it. When them papers started a-movin' I just"—she panted and gasped, as if she were hyperventilating—"I just jumped up and blowed the light out and jumped right over the bed. It was 'cause I was lyin', Pick. Don't you see? It was 'cause I was tellin' him a lie in the letter."

I didn't know what to say to this sudden spasm of guilt over a lie told some seventy-five years ago. We sat there in silent contemplation of all that had been told. So the mill owner's son had the hots for Mama Lucy and she never was that crazy about my grandfather. This was all fascinating but the morning was getting away from us and I still didn't understand what any of this had to do with Annie Laura and how she had gotten Mama Lucy involved with the strike.

"But what about that day in Eno? The day of the shootings," I finally asked.

"That was fifteen years later. I was a married lady and a mother. I should have been home with the children."

"Do it!" someone screamed from the mill window. "Shoot 'em! Shoot the rats!"

The tear gas was blinding. Lucy dabbed her eyes with her red bandanna and cupped it to her nose so she could breathe. People were running and screaming, scattering as a volley of gunfire erupted from the mill windows. She knew many of the men who were shooting at them. Many of the deputies and guardsmen were local boys, Jake Satterfield and Dalton's brother, Bud Cantrell, among them. She'd gone to school with some and church with others and worked side by side on the same shift with a few. Why in God's name were they firing on their own people? Clouds of smoke drifted up from the mill windows and mixed with the teargas drifting across the yard and the crowd. She scanned the stampeding crowd for Annie Laura and saw her brother Davis running toward one of the fallen strikers.

Above the din, she heard someone shout from a mill window, "Shoot, dammit! Stop them bastards!" Through the clouds of gas she thought she saw someone in a brown dress and yellow-and-white polka-dot scarf moving slowly toward her. Then she heard Annie Laura's voice shouting, "Run, Lucy, run!" Lucy turned toward her as another volley of shots rang out. Another body fell. "Lord God!" she cried, as Mrs. Copeland dropped to her knees beside her wounded husband. Annie Laura limped to her side, Lucy following. Annie Laura ripped the scarf from her neck to help stanch the bleeding. Lucy handed her the red bandanna she'd been using to cover her face. A moment later the mill windows thundered again. Then there was the wet smacking sound of a bullet striking flesh. Lucy screamed as Annie Laura slumped to the dirt. Her green eyes fluttered and blood trickled out of the side of her mouth. "Are you okay, honey?" Lucy pleaded. "Are you okay?" But she knew from the way Annie Laura's eyes were rolling back in her head and the way the blood was pooling beneath her that she wasn't okay.

Lucy screamed for help but people were fleeing toward the street and no one seemed to hear her. She glanced up at the mill windows, searching for the man who had shot her friend, but the face of the building was now blank. But she knew Dalton Earl and his brother Bud were up there somewhere. She turned back to Annie Laura, who, despite her glazed eyes, was trying to speak. Lucy leaned close, shaky with grief and rage, trying to make out Annie Laura's tortured words. She pulled her friend close and felt warm blood soaking into her dress. Annie Laura was ghastly pale. Lucy cradled her friend's head in her arms, uncertain whether she was still conscious. Annie Laura clutched her hand, pulling her close. She was trying to say something. Lucy, tears falling onto her friend's face, leaned close and placed her ear next to Annie Laura's lips.

"Go ahead, Annie," she sobbed. "I can hear you, honey." She strained to hear, knowing whatever Annie Laura said might be her last utterance on this earth, and praying that it would be something articulate and coherent, something personal that Lucy could hang on to forever when her friend was gone. What Annie Laura Gaskins said that day, what issued from the lips of Lucy Barlow's best friend as she lay on the ground dying, was one word and one word only. And though it wasn't what she had hoped to hear, it would stick in Lucy's memory, searing her conscience and haunting her dreams, and it would change her life forever.

"Union," Annie Laura gasped. Union. And then she was gone.

*   *   *

Lucy slumped back onto the sofa, her frail body bowed under the weight of the scene she had just described. I had many more questions but didn't know where to begin. I let the implications of her story wash over me. She had watched her best friend from childhood die in her arms, a martyr to the union cause. Mama Lucy sat there silent as a statue while the clock ticked ominously on the mantelpiece. She looked tired.

"I've got to go and let you get some rest now, Mama Lucy," I said. "Maybe I can come back some other time."

No response. "Mama Lucy, how are you feeling? Okay?"

"Fine," she murmured.

Something was wrong. Ordinarily, that question would have unleashed a torrent of symptoms and maladies and complaints, especially after her recent hip and heart problems and trip to the hospital, which is why I had learned long ago to avoid it. Mama Lucy had never done "fine" her entire life.

That was when it hit me that Lucy would not be with us much longer. To my surprise, I felt a great sadness, but also an urgency to get answers to questions I didn't even know how to articulate. But for now I felt I needed to leave her alone.

"I have to get going, Mama Lucy. I've got to pick up Wiley at school. Are you sure you're going to be okay?"

No answer.

"Mama Lucy, I've got to go now."

Her head sunk to her chest. "Mama Lucy!" I dropped to my knees in front of the sofa, grabbing her hands and trying to look directly into her closed eyes. Her breathing was labored and her face was peaked.

I grabbed the phone and dialed 911.

THE BURLINGTON
DYNAMITE PLOT

The paramedics took Mama Lucy to Alamance General, the hospital where my mother had endured her early psych-ward experiences. Buzz met me in the emergency room and the young doctor who examined her—Dr. Gurney according to his name tag, an intense bearded fellow—said her shortness of breath and swelling in her legs indicated heart trouble, but he was puzzled by the electrocardiogram.

He appeared disappointed as he looked at her chart, rubbing his beard and glancing nervously at Mama Lucy, who was sitting up now and breathing through an oxygen mask but seemed much better off than she had when the paramedics first arrived at the house.

"No evidence of a myocardial infarction," he said.

"What's that?" Buzz asked.

"Heart attack," Dr. Gurney explained in a thick Boston accent. *Haht attack.* We all glanced at Mama Lucy sitting there, alert but sedate, in the relatively calm emergency room. The doctor excused himself, then returned a few minutes later with another man. "I wanted Dr. Levin to take a look just to be on the safe side," Gurney said.

Dr. Levin, a short, balding, white-haired man with kind, mischievous eyes, removed Mama Lucy's oxygen mask and studied her chart. Then he looked at her eyes and her feet. "Having trouble getting your shoes on, Mrs. Cantrell?" he asked in a rich baritone, his accent native to the Upper South, as he studied her chart again.

"How did you know?" she asked, hiding her feet.

"They look mighty swollen. Have you been taking your digitalis and diuretics?"

Mama Lucy looked guilty. "Most days."

Dr. Levin peered at her over his reading glasses. "Mrs. Cantrell, have you been eating salt?"

"No sir," she insisted. "They told me not to put salt on my food and I ain't been doin' it. No sir."

"I already asked that, sir," Dr. Gurney interjected.

"Mmm," replied Dr. Levin, ignoring him. "Mrs. Cantrell, have you eaten any country ham lately?"

Mama Lucy flushed crimson. "I'll tell you the truth, doctor, I was cleanin' out my freezer and had some left over from our Labor Day picnic and I just couldn't resist. You ain't lived 'til you taste my country ham biscuits."

"I'm sure that's the truth, Mrs. Cantrell, but if you continue to eat salty foods like that, even a country ham biscuit, it may be your last meal."

"Well, I'll swan."

"Country ham biscuit," muttered the bearded young Bostonian.

Dr. Levin chuckled and began writing something on her chart. "These transplanted Yankee doctors aren't familiar with all our salty food down here. You got to know what questions to ask."

"I asked her about salt," Gurney reiterated.

"Any other complaints, Mrs. Cantrell?" Levin asked.

"She was having headaches, doctor," Buzz said.

" 'Bout to bust my head wide open. I liked to died when I run out of my Goody's."

"You worked in the cotton mills around here, Mrs. Cantrell?"

"Goodness, you a mind-reader or somethin'?"

"Are you still taking Goody's?"

She nodded and Gurney looked at him quizzically.

"You run into a lot of mill workers all through the Piedmont, especially women, with kidney problems from a lifetime of taking Goody powders headache remedy," Levin explained. "Goody's contains a compound called phrenacetin. Showed a little skull and crossbones warning on the package."

"We'd always take a Goody's at lunch," Lucy said. "Used to be advertised on radio on the *Grand Ol' Opry*."

"Then on their days off they'd go through withdrawal," Dr. Levin continued. "Mondays would be the worst day for headaches. Women seemed more susceptible than men for some reason."

"I'll swan. Why, some of my friends I worked with ended up with bad kidneys."

"We'll keep an eye on that, Mrs. Cantrell," said Dr. Levin, handing the chart back to his young charge. "Now, I'm gonna give you a diuretic. That's a water pill to help you flush that salt out of your system. And don't forget to take the pills your doctor prescribed. I don't want to see you back over here, now, y'hear?" With that he bowed and kissed her hand and said, "Have a good day, ma'am."

"Levin?" said Lucy without letting go of his hand. "That's a Jewish name, ain't it?"

"Yes, ma'am."

"Well, you don't sound Jewish," she said and I cringed, but Levin smiled. "Where you from?"

"Chapel Hill. Born and raised. I'm about retired now but just over here checking on a kidney patient on dialysis. Ran into this young man in the hallway looking for an attending physician. These youngsters need help with their bedside manner." He winked at Gurney.

"How come my regular doctors ain't never as nice as you, Dr. Levin?" asked Mama Lucy. Buzz and I exchanged amused looks.

After Levin left, Buzz and I stood there while Gurney, reasserting his authority, rechecked Mama Lucy's vital signs. Then, after giving her a stern lecture about her diet, he sent her on her way. Buzz drove her home while I headed back to Eno to pick up Wiley at school. When I got home I called my father and told him what had happened so he could alert the family. Then I called Sandy Murphy and set up an appointment to see her the next day.

Sandy wasn't surprised to hear that Mama Lucy had written a letter to FDR.

"You've got to understand the context," she explained, in her cramped little office in the basement of Manning Hall on the campus of the University of North Carolina. "People down here saw Roosevelt as a god. The South was already impoverished when the Great Depression hit in 1929. Nothing short of radical surgery was going to help. Roosevelt offered hope, a New Deal for poor folks, including textile workers like your grandmother."

"The National Industrial Recovery Act," said Russ Draper, who had joined us. "Wasn't that the legislation?"

"That's right. Offering higher wages and shorter hours—you can imagine the impact. Millworkers now thought they had powerful allies willing to help improve conditions in the mills. Hopes were raised and then dashed. When the National Recovery Administration failed to deliver on its promises, workers in Alabama walked out and touched off a nationwide strike that paralyzed the textile industry. The mill hands still thought a decent man like FDR, once he understood the injustice, would settle the strike in their favor. The letters I've seen are just heart-breaking." Sandy looked comfortable in the cluttered office with boxes of books stacked up and a poster of Eleanor Roosevelt on the bulletin board along with class and office schedules and a bumper sticker that read, *Unions: The Folks Who Brought You the Weekend.*

"I've got to admit the tone of her letter surprised me," I said. "So personal. So unintimidated. Like she knew him and expected a lot of him."

"Because of the fireside chats. Radios had just become affordable. Even poor people in the mill villages and hollows of Appalachia owned them. The radio was the only entertainment some of these people had. And with the rise of radio the popularity of country music grew, too, and helped mill hands develop a sense of group identity. Then along comes FDR on the radio. Folks listened. It felt like he was talking to them. Like somebody understood. A very powerful somebody."

"I wonder why she didn't mail the letter," I said. "Especially after sending the first one. I wish I could have seen that one!"

"Maybe you can," Sandy said. "We might have it right here at the Southern Oral History Project. We went up to D.C. to the National Archives where they've kept all those letters, and copied tons of them. You're welcome to look at them. They're housed at the Wilson Library. If we don't have it, the National Archives does."

"But why didn't she mail that one?" asked Russ.

"When I asked her about it she said something terrible happened in Eno."

"I thought she was bayoneted in Burlington. I assumed that's where she lived."

"Her brothers and sisters worked in Burlington. That's where she was stabbed. But she's from Eno."

"There was an incident in Eno," Sandy said softly. "A National Guard riot. A mob was set loose on the strikers. Some strikers were killed. It was sort of hushed up," said Sandy. "Repression, denial, mass amnesia, whatever you want to call it. People wanted to forget on all sides. It was an embarrassment to the authorities. Naturally, the Historic Eno Commission isn't going to publicize it. Does your grandmother know something about it?" Sandy asked.

"She was there," I said. "She lost her best friend that day. Annie Laura . . . something."

"Annie Laura Gaskins?" Sandy said.

"Yes, that's it."

"Who's she?" asked Russ.

"Martyr to the movement," Sandy explained. "One of the first killed in the 'thirty-four strike. One of the local leaders. A singer in the tradition of Ella May Wiggins. Ella May was murdered in the 'twenty-nine strike in Gastonia. She was a national cause célèbre. Wrote songs that by 'thirty-four were standards all over the cotton mill culture. 'Mill Mother's Lament' was one of her most famous. Pick, why didn't you tell me back in high school that you were related to the magnificent Lucille Barlow?"

"You didn't ask. And I didn't know."

"And she was there that day, September eighth, 1934," Sandy said. "A living eyewitness to the Eno massacre. Wow."

"Jesus, that's the same day she wrote the letter," I exclaimed. "I'm pretty sure that's what politicized her, her friend's murder, or at least got her involved enough with the strike to get bayoneted."

"We're planning to include Eno in our book but there's so little known, at least publicly or officially. Can you persuade your grandmother to talk to us?" She looked at me imploringly. "Time is of the essence."

"I don't know," I said, looking at Russ. I told Sandy about Mama Lucy's heart problems and how she probably wouldn't be with us much longer. "I don't know how she'd hold up. This stuff is pretty emotional for her."

"It would be a shame if we couldn't get her on the record," said Sandy. "Even if it was just audio. Things have taken a turn for the worse for us as well. There's pressure from the new chancellor. He's reviewing the efficiency of all departments. There's a very real possibility that we may have our funding cut off if we can't justify ourselves. This project is the sexiest thing we've got going. And an interview with Lucille Barlow, an eyewitness to the Eno massacre, now that's news!"

"I can't make any promises."

"I understand. We'll play it by ear. No pressure."

"Well, at least we know she wasn't hallucinating. Thank you, Sandy."

"Thank you. And if you like, I'll be happy to play facilitator for your upcoming speech at St. Stephen's. You can use me as a resource, research assistant, moderator, whatever. It's the least I can do."

"Oh, right. The speech."

"It's scheduled right after Halloween. Don't forget, Pick," Russ admonished. "We've had a lot of interest."

I was to wait for Russ, who was meeting with the chairman of the music department to recruit a new organist for St. Stephen's, and Sandy was late for a class but before we adjourned she gave me something in a brown manila envelope she said I might find interesting.

Russ left me at the steps of the Wilson Library and I made my way to the exquisite solitude and silence of the reading room in the North Carolina Collection on the second floor. Except for a couple of librarians at their computer screens, I was alone in the spacious room among the sturdy mahogany tables and chairs with elegant chandeliers dangling like antique jewelry from the high ceilings. I took a seat at a table surrounded by computer terminals, card catalogs, plaster busts, dictionaries, and portraits of the luminaries who founded the university and donated their personal libraries to start the collection. I was tempted to look up my namesake Pickard Barlow, who fought at Gettysburg with the famed NC 26th, in the leather-bound volumes of NC Regiments 1861–1865 that lined one wall, and I also wanted to search for Mama Lucy's first letter to FDR. But I was curious about the envelope Sandy had given me so I settled back in my chair and opened it.

Inside was a small, tattered pamphlet about four by six inches, yellow and faded with age, printed on cheap pulp paper. It looked ancient, as if it had been published in the early part of the century. Its cover showed a pen-and-ink illustration drawn in silhouette, in a depression-era style seen in magazines like *The Nation* or *New Masses*, depicting an explosion over some factory houses, and emblazoned in smoke in large hand-drawn block letters were the words, *Burlington Dynamite Plot*.

"By Davis Barlow," I read aloud. My god, I thought, this was written by my uncle Dave! On the back of the booklet the legend read, *Printed by the Labor Defender. International Labor Defense. New York. 14 Wooster Street. Greenwich Village, March 4, 1935.*

I opened it and began reading:

Everything I'm about to put down in this little book is the good truth. I wouldn't say it any different if it were the Judgment Day.

Six mill hands in our town of Burlington, North Carolina, were rounded up by the sheriff, framed by the mill-owners and their detectives and stool-pigeons, and sentenced to serve long years in the pen—all for a dynamiting they knew no more about than you do.

He then went on to outline a tale of conspiracy on the part of the mill owners to discredit the union leadership beginning when the strike came to Burlington.

And on the fourth of September, 1934, the workers on the night shift looked out of the windows, and there were a power of men and women in the streets. The flying squad from the union had come. They went over the mill fences like rabbits. So we knew the textile strike had rushed over Burlington at last. We stopped the looms and shut off the power, and came out into the streets.

The pamphlet described the origins of the uprising, how the Governor called out the National Guard at the request of the mill owners and how it turned ugly in Eno. He went on to describe Burlington and how they turned the hoses on the strikers and teargas and clashed at the mill gates with bayonets. He even mentioned what happened to Lucy after the massacre in Eno.

The guards took some of the women, including my own sister, and stood them on a truck, and rode them about town. They thought that would make them ashamed, and frighten away our women-folk from the picket-lines. But my sister stood there proud, knowing it was for the union.

So Mama Lucy was not only bayoneted, she was made an example to other women, humiliated by the authorities as well as stabbed. Nobody ever mentioned that before either. This little pamphlet was a treasure. In colorful language all his own, Uncle Dave painted a vivid portrait of life in the mill villages and showed how the authorities, both civil and religious, were in the pocket of the mill owners. He wrote about the inequities of the stretch-out, and the workers' disenchantment with the New Deal, but mainly he told the story of the Burlington dynamite case, how an explosion of dynamite late one night on the most violent day of the strike that "didn't do $15 worth of damage just knocked out a few window lights" was used to justify rounding up the union leaders, framing them for the dynamiting, and railroading them. He told how they arrested six "honest working-men" and charged them with conspiracy along with three "rats," no-accounts, kept and coddled by the mill bosses and detectives, who claimed to have conspired with the six others. "They fed them and cared for them, and drilled them in their dirty job." So that "when these stool-pigeons got on the witness stand, one of them would lie like a yellow dog, and the others would swear to it."

According to Dave, it was shown during the trial that company detectives dragged one of the six out of his bed at night, carried him to the Correct Time Inn, and got him drunk with bootleg whiskey. They told him they wanted his name written on a piece of paper so they could see if it was the same writing as on the bill of sale of a car he used to own. That was just a trick to get him to sign his name on a blank sheet. The next time he saw that paper it had a "confession" over the name.

It sounded from Dave's description like the classic tactics authorities have used in tumultuous times against "dangerous" groups like black militants or Klansmen, the kinds of tactics that I had condemned in my editorial cartoons for years. By infiltrating them with agent provocateurs who urge or even commit violent crimes, then arresting the leaders along with the undercover agents, thugs, and others with criminal records, and then striking deals with the plants in exchange for testimony against their true targets.

"The trial parted our town in two, like a plow making a straight furrow across a field," wrote my great-uncle Dave, and he ended with an appeal for support. "The mill owners think they've got us down and crushed us—but I can tell you right now, we're not humbling to them!"

The pamphlet was signed, "Davis Barlow, President, Local No. 1777, Textile Workers International, Workers Defense Committee."

I sat there staring at the booklet. It took my breath away. It was the voice of my people, of the Barlows and Cantrells, of the lintheads, of Karl Marx and Woody Guthrie and the prophet Jeremiah all rolled into one. It was my grandmother's voice, my daddy's, my own. The phrasing and cadences, the proud defiance and biblical sense of justice, lifted off the page simple and direct, and what moved and surprised me most was the unadorned prose style that shone through in spite of the rhetoric, the raw literary flair, the sheer sense of storytelling. It called to me from across the decades. Writers search a lifetime for such an aching authenticity, clarity and authority. My uncle Davis Barlow was a natural.

As I sat there in the filtered light of late morning in the august and imposing stacks of the North Carolina Collection of Wilson Library, surrounded by the vast resources of research and scholarship of a great university that in its generosity and benevolence had casually offered up a glimpse into the soul of my family, I knew that I had to get to the bottom of this story. I couldn't wait to tell Mama Lucy and find out what she knew about the Burlington Dynamite Plot.

Leaves fell in swirls of orange and gold as Russ and I left the library and walked back through the beautiful spreading white oaks of the old quad in the heart of the campus. The quad was called Polk Place after President James K. Polk, who lived in South Building when he was a student at Chapel Hill. I filled Russ in as best I could on the Burlington Dynamite Plot as we walked past the Old Well to the visitor's lot where we had parked.

"Slow down!" I shouted to Russ as we drove past the Carolina Club parking lot. "That's our car!"

"Where?" asked Russ, screeching to a stop.

"Back there," I said, pointing at the vast parking lot. But we were in no position to turn around with traffic backing up behind us. "I thought I saw a Volvo that looks just like ours. Cameron drives it to work. It had a New York tag and Wiley's Garfield sun visor on the side rear window."

"There are a gazillion Volvos and lots of out-of-state tags and Garfield sun visors in the Triangle, Pick. Especially around the university. Hell, you can go for days in Chapel Hill without even hearing a Southern accent."

"No, it was our car. But what would Cameron be doing at the Carolina Club? We certainly aren't members."

"Her company must've bought a corporate membership. She's probably wining and dining a client."

"No, that's her boss's job. She always takes her lunch to work—brown bags it and eats at her desk. I saw her packing her lunch this morning."

"They host lots of corporate functions," Russ said, turning up toward Franklin Street and heading home. "Maybe she had a meeting there."

"Maybe," I said, staring back at the plate glass and brick facade of the Carolina Club as we pulled away.

DRIVING MISS LUCY

After Mama Lucy's emergency room visit there was little disagreement in the family that she belonged in a nursing home, and the sooner the better. I was surprised to find myself in the loop on these discussions but my presence in the emergency room and recent rapport with Mama Lucy had embroiled me in the family drama. Cameron stayed out of it.

Everyone knew Mama Lucy would put up resistance, and the discussion centered around strategies to achieve the desired end. The direct approach—telling her what we were doing and dealing with her fulminations and recriminations—was out of the question, too painful and guilt-inducing and definitely not the Cantrell way. The phone lines burned up with Machiavellian plots and schemes hatched by her children. Mama Lucy, who had always complained before because her family never visited, was irritated now because they were constantly dropping by checking up on her. Now she couldn't get any peace and quiet, she claimed. Finally, Beth was delegated to take her some lunch and broach the topic. She returned totally thwarted.

"When I brought up Shady Grove, Mama Lucy said it was a plot and that we was all in on it and had been planning it for years."

The debate turned to more proactive measures.

"I say we just send the paramedics in and let them shoot her up with dope and kidnap her," Florence said.

"Well, I don't want to be there when she wakes up at Shady Grove. We can't do that to them poor nurses over there," said Lily.

After listening to this for a few days Buzz decided to drop by Lucy's to do his own reconnaissance. Afterward he called me with his report.

"She's ornery as ever, but guess what? She's taken a shine to the doctor we met at the emergency room."

"Not the twit?" I replied.

"No, the older, distinguished gentleman from Chapel Hill, Dr. Levin.

She's followed all his instructions religiously. 'Dr. Levin said this. Dr. Levin said that.' He's all she can talk about. Can you believe it? No salt. No more country ham biscuits. It gave me an idea for handling the nursing home problem. I got Dr. Levin's phone number and explained the situation and we arranged an appointment in Chapel Hill at his clinic on Monday. Lucy's excited about it. I told her it's a follow-up. Of course, she doesn't know the hidden agenda. But maybe, just maybe if he brings up the nursing home she'll listen to him."

"Great!" I said.

"She asked if you would drive her."

Of course, I had my own reasons for chauffeuring her. I'd been looking for a chance to follow up on the Eno Massacre. I also wanted to find out what she knew about the Burlington Dynamite Plot and to learn more about her arrest and confirm the story about her being paraded around town on a truck. I knew I had to ease into it, but I would have all morning. As long as she didn't get the idea I was trying to put her in a nursing home. It would be tricky.

Mama Lucy was giddy with excitement over her appointment with Dr. Levin. When I arrived at 8:15 Monday morning she was all decked out in a beige Sunday dress with white shoes and hat, carrying a little white purse as though she was going to church. She talked my ear off the entire drive from Burlington to Chapel Hill. Dr. Levin saw us at 9:00 A.M. sharp. In his presence Lucy looked and acted twenty years younger. She flirted and chatted him up like a schoolgirl while he examined her. Dr. Levin himself was the soul of grace and I realized he had probably been in this situation a thousand times before.

I sat in the room while they discussed her ailments. His courtly manner worked beautifully. He was never didactic or direct. He never said, "You should do this or that." He just talked. He told her stories of folks her age and of the problems they faced living alone, stories that, if you read between the lines, illustrated the exact points we had tried so hard—and failed—to make. Mama Lucy was rapt because he told them like they were clothesline gossip, the inside scoop. He discussed the natural decline of functions with aging and empathized with her wish to be alone. He didn't put the hard sell to her but I could tell he had given her food for thought. Then he asked if he could speak to me alone. Lucy watched her morning soaps in the waiting room while he and I talked.

"This won't be easy," he said. "You and your family have a tough decision before you. She needs care. But she still isn't convinced she can't do it herself. And frankly, I'm not, either. The best thing would be if she went voluntarily; I'm not a believer in circumventing free will. But there's never a perfect way to do it. It's painful enough for adult children to see the diminishment of parents but this makes it even tougher. I don't know how much good I did but I gave her something to chew on. I'm available if you need me."

"Pick," Mama Lucy pleaded as I buckled her into her seat belt in the clinic parking lot. "Don't let them put me away. Promise me that. Don't let them put me away." Her words sent shivers down my spine. They were the same words my mother had uttered when the family threatened to commit her to Appalachian. It was an unpleasant reminder of the enmity that had festered between my grandmother and me for so long, and it was ironic now that Mama Lucy was on the receiving end of it and that she was turning to me for help. Even at her age she was sturdier than my mother ever was. But I could tell by the way she pleaded that Dr. Levin's talk had made an impression. For the first time in my life Mama Lucy sounded unsure of herself. She was scared.

Before we hit the road back to Burlington, I stopped at the Dairy Queen and bought her a vanilla milkshake.

" I thought we could go through Eno on the way home, Mama Lucy," I said when we were back on the road. "Maybe you could give me a tour." I watched carefully for her reaction but she registered nothing, though I thought I saw her eyes darken. I had learned to tread lightly if I wanted information. The direct approach had never worked with Mama Lucy.

"I cain't stay gone long now," said Mama Lucy, sipping purposefully on her straw as we turned onto Interstate 40 and headed for Eno. "I cain't miss my stories."

"You won't miss your soaps, I promise. It's on the way. I just want to drive you through town and maybe show you our house. Anyway, I gotta get back to pick up Wiley at school." I took her lack of protest as an OK. We made our way through the gauntlet of fast-food franchises that had sprung up around the Eno interstate exit like poisonous mushrooms.

"I bet none of this was here when you were a girl," I said.

"Lawd, it's been sixty years, Pick. It's sho' growed up."

"What made you want to leave Eno?" I asked.

"It was time to move on, and Burlington was as good a place as any to live."

Mama Lucy seemed engrossed as we crossed the New Hope River and entered downtown on Cheshire Street, with the historic markers planted along the street.

"There's the old courthouse, Mama Lucy, you remember that?"

"I do."

"Isn't that where Granddaddy worked as deputy sheriff?"

"It was."

We cruised slowly down West Cornwallis past the law offices, tanning salons, Dual Supply Hardware, the old Masonic Lodge, Cedar Lane Antiques and approached the Eno House Inn.

"Khoury's Dry Goods used to be there," she said, pointing at Dual Supply. Then she indicated the facade of the old inn, a bed and breakfast that served home-style cooking, one of the few tourist attractions left in Eno. I had met the new owners at the Strudwick party. "And that there was a welfare hotel back in my day. That's where me and the young'uns lived for a while during the depression when Dalton was gone to look for work after the sheriff let him go. We couldn't afford nothin' else."

Good Lord, I thought. Did the trials and tribulations of our family never end? We continued down West Cornwallis to Hillsborough Street and turned left. Lucy scanned the houses on both sides. We were getting close to the West End.

"I remember this," she said. "That over yonder is where the Copelands lived. And that's where the Sykeses lived. And there's the cemetery where the colored folks got buried." To our right was a weed-infested lot with a marker that said Old Slave Cemetery. This, I realized, was where the slate headstones for the Strudwicks' patio were stolen from.

As we moved slowly down Hillsborough Street, Mama Lucy began to recognize more landmarks, remnants and vestiges of her past. When the road emptied out onto a small town square–like strip of abandoned storefronts and pool halls perpendicular to the railroad tracks, we pulled over to the side and stopped.

"There." Mama Lucy pointed at an abandoned store front. "Where it says 'Bluebird Cafe.' That used to be a boardinghouse upstairs the old man's first wife run."

I stared at the empty cafe with the faded letters peeling off the whitewashed brick and tried to imagine my ancestors hanging around this ghost town less than a mile from the house I now lived in.

"And that's Scott's store next to the depot," she said excitedly, indicating another boarded-up storefront. "Or used to be."

"Where's the mill?" I asked. I had walked over here on my own in those first few weeks of getting to know the town but had never ventured across the tracks.

"Back up yonder." She pointed across the railroad tracks. We followed the road under a trestle and began curving up a hill. "There it is. Up there. That's the Bellevue mill. And this is the way we used to walk to work."

We drove up the steep hill and moved along the street that passed in front of the plain brick building. The evidence that it was abandoned was abundant. Windowpanes were punched out and much of the surrounding land was overgrown with weeds and kudzu. The rapacious vine, a vegetative form of cancer, the poet James Dickey called it, covered the ground like a faded green blanket, although its leaves were thinner than they were in summer and starting to wither and turn yellow, allowing the thick tangle of root and vine beneath to show through. The cover spread from the road where we were parked all the way up and across the chain-link fence onto the grounds and across the mill yard to the building. Climbing the brick wall like ivy, its relentless tendrils insinuated themselves inside and out the shattered front windows. On the left, behind the main structure, a bulky brick smokestack rose up like a doric column partially covered with kudzu. On the far end of the building, lending a crude balance to the plain, unadorned architecture, stood a dilapidated water tower rusted out and festooned as well with the dying leaves of the indefatigable vine.

As we took in the full panorama of this once-proud factory that had long ago teemed with mill hands flush with industry and productivity, I could feel Lucy growing silent, sinking into herself and her memories in the passenger seat beside me.

Lucy stuck her head in the foreman's office soon after the lunch whistle blew. "Mr. Sumner?"

"Yeah?" He grunted, without looking up from his detective magazine, with a picture of a scantily clad blonde on the cover being held with a knife to her throat.

"Mr. Sumner, may I speak with you a minute?" Lucy slipped inside as the mill hands filed noisily down the hallway for their lunch break. L. B. Sumner smiled, his yellow teeth peeking out from behind his fleshy lips. He leaned over and spit a wad of tobacco juice into a Coca-Cola bottle on the floor, and raked his fingers through his greasy black hair.

"Why, sure you can speak with me, little girl." He grinned, sitting up and straightening the papers on his desk. Lucy had never before been to the foreman's office. She avoided it as she avoided its occupant. Mr. Sumner had a reputation as a harsh taskmaster and a severe steward of the company's interests. Now she was talking to him for the second time that week.

"What can I do for you, Miss Barlow?" he asked with oily concern.

"It's not for me, Mr. Sumner," she explained. "It's for my friend, Annie Laura."

"Oh."

"Are they lettin' her go?"

"C'mon now, Lucy." He flipped through his magazine. "That ain't no concern of your'n."

"I heard you was gonna lay her off."

"It ain't up to me."

"She needs that job, Mr. Sumner."

"She ain't pullin' her weight in the weave room."

"She's better than me," Lucy pleaded. "She's nimble, too. She ties off warp threads a sight better'n me or anybody you got out there and she's more particular, too. She can watch over more machines with a sharper eye."

"She cain't climb up the loom to get to a loose thread, now, can she?" said Sumner, looking up.

"But she's only got one leg." Lucy could tell by the way Sumner looked at her, that mentioning Annie Laura's disability was a mistake. He just grimaced, and went back to his magazine.

"Send her back to the spool room then," Lucy urged. "Set her up again back there with me and Miz Copeland."

"Cain't do it. We full up back there. Look, this ain't no charity," Sumner snapped. "We kept her on after her accident 'cause her daddy was a good man, but he's gone now and she's gittin' to be more trouble than she's worth. A body's gotta pull they weight, simple as that. You gotta trim the fat if you gonna compete in textiles today."

Sumner spoke with such an air of benediction that Lucy took it to mean that the subject was closed. She started for the door, but then, in a final act of desperation, she whirled around and cried, "Lay me off instead."

"Huh?"

"Lay me off. Annie Laura needs the job worse'n I do. I can go back to school. Please, Mr. Sumner. She needs the paycheck. She's got brothers and sisters at home dependin' on her."

"That ain't my trouble. If she cain't do her job they's some who can." Lucy just stood there as the finality of what he just said sank in. Defeated, she turned to leave. Sumner glanced up at her, appraising her as she turned away in her pretty yellow dress, her brown hair slipping out of the bun and falling to her shoulders. As she opened the door he said, "Hold on, girl." Then he got up, laid the magazine in his chair and walked over to her.

"I'll tell you what, Lucy." He brushed her cheek with his arm as he closed the blinds to the weave room. He stood a foot taller than her and smelled of sweat and tobacco and she even thought she detected a whiff of whiskey on his breath when he spoke.

"Tell you what I'm gonna do." He turned her toward him and pinned her against the door with his meaty hands. She averted her gaze but she caught a glimpse of his bloodshot eyes peering down at her. He was breathing heavily, and so close now she could smell the sour odor of chewing tobacco on his breath. He whispered hoarsely, "I'll be nice to your friend, Lucy, if"—he took his big rough hand and brushed the strand of hair that had fallen across her eyes—"if you be nice to me."

"Is this where it happened, Mama Lucy?" I gazed at the windows staring at us like hollow eye sockets, trying to imagine the deputies and guardsmen and snipers gunning down the strikers gathered on the road where we sat now.

"Yes," she said.

"And where was Annie Laura killed?"

"Right there." She pointed to a weed-covered spot a few yards away.

"I've got so many questions. You said it was after that you got involved in the strike?"

"Yes."

"And that was what led to your bayoneting over in Burlington?"

"Yes."

"Do you remember anything about a dynamiting in Burlington?"

She looked at me. "A what?"

"There was a case brought against the leaders of the strike," I explained, "charging them with dynamiting a plant in Burlington. Uncle Davis wrote about it. He called it the Burlington Dynamite Plot."

Mama Lucy gazed at the old mill like she was trying to recall something. For a moment I thought she didn't know what I was talking about.

"This dynamiting," I added, "you may not have heard about it if you were over here in Eno."

"Oh, I remember it," she said, snapping out of her reverie. "Davis was lucky he won't sent to prison. It started for me at Chicken Bridge. Nearby here. If it's still there."

I wanted to question her about it but I didn't want to spoil her visit to her childhood home. We drove to the back of the original mill. I soon realized the back section of the complex beyond the old loading dock had been built up. There was another modern building, a plant and a set of warehouses with a loading dock and semis and trucks parked in a lot surrounded by chain-link fence with a discreet sign that read: EDEN ENTERPRISES, NO TRESPASSING.

Beyond the fence was a vast parking lot full of cars.

"Eden Enterprises," I repeated. Oh, my god, Garden of Eden. This must be Nathan Price's sex-toy factory. I wasn't about to explain to my grandmother that a company that made artificial penises, vibrators, and anatomically correct life-size dolls had replaced her looms and spindles.

"It's sure not a cotton mill anymore," I said vaguely, speeding us past.

"Probably some foreign company," Lucy speculated.

"Where did you live growing up?"

"Right up yonder." She pointed across the tracks to the hill called New Hope Mountain. The mountainside was covered with trees, underbrush, weeds and more kudzu. "But I don't see no houses."

"Maybe it got covered up. You'd have to take a bush hog to that to see what's back up under there. Where did you live?"

"When I was a young'un, there on the hill. In the old days, when I first started at the mill, the mill owner lived back up yonder in a big old house overlooking the village. But after a while he and his family moved into town." She seemed distracted now, confused.

"You okay?"

"It's gone, Pick. The house papa built, the Baptist Church. Even Panther's Den. All gone now."

We were heading back down the winding road past the mill toward the West End when I spotted a familiar figure jogging toward us with a big yellow lab on a leash. I pulled up beside them and lowered the window. "Hey, Russ." I introduced the rector to my grandmother.

He grinned an expansive pastorly grin and extended his hand. "Mrs. Cantrell, pleased to meet you! I've heard so much about you." Lucy straightened up in her seat and smoothed her hair.

"Just the man to answer some questions for us," I said. "Mama Lucy was wondering what happened to the mill village that used to be up on New Hope Mountain."

"Oh, it's still under there. Under that growth. That's where I walk Ginger. The path winds along the New Hope. Runs along the river through town under the bridge and snakes back behind where you live, Pick. I was just headed up there on my morning constitutional."

Lucy turned to me, her energy reignited. "That's the path we used to take to Panther's Den." She turned to Russ. "It's a clearin' overlookin' the river."

"Yes ma'am, Ginger loves it up there. She comes back just covered with ticks."

"See, Pick, I told you it was up there."

"I've been trying to get your grandson to walk up there with me. Maybe you'd like to accompany me instead, Mrs. Cantrell," Russ said.

Lucy blushed and looked at me. "Aw, I'm too old. But Pick better go. I want him to see what I seen when I was a girl. It's beautiful up yonder, ain't it?"

"Yes, indeed."

"Do the mountain laurels still grow?"

"Every spring. It's gorgeous. Get Pick to gather up some for you."

"We rode past the old Bellevue mill," I said. "Is that . . . um . . . what I think it is?"

"You got it. The biggest industry in Eno now."

"A foreign company?" confirmed Lucy.

"Yes, ma'am, you might say that."

"See Pick. I tole ya."

"We better go," I said.

"Mrs. Cantrell, it's a pleasure to meet you."

"Say, young man. Where about's Chicken Bridge? Which way from here?"

"Chicken Bridge? Straight out Dimmock's Creek and then right at the junction of old State Road One-fifteen, about a mile down. You are a native, aren't you, Mrs. Cantrell. Not many but natives know about Chicken Bridge. Or call it that if they do."

"Why is it called Chicken Bridge?" I asked.

"It's a narrow, one-lane bridge and I guess it got its name because rowdy teenagers are occasionally tempted to barrel down off One-fifteen and tear across it full throttle without checking to see what might be coming from the other direction. Play 'chicken,' as it were. Another explanation has it that a poultry truck turned over crossing it, plunged into the river and lost its cargo of chickens."

"That's the real story," said Mama Lucy, matter-of-factly. "I seen it with my own eyes. I was about ten years old. We all traipsed up there after it happened to watch 'em fish the truck out. Chickens everywhere. My papa brought two back that very day. Ones we couldn't catch just stayed in the vicinity. You could hear 'em and see 'em peckin' and scratchin' along the river lookin' for food for right smart after. 'Til they died of starvation, I reckon, or got ate themselves by bobcat or whatnot. Or caught by hobos for fryers. Pick," Mama Lucy said, "drive me down there."

"Careful out there, Pick, it's one lane," Russ said. "The bridge is a tad rickety. Nice meeting you, Mrs. Cantrell." We both waved good-bye and I turned the car around.

"Before I forget, Mama Lucy, I was wondering, could I borrow that letter you wrote FDR?"

"Ain't got it. I give it to your cousin Talbert Bailey. After you was at the house that time he come by to borrow some money."

"Borrow money? From you?"

"Just a little. You know I cain't say no to my grandyoung'uns. Them boys is always in debt. They ain't blessed with talent like you was, Pick. They always had to struggle to make a living."

"Getting an actual job might help," I said.

"Anyways," she continued, "he seen it sittin' on the kitchen table and I told him you brung it down from the attic and was real interested in it and that's when he asked if he could borrow it. He wanted to show it to his brother."

I wondered what those two would want with the letter. "Mama Lucy, did the reason you didn't send that letter have something to do with what happened in Eno?"

Her expression was answer enough.

"Mama Lucy, there's a Carolina professor named Sandra Murphy who's done a lot of research on the strike. I'd like to show her that letter. She's a friend of mine. Would you mind letting her interview you? She knows a lot about you and Davis."

"How does she know something I ain't told her?"

"She's a scholar. It's her job to study such things. Apparently you and your brother made quite an impression on a lot of people back then. And she's very sympathetic. Her granddaddy worked in the mills."

"Whereabouts?"

"I don't know. Delaney maybe. He died of brown lung. We can ask her."

"Probably Burlington. Dalton's brother John Wesley died of it. That's where he worked his whole life. They had it the worst. If you went in there, you'd come outta there just a-gaggin', the air was so thick with cotton dust."

"So you'll talk to her if I bring her by?"

"If she lost kinfolk to the brown lung I reckon she's like family." She stared out the window at the autumn leaves on the trees rising up on both sides of the old state road. "Davis used to drive his motorcycle on this road." The thought seemed to trouble her.

Not wanting to get distracted, I asked, "The letter to FDR, Mama Lucy, I found it in a high school English textbook with your name on it. I thought you didn't go to school beyond the eighth grade."

"I didn't."

"Where did you get that book then?"

"Somebody give it to me."

"Who?"

"I can't remember."

"I read that in Burlington the sheriff put you on a truck and paraded you around town."

"I ain't thought about that for years."

"Is it true?"

"I reckon." She gazed off into the distance before she answered. "I stayed out of it as long as I could. Even after I got stabbed and ever'body was makin' a fuss over me and all, callin' me a martyr to the cause, and wantin' me to speak out at rallies and ever'thing, I reckon I really didn't feel like I had the right. Not like Annie Laura. I just wanted to be at home with the young'uns."

"But you'd worked in the mills all your life. Didn't that give you the right?"

"I reckon."

"You were union, weren't you?"

"My brothers and sisters was right in the middle of it. I couldn't stay away. Not after what happened in Eno. That was the beginning of my troubles with the old man. And his family. It was his brother that done it. But," she finished wearily, "that's a story for another day."

"Okay, okay. I ask too many questions."

She stared out the window with a hint of a smile. "You always did."

We followed the highway through wooded terrain. The trees fell away as we approached a gorge and a wide stretch of the New Hope River. There the road abruptly choked down to a narrow wooden one-lane bridge, supported beneath with elaborate trestling, and with low waist-high railings along both sides. The bridge ran about seventy feet above the river and stretched for about a hundred yards before the road widened again and disappeared into the dark forest of pines and hard-woods. We pulled to the shoulder.

Spread out before us was the river basin gorge of trees and rocks and water doused in the vibrant autumn hues. Mama Lucy seemed lost in reverie.

Finally I broke the silence. "You thinkin' about those chickens?"

"Naw. I was thinkin' about a Halloween party. We'd have a pumpkin carvin' here ever' Halloween. Ever'body from the mill village would show up and pitch in. We'd carve jack-o'-lanterns and set 'em out on this bridge. It was a sight. Hundreds of jack-o'-lanterns just a'glowin'. Prettiest thing you ever saw. Mr. Webb's boy, the one who brung me the special delivery, we met here right after. I'll never forget it."

CHICKEN BRIDGE

The bridge lighting was an annual event. Nobody in the West End missed it and folks even came from miles around—Efland, Mebane, Saxapahaw, some as far away as Burlington—to see. There was party food, cakes and pies, and soft drinks and hot apple cider. Sometimes if a string band was playing, there'd even be dancing.

Lucy and Annie Laura hitched a ride on one of the flatbed trucks, piled high with pumpkins, that left from the Bellevue loading dock that Friday afternoon right before sundown. Lucy's sisters, Eunice and Icy, came along with them as did Annie Laura's younger brothers, Fetzer and Eugene. When they pulled up, night was falling along with the temperature, as it always did at dusk that time of year, and their teeth were starting to chatter. But they soon forgot the nip in the air, for the sight of the eerie luminescence leaking through the trees sent a charge of excitement through the group. What looked from the road like a gigantic bonfire turned out to be the warm glow given off by a huge pile of jack-o'-lanterns stacked up in a clearing next to long tables loaded with food and drink. People ate and drank and carved and scooped out and carefully placed candles inside each pumpkin, then set the glowing jack-o'-lantern in the pile to be taken out and set up on the bridge railings.

Annie Laura searched for a pumpkin to carve. It had to be right. She had worked out a design, but she was keeping it to herself. Annie Laura was the most artistic of Lucy's friends and for some reason this year she was the most serious about this contest. For weeks she had bombarded the lady who ran the contest with questions, to make sure she understood the rules for eligibility and the criteria for selection of winners. Lucy, on the other hand, wasn't interested in entering but enjoyed seeing what everybody else came up with.

The others went straight to the food table, and after loading up with potato salad and country ham biscuits and cakes and pies and cider, they all headed straight to a table and began carving. Many of the children had brought sketches and blueprints of their designs which they'd drawn up on butcher paper and paper sacks. Lucy supervised the children's carving, while Annie Laura meticulously transferred her design to her pumpkin. After a time Lucy picked up a jack-o'-lantern from the glowing pile and joined the revelers heading toward the bridge. As she emerged from the trees she heard somebody call her name.

"Lucille Barlow! *Pssst!*"

She looked around in the gathering darkness but saw no one she knew. She started toward the bridge again, moving past a flatbed truck that had just arrived with more supplies.

"Hey, you!" said the voice again. A figure jumped down off the back of the truck, startling Lucy. The young man grabbed her jack-o'-lantern and stood there with it under his arm grinning sassily at her. It was Spencer Webb. "I was hoping I'd see you here." He turned around and headed for the bridge. Not knowing what else to do, Lucy followed him. They arrived at a row of lit jack-o'-lanterns on the rail of the bridge. He placed Lucy's on the railing, extending the orange glow farther out over the river.

"Cat got your tongue?" he asked. Lucy silently corrected the angle of one of the jack-o'-lanterns. ⸺

He smiled. "I hope that special delivery letter was the fulfillment of all your dreams."

"That's none of your business," Lucy said.

"Well, I reckon it is my business, if I work for the United States Post Office. That's exactly my business."

"Snoopin's a federal crime. Even if you do work for the P.O. Everybody knows that."

"Aren't you the smart one tonight? Halloween's turned you into a haint."

"You're the haint," Lucy said. "Snooping around people's personal mail."

Spencer Webb stood there grinning. "What are you staring at?"

"Smile," Lucy said.

"Huh?"

"Smile," she repeated.

He did as she asked. She cast her eyes downward.

"What is it? Tell me." Then he reached over and lifted her chin with his index finger so he could see the expression on her face and the soft orange glow reflected in her eyes.

"It's just"—she looked at the ground again—"I ain't seen that many boys my age with all their teeth before. It's . . . It's so pretty." Embarrassed, she turned back to the railing and gazed at the river running below.

When she looked back Spencer seemed at a loss for words. He stared at her as if something was sinking in, some recognition and understanding that had escaped him in the giddy heart-pounding rush of adolescent infatuation. She hoped she hadn't embarrassed him. Lucy had a good sense of humor, everybody said so, and she tried to make light of it.

"No offense," she said. "But a full set of teeth is somethin' to see. Most boys I know look like them jack-o'-lanterns. Except the pumpkins got better smiles."

Spencer snapped out of his spell. "Come on," he said, "I want to show you something." He pulled her toward the darkness on the far side of the bridge.

"I cain't."

"Sure you can. Come on!"

She glanced over her shoulder. "But my friend and my sisters—"

"They'll be fine. They won't even know you've been gone. You've gotta see this."

He led Lucy down an embankment to an old logging road. The road degenerated into a trail that turned into the woods and rose along a cliff that dropped straight down to the river's edge. She followed Spencer onto the ledge. "Now, close your eyes," he said. He took her by the shoulders and turned her around. "Open your eyes."

The entire bridge was aglow with dozens of jack-o'-lanterns, the clear harvest moon hanging in the sky. It was dazzling. Spencer gazed at the view alongside her.

"Oh, my goodness," she gasped. "It's beautiful."

"You can see the bridge lit up from the road," he said, "and from all different sorts of angles and they're all pretty spectacular, but I think this is where you get the very best look at it."

Lucy sighed. "It's the prettiest thing I ever saw. It's magical."

"It sure is. This is my favorite holiday. It's like some pagan bacchanal. The only holiday the preachers aren't hovering over and granting dispensations to have fun."

"Oh," said Lucy, pretending she understood what he was talking about.

"I like the fact we can leave these jack-o'-lanterns out here night after night and nobody messes with them. It's nice. Folks respect the beauty of it, the spontaneity. To me it looks like a little Brooklyn Bridge at night. Eno's version."

"You've seen that?"

"One time. On a trip to New York with my father." Spencer smiled.

"New York." Lucy sighed. "I ain't never been nowhere but Alamance County. Here I am nearly fifteen years old an' never seen nothin' but Burlington. But I will someday. I've read about lots of those places: New York. Paris. London."

"You like to read?" Spencer asked.

"I do. It's like takin' a trip."

"I should have guessed. Every time I've seen you come in the dry goods store you've got a different book. *Treasure Island. A Tale of Two Cities.*"

"My brother Davis give 'em to me. He wants me to go to school."

"Why don't you?"

"Gotta work. Help out at home. I owe it to Mama and Papa. But now they talkin' about layin' off Annie Laura," Lucy said, "but they cain't lay her off!"

"The one-legged girl? The one I see you with in the store?"

"She lost family to the flu and her papa's too sick with TB to work now. She's got younger brothers and sisters dependin' on her."

"I heard something about layoffs. Not many, though. It's all the competition. It shouldn't be too bad."

"Unless it's you."

"Of course," he replied sheepishly. "But why her?"

"Mr. Sumner said she's too slow but she's not."

"Sumner's a shit," declared Spencer. Then catching himself, he said, "Pardon my language but I've seen the way he talks to people. And then tries to kiss up to my father."

"You don't know how it is in the weave room. I talked to him about Annie Laura's situation."

"Will he do anything?"

"If I'm good to him," she said. Then, suddenly nervous, she blurted, "I don't want to get nobody in trouble. I'll lose my job."

"What did Sumner say to you?"

"It ain't just me. He's friendly with all the girls. But I just can't do it. Now he says it's gonna be my fault she loses her job. And I don't think I can stand bein' the cause for that, too." Tears threatened but Lucy fought them back.

"Too?"

"It was my fault she lost her leg. The train hit her 'cause I was too slow gittin' back to work."

"C'mon. What did Sumner say?"

"He said if I was nice to him he'd be nice to me and Annie Laura."

"What did he mean 'nice to him'?"

"Let him touch me."

"He said that?"

"Not in so many words."

"That's disgraceful. If my daddy knew he'd—"

"You can't tell him," blurted Lucy in a panic. "He'd know where it come from and I'd get fired."

"You're not going to be fired. And don't worry. I can't tell my daddy. We're not supposed to fraternize."

"Fraternize?"

"Make friends with mill hands and their families. I don't understand. Seems to me like we're all in this together."

"What would your daddy say if he knew you was talkin' to me?"

"It doesn't matter."

"Why not?"

"I never listen. And he's not going to know. C'mon, I'll take you back down to the party."

They had already started back down the trail when Lucy turned to Spencer and said, "Maybe I should go first." Lucy turned down the path. She felt Spencer grab her arm. She turned around. Spencer was looking at her tenderly. He pulled her close and kissed her. Lucy had been kissed before but never had she been so surprised or so willing. It was a long, deep kiss and when Spencer let go she could see the flickering glow of the jack-o'-lanterns reflected in his eyes.

She breathed deeply, wondering if he did this with lots of girls, but the surprised look on his face told her different. "I better go," she said.

"I—I'll hang back here for a minute," he said. "You go on ahead."

Lucy made her way down the trail and back to the bridge. The glow of jack-o'-lanterns now reached nearly three-quarters of the way across the bridge. She saw the silhouetted figure of a girl running toward her. It was her sister Eunice. "I'm tellin' Mama on you, Lucy," she crowed.

"Tell her what?"

"That you talked to that Webb boy."

"It's a free country, ain't it?"

"I'm tellin' her you run off with him."

"He showed me the bridge, that's all."

"You were gone an awful long time."

"Not more'n five minutes," Lucy said, though she knew it had been much longer. But she also knew her sister didn't have a watch and was prone to exaggerate. She grabbed Eunice's arm. "C'mon, where are the others? Let's get somethin' to eat."

"Dave's here," said Eunice. "He was lookin' for you. He drove over from Burlington on his motorcycle."

"Where is he?"

"Where have you been, girl?" asked Annie Laura when they got back. "We been lookin' all over for you."

"Nowhere," Lucy replied.

"She was out sparkin' with Mr. Webb's boy," Eunice said.

"I was not."

"C'mon, Lucy," Annie Laura said, "help me finish carvin' the pumpkin for the contest." Annie Laura led her to the table where the girls were dipping snuff and chattering away like they were at a quilting bee. Annie Laura spit into a Coke bottle and offered her friend a dip of Tube Rose. Lucy turned it down.

Annie Laura took a pinch and said, "I ain't never knowed you to turn down a dip before. Who you tryin' to stay sweet-lipped for? Dalton Earl?"

Lucy shushed her and sat down at the table. "Annie Laura, did you do this?" Lucy had never seen a jack-o'-lantern with bats for eyes, nose, and mouth. Her friend blushed and grinned and spat again into the Coke bottle. "You gonna win for sure, girl," Lucy said.

Annie Laura picked up her knife and went back to work. "I ain't finished. I got more to do on his mouth." Lucy was amazed at Annie Laura's blossoming natural talents, artistic, musical and culinary. She had hardly revealed them when they were younger but right after she lost her leg she had started turning out paintings and pots and casseroles and writing poems and songs like she was possessed by a demon. It was as if she'd been given the go-ahead from God Almighty Himself to use her creative powers. Davis said she was compensating for her lost limb but Lucy thought she was doing it more as a form of prayer and gratitude, like folks at the hard-shell Baptist church speaking in unknown tongues, ecstatic and grateful she was still alive.

"I been lookin' all over for you to set with me," Annie Laura whispered as she carved. "I was afraid Jake Satterfield would come over here and sit down. I think he's a-scairt of you."

"He's a-scairt of my brother is what he is." Lucy stared at the Coca-Cola bottle spittoon and the beautiful way the light from the bonfire and the bridge reflected in it. Nobody messed with Davis Barlow's little sister or they had to answer to Dave. Even Jake Satterfield was wary of him.

Annie Laura pointed with the knife blade. "Jake's over yonder with Bobby Joe Hullender carryin' on at the bonfire, both of 'em drunker'n a skunk." Just then Jake looked their way.

"Uh-oh," Annie Laura said. "He seen me pointing at 'em. They comin' over."

"Well, look who's here," said Jake as he and Bobby Joe shambled over to the table. "Miss Annie Laura Gaskins and Miss Lucille Barlow. The goddamned Belles of Eno."

He stared at Annie Laura's handiwork. "Well, what do we got here?"

"Leave it alone, Jake," Lucy ordered. "She's entering it in the contest."

"You don't say." He walked around behind her, and snatched the Coke bottle she was fingering off the table. "You gonna let me have a swaller of your Co-cola tonight, ain'tcha, Miss Lucille?"

"It ain't mine," replied Lucy.

"I don't care whose it is," declared Jake, "I'm mighty goddamned thirsty."

"I wouldn't drink it if I were you," Lucy said, glancing at Annie Laura, who was still focused on her work.

"What you gonna do?" Jake taunted. "Call your big brother and squeal on me?"

"We don't want no trouble," said Lucy. "Why don't you just go on and leave us alone?"

"I'll go when I'm good and ready, Miss Lucy High and Mighty. I seen you out there on Chicken Bridge smoochin' with the Webb boy."

Lucy froze.

"Like some road whore," Bobby Joe chimed in.

Annie Laura stared at Lucy and everybody around the table stopped working and looked at her, too. Lucy glared at Jake. He had an audience now and was playing it for all it was worth.

"Yeah, I reckon you got your eye on the boss man's son," Jake drawled, "givin' him a little taste of what he can have if he moves you into that big fine house over there in town."

"Shut up, Jake," Lucy snapped.

"Leave her alone, " Annie Laura pleaded.

"Yeah, I wonder what it'd be like to have me a taste of some of what you got," he continued, the spotlight feeding his predatory instincts. He lifted the Coke bottle to his lips, and with his legs spread and one hand on his hip, threw back his head, and in one swift gulp guzzled down the bottle's entire contents. Instantly, he was gagging and coughing and spitting.

"Goddammit, Lucy!" he screamed. "What the hell is that?"

The whole table doubled over with laughter. Lucy said, "What's the matter, Jake, don't you like snuff?"

"I oughta kill you, you bitch," Jake snarled. Saliva foamed from his mouth. "You think you better'n me, but you ain't nothin' but a linthead and a road whore. I seen you kissin' up on your rich boyfriend at the bridge, puttin' on airs like you better'n the rest of us."

"I did not. He just showed me a view of the bridge."

Just then a deep male voice, rough and scratchy like sandpaper, rasped at her out of the darkness. "Who showed you a view of the bridge?"

Jake started.

"Davis!" squealed Lucy, running to hug her brother. Jake melted into the confusion of the party.

Davis Barlow was seven years older than Lucy, the eldest of the Barlow brood, but he was devoted to Lucy and she to him. Though still a young man, he had returned from the Great War with a weariness beyond his years. Although he was not what you'd call a handsome man, he had a way about him that was cocky and self-assured, like somebody who thought he was the best-looking thing on God's green earth, and that gave him an appeal that the ladies mistook for handsome. He was medium height, but of muscular build, always wearing overalls that made him look stockier than he actually was. He had stopped wearing his military uniform, the one he used to parade around in before he went off to the war, the one Lucy remembered he looked so handsome in, and he now walked with a slight limp from a shrapnel wound he took in the trenches of the Argonne Forest. But the injury didn't inhibit his wild ways or stop him from riding a motorcycle, which worried his mama half to death and put even more years and lines on the face of his papa. Davis too had his share of scars on his face, not from fighting Germans, but from too many knife fights on Saturday nights in pool halls all over Alamance and Eno counties. He was known to run with a rough crowd but was considered smarter than most and he could outtalk a preacher. Nobody could tell a story like Davis Barlow. Even drunk. Especially drunk. And he was bad to drink. But his little sister loved him anyway.

He swung her around, laughing his raucous pool hall laugh, and she could smell the whiskey on his breath. Then he reached in his pocket and gave Lucy, Eunice and Annie Laura each a stick of Juicy Fruit.

"Spencer Webb, the mill owner's son!" Eunice shouted gleefully. "That's who Lucy run off with!"

"Shush, Eunice," Annie Laura said. "Let's go put my pumpkin on the bridge."

"Well, now, is that right, Lucy?" Davis asked. "Are you courtin' Mr. Webb's boy now? I thought you was already engaged."

"I'm gonna kill you, Eunice," Lucy said. Annie Laura pulled Eunice away.

"I gotta say I'm mighty glad you're not takin' this marriage business with Mr. Dalton Earl Cantrell serious like Mama is. But still you got no business talkin' to somebody like the Webb boy, neither. What am I gonna do with you, girl? You think he's gonna invite you up to that big ol' house of his on the other side of town?"

"Oh, Davis, don't listen to Eunice. She's just jealous. It won't nothin'."

"You listen to me, now. You stay away from the boss man's boy. He'll try to take advantage of you, Lucy, y'hear? You belong with your own people, you understand?"

"You're not the boss of me, mister." Lucy punched his arm.

He pulled a bottle of moonshine from his coat pocket and took a swig. "Did you get that package I left with Papa?"

"The books. Yessir. Thanks."

"When you goin' back to school, girl?" he demanded.

"You know I cain't. Papa needs me to work to help out at home. Anyway, I'm no good in school. I want to stare out the window all the time and be outside."

"You tellin' me it's harder than workin' the weave room."

"It's different. That's all."

"You finished the eighth grade, Lucy. You need to go on to high school. College even. It's a great big world out there and you're smart. You can do anything you want. You deserve better than workin' in the mills."

"Oh, Davis, you're drunk."

"You ain't seen drunk, darlin'. Now you promise me to finish school."

"C'mon, Lucy!" Annie Laura called from the bridge. "The judgin's almost done and they're fixin' to announce the winners!"

"You promise me now, girl!" shouted Davis as he turned to head back out to the bridge to drink with his friends. "And don't you go gittin' married!"

The crowd swarmed toward the glow from the clearing in the trees. The others had run ahead leaving Lucy behind. "C'mon, Lucy. It's time for the contest," Annie Laura said.

Lucy had just started toward the others when Dalton Earl Cantrell slipped up behind her and took her by the arm. "Where's the fire?" he said.

"Dalton," Lucy said. "What are you doing back from Danville?" She hugged him awkwardly.

"I wanted to see you. And I didn't want to miss Chicken Bridge. I made every single Halloween come hell or high water for I don't know how long. I won't gonna miss it this year."

"Well, you're just in time for the winners of the carvin' contest to be announced," Lucy said.

"You got a pumpkin in there?"

"I'm gittin' too old for such. Annie Laura does, though."

"I ain't heard from you, Lucy. It gets lonesome up there."

"I know you sent me that special delivery," she replied, praying she didn't look as guilty as she felt. "They got it to me at work and all." She brightened. "I was Miss Somethin' gittin' that at work."

"I don't know what happened to all the other ones I wrote. But I meant what I said about settin' a date for the weddin'."

"C'mon, Dalton," Lucy said. "We gon' miss the winners."

"Hold on. I brung you somethin'." He handed Lucy a small box.

Lucy held it like it was a hot coal, staring at the ribbon and bow on top, fearful of what was inside. "Lord, what have you done, Dalton Earl?"

"Go ahead," Dalton said. "Open it."

Lucy was speechless when she saw the ring. It looked like a diamond but she knew he couldn't afford that. Still, the stone was beautiful, and looked expensive, the light from the party catching and caroming off it. She didn't know what to say.

"Lucy, you comin'?" It was Davis. She could see him silhouetted against the glow of the bonfire flaring behind them.

The blaze at the center of the clearing had been lit to replace the rapidly diminishing pile of jack-o'-lanterns whose glow had been depleted as one by one each pumpkin was removed to decorate the bridge. From a distance the pumpkin luminaries on the railings hung motionless in the blackness like frozen fireflies, and Lucy realized she and Dalton standing there must have looked like furtive conspirators relegated to the margins of visibility, their features faint, mutable, half-hidden, flickering in and out of the blackness with the fickle intensity and brightness of the bonfire flame. But even from there in the eerie half-light she could tell what was going on. Suddenly the sound of footsteps and the judges who had spent the last few minutes walking the bridge voting on the winners brushed past Dalton and Lucy.

"Howdy, Dalton," said Davis, approaching as the last judge slipped past him on the narrow path to the clearing.

Dalton nodded, friendly but guarded.

"What you got there, Lucy?" Davis asked, pointing at the package in her hands. Lucy flashed the ring still in the box. "It's an engagement ring."

"You robbin' the cradle, ain'tcha, hoss?" Davis said.

"Don't you think that's up to Lucy, Davis?" replied Dalton.

"Then why are you speakin' for her, Slick?"

"Davis!" Lucy cried. She could feel the tension flashing between them and she knew Davis could turn mean in an instant when he'd been drinking.

"Lucy's old enough to make up her own mind," Dalton answered. "I've already spoken to her daddy about it. If it don't bother him, I don't see why it should bother you."

" 'Cause she's too young to make a decision like that for herself," said Davis, staring at his sister. He knew her and he knew she had doubts. "She don't have any idea what's best for her."

"And you do?"

"I know she's got no business gittin' married. She's got a head on her shoulders. And she should go to school."

"She can go to school if she wants. I ain't gonna stop her."

"She'll be knocked up quicker'n a jackrabbit in springtime. And you know as well as I do once that happens there's no turnin' back."

"It's a free country," Dalton said. "She can go to school or have babies and it ain't up to you or me."

"Then why don't you wait? You love her so much waitin' ain't gonna hurt nothin'."

"That's up to Lucy."

"Horseshit!" Davis exploded.

A flatbed truck drove by spewing gravel from beneath its tires. From the back of the truck Spencer Webb waved to Lucy. She waved back as it pulled out onto the highway and disappeared into the night.

"Who's that?" asked Dalton.

"Just a friend," answered Lucy.

"What friend?" Suddenly it was as if Davis wasn't even there.

"Mill owner's son," explained Davis. "Spencer Webb. I hear he's a fine young man."

"You talkin' to him, Lucy?" asked Dalton.

Lucy crossed her arms and turned her back to both of them. "I don't have to answer to you or nobody else."

"Y' see, Cantrell. A smart, pretty girl like Lucy's got more options than her mama and daddy did who are tryin' to marry her off. She's got a good head on her shoulders and more goin' for her than you or me either one. She's got a chance to make somethin' of herself. And if I'm the only one who sees it, so be it. You're right—she's got no business messin' with the mill owner's boy. But truth is, she's got no business messin' with you, neither."

"I reckon you're entitled to your opinion," Dalton said. He turned to Lucy. "Why don't you put that ring on, Lucy?"

"Give it back to him, Lucy," Davis said.

"Put it on, Lucy."

"Give it back."

Tears welled in Lucy's eyes. She couldn't take it. "Y'all just leave me alone." She slapped the box back into Dalton's hands and ran toward the bridge.

"Lucy!" Dalton shouted. Lucy ducked behind a tree and peered back at Davis's and Dalton's shadowy figures flickering against the firelight.

Davis cut him off. "Leave her alone, Cantrell!"

"Out of my way!" Dalton shoved past him. Davis fell over a bush, then bounded to his feet.

"Cantrell!" Davis shouted. Dalton turned around and saw the glint of cold steel in Davis's hand. A cheer erupted from the crowd gathered around the bonfire, but Davis was oblivious. "You ain't goin' nowhere, Hoss!"

"I'm goin' to get Lucy," Dalton answered. Davis stood between Dalton and the bridge, edgy and alert in the crisp October night air.

"You gonna have to get past me first, Hoss."

Lucy had seen before how violence sobered Davis up and was fascinated and frightened by it. A cold animal glint entered her brother's eyes. Dalton, his tall slender frame frozen and still, was unarmed, vulnerable against the knife-wielding Davis. Older than his adversary, Dalton disliked physical confrontation but seemed remarkably calm in the face of it. The two men stood there taking each other's measure, regarding each other for what seemed to Lucy like an eternity.

"You're drunk, Dave," Dalton said finally. "Put down the knife."

"You take it from me, buddyrow, and it's all yours."

A flurry of footfalls upon the path broke the spell, as Annie Laura brushed past Davis on her crutches, the other girls not far behind.

"Lucy," Annie Laura shouted. "I won!" she looked around. "Where is she?" Lucy emerged from behind a tree. Annie Laura, her face alive with excitement, said, "I won! I never won nothin' before." Then she saw the knife in Davis's hand. She gasped.

Lucy ran up behind Dalton. They all stood around awkwardly as others arrived, the excitement of Annie Laura's triumph punctured by the blade's presence. Davis, aware of the pleading eyes of his sisters, looked hard at Dalton, pulled his bottle of moonshine from his jacket, took a long swig, and stalked away, disappearing into the raucous confusion of the party. Lucy rushed to Annie Laura and hugged her as Dalton slipped the engagement ring back into his pocket.

My head was swimming with my grandmother's stories as we drove back into Eno from Chicken Bridge. I was struck by the vividness of her recollections, the clarity with which Mama Lucy resurrected long-ago incidents, as if she were watching them play out on a giant movie screen in her mind, digitally enhanced in 3-D and Technicolor, Dolby, and SurroundSound. She seemed to have the opposite of Alzheimer's. She remembered everything. And I was intrigued by the way her memories nurtured and sustained her, that her internal mental tapestries seemed, in fact, to be more concrete and palpable than the reality around her.

Her visual gifts were quite profound as well. She had the eye and ear of an artist or poet, if not the means of expression. It was as if everything that ever happened to her of emotional significance had registered deeply, had been indelibly etched in her mind, singeing her synapses and searing her consciousness, so that ancient joys and traumas were not only recoverable but were instantly retrievable and stood out in sharp relief.

For the first time I was beginning to see myself in my grandmother and to recognize my own reflection in her and her gifts and I was astonished at the thought that I might have inherited that which I most valued in myself from my childhood nemesis.

Driving home from Chicken Bridge that crisp autumn morning, with leaves swirling on the highway and the smell of bonfires and woodsmoke in the air, I felt an urge, a stirring I had not felt in months. It was pure and clean and unbidden and strange. I wanted to draw.

As we passed the former Bellevue mill and reentered the terrain of her youth Lucy seemed shaken. The little town had changed. She turned away from the window and her chin sank to her chest. Her eyes closed. When I glanced over at her again she appeared to be sleeping.

"I'm sorry we couldn't see the house on the mill hill, Mama Lucy," I said. "Too bad that area's all covered up now."

"Won't much to look at anyway," she muttered, still refusing to look out the window. But as we retraced our route, pulling back up along Hillsborough Street toward Cornwallis, Lucy sat up and squinted through the windshield at an old house covered with canary yellow aluminum siding.

"Hold it, Pick. There, that's where me and the old man lived when he was deputy sheriff. It ain't the same house but that's the lot."

I pulled over so we could get a better look.

"That's where the baby died."

"The one you lost to the whooping cough?"

"It was the saddest thing. Little Sara won't but a month old when she come down with the croup. You'd look over at night when she was layin' there in her crib and just a-coughin' and see her little arm just a-jerkin' each time she coughed and there was nothin' you could do about it. It liked to broke my heart." She stared at the house, lost in memory, then sighed, and with a well-earned stoicism, said, "Life is hard, ain't it, Pick?"

"You're tired, Mama Lucy."

Returning through town it began to sink in for the first time how much of my own family history had played out on this particular piece of real estate in the West End, and how little I knew of it until fate brought me back. On Cornwallis Street yuppie tourists gathered under the narrow columns of the Eno House Inn, obliviously occupying the renovated square footage that once served as the scene of our family's destitution. We passed Cheshire Street, with its antiques and boutiques, and drove past the old brick courthouse.

We passed the county jail and then the modern, low-slung post office, quite a contrast, I imagined, to the P.O. window in Khoury's Dry Goods store. Then we turned off Cornwallis, passing St. Stephen's Church, and moved slowly down Bennehan until finally we arrived at Oaklawn. The old house, set back in the newly mowed lawn and surrounded by huge two-hundred-year-old trees, looked majestic as we pulled up the drive.

"Well, this is it," I said, smiling as I came around to the passenger side and opened Lucy's door. Lucy sat there frozen, staring straight ahead.

"Come on, Mama Lucy. Let me show you the house."

"I want to go home."

"But we just got here. I thought you'd want to see the work we've done."

"No. I cain't. Take me home, please."

"At least let me walk you through. It would be a shame to—"

"No," she said, cutting me off.

"Are you breathing all right? Is it your heart?" I had to remember, despite her robust spirit, that she could only take so much.

"Don't you know, Pickard?" she said finally, her voice cracking. "This is the Webbs' house. Spencer Webb lived here."

PART III

SPOOLER'S SONG

HAUNTED HOUSE

That night, between my rekindled desire to draw and the sudden revelation that Oaklawn had belonged to the owners of the Bellevue mill, whose scion once had fancied my grandmother, I could hardly sleep. I tossed and turned all night and arose before dawn and surprised Cam and Wiley with a big hearty breakfast of pancakes, bacon, and eggs. By the time Cam left for work and Wiley got off to school I knew what I wanted to do.

It was another bright and crisp morning and the old highway out by Chicken Bridge was deserted. I parked my pickup along the shoulder and scouted the vicinity along the river for a good angle from which to draw the old trestled bridge. After checking out several perspectives from above and below the bridge's span, I skidded down the riverbank and chose for my first vantage point a large shelf of rock jutting out above the swift, sun-dappled waters about fifty yards downstream.

I drew without deadline or purpose or agenda, conjuring in pencil and charcoal and sepia rough, spontaneous images of the deserted bridge, drawing just for fun, for myself, as I had when I was a child. The effect was exhilarating, liberating. I was a bit rusty, but soon the lines and textures and quaint grandeur of the bridge took me over, and my eye and hand and brain got lost in the task of capturing it all on paper.

After accruing several pages of drawings from different points of view, I crossed the bridge and walked along a trail that forked off into the woods and led up and around a bend and onto a promontory that opened onto the river again—the very spot, I was convinced, where Spencer Webb and Mama Lucy had rendezvoused so many years ago. The vista was still spectacular, even during the day, and I could imagine what the bridge must have looked like aglow with jack-o'-lanterns, their twinkling lights reflected in the river below.

Emboldened by a newfound sense of artistic urgency, I decided to attempt to capture the nighttime scene on paper. Switching from pencils and charcoals to pens and markers, a riskier medium, since each stroke was committed indelibly to paper, I plunged ahead. Working from Mama Lucy's vivid descriptions, I let my imagination take over, supplying from memory with intricate shading and cross-hatching the shadows and blackness of a crisp October night lit up by the magical incandescence of the jack-o'-lanterns and the glow and reflection of moonlight and candles on water. Before long the scene began to take shape, and I liked what I saw.

Soon a sheen of sweat beaded on my forehead and the sweatshirt I was wearing grew uncomfortably warm. Looking up I saw the sun high overhead and realized I was hungry. Three hours had passed without my noticing. I had spent almost the entire morning shading and refining one drawing. It was time to go home.

Halloween arrived at Oaklawn in a jumble of frenetic activity. Pumpkin-carving, house-decorating, costume planning, party scheduling, and cupcake-baking suddenly took over our schedules. Cameron and I, believing in the fundamental right of every seven-year-old, in spite of his parents' problems, to experience an old-fashioned, small-town Halloween, set aside our daggers and declared an unspoken truce.

The holiday fell on a Friday and I spent the morning setting up a makeshift gallows in the front yard by looping nooses over the lowest limb of one of the oaks and hanging a couple of dummies dressed up as Regulators in colonial tricorns, waistcoats, and knee stockings. When Wiley got home from school he and I decorated the front porch with jack-o'-lanterns and the door with a life-size drawing of Frankenstein.

Later that evening we attended a party for the kids at St. Stephen's. The children busied themselves apple-bobbing and had a quick dinner of hot dogs and potato chips. "Russ is having a little service in the graveyard to send you all on your way," Cam said. She was due at Sassafras to assist Ruffin Strudwick with his haunted house. "Don't let Wiley out of your sight." I assured her I wouldn't and returned to touching up the kids' ghoulish makeup in the downstairs bathroom.

Wiley and Malcolm appeared at the door to ask when we were leaving. "Soon," I said.

I touched up Wiley's wolf nose and Malcolm's vampire's eyes and told them to wait for me at the cemetery entrance. "I'll be along in a few minutes." A few more kids passed through on their way to the service. As I applied pancake makeup to the face of a miniature Phantom of the

Opera, a sexy witch with green skin, red lips, and a tight black dress stuck her head in the door and asked, "Is this the makeup room?"

Recognizing the smoky voice of Lisa Price, I said, "I didn't know you were an Episcopalian."

"I'm not. Russ lets me come play surrogate mom. Nathan's working as usual, so I'm on my own tonight. How about you? Staying busy?"

"This looks like my last one," I said, patting the Phantom on his head.

"How's the pooch?" Lisa asked.

"Hanging in there," I replied. "She gets the staples out next week."

"Poor thing."

The Phantom's mother retrieved her son and gave Lisa the once-over before leaving.

"It's a miracle Flappy survived," I said, putting away my tools. "Cameron's a great dog mommy."

"She sounds like a saint."

"I wouldn't go that far." I returned charcoal sticks to the cigar box, suddenly feeling disloyal for divulging any hint of our recent estrangement. I washed my hands in the sink. "How have you been?"

"Fine, I guess. I love Halloween."

"Oh, were you here?"

"You didn't see me but I saw you. I was serving punch in the kitchen. Orchestrating the *pinata* for the little ones. Vicarious mothering. Russ is a sweetheart for letting me help out with the party."

"You're not a member of St. Stephen's?" I inquired a bit redundantly.

"No." She laughed. "Hence my disguise. I'm too controversial. Even for Episcopalians. They'd die if they knew the Dildo King's wife was serving punch to their kiddies. Speaking of the Dildo King, Nathan wants to meet you. He'll probably drop by Ruffin's later on."

"I look forward to meeting him."

"Russ was upstairs touting the marvelous monster makeup of Pick Cantrell so I dashed down to say 'hello' and retouch my witch makeup before heading over to Strudwick's. I'm one of his army of haints."

"So's Cameron," I replied. "She got drafted. You'll see her over there."

"Will you be there?"

"Later. I'm going to take Wiley on his rounds. I'll drop by afterward to see the famous Strudwick haunted house."

"It's wild, all theater and pageantry. You know Ruffin." She leaned toward the mirror and touched up her makeup. "Pick, do you have any more greasepaint left in that box of yours? I ran out of green." I dug into the cigar box and retrieved my well-used bottle of green.

"Would you apply it for me?" she asked. "I left my contacts at home and can't see a thing."

"Sure."

"Shall I sit on your throne of the anointed?"

"Be my guest."

She sat down on the toilet seat cover. I situated myself on the folding chair, and trying not to notice the way the slit of Lisa's skirt bared her thigh, dabbed green paint along her cheekbones and added blush to her cheeks. The intimacy of applying makeup to a grown woman made me feel a little uncomfortable.

"So you don't go for the warty nosed, wrinkly witch look, huh?" I asked, trying to keep the conversation light.

She smiled. "I always identified with Glenda in *The Wizard of Oz*, although I wouldn't say I'm necessarily good. I'm still vain enough to want to look sexy in my Halloween costume."

I reached into my box for more paint. "Well, you certainly give that sickly pallor a certain charm. You look quite fetching, even green."

"Why, thank you, sir," Lisa drawled in her best Scarlett O'Hara voice. "You're going to make me blush."

"Wouldn't want to turn that carefully cultivated green a rusty orange-brown." I applied the green around her temples while avoiding looking into her emerald-green eyes.

"Pick, while you're at it, would you mind touching up my lipstick?" she asked, glancing at herself in a hand mirror.

I smoothed her temples with my thumb. "Sure, I can do that." I was trying to seem nonchalant as she handed me the tube of cherry lipstick she retrieved from her dress pocket. Outside in the graveyard Russ and some of the parents were performing a skit about King Saul and the Witch of Endor. Instead of being upstairs with them, I was easing out onto very thin ice. Working with professional precision on Lisa's full, perfectly shaped lips, I felt a stirring in my loins. I sensed her watching me but I kept my eyes on my work. She was extraordinarily beautiful even through the green makeup. I steadied my left elbow and she shifted in her seat to accommodate me. I felt the alarming press of her full bosom against my elbow.

"Your hand is shaking," Lisa said.

"D.T.'s."

"I thought artists had to be steady of hand."

"Not me. This is how I get my patented Cantrellesque squiggly line." I capped the lipstick. "There."

"Pick," she said, gazing into the hand mirror again, "don't you think I should have a missing tooth? All witches, even fetching ones, could use a gapped tooth."

I hesitated for a moment. She handed me a small pencil she had in her pocket. "Use this eyeliner. It should take." Outside Russ was leading everyone in the singing of the old children's hymn, "I Sing a Song of the Saints of God."

I lifted her chin and she gave me a perfect white smile. I darkened one of her incisors and smoothed it with a finger. Lisa nipped my finger and giggled mischievously. Then she enveloped my finger between her full lips, and looked me directly in the eye. The effect was electric.

Flustered, I plucked my finger from her mouth. She held my gaze. Just then I heard Wiley calling to me from the stairwell, "Dad! C'mon, let's go. It's time to trick-or-treat. Everybody's in the parking lot."

Lisa held out her hand for her eyeliner. "You'd better get going, Dad."

"I guess so," I said, fumbling the remaining sticks and colors back into the box.

Lisa adjusted her witch's hat in the mirror, then gave me a smile from the door. "Well, how do I look?"

My heart was beating and I was waiting for the tumescence in my jeans to go away before I stood to leave. "Great!" I coughed.

"Now I have an original Pick Cantrell! Thanks." She kissed me on the cheek, then rubbed off the lipstick smear. "See you at Ruffin's, right?"

"Yeah, right."

Lisa disappeared into the hallway and Wiley the Wolfman appeared at the door. "C'mon, Dad! Bring the flashlight. It's dark out."

Flashlights blazing, Russ and I led a pack of about a dozen goblins across the bridge and meadow and through the woods to Oaklawn. I was grateful for the chaperoning duties, which required little of me but my presence. The encounter with Lisa had left me rattled. Crossing the meadow I glimpsed through the trees the headlights of a vehicle pulling up our drive.

"Look, Dad!" said Wiley. "Trick-or-treaters! Maybe we'll get some tonight after all." But as we made our way through the woods the red glow of the vehicle's taillights disappeared down the drive. Tires squealed when rubber hit the pavement. Flappy barked mournfully from the house as our band of costumed revelers spilled from the trees onto the lawn.

The house looked spooky in the darkness with the lynched Regulators swinging in the breeze and the lit jack-o'-lanterns grinning from the front porch. Creepy music and moans emanated mysteriously from the jambox I had hidden behind a bale of hay. Wiley and the other kids, after pausing to take in the eerie panorama, attacked the bowl of treats I had left on the porch. I went inside and checked on Flappy, who was confined to a box in the kitchen, and found her uncomfortable but otherwise OK. When I returned more kids were hiking up the hill and I could hear more coming up the street behind them.

Wiley and the others were running around on the lawn urging us to hurry up and come on. Russ offered to take the kids on ahead while I stuck around to deal with trick-or-treaters. I could catch up with them later or we could meet at Sassafras at eight o'clock if we didn't cross paths before then. After the encounter with Lisa I needed some time to myself.

Russ and the church kids disappeared up the street and a group of six or seven revelers ambled up the driveway toward us, shouting, "Trick or treat! Happy Halloween!" Despite their festive costumes there was something different about these kids.

A familiar voice in a Freddy Krueger mask called, "So this is the house everybody's gossipin' about."

"Buzz! You son of a gun!" I said, genuinely happy to see him. "Put that mask back on. You're gonna scare the children."

Buzz laughed, indicating a slim young woman wearing a Tweety Bird mask. "You remember Violet, my youngest, don't you? These are her special ed kids." He scanned the Oaklawn acreage. "Good Lord, Pick, you sure got your hands full around here. This is a sight more lawn to mow than Mama Lucy's, that's for sure."

Violet spotted a child trying to climb the Regulator tree as the others finished raiding the bowl of treats. "Dad, we better get going. I'm not going to be able to restrain 'em much longer."

"Where y'all going?" I asked.

"Just gonna hit a few more houses before we head back," said Buzz.

"Hold on—I'll come along!" I said. "I've got to catch up with Wiley."

I left a help-yourself note for trick-or-treaters next to the candy bowl and caught up with the pack near the bottom of the driveway. We proceeded up Bennehan Street past the new county office building and the old jail across from the courthouse, where the two men accused of assaulting the gas station attendant had recently been sentenced to twenty years in prison.

Buzz said, "Last time I was over here was when Talbert got arraigned and did time at the state pen for grand theft auto. Damn fool stole the car in broad daylight. Mama Lucy sent me over here with a certified check to get him out before he went to trial."

"Good Lord."

"Mama Lucy'd do anything for her grandyoung'uns," Violet said. "Even the sorry ones."

"Especially the sorry ones," said Buzz. "Went into her savings. All that support money Granddaddy gave her over the years. Talbert said he'd pay her back but I don't think he ever did. But he sure spent time in that old jailhouse yonder."

As we walked from house to house watching Violet's charges swarm like locusts upon each well-lit stoop with their bags in tow and eager faces, I marveled at her unceasing student-teacher patience. She tended to the children like a friendly sheep dog, with boundless energy and stamina. Buzz too had a naturalness in his approach with these challenging kids. He talked to them and disciplined them without the slightest sign of condescension. I was moved by the decency that flowed between Buzz and his daughter, from one generation to the next.

We marched up and down the next few streets and finally caught up with Russ, Malcolm, and Wiley in a neighborhood off Cheshire not far from our house. Wiley wanted to continue trick-or-treating with the Fitch twins and their father. I told them to meet me at Sassafras at eight o'clock, and Buzz, Violet, and I headed off for the haunted house, kids in tow.

By the time we got there the children were exhausted and a little apprehensive. Sassafras had been transformed into a real haunted house. The long tree-lined drive was decorated with jack-o'-lanterns and crowded with adults and children. Organ music emanated from an upstairs window. Ghostly female figures in diaphanous shrouds, Cameron among them, rollerbladed across the front porch, weeping and wailing and gnashing their teeth. Ruffin himself, dressed like a

Confederate officer and ghoulishly made up in white pancake with dark circles around his eyes, greeted visitors at the door with his entourage of wailing zombie mourners.

Outside, Lisa perched on a swing, her witch costume adjusted to reveal more spike-heeled pulchritude. A vampiress in a low-cut dress passed us carrying a plate of cookies, bade us hello, and urged us to join the party.

Buzz stared after the shift and sway of her dress. "Who was that?"

"I don't know," I said.

"I wish I did," Buzz murmured.

"Go talk to her," Violet said, then turned to me. "He never goes out, but women adore him. All my friends ask about him."

"They want to set me up with their divorced mamas. No thank you." Violet left to attend to some of the younger kids who were crying, afraid to enter the haunted house.

"Vampirella there don't look like nobody's mama," I said. "Go say hello."

"Naw, Pick," Buzz said. "We better get these young'uns on back to Saxapahaw. You go ahead on."

Fretful kids notwithstanding, I could feel Buzz's reluctance as he took in the opulence of the house. The diffidence I sensed was the old "lint-head" feeling of intimidation in the face of wealth and privilege, a feeling still alive in my generation of Cantrells—even in the Cantrell who had identified for me the Southern Disease. We said our goodbyes.

Inside the house was a series of dioramas illustrating the Seven Deadly Sins acted out by Ruffin's friends, each tableau in a different room. I moved past Lust, Sloth and Vanity. Many of the performers and guests were loaded from the green punch bubbling in a bowl of dry ice. I had seen little of Strudwick's house at the September party and was considering making the tour when Ruffin waylaid me and asked, "Pickard Cantrell, where on earth is your costume?"

"I'm afraid this is it."

"Not very imaginative. After our last gathering I was afraid you'd show up as a pugilist."

"Sorry to disappoint you, Ruffin."

"Don't be. I'm always delighted when we don't have to call the cops. Although I did expect something a little more festive from a political cartoonist. Where's your creative spirit?"

"I figured you have enough for both of us, Ruffin." I tried to sound jovial, as I moved to excuse myself.

Ruffin, giddy with the spirit of the occasion and dying to share a tantalizing bit of fresh local gossip, glanced over his shoulder and whispered, "Speaking of cops, did you hear there was another break-in? At Burnside. Third historic home in town since August. It's enough to make me start locking my back door."

"Thanks for the tip," I said as I turned to clear out, but Ruffin halted me and tapped another man who was talking on a cell phone on the shoulder. "You're not leaving us, are you, Nathan?"

The Dildo King returned the cell phone to his breast pocket. "I have to go. Business. Don't worry, Ruffin. Lisa's got her Beemer. She's not abandoning you."

Ruffin introduced us and I saw a glimmer of recognition in the man's dark eyes. He was older than I, fiftyish or thereabouts, short and beefy, with long sideburns, and had camouflaged his balding pate with a comb-over. He was dressed impeccably in an Armani suit and tie.

"Pardon my bluntness," he said to me, "but I'm a cut-to-the-chase kind of guy. Y'know, it's a shame a man of your gifts is in such a position where your talent goes to waste. Has Lisa spoken to you?"

"She said you wanted to talk to me."

"My wife may look like a bimbo but she's a good judge of people. She has a state-of-the-art bullshit detector and she likes you. If you've got a minute I'd like to run an idea by you." He turned to our host. "Ruffin, if you'll excuse us, this is private."

"Of course." Ruffin, stunned at being excluded from a conversation at his own party, slinked away.

"Listen," Nathan said, ushering me into the shadows of Ruffin's porch. "I don't know anything about your job prospects but I have an idea that I think could make money for both of us."

"I'm listening."

"Do you know anything about the AIDS epidemic?"

"Only what I read. And I've had some friends who died."

"A common problem for these patients in advanced stages is incontinence."

I nodded, curious to know where this was leading.

"And, of course, gay men are the funniest people on the planet. Like Ruffin. Wicked, scathing wit. Yet this whole thing, this tragedy and plague mentality, has gotten so somber, so heavy. My idea is this." He looked around again to make sure nobody was listening, and whispered, "Funny diapers."

"Excuse me?"

"I want to manufacture diapers with cartoons on them for adults," he said, as if he were teaching an especially slow student. "Incontinence is one of the most humiliating aspects of the disease. Adults are mortified about soiling themselves. I say make light of it. Scatalogical humor. Incontinence jokes and cartoons. I think there's a real market. For cancer patients, too. Distribution through clinics and sex ed. Are you with me?"

I tried to imagine my work decorating Depends. "I don't know."

"Well, don't think too long. Somebody's going to make a fortune on this. I've got the marketing know-how. You've got the humor and drawing ability. Let's team up. Here's my card. Call me. I always wanted to work with cartoonists. I tried to license cartoon characters for condoms once—Snoopy condoms, Garfield condoms, Calvin and Hobbes condoms—but I couldn't get past their syndicates. I always figured if I could get to the cartoonists themselves they'd see the opportunity." He seemed to sense that he'd overplayed his hand and backed off. "But that's a subject for another day. Anyway, call me." He grabbed his cell phone and headed for the street, punching in numbers.

I was moving back inside when a wail arose behind me. Turning, I saw Ruffin, Cameron, and an army of goblins swinging back into action for the benefit of a large crowd coming up the path. A ghoulish butler with an eyeball dangling down his cheek was talking to a pretty ballerina next to a casket by the front door. The ghoul was Roland Jameson, the honcho from WeltanCom, who had flirted with Cameron at the last Strudwick party. The scantily clad vampiress who had so bewitched Buzz was standing with a group in the hallway. She turned to me with her black tresses and bloody fangs and said conspiratorially, "Are you ready for our talk on Sunday?"

I stared at her blankly.

"It's me, Sandy."

"Sandy Murphy! No way!" I sputtered, totally disoriented. "You sure fooled me."

"It's the hair. Nobody recognizes me."

"No," I said, trying not to stare at her decolletage. "You look . . . good. You should dress like this more often."

"We academic types seldom get a chance to play dress-up. I try to take advantage."

"I'd say the dress takes advantage of you."

After a few minutes, I excused myself and continued my tour of the house. Ruffin had decorated the place with the finest antiques of the period in which Sassafras was built—Aubusson chairs, Louis XIV sideboards and tables, Thomas Day mantelpieces, and mounted over the living room fireplace, an original Gilbert Stuart portrait of Thomas Jefferson.

"Pick Cantrell, right?" Standing behind me, smiling warmly and extending his hand, was a pirate. His tricorn was marked with a skull and crossbones, and there was a stuffed parrot perched on his shoulder. "I'm Franklin Webb. We met at Ruffin's last big do."

"I remember. How are you, Franklin?"

"Fine. I was just taking in some of the family heirlooms myself. That Jefferson portrait used to hang on the wall at Oaklawn, you know."

"Really? Your family lived there at one time, too, am I right? I suppose they collected some great art."

"My ancestors did, yes. Before they fell on hard times and all the money went to the Strudwick side of the family. My great-grandfather, DeWitt Webb, was the last to live there."

"Spencer Webb's father?"

"Yes, the owner of the Bellevue mill. Spencer, my grandfather, grew up at Oaklawn but never inherited it. Nor the business. He and his father, Dewitt, had a falling out. What made you buy the place?"

I told him how Cameron and I fell in love with photos of the house and bought it after my trouble at the paper but how I was now discovering family ties to the town I never knew existed. I didn't even know this man, but I instinctively liked him, and there was something about his easy manner and sad eyes that made me feel comfortable opening up to him.

"It's a beautiful place," he replied.

"Yeah, the more I learn about it the more I wonder if there wasn't some genetic tug transmitted visually. I don't know. Tell me, what happened between DeWitt Webb and Spencer?"

"It's a little sketchy. A lot of speculation. But it was ugly. Classically Oedipal. The younger was close to his mother and his father was an asshole. The daughter was more like the old man and married someone just like him. Ruffin's grandfather. The asshole legacy continued even if the name didn't."

"But what happened?"

"I'm not sure. My father was a historian, but British history, Cromwell, Church of England, that sort of thing. He stayed away from the family story. Too sensitive, I guess. Wounds were too fresh. Didn't want to stir up resentments. I grew up in Boston where my father taught and came down here to go to law school at Chapel Hill and decided to stay. What I know I discovered on my own."

I asked him what he knew about the Eno massacre.

"There was a riot of some sort at the mill. DeWitt Webb panicked and sent in a lot of trigger-happy deputized locals along with the National Guard to put down the strike and a lot of people got hurt. Several killed. It was a huge embarrassment. The other mill owners were furious with him. Some even questioned his sanity. He had just lost a child. It was a crib death. Probably what they call SIDS today. It was a boy. He suspected the union was behind it. Thought they smothered the baby. Who knows? Like I said he was a little crazy with grief. Blamed my grandfather for it somehow."

I recalled Mama Lucy telling me about her conversation with Spencer the day Annie Laura was killed. Franklin continued, "I always suspected Spencer was sympathetic to the union. He'd gone off to UNC in the early twenties and was expected to return to take over the family business. But he was an intellectual, and he fell under the influence of friends like the playwright Paul Green, and Dr. Frank Porter Graham, the great humanitarian who later became president of the university. I think Graham became the father Spencer never had. My grandfather went to law school at Yale but instead of coming home and running the mill he stayed up north to work in a law firm in New York. He returned to Eno briefly during the strike but disagreed with his father's handling of it. Not long after that he was disinherited. Bates Strudwick, Austin's daddy, who had been working for DeWitt as his plant superintendent and married his daughter, was there to step in. And the rest is history. It was tense for a while between us Webbs and the Strudwicks. Spencer's progeny all went into education. The Strudwicks tended the family money. Until Ruffin. When he got famous he reached out to the Webbs, and that's why I get invited to his parties."

"Decent of him."

"I suppose. It's always nice when you can lord your good fortune over your relatives and appear gracious doing so. Also, it really irritates his father."

"My grandmother knew your grandfather," I said. "She was a millworker in the thirties. She met him at a dry-goods store when they were kids. She thought highly of him."

"Well, I'll be damned."

"Oh, Franklin," Ruffin shouted from the porch. "Can you grab some dry ice for the punch?"

"My master's voice." Franklin smiled and started toward the kitchen. "Perhaps I could meet your grandmother sometime."

"I'll mention it."

I wandered out by the swing hoping to see Lisa, but the swing was empty. Cameron and Ruffin were talking on the porch. I gazed up at the clouds moving across the harvest moon, and prayed that Wiley would show up soon so we could go home. A low intimate voice chastized me from behind the tree. "I was wondering when you'd show up."

I saw the red glow of the cigarette before I saw her. "I want to apologize for what happened at the church," Lisa said, stepping into the light from the porch. "I hope you don't think me a wanton woman." She stubbed out her cigarette and tossed the butt into Ruffin's boxwoods.

"No, it just caught me off guard."

"I don't know what's gotten into me lately." She retrieved another cigarette from her purse and slipped it between her sensuous lips. "I'm a little freer with my sexuality than most people. Not to say I'm promiscuous. But if I like someone, which I hardly ever do, I let 'em know."

"I-I'm married," I said.

"So am I," she said, her face suddenly illuminated by the lighter flame.

"Happily," I said, wishing it were true.

"It was probably the season. Full moon and all." She took a long drag on her cigarette and exhaled slowly.

"Let's be friends," I said to break the silence.

"I thought we already were."

"Look, you're an incredibly attractive and sexy woman . . ."

"I know," she said, with no trace of irony or pride.

"I've already got enough problems."

"I would never want to be a problem for you, Pick. I like your wife. And more importantly, I respect her. I'm not the kind of woman who goes after other women's husbands. At least I don't like to think of myself that way. I just connect with you."

"What about your husband?"

"Ah, Nathan. That's about something else," she said, moving around to the front of the tree and slipping into the swing. "Our marriage is something I need very much and would never jeopardize. Believe me. But I think I know where you are and what you're going through. If you want more from me, I'm available."

"I—I hear you," I said, regarding the voluptuous figure in the swing. The breeze caught her skirt and lifted it up over her thighs in the moonlight. I felt a tingle.

"Did Nathan tell you his business proposition?"

"Yes."

"Be careful. It's his way of regaining the upper hand. He wants to incorporate you. Like a one-celled organism. It's his defense. He senses I like you."

"I think he could tell I wasn't interested in the work."

"Good." She pushed back resuming her role as the witch on a swing. "You're better than that."

I glanced back at the house and saw the performance was on break. I excused myself and went to check in with Cameron.

As I approached the porch Cam asked, "Pick, where's Wiley?"

"With Malcolm and the Fitch twins."

"I thought you were staying with him." She was angry but I also saw a trace of fear in her eyes for Wiley. When Cameron was a girl she and her best friend were riding bikes when a drunk driver sideswiped her friend and killed her. Adult supervision was no guarantee against such tragedy but I knew a deep chord of primal anxiety had been struck. Maybe Cameron was right and I had been remiss, but I wanted to reassure her.

"He's fine, Cam. Fitch's responsible and Russ said it was safe."

"I don't care what Russ thinks," Cam snapped. "I left him with you."

I noticed for the first time dark circles under Cam's eyes and wondered if she was getting enough sleep. Her work was turning out to be more stressful that she had anticipated. "Don't worry. He'll be here at eight."

"It's eight-fifteen."

"Shit."

I jogged to Russ's house but nobody was home. My irritation shifting into alarm, I sprinted through the churchyard and across the meadow, retrieved the Volvo from Oaklawn and cruised the Eno streets, searching the faces of lone children moving from house to house. I pulled up to a band of spooks and goblins and rolled down my window and said, "Do any of you kids know Wiley Cantrell?"

Negatives all around. The night was growing damp and fog was settling in. A light mist was falling and the crowds of trick-or-treaters were thinning. I retraced the path we had taken that evening and asked a group of children, "Have any of you seen Wiley Cantrell?" Finally one of Wiley's classmates, a pretty young girl named Carla who was dressed like a fairy princess, said she had seen him and Malcolm Draper and the Fitch twins over on Tryon Street about a half hour ago.

"Which way were they headed?" I asked.

Her mullet-haired father with his Metallica T-shirt, exhaling cigarette smoke, pointed in the direction of the West End. "Towards Hillsborough Street."

I scoured the streets, high beams blaring, feeling more and more frantic. Wiley was nowhere to be found. Soon my dark imagination started to kick in. What if Fitch, trying to keep up with his twins, lost track of Wiley? What if something happened to him? What if Wiley was right now wandering the dark streets of the West End, lost and frightened?

After retracing my earlier route and combing the likely neighborhoods I headed over to the Drapers. Lorraine came to the door still dressed in her Raggedy Ann costume. She looked surprised to see me. "Is Wiley here?" I asked.

Then Malcolm rounded the corner, his mouth full of candy and his face covered with chocolate. "His cousins picked him up and said they would take him home."

"Was there a young woman and some kids with him?"

"No sir, it was two men in a truck."

My mind raced. "What were their names, Malcolm? Do you remember their names?"

"No, but one of them was chewing tobacco."

My heart catapulted into my throat. Jerry and Talbert. Jesus Christ. So that's who I saw cruising through Oaklawn earlier. I jumped into the Volvo and raced back to Oaklawn. The house was empty. I hopped back into the car and tore up and down the streets, shooting past thinning ranks of revelers.

"Watch it, mister!" a chaperone shouted at me from the sidewalk. "There's kids out here!"

I slowed down and circled the block where Talbert and Jerry had picked up Wiley. Nothing. As I turned onto Bennehan Street to make another sweep I caught a glimpse of taillights in our driveway. "Please let it be him," I prayed.

When I pulled up there was a pickup truck parked in front of the porch and Wiley, still in his Wolfman costume, was standing on the steps. Talbert, looking up at the second story of the house, stood beside him. Jerry sat on the hood of the truck drinking a bottle of Mad Dog 20/20. My relief turned instantly to anger.

I slammed the car into park, and threw open the door. "Where the hell have you been, Wiley!"

"Look, Dad," said Wiley, clutching his bag of treats in one hand and holding out a plastic toy with the other. "I got a Happy Meal."

"Hope you don't mind, cuz," drawled Talbert. "He said he was thirsty so we took him to McDonald's."

"I got sick, Daddy."

"Puked in the truck," Jerry added. "All that candy. Had to stop at the Shell station and hose down the floormat."

"I was chewing tobacco," explained Wiley.

"He asked for a chaw and Jerry give it to 'im," Talbert explained. "Boy's gotta learn sometime."

Jerry sipped his cheap wine. "I tole 'im not to swallow."

"Wiley," I said, "go inside."

"I wanted to show Mom my Wolverine."

"Get in the house. Now!"

Wiley slunk inside with his new toy and bag of treats. Talbert said, "You ain't mad at us, are you, cuz?"

I could feel my jaw muscles clenching and my response leaked out between gritted teeth. "I just wish I had known where my son was, Talbert. I've been looking all over town for him."

"We thought we was helpin' you out, didn't we, Jerry? Y'know, you shouldn't let a boy his age roam around at night without some adult supervision. Even in a safe town like Eno they's a lot of nuts out there."

"Speaking of which, what are you two doing in Eno?" I asked.

"Just headin' out to meet a buddy at the Gaslight out by the Interstate. They celebrate Halloween in style. Half-price drinks and they bring in girls from their other clubs and all. While we was in the area I thought we'd drop by and check out this big new house ever'-body's talkin' about." He indicated Oaklawn with a grand sweep of his hand. "This is high cotton, man."

Even from several feet away I could smell the alcohol on his breath. "How did you find Wiley?"

"When nobody was home we figured y'all went out tricky treatin' so we just drove around 'til I spotted him."

"How did you pick him out in a crowd of kids in costumes?" I was starting to sound like a prosecutor cross-examinining a witness, but I didn't care. I was furious.

"Aw, we know family, ain't that right, Jerry?"

"At night? In costumes?"

Jerry's eyes narrowed. "You sound right ill, cuz. You don't want your boy around his family, is that how it is?"

"Hell, we didn't mean to upset you, Pickard," Talbert said.

"Forget it. Look, I'd give you the tour, but Cameron's not back yet and it's past Wiley's bedtime."

"That's all right. We'll just come back some other time and see the Ponderosa, won't we, Jer'?"

Jerry grinned. "You bet."

"Oh, by the way, Pickard, I got somethin' for you." Talbert pulled a crumpled envelope from his back pocket and handed it to me. "Mama Lucy said you was interested in this."

I opened the envelope. Inside, folded carelessly and damp from the humidity and Talbert's sweat, was the letter Mama Lucy had written FDR.

"Ain't she somethin'?" Jerry said. "Mama Lucy writin' the president of the United States like they was pen pals or somethin'."

"What you want with somethin' like this?" Talbert said.

"I was just about to ask you the same thing, Talbert. You're the one who took it."

"I was curious. Like you."

Another car pulled into the shadowed driveway and cut the lights. The passenger got out and moved around to the driver's side where the two engaged in conversation.

"Whooee!" Jerry said. "Who's that?"

"Whoever it is drives a Ferrari," Talbert said.

It was Cameron. I could just barely make out her white gown as she stood in the darkness at the driver's side window. I wondered who was behind the wheel of the Ferrari. I got the same queasy feeling I had when I spotted her Volvo at the Carolina Club.

"Well," Talbert said, "we better git on home. Nice plantation, cuz.

Say howdy to the little lady for us. I'll tell Mama Lucy I give you her letter." They hopped back into their truck and revved the engine. Talbert grinned at me and took a slug from Jerry's bottle of MD 20/20. Then he gunned the gas, shooting up gravel as the truck careened past Cameron, and nearly sideswiped the sleek black sportscar backing into the street. Cameron stared at them incredulously, then trudged up the driveway, the train of her costume wedding dress dragging through the dirt behind her. Red taillights faded in the distance.

"Where's Wiley?" she called to me. "And who the hell was that?"

"I was just about to ask you the same question," I said. We stared at each other a second, then turned and headed for the house.

Cameron did not attend my talk at St. Stephen's on Sunday morning. When she learned that Talbert and Jerry had "baby-sat" her son on Halloween night and taught him how to chew tobacco she was furious. I had my own questions about the mysterious Ferrari but my battered pride and embarrassment over the lapse with Wiley, even if it wasn't entirely my fault, prevented me from bringing it up.

The St. Stephen's parking lot was full and the fellowship hall packed when Wiley and I arrived. I immediately regretted not preparing more for the occasion. Russ himself was beaming and said this was the largest audience he'd ever drawn for one of his Sunday colloquia.

After Wiley slipped off to Sunday school Sandy and I huddled in the outside hallway to go over the order of our talk. My father tapped me on my shoulder. He looked tired and a little apprehensive with my aunts at his side.

"I should have called," he explained sheepishly. "We had to come over this weekend to deal with Mama Lucy."

"What's wrong?"

"Lily found her passed out on the sofa yesterday afternoon with the gas oven on. We can't go on like this. Lily and I are taking her to Shady Grove tomorrow."

"Does she know?"

"We're just going to show up with an ambulance in the morning. It's better not to give her time to think about it." Just then Russ approached the podium and Sandy and I took seats up front facing the audience.

As Russ made the introductions and stragglers filed in Sandy and I scanned the crowd for familiar faces. Right up front were Ruffin, Austin, and Merlie Strudwick. Franklin Webb was there, too, along with others

I had met at Ruffin Strudwick's parties. An elderly group of Bellevue mill veterans and interviewees from Sandy's oral history project were also sitting up front, looking out of place in the upscale church surroundings.

Buzz was there, too, beaming in a coat and tie, seated next to Violet. Beside them was a disheveled, disconsolate-looking man who looked familiar but whom I couldn't place until he leaned over to speak to Buzz and I realized it was Wallace Cantrell. What on earth, I wondered, was my cousin, the unemployed drunk from the reunion, doing here? I didn't know Wallace very well but he didn't strike me as a history buff. An older gentleman seated behind my two cousins smiled at me. It was Dr. Levin. Mama Lucy would be disappointed she missed him.

I was surprised and a little discomfited when I spotted Lisa in the back row. Even dressed down in jeans and a sweater, and wearing no makeup, she still stood out from the crowd like a peacock among sparrows. She was doing her best to blend into the crowd. Since our Halloween night encounters I had been unable to get her out of my mind and her presence was hampering my ability to concentrate.

Sandy led off with a masterful presentation, breezy and informative, on the history and conditions of the cotton mill culture in the South in the early part of the century and revealed how things like the short flapper hemlines of the 1920s brought on the hard times, including the harsh stretch-out conditions that led to the General Textile Strike of 1934 and Eno's part in the strike. Her personal charm and passionate enthusiasm for the topic transformed what could have been a snooze of a lecture into a delightful entertainment. She possessed the unique talent of all great teachers to appear, no matter how familiar the subject, as though she were discovering it for the very first time. And she put the stories I had recently heard in a context that helped me understand the events in a larger framework as well.

She described the coming of the New Deal and the rise of radio, with Roosevelt's fireside chats and his repeated urgings to ordinary people to write to him, which resulted in the remarkable letter-writing campaign Mama Lucy participated in. And when the promises of the New Deal raised expectations, only to be dashed, how it led to the uprising of 'thirty-four, the largest strike in our nation's history.

"Half a million textile workers across the South went out on strike, along with a goodly number up north, paralyzing the textile industry, and stunning the mill barons, who responded swiftly and brutally. It was all over in three bloody weeks and one of the worst episodes took place right here in Eno. Pick's grandmother was witness to it," she said, then concluded with "but I'll let him tell you about that."

I told them what I knew about Mama Lucy, how she was bayoneted and blacklisted and paraded around town in a wagon, but how the day she saw her best friend, Annie Laura Gaskins, shot down in Eno with all the others was the day she got involved in the strike. At Russ's urging, I told them too what I knew about the Burlington Dynamite Plot. Sandy talked about the mass amnesia that had taken over after the incident and how difficult it was for her to find people who were willing to discuss the strike, much less the Eno massacre. The audience was riveted, and when we finished the discussion there was an eager outpouring of questions and comments.

Not surprisingly, Austin Strudwick was not pleased with our characterizing what happened in Eno as a "massacre" and denounced our speeches as inflammatory left-wing anti-business propaganda. He defended how workers were treated in the old days, rhapsodizing about the Christmas gifts and Thanksgiving turkeys and Halloween pumpkins distributed to mill children during the holidays. He talked about how the mill owners enforced a morality that was good for the community as a whole, how alcoholism wasn't tolerated, how in the old days one owner used to walk through the villages and enforce lights out at eleven o'clock. He explained how churchgoing was encouraged, that the mill owners, though by no means perfect, more often than not expressed a healthy concern for their workers' spiritual and physical well-being.

"What about brown lung?" one of the mill veterans wheezed. "What about the physical well-being of their lungs?"

Austin bristled but otherwise ignored the questioner. Sandy took the opportunity to wrest the floor from Austin and gave a general description of the effects of cotton dust on the lungs and how bysinnosis, the formal name for brown lung, was not recognized by the enlightened management of the textile industry until as late as the 1970s.

"Poppycock!" Austin exploded. "Communist propaganda!"

"Oh, Daddy, please." Ruffin sighed. "Give it a rest."

Finally Russ thanked the speakers and invited anyone who wanted to continue the conversation to stick around for coffee and cookies.

Afterward, Sandy and I were surrounded by clusters of well-wishers. Lisa slipped off without saying hello and I was relieved. Several people had brought in some of my old cartoon collections for me to sign, a bittersweet reminder of what I no longer did for a living.

Franklin Webb stopped by and apologized for Austin's tirade. "He's just defending our forebears, the so-called enlightened management who used to dwell at Oaklawn."

My father pushed through the crowd and told me that he and my aunts were leaving. We'd talk later about Mama Lucy.

Dr. Levin took advantage of an opening to congratulate me on my speech and ask about my grandmother. "I was hoping I might see her here," he said. "How's she doing?"

"The family's decided to put her into Shady Grove," I told him.

"Your grandmother's got more spirit and spunk than physical strength. Her spirit's outlasted her protoplasm. It makes it tougher. Will she go?"

"Not willingly, I'm sure. What would you do?"

"I don't know."

As the crowd thinned out I spotted Buzz and Violet hovering near the exit.

"Nice talk, Pickard," Buzz said. "Mama Lucy'd be proud. Where's Cameron?"

"She wasn't feeling well," I lied. "Buzz, have you met Sandra Murphy?"

"No, but I sure enjoyed her talk," said the shy but courtly Buzz.

"She was the Vampirella on Halloween," I whispered to him as someone pulled Sandy away.

"Oh." He did a double-take, checking out Sandy's outfit, then said, "Speaking of Halloween, I heard you had a run-in with the boys."

"Word travels fast."

"Hey, if you don't mind, Wallace would like to speak to you." Our cousin was standing by himself smoking a cigarette. "He actually sobered up for your talk."

I felt perplexed and wary. I didn't know Wallace but he had not struck me as the most stable of my distant cousins. But if he had made the effort to come here, the least I could do was talk to him.

"Hey, listen," said Buzz, "we're gonna show Violet the sights. We'll be back shortly to pick him up. Send him on around to the parking lot when y'all're done."

Just then a little old lady I'd seen talking to my father earlier and her husband came up. She slipped her hand into mine. "I didn't want to speak up in the meetin'," she whispered, "but I knew your mama. She had a wonderful sense of humor, just like you. You look just like her.

You've got her eyes. I worked as a nurse on the eighth floor of Alamance General. She didn't belong there. She took care of everyone else on the ward. You should know that. I saw in the paper when she died and I was sorry I couldn't make the funeral."

She smiled and squeezed my hand. "God bless you." Then her husband tugged her away and, before I could gather my thoughts to respond, someone else was asking me to sign a cartoon book.

Wallace dropped his cigarette butt in a Styrofoam coffee cup and walked over. "I hear Talbert an' 'em's been botherin' you like he does me."

"I can handle Talbert," I said.

"I just thought you should watch yer back, is all. You should see some of them he runs with."

"Buzz said you had something to tell me, Wallace. Was that it?"

"I heard you was askin' around about the troubles back in Lucy's day and I thought I might know something you'd be interested in."

We drifted among the gravestones in the old cemetery behind the church where the Bennehans and Ruffins and Strudwicks and Webbs and all the old families of Eno were buried. Russ was walking Sandy to her car when she spotted me and strolled over. "Pick, that grave you're standing in front of. It belongs to Duncan Bennehan, the guy who built Oaklawn. Do you know anything about him?"

"Just that he was one of the largest slaveholders in the South. One of the state's founding fathers. Laid the railroads and was on the university's board of trustees."

"Did you know Bennehan also bankrolled not only the Bellevue mill in Eno but the Burlington mills too?"

"No way," I said.

"You moved into the house your grandmother's oppressors built," said Russ.

"You know who my grampaw is, don't you?" asked Wallace when we were alone. "Bud Cantrell. Your granddaddy, Dalton Earl, was his older brother. He's gone now but Grampaw raised me when Daddy died and Mama went in the hospital. When I got older and was workin' the weave room he used to tell me about the old days in the mills. We was real close. He hated millwork, though. Didn't want me a-workin' there, but I didn't mind. That was interestin' hearin' about all that today. I ain't never heard nobody talk about it but Grandpaw. He told me your grand-maw Lucy never got over him bein' in the guard that day in Eno. She never spoke to Grampaw again the rest of his life."

"She barely spoke to my own granddaddy either."

"I know. She always held it against him, too." Wallace stubbed his cigarette out on the ancient gravestone of Duncan Bennehan. "I reckon that's why I'm here. Before he died Grampaw told me what happened that day. The day of the shooting. Inside the mill. It ain't what she thought."

Bud's heart was pounding and his brain was racing when they were ordered to set up in the second-floor windows. Sweat poured down his face from beneath his helmet. He could still feel the cool of the morning but perspiration had already pasted his uniform to his back. He wished now he'd gone to the outhouse before he left home because he had to pee bad, but there was no time now. Bud saw Dalton off in a corner arguing with one of the mill supervisors and couldn't catch his eye.

Just then a cry went up below. "They're handing out picker-sticks!" Bud looked down and saw that a fight had broken out at the end of the building in front of the windows on the first floor. Some men inside were passing bundles of picker-sticks through the window to supporters below to use for weapons. Then scuffling broke out all over the yard and Bud was transfixed by the spontaneous combustion of the crowd before him, like popcorn popping, when suddenly he heard gunfire.

Bud Cantrell was comfortable handling a rifle. He'd been putting food on the table since he was eight years old and everybody in Saxapahaw knew he was a crack shot with his trusty thirty aught six, and he was superstitious about using any other weapon. He was hardheaded and his sergeant long ago gave up arguing with him about it and let him use his own weapon instead of the government issue, figuring it just saved the taxpayers' money. Now that sergeant was yelling at him to use it.

He was scared and wanted to melt away and disappear but he couldn't. In his eagerness he had maneuvered himself to the second window from the end, over the crowd in a prime sniper position, perfect for a sharpshooter like Bud Cantrell. The confusion must have made him hesitate because the next thing he knew the sergeant was standing right behind him and screaming in his ear, "Fire, Cantrell! Fire!"

"Shoot, you son of a bitch!" The mill man next to him pointed into the crowd, and his sergeant echoed, "You heard him, soldier, do what you're told!"

Bud's heart was pounding and his mouth was dry as dust. He had shot squirrels and quail and doves and deer, but he had never shot a human being before and he didn't know if he could do it. His hands were shaking, and his gun was unsteady. Bud glanced to his right and saw Jake Satterfield squatting in the window, steadying his gun with his elbow propped up on his knee. There was a look of brute ecstasy on his face as he squeezed off round after round.

Bud moved his gunsight over the crowd. Clouds of smoke and gas drifted across the yard adding to the confusion. He sighted down upon a small, dark figure about thirty yards away. The person's face was obscured by a red bandanna. His sergeant screamed in his ear. "Shoot, Cantrell! Did you hear me, son? Open fire!"

But Bud couldn't shoot anybody in the back. He lowered the sight to aim at the person's leg but it was hard to draw a bead because the sweat in his eyes was blurring his vision.

"Do it!" screamed the mill man. "Shoot the rats!"

Bud steadied his rifle, gazing hard down the barrel, realigning his shot. Then, just as he was about to squeeze the trigger, the bandanna came off and through the sweat and the tears and the smoke and the gas the face of his target came into focus. And he froze. It was his brother's wife—Lucille Barlow Cantrell.

"Oh, my god," I interrupted. "He was aiming at Mama Lucy."

"But he couldn't pull the trigger," Wallace replied. He leveled his bloodshot gaze at me and said flatly, "Grampaw swore he never shot nobody."

REPERCUSSIONS

I trudged home from St. Stephen's in a fog. Wallace's story had introduced another discordant note to the cacophony in my mind. I had been pleasantly surprised by how well the talk had gone but I was haunted by the encounter with the woman who had taken care of my mother. I snapped out of the fog when I saw a black Ferrari parked in our driveway. I entered the house. I heard an animated conversation from the kitchen. Rounding the corner, I saw Roland Jameson seated at a table covered with papers. Cameron was leaning hard on his shoulder, pointing at one of the sheets he was scanning. Her other hand rested casually on his shoulder. A stab of jealousy shot through me like a high-voltage electrical jolt.

"Where's Wiley?" I said.

"Pick, you're home!" Cameron's smile dissolved when she saw my grim demeanor. "Wiley's watching a video. How'd it go?"

"Fine." I pretended to look for some juice in the refrigerator while trying to tamp down my fury at finding a strange man in my home alone with my wife, a man I suspected had the hots for her. This was why she hadn't come to the presentation at St. Stephen's?

"I'm sorry I missed your little talk," said Roland through his gleaming forced smile. He came over and administered another one of his bone-crushing handshakes. "But I'm on a tight schedule this week and today was the only time I could work this in."

"Work what in?" I asked, coolly.

"Roland called this morning to see if we could go over the budget for our shoot today because his board meets tomorrow morning," explained Cameron. "I invited him over to take a look."

"Our shoot?"

"Didn't I tell you?" Cam said excitedly. "Roland hired Oleander to shoot his new national spots for WeltanCom. Isn't that great?"

"Great," I said.

Jameson switched to his hearty, backslapping Jaycee mode. "Nice house you've got here, Cantrell. It reminds me of the one my wife and I renovated when we first moved down here. Went through three architects before we got it right. Who are you using, if you don't mind me asking?"

"I'm doing it myself."

"That's brave of you." He chuckled sardonically, revealing his skepticism, before catching himself. "But Cam tells me you're handy. I bet you'll know all the shortcuts."

"I don't take shortcuts."

Cameron glared at me.

"Of course you don't." Roland, his antennae aquiver at last, glanced uneasily at Cameron. He quickly checked his watch. "Listen I've really got to run." He kissed my wife's cheek in a too-familiar gesture. "But the numbers look good, Cam. If you can pull off shooting in Penn Station I think I can get the board to sign off on the budget. We'll touch base on Monday."

"Call me and let me know how the meeting went," Cameron said, clearly irritated that I had busted up their little party.

"She's a genius, Pick." Jameson winked as he brushed by.

"Yeah," I agreed. "A regular Einstein."

"I'll show you out, Roland." Cameron trailed behind him, scowling at me as she passed.

My mother was buried beside the graves of her mother and grandmother in a family plot in the rear corner of the cemetery. It had been so long since my last visit that it took me a while to locate the simple polished marble stone that served as her marker. It was one of many such gravestones and would have been indistinguishable from row upon row of others had it not been situated between a magnolia tree and a couple of Chinese firs planted incongruously in that remote part of the cemetery. I had last been here in the early eighties, when I'd given a talk at the journalism school in Chapel Hill and made an impromptu detour to Burlington on the way back home to Charlotte. The gravesite was overgrown then. Looking forlorn and abandoned, it had reminded me so much of my mother in her final years that it broke my heart. There'd been no flowers on her grave as there were on others and I'd felt guilty for failing to bring any along. Today, I had picked up some daisies, my mother's favorite flowers, at a roadside market, and a pair of garden shears from Oaklawn in case the weeds needed trimming. The last time I'd done it by hand. Now the gravesite was not quite as overgrown and I was surprised to find a bouquet of lilies had been placed here recently. I wondered if my father had left it.

Although the weather had been mild and clear that morning, a cold front had moved in that afternoon and by the time I arrived at the cemetery the day had grown austere and foreboding. As I stood there with my hands in my pockets and my back to the breeze, staring at the headstone, I realized it had been a cold day in November, dark and brooding, just like this one, when we buried my mother. I'd been a pallbearer, along with Buzz and some of my uncles, and I'll never forget carrying the beautiful walnut casket from the hearse to the gravesite, with the wind whipping through our hair, and how we had to brace ourselves at times to keep our balance and how heavy the coffin felt and how I couldn't believe it was my mother inside. I don't know who was in worse shape at my mother's funeral, my father or me. I suspect he was on some sort of medication beyond alcohol, just to get through it all. Rage was my anesthetic.

"Your mother's dead," my father had mumbled when he called me at school to break the news. He was distraught and I could hardly make out what he was saying over the shouts of the guys in the locker room and showers as I sat on the edge of the desk in my coach's office at FSU. The look on coach's face when he'd pulled me from passing drills had warned me that something was wrong. "She died last night at Appalachian," said my father. "I tried to call earlier but you were in class, and I didn't want to leave a message at the dorm."

"How?" was all I could muster in reply.

"She died from a reaction to her medicine, complications arising from the neuroleptics they had her on," he explained through sobs, lapsing into the medical jargon he felt comfortable with, a habit from his war days that I later realized helped him to objectify the trauma and distance himself from the pain. Sudden deaths happen occasionally in mental institutions, the authorities at the hospital had told him. They had not had one at Appalachian in a while but "these drugs have side effects," my father offered feebly, and there was "no way to anticipate" everyone's reaction. He sounded as if he was defending the hospital.

"Why the hell did they put her on them then?" I demanded, searching for a place to put my frustration and hurt.

"They put everybody on Thorazine. Your mother was frail. She couldn't handle it." They weren't sure how it happened, or if she had shown any signs of problems before but apparently she died in her sleep and was found by a nurse the next morning. Further investigation revealed that the attendants who normally checked on the sleeping patients had failed to check on my mother that night. Unlike some of the other patients, they claimed she didn't require such close supervision. "She didn't belong there," the woman at St. Stephen's had remarked about my mother's stay at Alamance General, but I had heard it before. It was a reaction shared by many who encountered my mother in the mental wards, and it was mine, too. She seemed so much more competent, more normal, than those around her and she gained the trust and confidence of other patients and the hospital staff. For whatever reason, out of some vestigial pride or misguided need to please, or not to burden, my mother successfully hid the severity of her depression from others. I suppose to the night staff at Appalachian she didn't appear to be the kind of patient who needed to be checked up on regularly, but that wasn't how I felt then. My mother's death, so absurd and pointless, only reinforced my own sense of the indifference of the fates, the arbitrariness and capriciousness of life.

By the time the funeral came around I was numb with grief and guilt. The last time I had seen my mother alive was on the day we drove her to Appalachian. I never got to say good-bye because I hadn't gone inside with my father to check her in. And I was still enraged at the circumstances of her death. Although I couldn't prove it, I was convinced the hospital was negligent and I was furious—at the hospital, the doctors, my father for putting her there, myself for going along with it, and Mama Lucy, of course, who had first suggested committing my mother and then didn't even have the decency to show up for the funeral. I wanted to sue the hospital but everyone in the family said it would be expensive and fruitless. Mary Alice couldn't be brought back by such an action. What was done was done. Better to put this behind us and move on. "They should have checked up on her," I insisted. "And what about the other patients? Don't we have a responsibility to them and their families to expose this so it doesn't happen again?" To the family, my rage and resentment was a natural expression of an only son's grief, one of the phases of mourning, difficult yet understandable, and best ignored.

I flew in from Tallahassee the night before the funeral to attend the "visitation," as the traditional wake is called in the South, held at the funeral home in Burlington. When I approached my father and my aunt Florence at the airport in Greensboro, they seemed not to recognize me at first. With my long hair, denim work shirt, jeans, sandals, and green army fatigue jacket with the American flag sewn upside down on the back, I looked like a stranger to them. Like so many others of my generation who went off to college in the tumultuous sixties I returned home for the first time already transformed. I had let my hair grow since summer, an act that already made me suspect around the FSU locker room, but my metamorphosis from central casting's Mr. All-American football hero into a hippie weirdo was especially jarring to my "Love It or Leave It" family. My change in appearance, coinciding as it did with the sudden loss of my mother, disturbed my father, and on some level must have seemed to him a sign and symbol of her loss, as if my mother's madness and deterioration correlated with a madness and deterioration set loose in the land—and his son was Exhibit A, linking the two in his mind.

The visitation was attended mainly by family and my mother's old high school friends, whom she had lost touch with after she moved to Delaney. I kept to myself as much as possible, not wishing to be a focus of attention, but lots of well-meaning family members, strangers mostly, sought me out to express their condolences and their memories of my mother's sensitivity and wonderful sense of humor. Occasionally, someone I didn't recognize would come up, identify himself as a relative, and whisper something bizarrely inappropriate like, "You know your mama always was too sensitive for her own good," or "I remember Mary Alice's mama had trouble with her nerves, too."

The Baptist preacher who delivered the eulogy the next day was in over his head. He didn't know my mother, and after listlessly reciting the facts of her life and mispronouncing the names of various family members, he seemed at a loss, so he launched into a generic sermon and wrapped it all up with an appeal to one and all to accept Jesus Christ as their personal Savior. The next thing I knew the organ was playing and I, furious at myself for not speaking up and at my inarticulate family for choosing such a poor eulogist, was being escorted to the cemetery.

The pain flooded back as I stooped down and cleared the leaves and trimmed the overgrown weeds around my mother's headstone. Tears formed in my eyes and my throat tightened. My mother deserved better. I forced those feelings down, the same way I always had. My thoughts turned to Mama Lucy and the resentment I had harbored toward her all those years. I had spent a lifetime avoiding her and blaming her for my mother's death, for being the first to suggest "putting Mary Alice away." Now I sought out Mama Lucy and had even developed an appreciation, a grudging respect for her. I wondered whether this newfound rapport, this wary acceptance, was in some ways a betrayal of my mother's memory, whether it was really real.

I finished trimming the weeds, tidied up the grave, and placed the daisies up against the headstone next to the lilies. Then I murmured a prayer for my mother's sad, tortured soul, and left.

I arrived at Mama Lucy's mid-afternoon, half expecting to find a coterie of relatives there, but I realized when there were no cars out front that since my father and his sisters had decided to put her in a rest home, they couldn't bear to face her again until they had to. Lucy seemed surprised to see me. Nevertheless, I could tell when she opened the door and returned to the family room that she was in a sour mood. She eased onto the couch in front of a TV tuned to some old black-and-white movie.

I sat across from her next to the TV. "How you doing, Mama Lucy?"

"I been better."

"I heard you fainted."

She picked up her magnifying glass. "I did not. I fell asleep is all."

"Daddy and 'em said you fainted and left the gas range on. Gave 'em a scare."

"They lyin'. Just lookin' for an excuse to put me away." It was as though she knew the ax was about to fall. She put down her magnifying glass and stared hard at me. "What are you doin' here, Pickard? Gonna try to talk me into goin' into that home like the rest of 'em?"

I couldn't look her in the eye. If they hadn't told her what was going on I wasn't going to be the one to break it to her. "That's really none of my business. I was just dropping by." I was telling the truth. I was there because I wanted to follow up on some of the questions still lingering from our last conversation. I was dying for answers but on the other hand I felt a little cheap and hypocritical talking to her as if nothing was up, trying to get answers to my questions when I knew what was in store for her. I changed the subject. "On the way over I stopped by Mama's gravesite."

"Well, it's about time." Lucy fingered her magnifying glass. "I hope my children take better care of my grave than you and Clayton's done with Mary Alice's." Her remark stung. Despite her current fragility, Mama Lucy still had an unerring instinct for the jugular.

"Buzz said he was over there last week," she continued, "with some lilies for his mama's grave. Said he left some for Mary Alice, too. Said it was a sight, though."

I didn't want to fight with her, not today, so I changed the subject again. "I was hoping we could talk some more about the 'thirty-four strike and what happened in Eno. I've got a lot of questions."

"Not now, Pick." She squinted through the magnifying lens. "Cain't you see I'm tryin' to watch the TV."

"You told me when we were driving around Eno the other day that you were prevented from going back to work at the mill after the strike." I knew not to dive into her relationship with Spencer Webb, to keep the topic general, yet about something I wanted to learn more about.

"I don't want to talk about that," she said.

I forged ahead on another front, hoping to bust through her resistance by sheer force of will. "You never did tell me what happened that day you got bayoneted. You promised, but you never got around to it."

"I'm through talkin' to you about that, Pick. I got nothin' else to say. Your questions make me tired. Florence and 'em said I don't have to answer if I don't want to and you shouldn't be burdening me with all this."

"Florence and who?" I flared, furious that Florence and her reprobate sons were interfering with this fragile dialectic. "Talbert? Jerry? You think they've really got your best interests at heart?"

"They do," she said.

"Then why were you complaining before that they all wanted to put you in the home?"

Mama Lucy glowered and returned to her movie.

Swell, I thought, retreating to the kitchen for a glass of iced tea. Petey stared at me morosely from his cage. I poured the tea and paced the floor. This might be my last chance to talk to Mama Lucy alone, and the whole interview had gotten off to a shaky start thanks to my busybody aunt and meddling cousins. Here was a chance to shed some light on long-ago events that shaped the lives of our entire family. What right did they have to suggest I was taking advantage of an old woman? I grew irritated just thinking about it. Or maybe I felt guilty because I suspected they might be right. I returned to the family room and took my seat. I had to calm down, plow ahead, and hope that something I brought up rekindled her interest in our conversation. I watched television with her until an opportunity presented itself.

"You know," I said at the first commercial break, "Wallace told me something about what happened that day when Annie Laura was shot."

"Wallace don't know," she said, getting up to check on Petey, who had been calling from his cage ever since I left the kitchen.

"He seems to believe what granddaddy's brother Bud told him," I shouted.

"Bud was lyin' to cover for Dalton. And vice versa. They lied for each other all their lives."

"But why?"

"Bud's the one that done it," Lucy said when she returned to the sofa. "And Dalton was up there with him and he might as well have pulled the trigger hisself. He knew when I found out it'd be all over 'tween him and me and they started coverin' up for each other the minute they come down outta there. Now I don't want to talk about none of this no more, Pickard. It's water under the bridge." She picked up her magnifying glass again, wielding it like a crucifix against a vampire. I hadn't seen her in her old form as much lately—prickly, obstinate, opinionated—and it reminded me of what I never could stand about her. I could see that no matter how desperate I was to put the pieces of this puzzle together before she slipped into senility or was gone for good, she wasn't going to cooperate. At least not today. At the same time I noticed she seemed more full of herself, more feisty than she'd been in a while. It was as though her old belligerence were fueling her spirit. When she was a contrary-assed, ball-busting bitch she was more her old self. Mama Lucy Classic.

"You know I was at my mother's grave today," I said, changing course again, this time playing to her fire.

"You told me."

"I got to thinking, Mama Lucy. How come you and my mama never got along?"

"Who said we didn't? We got along fine. I was good to every one of my in-laws and I was good to Mary Alice, too."

"That's not how she felt."

"She was too sensitive."

"That's what everybody says. What my family always said about me, too, growing up." I gazed at the TV and bit back my anger. "You know what I think?"

"No," she said not looking at me.

"Do you want to know?"

"Not particularly."

"I think you would have given a hard time to anybody Daddy chose to marry. He was your firstborn son. That's to be expected. But I think there was more to it."

"I'm watching a picture show, Pickard." In other words, Shut up, Pick.

I started in again at the next commercial break. "Maybe all this talk about putting you in the home reminded me of it. The way they talk about you now. It reminded me of how they treated my mother. In fact, Mama Lucy, it reminds me of how you treated my mother."

"Your mother was a very sick woman, Pickard."

"That's what they say about you now."

"It's not the same."

"They want to put you away and you don't want to go. How's it different?"

"Stop it. Leave me alone. Can't you let an old lady have some peace? Why are you dragging up this old business now?"

"All I know is that you wanted to put her in the mental hospital from the beginning and she wound up there and she died there for no reason. And for the longest time I blamed you."

"Pickard, you can be so cruel."

"Maybe. But you were cruel to my mother, too. When I was a kid I hated you for that. She was crippled and you seemed to hold that against her."

"I did not."

"I used to think you were just mean. But now—"

"—Pick, I can't stand this—"

"—I think my mother reminded you of somebody."

"Don't be silly."

"I think her bad leg reminded you of somebody you didn't want to be reminded of. I think she reminded you of Annie Laura. And you held that against her." Her face blanched and I knew I'd scored a hit. "What I don't understand, Mama Lucy, is if your friend was so important to you and she was crippled, why you didn't have more sympathy for my mother."

"Why are you doing this to me?" Mama Lucy pleaded.

"I just felt like you should know how I always felt. People should know about the damage they inflict. No matter how unintended."

She shook her head, tears showing in her eyes. "You don't know what you're saying," she said. "Your mother was—"

"My mother was what?"

"Nothing."

"Say it. Admit how you felt about her. If I'm telling you how I felt about you, then you have a right to tell me about how you felt about my mother."

"She was a danger to herself."

"A danger to herself and others, right? The legal justification for commitment. That's how you all rationalized it. She was a danger to nobody, Mama Lucy, and you know it."

"She was!"

"Bullshit."

"She took her own life, Pick."

I gaped at her. I felt as if the wind had been knocked out of me.

"She committed suicide, you know that?" She was looking at me imploringly.

"What are you saying?" I had never allowed myself to consider such a thing. It was the hospital's fault. My mother was depressed, certainly, but when she was herself she was too much in love with living. Too much an appreciator of life's gifts. She never could have taken her own life.

Mama Lucy turned off the television and looked over at me, her eyes watering like spring runoff after winter ice has melted. I must have looked devastated. "You didn't know, did you?" she whispered. "Your daddy never told you, did he?"

I leaped to my feet, started pacing. "It was an accident. 'Sudden death.' It happened all the time back then, they said. She died of negligence. If anything it was murder. You're just saying that to cover your ass. Because you feel guilty for putting her in the place that killed her."

"She died of an overdose, son. Pills she saved up over a long time. Thorazine. She even stole a bottle of concentrate from the nurse's cart—"

"No—"

"—and guzzled it to wash down the pills."

"NO! She died of negligence and stupid bureaucracy and inadequate training. Daddy got the whole story from the doctors."

"We didn't want to tell you the truth because we were worried about you. You were so close to her. We didn't want to hurt you. Ask Clayton. He'll tell you."

The idea of my father and grandmother conspiring to keep the circumstances of my mother's death from me hardened my battered carapace of defense and a dark knot of rage rose up from deep within me.

"NO!" I slammed my fist into the wall where the picture gallery hung, smashing a hole in the plaster and causing the photo of my uncle Donly to crash to the floor. My grandmother cowered in the corner of the sofa, covering her face with her liver-spotted hands. Cradling my bleeding fist, I shrunk back in horror at what I had done then doubled over and collapsed, shaking and sobbing, onto the sofa. "You had no right!" I cried out. "You had no right to keep something like that from me."

"Your mother was much worse off than you knew, son," Mama Lucy said softly, stroking my hair. "Your daddy kept it from you but that wasn't the first time she tried it. Those times she come over here to Alamance General was after he found her at home asleep with a empty bottle of pills lying next to her."

"You had no right," I said. "No right."

"Mary Alice made your daddy promise not to tell you. Your daddy suffered over this, son. I guess he thought he was doing what was best."

I sat on Mama Lucy's sofa for I don't know how long, as tears streamed down my face in an unstoppable flow. The only other sound besides my weeping was the old clock on the mantelpiece, its ticking drowned out intermittently by my sobs, returning when I gathered breath. "I'm sorry, Pickard," Mama Lucy said. "I'm so sorry."

I had never cried in front of my grandmother as an adult and it felt strange, vulnerable but somehow oddly appropriate. Mama Lucy hugged me close, stroking my head and patting my shoulders. After a long while I heard her say, "Pickard, are you okay?"

"Yes, ma'am," I said.

"Pickard?"

"Ma'am?" I said, looking at her through a prism of tears.

"I'm ready to talk about the blacklist now, son, if you want me to. I'm ready to answer your questions. That is, if you still want me to."

Lucy stumbled through the lingering smoke and teargas in a state of shock. In the aftermath of the shootings, the National Guard busied itself clearing people away from the mill, tending the injured and collecting the bodies of the dead. Lucy looked for Davis but couldn't find him. She heard later that the injured had been taken by ambulance to a hospital in Chapel Hill. On her way home she saw Spencer Webb's yellow roadster parked outside the West End train depot. She did not stop. At home, she found a note from Bessie, informing her that she had taken the children to Grandma Barlow's. Using the phone Dalton put in for police business, she called around inquiring about who had been hurt. She didn't know when Dalton would get home and didn't care. She called a neighbor of her mama's and told them to tell Bessie she was all right and to stay there with the children until she came to get them. No sooner had she hung up than the phone began to ring. She picked up the receiver, fearing it might be Dalton Earl, and wondering what she would say to him if it was.

"Lucy," Davis said. "We need your help. The funeral homes in Eno refuse to accept the bodies of the dead strikers and other arrangements have to be made. The union sent word out for help but we need somebody to do the autopsies. Can you talk to that feller you used to go with worked at the funeral home?"

"Linwood Copeland? Davis, he lost his daddy!"

"Do you want Annie Laura to get the kind of burial she deserves?"

"Of course, but—"

"Who was that colored fellow Annie Laura used to talk to, whose daddy run the dry goods?"

"Sam Khoury. He won't colored. He's A-rab. He went off to medical school in Nashville. I lost track of him after that."

"He's back doctorin' in Chapel Hill. He brung a petition over to Burlington signed by students and faculty at the university supportin' the strike. Can you call him and have him contact me at strike headquarters?"

"What can he do?"

"Maybe he can help us with the autopsies—or knows somebody who can."

Spencer Webb was the only person Lucy knew who might be able to get in touch with Sam. But she hadn't seen him since that morning. And that was the first time in a long while. And contacting him was another matter. "I can try."

"Are you coming to the funeral?" Davis asked.

"Of course."

"Lucy, will you do something for us? Will you sing like Annie Laura always done?"

"I can't believe she's gone," Lucy sobbed. "It won't be the same. Nobody could sing like her."

"We're lucky to be alive," said Davis. "You know that, don't you, sister?"

"I-I guess."

"Will you do it, Lucy?"

"Dalton won't like it."

Davis's voice turned cold and steely. "What does Dalton have to say for hisself now?"

"I don't know. I ain't seen 'im since it happened."

"Will you sing, Lucy?"

Lucy sighed. "If I can hold myself together."

"You can do it, sister. And don't forget to try to get in touch with Khoury."

Lucy hung up the phone, slid open the bottom chest drawer, and retrieved her writing box from under the linens. She removed a clean sheet of stationery from the box, and using the sharpened yellow pencil she always kept inside, scribbled a note to Spencer Webb. When she was done she slipped the letter into an envelope and wrote his name on the outside. From the closet she retrieved a drab gray dress she used to wear to work that wouldn't attract attention. After washing up, she changed, and put the envelope in her pocket, pulled a scarf over her head and headed out the door.

She walked to Cornwallis Street, turned right, and marched away from the West End, with her head down and hands deep in the pockets of her dress. The streets had emptied around the depot, but tension still lingered in the air. She walked down Cornwallis toward Eno proper. Truckloads of stunned-looking guardsmen rumbled past her on their way out of town. Downtown Eno had come to a halt. A few people still milled about wary and watchful, talking to each other in hushed tones.

When she reached the Seed and Feed on the corner of Cheshire Street, she ducked through the doorway and hid behind a stack of fertilizer bags, scanning the street outside the courthouse for Dalton's car. Not finding it, she darted across Cheshire and hurried past the courthouse. The old clock struck twice—two o'clock. Lucy picked up her pace, hurrying past the remaining houses to where the street dead-ended at Bennehan. Up the hill a church steeple poked above the treetops, its brick edifice visible through the branches. A wave of doubt washed over her. She had never been to the Webb house before, although she knew where it was, and she felt like a trespasser. She wondered if she was making a mistake, or worse, a fool of herself. She took a calming breath, felt the letter in her pocket, and pressed on.

The mid-afternoon sun beat down on her. To her left trees newly flecked with gold undulated in the breeze. On the right was a field of withered wire grass and weeds. Ahead, woods and fields seemed to stretch all the way to the river. Then, on the left just beyond a kudzu-choked embankment a driveway suddenly appeared, rising up between two brick pillars. A drive ascended from the road to a big white house on the hill. The Webb place. Lucy, more nervous than ever now that she was finally here, rose up on her tiptoes for a better look. A flash of yellow and chrome through the foliage filled her with relief. Spencer was here, his roadster parked in front of the house. But as she turned up the drive she saw a shiny black Ford parked just inside the gate barring the way. Two burly men, one short and one tall, in brown fedoras stood beside the car smoking cigarettes. Lucy froze as the men whirled around, their hands gripping the pistol butts protruding from their leather shoulder holsters.

The tall one looked her up and down, adjusted his hat and straightened his tie. "Help you, ma'am?" His partner stubbed out his cigarette. She didn't like the look on the face of the man coming toward her and he didn't sound local.

"Is young Mr. Webb here?" asked Lucy.

"The Webbs are out of town." The tall fellow drew up close to her. "Ain't nobody here."

Lucy fingered the envelope in her hand. "Spencer Webb. I have a letter for him."

"We'll take that." The man reached for the letter.

Lucy stepped back. "No, it's a . . . a special delivery."

"There's been some trouble in town," the man said. "We're Mr. Webb's private security. So I'm afraid all correspondence must go through us."

"Who are you?" asked Lucy as the short one came down the drive.

"We're a special detail in charge of interceptin' Mr. Webb's mail." A smirk rose on the stubby man's thick lips and he snatched the letter from

Lucy's hands with the swiftness of a striking copperhead. Lucy, shocked and angry, wanted to say something rude, but thought better of it.

"Would you please make sure he gets it?"

"Absolutely," said the tall one with the Yankee accent.

Lucy fled.

"Where you goin', little lady?"

When she finally looked back she saw the men tearing open the envelope. She knew all they would see were words they wouldn't understand. She just hoped that Spencer saw it in time.

Lucy arrived at Panther's Den at four o'clock. She sat on a rock next to the small cave on New Hope Mountain and gazed at the last of the summer's mountain laurel. She prayed that Spencer would show up. The cave was nothing more than a shallow indentation in the rock on the hillside, but its mouth, set back on a bluff, afforded a view of the swirling waters of the New Hope River below. The only way to reach the secluded spot was by a hunting trail on the back side of the mountain opposite the slope occupied by the mill village. Its remoteness guaranteed a much-prized privacy in a community where everyone knew everyone else's business. Panther's Den had served the local teenagers for years and she always remembered it as pristine and untouched. But it had been fifteen years since the last time she had met Spencer here, and she now noticed beer bottles and candy wrappers on the ground, and beside the path leading up the hill she'd seen the rusted-out remains of an old automobile tangled with kudzu.

For a brief time, before she finally told Dalton she'd marry him and broke Spencer's heart, she and Spencer had met here at Panther's Den to kiss and hold each other and stare out over the river and hold hands and talk about their dreams and plans and frustrations, their secret longings and desires. Sometimes they would discuss the books Lucy had read or wanted to read, the ones Davis had given her, and Spencer would tell her about ones he liked and sometimes would bring her one of his favorites—*Silas Marner*, *Great Expectations*, *The Count of Monte Cristo*, or *Huckleberry Finn*—for her to keep. He sometimes brought her flowers or candy from Khoury's, but her favorite gift, the gift she treasured above all others, was a used schoolbook from Eno High, a book of stories by different authors that she would have studied had she stayed in school. Each night, she would read a story and return to talk about it with Spencer, who seemed to have read everything, and they would speculate about the lives of the characters and what they were like after the story was over and the kind of person the author was who could make up such a glorious tale. Sometimes Spencer would even read to her from his journal, a notebook he carried with him all the time and kept like a diary, recording his thoughts about things going on around him. She enjoyed that the most.

But that was another lifetime, before their lives had diverged and followed the paths that were intended for them from the outset by forces and wills much larger and stronger than their own.

Lucy had only been there a few minutes when she heard somebody approaching.

"You came!" Lucy said.

"Of course I did." Spencer, reaching the clearing, mopped his brow with his handkerchief. "Thank God you're okay. I was worried. I drove by your house after the shooting but nobody was home. I got the note."

"Spencer, what happened?" cried Lucy, rushing to him and burying her head in his shoulder. "Who ordered those men to shoot?"

"I don't know." He held her and gently patted her back. "I begged my father not to deputize those men, but he wouldn't listen to me. He left it in Strudwick's hands, the superintendent, and the detectives they hired. Then he left town with Mother and my sister."

"How could you allow such a thing?" Lucy asked.

Spencer held Lucy at arm's length and looked into her eyes. "Lucy, listen to me: I had nothing to do with this. You know that, don't you? There was nothing I could do."

She looked down, unable to engage his eyes. "Annie Laura was killed," Lucy sobbed, "shot in the back like a dog. The funeral home won't even bury them. No one will even do the autopsies."

"What about Linwood?" Years ago, Linwood Copeland had apprenticed himself to Mr. Dickens at the funeral home to learn the undertaker's arts of embalming and grave digging, swapping a life in the weave room for the more steady and dependable work of a mortician.

"Linwood cain't even bury his own daddy," Lucy said. " 'Cause his daddy was union. That's how bad it is." She steeled herself. This was the reason she'd come here. "Spencer, could you . . . contact Sam Khoury for me?"

"Of course. It's the least I can do." Spencer turned back to the river, sadness and frustration etching his face. "I wish I could do more. I've been gone too long. Strudwick's in charge . . ." Then turning back to Lucy, he smiled, "But then again, he's not a Webb, is he? I am. I'll have to be careful, but . . . with my father out of town I may still be able to work behind the scenes."

"Spencer, who were those men, really?"

"Detectives. Bodyguards my father hired. Ostensibly to protect our family. Thugs, really. To give them the slip, I walked down to the back of our property and followed the river trail all the way over here."

Lucy smiled. "Just like the old days."

Spencer's face darkened. "Except it's more serious now."

"Remember the last time we were here?"

They'd been teenagers then, and Panther's Den was the only place they could meet and not get caught but only if it was the right time of day when no one else was around and the right day of the week when there was a baseball practice or school track meet and the older boys were too busy to bring their girls up here. Four o'clock on Thursdays, just after shift change, was that time for Lucy. She was working first shift then and got off at three. She would rush home and change into something pretty and flattering and slip off up to Panther's Den for their rendezvous. It was dangerous and exciting and could lead to nothing but trouble for both of them, as Annie Laura had told her more than once at the time, but she hadn't listened until it was too late and by then they were falling in love.

"We've got nothing to be ashamed of, Lucy," Spencer said. "You didn't betray Dalton."

"But I wanted to. The Bible says if you done it in your heart it's good as done."

"Bible says a lot of things, Lucy. You're a good and decent woman and your husband has nothing to feel but proud of you."

Lucy stared at him, awash in memories. "I'm a mama now, Spencer. I got six young'uns, but I still feel like that girl you kissed at Chicken Bridge fifteen years ago."

"We were both young, Lucy. Wait a minute." Spencer moved to the edge of the bluff, looked down the mountain in the direction of the trail, and raised a finger to his lips. "Did you hear something? I thought—"

"It was just the wind. Or a limb falling. Or squirrels storing nuts."

"I better be getting on back," Spencer said. "Strudwick and some mill representatives are meeting with the sheriff to discuss how to handle the killings. They're panicked. The last thing they needed was martyrs." Lucy, wondering if Dalton would be there, said nothing.

"Lucy," Spencer whispered, taking her hands. "Did anybody see you come here?"

"I don't think so," she answered.

He smiled—sadly it seemed to Lucy. "Good. Your brother's a strike leader. My credibility's already suspect around here. I can't be seen fraternizing with the enemy. But I'll try to reach Sam Khoury as soon as I get home."

"Thank you, Spencer Webb." They stood hand in hand, staring at each other. After a long moment, he leaned over and kissed her softly on the cheek and disappeared down the trail.

By the time she got back to the West End, the sun was setting. She went to her mother's house to check on the children. Dalton had come by, but he'd said nothing about the killings. The mill was shut down until further notice. The afternoon shift had been turned away and told to come back when word was posted. Lucy sat at the kitchen table, eyeing but unable to eat the sandwich Bessie had made for her. The children swarmed about and the little ones crawled all over her. Her mama, sensing her exhaustion, sent her home to get some rest.

At home, Lucy collapsed on top of the chenille bedspread and fell immediately to sleep. Her dreams were haunted with images of Annie Laura lying in a pool of blood and smoking guns poking through the mill windows, serpent-like, while Dalton and Bud peered out at her from behind the black, deadly portals.

She jerked awake, sweaty and disoriented. The house was silent and empty, dark now that the sun had set. Worried that she'd slept through her shift, she scrambled to the bathroom and washed her face before realizing that her shift had been canceled. She stood in the tiny bathroom in the pale evening light and stared at herself in the small medicine cabinet mirror. The face looking back at her was almost unrecognizable. Dark circles ravaged her eyes. She looked like she'd aged ten years. Still half-asleep, she splashed cold water on her face to wake up and suddenly recalled where everybody was—the children at her mother's, Dalton at the courthouse, and Annie Laura lying dead on the ground with a bullet in her back. She ran downstairs.

The living room was dark, empty, and desolate. The only light filtering through the window curtains came from a street lamp outside on the corner. The shape of the RCA Victor radio console set up in front of the window cast a shadow like a tombstone on the living room floor.

Lucy stood there in the dark, thinking about how just the Sunday night before she and the children had gathered around the radio and listened to the president talk about the strike. Lucy had missed few of the president's "fireside chats" since they first started and they were always discussed around the spinning frames at work the next day, almost as much as the Saturday night "Grand Ole Opry." She liked the sound of the president's voice when he delivered his radio addresses and what he said about improving conditions for the working man and better days to come. He always sounded far off but clear-spoken and personal and high-toned, like one of those Hollywood matinee idols in pictures about rich people in Philadelphia or Boston or New York City. And she liked to imagine him sitting in the Oval Office by the fireplace with his little dog, Fala, by his side.

A few months ago Annie Laura had talked her into writing a letter to President Roosevelt. Annie Laura was convinced that if they just found the right words to express how they felt about the stretch-out and if they said it just right, he would know they were speaking from their hearts and being an honest man would have no choice but to do something about it.

But now Annie Laura was gone.

As Lucy stared out into the gloaming the darkness deepened in her living room and the injustice of her friend's death settled in like the shadows all around her. Then an idea clapped through her mind like summer lightning. She would write another letter to Mr. Roosevelt. Only this time she didn't have Annie Laura to help her form the words. But this time she was sure she wouldn't need anybody's help.

She sat down at the desk in her room, spread out the paper, turned on the little lamp next to the window addressed the envelope. Then, she carefully inscribed his name again at the top left of a clean page: *President Franklin D. Roosevelt, The White House, Washington, D.C.* On the right, in a column under her return address, she wrote the date: *September 8, 1934.*

Dear President Roosevelt, she began and a chill came over her.

> *I know I wrote you before and I know you are busy but things down here got a lot worse. As you know, the strike started up a few days ago because people just couldn't take it anymore. Now everything's gotten out of hand.*

I don't know where else to turn, Mr. Roosevelt. I believe you are a god-sent man and as far as I can see you are our only hope.

Suddenly an exhaustion smothered her like a heavy quilt and she knew she couldn't go on. She had underestimated the toll that committing the horrific experience to paper would take on her. She felt small and frail, foolish for thinking the president of the United States would care about anything she might have to say. She returned the letter the envelope and slipped it into her writing box, tears streaming down her face. She sprawled across the bed, and with memories of the sounds of gunfire ringing in her ears and the smell of tear gas in her nostrils, fell into a deep dreamless slumber and did not wake until late the next morning.

The town was in shock and the mood was somber after what had happened at the Bellevue mill. The authorities had declared martial law and issued a curfew and the only people allowed on the streets after dark were the National Guard and deputy sheriffs in their black Fords.

The newspapers were subdued in their coverage of the strike, and most of what Lucy learned was by word of mouth. Dave said the newspapers were in the mill owners' pockets just like the sheriff and the funeral homes and not to expect much insight or outrage there.

But word had spread throughout the region about what happened in Eno and by ten o'clock Saturday morning, the day of the funeral, cars, some with license tags from as far away as Georgia and Alabama, began backing up along Cornwallis Street as far as the eye could see.

Ten thousand people showed up that day.

Linwood in his undertaker black and Lucy and Mrs. Copeland, both dressed in black and wearing hats with veils, walked together along the road arm in arm with swarms of other mourners moving silently around them. When they reached the top of the hill overlooking the West End Lucy looked back and saw the crowds and vehicles filling the streets. She'd never seen so many people. Cars pressed forward through the crowds like ships lost in a sea of humanity, moving slowly along the street among the multitudes. She hoped she would see Spencer's car somewhere along the way, but he seemed to have disappeared after their rendezvous and she didn't even know if he was still in town. Police and National Guardsmen patrolled the streets. Just before she and the Copelands reached the road Dalton came up behind her, hooked her arm, and pulled her aside.

He was wearing the dark suit he'd had on when he left the house on the morning of the massacre and it looked like he'd been sleeping in it, and it smelled like it too. His deputy's badge shone on his breast pocket next to his lapel, catching the reflection of the sun. "What are you doing here, Lucy?" he asked.

"Where you been, Dalton?" she said.

"I'm sleepin' down at the courthouse until this is over. Sheriff wants us on twenty-four-hour call. Didn't your mother tell you?"

"All I know is I ain't seen you in days," she said.

"How are the young'uns?"

"They're with Bessie and Mama," Lucy said.

"That's where you oughta be." Dalton scanned the throngs still arriving. "Go back home to your mother's until this is over."

"I can't and I won't," Lucy said. "I gotta be here for Annie Laura and the others."

Dalton fixed her with his blue eyes. "It ain't smart, Lucy. You been talkin' to your brother again, ain'tcha?"

"Now listen to me, Dalton. I don't need you to tell me what's smart—"

"You know what I'm talkin' about."

"You was up there, Dalton!" she snapped. "You was up in those windows!"

"I had to be," he said, looking away. "I didn't shoot nobody."

"Most of 'em were shot in the back. Mr. Kershaw's boy was shot five times. Two in the front, three in the back. Some say he was killed because his brother-in-law is union."

"It won't like that, Lucy," Dalton said. "It was all confusion and panic. You ought to know that. You was there."

Now it was Lucy's turn to look away. He continued, "I told you to stay home then and I'm telling you again now." He grabbed her by the shoulders, shouting at her, "Dammit, Lucy, you're lucky it warn't you gunned down!"

"I wish it had been me instead of Annie Laura! She didn't deserve what happened to her. And neither did Mr. Copeland. You on Mr. Webb's payroll, too, Dalton?"

Dalton stared at her. "I'll be at the courthouse if you need me."

"Don't you turn your back on me, Dalton Cantrell!"

Dalton whirled around and grabbed her chin, snapping her head to the side. Clusters of men, two of whom Lucy recognized from Spencer's house, were moving among the cars and scribbling things in notebooks. "See that," Dalton said. "Those are Webb's men. They're taking down license plate numbers and the names of those who showed up. They're putting together a list, Lucy. They ain't playin' games. Mr. Webb's gonna remember who was with him and who was against him. And these folks"—he waved his hand toward the throng gathering under the funeral tent—"are against him."

"They're not against him," Lucy protested. "They're just paying their respects to their friends and neighbors and loved ones like any decent person ought to."

"That ain't the way he sees it. I'm just warning you, Lucy, stay away from that funeral. Pay your respects in private. We got mouths to feed. Annie Laura would understand."

Lucy pulled away. Dalton had taken part in the massacre. He wasn't going to tell her how to mourn her best friend. She marched off toward the tent.

The funeral service had been paid for by the union just as they paid for the autopsies and caskets because none of the churches or funeral homes in Eno would have anything to do with it. The canopies were set up under the spreading oak near the top of the hill but the crowd was so large it couldn't fit under the tent and it spilled out across the pasture and onto the baseball field. American flags were everywhere waving in the breeze and people were holding placards bearing the names of the fallen and slogans like REMEMBER THE ENO SEVEN and others that read, SUPPORT THE STRIKE and STOP THE STRETCH-OUT!

Parked along the road were seven black hearses with their tailgates open. Inside the tent seven identical pine coffins sat side by side, great sprays and bouquets of flowers piled on top. Annie Laura's coffin was the third from the left. Lucy knew it was hers because it was covered with a spray of white lilies, her friend's favorite flower. The families of those killed were sitting up front. Lucy sat beside Annie Laura's younger brothers and sisters, her heart breaking at the sight of all of them sitting there, from the oldest to the youngest, trying to put on a brave front just like Annie Laura would. Off to the side next to the coffins were Sam Khoury, looking solemn in a dark suit and tie, and another man who Lucy thought was the funeral director. When Sam, seeing Lucy looking at him, nodded, she knew that Spencer had done what he promised.

A preacher sympathetic to the strike was brought in from Durham to conduct the service and representatives from the TWI read statements over the loudspeakers. The weeping and wailing from the mourners was so loud that even with amplification you could barely hear the eulogies. Lucy had known four of the seven killed, including Annie Laura, and the others she knew by face if not by name. Most of the eulogies were brief. When it came their turn Annie Laura's brother Fetzer stood up and said a few words about his sister's sacrifice for their family, with both their parents gone, and how she had raised them on her own after their daddy died of TB.

"My sister was a Christian and would have asked all of us to forgive the one who done this to her, and I don't know if I can do that, but I'm gonna try because I know that's what she would have wanted."

Annie Laura's sister and brother-in-law and their kids, who had lost their home because of Annie Laura's union activities, wept as they listened to Fetzer tell how they all would miss her and would try to carry on in a way that would make her proud. By the time it was over and Fetzer returned to his seat Lucy was sobbing. Finally, Davis got up and spoke eloquently of the price paid by those who were killed, and of how freedom was bought with the blood of martyrs over and over again, from Bunker Hill to the Argonne Forest to the streets of Eno, North Carolina. Lucy swelled with love and pride for her brother and with grief for her friend and when Dave nodded to her to come up and sing she was ready, though still scared. The largest crowd she'd ever sung for was less than a hundred in the Baptist church. Today she would be singing for thousands. To ward off her stage fright she focused on the shining faces of Annie Laura's brothers and sisters. Lucy's a cappella version of "Mill Mother's Lament," though quavery at first, grew stronger as she gained confidence. She found her voice in the faces of those children who had depended on their big sister to see them through and were now on their own. By the final verse her voice, strong and sure, boomed out over the crowd, many of whom were singing along—

Now it grieves the heart of a mother
You everyone must know
But we cannot buy for our children
Our wages are too low

As scared as she was, and as inadequate a singer compared to Annie Laura, Lucy was proud that she sang that day because it released something in her and helped soothe the ache she felt and ease the hurt in others. Still, no amount of balm could alleviate that much loss. And as the family members paid their final respects, some of the wives and mothers swooned and fainted in fits of grief. Some even threw themselves onto the caskets and tried to climb inside the pine boxes until they were restrained by their families. When it was their turn, Annie Laura's siblings passed before their sister's casket weeping with a quiet dignity that reminded Lucy of Annie Laura herself.

"It liked to broke my heart seein' them young'uns like that, Pick, all them mouths to feed and Annie Laura gone and for what? An' when I looked up and seen Mr. Sumner movin' among the cars parked on the ball field, a-writin' down license tag numbers in his notebook, it made me sick."

"But you still had a job, didn't you?"

"I thought I did. Even if I didn't want to have nothin' to do with that mill after that, I had mouths to feed."

"But you had to cross the picket line, right? To go back to work?"

"I didn't want to, Pick. Not after what happened to Annie Laura. And what she said to me. After that I wanted to stay at home and crawl up into a hole. But Dalton made me go back to work at Bellevue. He said we couldn't afford to go on the dole with six young'uns. He said they'd be waitin and watchin' for any slip-up from me. If I missed a day they'd use it as an excuse to fire me. I couldn't sleep worryin' about it. It was like Annie Laura was watchin' me. I didn't want to let her down but I couldn't let my babies down, neither. It was the hardest decision I ever had to make, crossin' the picket line after what happened. But I made up my mind to do it for the young'uns an' I went back and just prayed Annie Laura would forgive me. I regret it to this day."

When Lucy showed up for her shift at the mill Monday night the tension in the air was almost palpable. Machine guns were mounted on trucks on either side of the gate and National Guardsmen were lined up behind the wire-mesh fence with their bayonets fixed. Strikers were gathered in front of the gate chanting and carrying placards though less rowdy than before. A table was set up inside the gate with guardsmen and armed deputies with sawed-off shotguns placed at either side. At the table Mr. Strudwick hovered over a ledger book he marked in and Mr. Sumner had some kind of list that he checked as each hand signed in for work. When Sumner spotted Lucy in the crowd, he set down his coffee and leaned over and whispered something to Strudwick.

"Lucy Cantrell," Sumner bellowed so everyone could hear him. "Lucy Barlow Cantrell." He sipped his steaming coffee and held up the list. Lucy, shuffling forward, saw a black dot beside her name, and beside that a list of crimes: Insubordination. Insurrection. Rioting. Treason. Disturbing the Peace.

"What's this, Mr. Sumner?" she asked.

"Looks like you're out of work, Lucy."

Lucy's throat contracted and her heart felt like a lead weight. "Why?"

"You know why."

Lucy's face burned with anger and humiliation as everyone—deputies, guardsmen, millhands—stared at her. "I'm a good worker, Mr. Sumner, you've said so yourself."

"Not according to this, Lucy."

"Then it's a lie."

"You calling Mr. Webb a liar?"

"I'm saying I'm a good worker and you know it."

Sumner's grin was vicious. Lucy turned to the superintendent, who was writing in his ledger, and begged, "Please, Mr. Strudwick, I need this job. I've got six children. My husband works for the sheriff. He'll tell you I'm a good worker. I've worked for Bellevue my whole life."

Strudwick turned away and mumbled something to a nearby deputy as Sumner said, "You read what it said, Lucy. You're holding up the line."

Lucy looked at Strudwick's back and the deputy's smirking face. The glint in Sumner's eye was evidence enough that he was enjoying her discomfort. "You heard me, Lucy. Git!"

Righteous indignation boiled up within her. Her feelings of guilt and shame for crossing the picket line and anger at the ones who killed Annie Laura were now superseded by a ferocious sense of injured pride.

Lucy grabbed Sumner's steaming cup of coffee and hurled it into his face. Sumner screamed, reeling in pain as the deputies and guardsmen leaped forward and shoved Lucy to the ground. A roar arose from the picket line and the guardsmen closed ranks to prevent anyone from breaking through.

Sumner, his face the color of a port wine stain, hissed at her while guardsmen pinned her to the ground with bayonets, "You got a lot of nerve showing up here, woman. You better watch yourself or you'll wind up like your friend Annie Laura Gaskins. I shoulda got rid of you two a long time ago, Lucy Barlow."

Strudwick turned away, and without a word headed back to the comfort and quiet of his office.

A PIECE OF BAD CLOTH

As the afternoon wore on, Mama Lucy grew more and more ener-gized. The revelation about my mother's suicide had crumbled the wall between us, and her voice took on a new intimacy and urgency. I realized she was probably recounting things that had happened to her that she had never told anyone before, fitting it into a narrative whole, weaving her memories into a piece as satisfying for her to tell as for me to hear. Inside on the mantel, the old clock marked time as, outside, the afternoon shadows edged toward evening.

"I was surprised at how bad it tore me up to get laid off," said Mama Lucy, sipping her iced tea. "I'd worked there since I was a girl and woulda done anything in the world for that company when I was younger. But to be treated that way, tossed aside like a piece a bad cloth, hurt my feelings."

"All because you went to the funeral?" I asked.

"A lot of folks lost jobs 'cause they went. I won't the only one."

"But you weren't even in the union or on the picket line!"

"I sung at the funeral. That's all it took. I suspect the boss man, Mr. Sumner, was still mad at me 'cause I wouldn't go in the back with him. And for tattlin' on him to Spencer Webb."

"But that was years earlier."

"And he never forgot it. I don't know what Spencer done but Sumner got in trouble with Mr. Webb. He never touched me again after that and he didn't lay Annie Laura off. I knew he carried a grudge all those years, but he couldn't do nothin' to me. First chance he got he did, though. Everything changed after the shootings. The first week, those first few days of the strike had been real excitin'. It was like a carnival atmosphere on the picket line, like a tent meetin' or the county fair. Of course, I couldn't take part but I never seen Annie Laura so excited. There was singin' and dancin' an' they was servin' coffee, bringin' food and cuttin' the fool and carryin' on. Ever'body singin' 'We Shall Not Be Moved.' It was like the Fourth of July, there was so many flags an' speeches. Felt like when Davis went off to fight the Germans. Ever'body was so full of hope. They was all in it together, standin' up for what was right and riskin' it all."

"But not everybody was on the picket line."

"Oh, no. Remember, I was workin' that first week. And the ones like me that kept on workin, most of 'em didn't like the union. I didn't mind the union, of course, but I just couldn't go out. Some others was sympathetic to the strikers but didn't think the strike would work. Management made like we was the true and loyal workers. Strudwick and Sumner brought a big box of new picker-sticks in there in the weave room and told us, 'Now if them flyin' squads goes to stickin' their head in them windows, start crackin' heads an' the company'll stand behind you.' "

"Divide and conquer."

"The company portrayed itself as peacekeepers—but they woulda been happy to see us fight with the strikers. Only the Catholics and the Jews from up north supported the strikers. Outside agitators is what the mill owners called 'em. Or worse. Communists. Bolsheviks. Like they was the cause of our unhappiness. Like we couldn't figure out ourselves we was bein' taken advantage of. But Pick, who else was gonna help us? I didn't see no Good Samaritans among the boss men offerin' to help us get a decent wage. Some of the churches sent out street preachers to preach hellfire an' damnation at the picket line. Told the strikers what they was doin' was wrong, lookin' for justice in this world, that they was none to be had until the sweet bye and bye. Annie Laura was right in the middle of it, a-quotin' scripture right back at them street preachers about how Jesus was a workin' man, an' how he preached good news to the poor and settin' free the captive. Won't nobody gonna out-gospel Annie Laura Gaskins."

"Lord helps those who help themselves."

Lucy nodded and her face turned solemn. "After what they done to Annie Laura and then layin' me off for goin' to her funeral, after the shootings, folks got opinionated. Some of those who had been neutral before the shootings were suddenly sympathetic to the union. Others thought it served us right. Folks you'd known all your life would pass you on the street and not speak to you. Later, as the strike wore on and the paychecks stopped comin', folks started goin' hungry. Flyin' squadrons could shut down the looms and call people out but they couldn't feed nobody. Union started takin' up collections for the ones that were the worst off, the ones with sick children and babies an' all, but it was like squeezin' blood out of a turnip."

"How did you wind up in Burlington?"

"My brother Charlie was a-weavin' there in Burlington and so was my sister Icy. And Dave asked me to come over there to show my support. He was workin' full time for the union by that time, but he'd worked in all the mills around Burlington. Dalton was mad as a hornet, but so was I after the killin's an' losin' my job so I left the young'uns with Mama and went over there one day."

"What exactly happened?" I had an idea from Dave's pamphlet but I wanted to hear it from her.

"The first day I got arrested. We was at the Plaid mill and no sooner did the first shift come on and we was outside a-picketin' than the soldiers pulled up in their trucks and rounded us up and put us on a flatbed truck. The sheriff paraded us around town to shame and embarrass us. He was sayin' to other girls this is what happens when you git mixed up with the union. Not that it mattered. By that time I was right outspoken. And after I found out what happened to Icy—"

"What happened?"

"They took Icy and some of the others out to Camp Claiborne and held 'em behind barbed wire without chargin' 'em with nothin' or lettin' 'em git in touch with their families or nothin'."

"They were put in an internment camp?"

"Internment. That's what they called it. Like a p.o.w. camp. That's where they put German prisoners durin' the war. Tryin' to discourage us. They was sayin' we was no better than enemies of our country. All it did though was rile ever'body up. The next mornin' we was out in force on the picket line. This time in front of the Pioneer plant. The tension was thick. We was already tradin' words with the shift change when the soldiers pulled up at the gate and piled out. Some was yellin' 'Scab' and 'Traitor.' Not me, though. I knowed what it was like to be on the inside and out."

"Pretty dicey, huh?"

"Oh, it was. Machine guns at the gates. Deputies ever'where with their sawed-off shotguns. Some fistfights broke out and tear gas was set loose."

"Good Lord, Mama Lucy, you must have been terrified after what happened in Eno."

"I was. But tempers was runnin' high just then and I was madder'n I was scairt that day. September fourteenth, 1934. I'll never forget it."

"Move!" said the soldier as he and his platoon shoved their way through the line of picketers along the wire-mesh fence. Lucy was at the front of the line near the entrance to the Pioneer plant when the soldier shouted at her and shoved her back. "Move along, you rats!" she heard him say.

Lucy stood her ground. "I won't. And you ain't big enough to make me."

The soldier shoved her with the butt of his rifle. "You're breaking the law. Git off the mill property."

"I ain't on the mill property and I ain't goin' nowhere. This is a free country and I got a right to be here."

Then another voice behind her yelled, "You heard the man, you little bitch! Move it!"

It was Jake Satterfield. She would know his voice anywhere. She looked at the other soldiers but didn't recognize anyone else.

"I ain't leavin', Jake!" she shouted. "I've got every right to be here!"

"I said to move along!" Jake nudged her with the flat of the bayonet blade. Furious, Lucy swatted the blade away and grabbed the barrel of the gun, almost yanking it out of his hands.

"You crazy bitch! This thing's loaded!" Jake yelled.

"Murderer!" Lucy screamed, still gripping the gun.

The look on Jake's face was pure contempt. "Git outa here, you whore!"

"Murderer! You was up in the windows at the Bellevue mill, Jake! I seen you!"

The other soldiers gaped at Jake, wondering what to do. They were used to acting as a group and being assailed as a group, not being singled out for abuse. This woman wasn't playing by the rules.

But for Lucy it was personal. Here now was her best friend's killer. Her enemy now had a name and a face. All of her grief and fury focused on this man, the town bully, someone she'd known all her life.

"How could you fire on your own people, Jake Satterfield? Your own people! How could you?" Lucy's face was red and her eyes flashed with tears of fury. "What kind of person are you?"

Jake's face twisted into a mask of hatred. His eyes went blank, the light in them dying and something unholy replacing it.

"Hey, Lucy," he said in a flat, lifeless tone. "Bud done it."

"What?"

Jake yanked the rifle back out of her hands, nearly knocking down the soldier next to him. Then in one quick motion he stepped toward her and jabbed the bayonet point into her side just below the ribs. The picketers let out a collective gasp. The other soldiers looked away. Lucy gaped at Jake in shock and disbelief as a warm wetness spread on her blouse near the belt line. She touched the wound and her fingers came back bloody.

"You son of a bitch!" she cried.

"Git movin' or I'll do it again."

"You try, you murderer!" she said, but she was already growing woozy. Then her knees buckled and she fell into the arms of another picketer. The man laid her out on the grass as others hovered around, clamoring to give her air.

"The last thing I remembered before I passed out was Jake Satterfield staring down at me. 'Bud done it, Lucy,' he said, 'Your own husband's brother. He killed Annie Laura. I seen 'im. He killed her. I was there.' "

"What an asshole!" I said "Did you believe him?"

"I did. I had my reasons."

"But Mama Lucy, what if he was lying?"

"You had to know Jake. He woulda liked nothin' better than to take credit for it."

"But Wallace says Uncle Bud claimed he didn't shoot anybody."

"Wallace don't know," Mama Lucy said. "Bud was a crack shot. He and Dalton both denied it, but they didn't know I got evidence Bud done it. Sam Khoury got a doctor from Chapel Hill he knew to do the autopsy. I didn't find out 'til later but the doctor told Sam the bullet that shot Annie Laura was from a different gun than the others. It won't standard issue army. It was one of Bud's. Thirty aught six. Dalton and Bud come up with that story to cover for Bud."

I couldn't argue with her. She'd had a lifetime to wrestle with these events and I could barely process all the information I was receiving. Every time I talked to her more of the story tumbled out and I still hadn't asked her about Davis and the Burlington Dynamite Plot.

"What happened after you passed out?"

"First thing I heard was someone callin' my name."

*   *   *

"Lucy, can you hear me? Lucy . . . ?"

She woke up at Alamance General to see Davis's face hovering over her. He was holding her hand. Surrounding her bed were a nurse, a doctor, and several other men.

"How you feelin', sister?" Dave asked.

"You're a very brave young woman," said a man behind her.

"And very lucky," said the doctor, checking her vital signs. "A few inches to the left and you might have lost more than blood."

"Hello, Lucy." It was Sam Khoury. A warm smile lit up his brown face.

"You don't have to worry about the hospital bills, Lucy. The union will take care of it," Dave said.

"The university community will pitch in, too."

"Lucy," Davis said, indicating the man who had just spoken, "this is Mr. Paul Green. He's a professor and a playwright over at the university. A friend of the working man."

"When you're feeling better I'd like to ask you some questions," said Mr. Green. "I'd like to write a piece for the newspapers about your bravery."

"And this is Mr. Norman Thomas," Dave continued, introducing a white-haired man with piercing eyes. "He's a supporter of the strike down from New York. He's speaking at the rally at the courthouse tomorrow."

"We appreciate your sacrifice, young lady," said Mr. Thomas. "You remind me of Ella May Wiggins. I met her in Washington once. You sang her song at the funeral on Saturday."

"You was there?" she asked weakly.

"Oh, yes." Mr. Thomas glanced at the others. "We all were. We heard you sing. I was told then you had children at home like Ella May. That you're a real firebrand."

Davis laughed. "That's my little sister, all right."

"Gentlemen, we should probably let her get some rest," the doctor said.

After thanking her for her contribution to the cause, the visitors left. Dave stayed on and sat with Lucy while she ate some canned pears. He told her about the men who'd just left and how important they were to the strike and their plans for the rally the next day on the the steps of the Alamance County courthouse and how proud he was of her.

"Oh, before I forget, sister, I brung you a book." Dave produced a worn copy of *Les Misérables*. "I'm afraid it ain't Mr. Dickens. I knowed how much you liked *Oliver Twist*. But I think you'll like this story."

Davis was always full of energy and talk ever since he gave up drinking years ago and tonight was no exception. She knew he wanted to get back to his meetings and "stractics and tategy" sessions, as he called them, but felt guilty for what happened to her, as if he were responsible, so she let him talk because it seemed to do him good. From their conversation, Lucy gathered that Davis still didn't know it was Jake who had stabbed her. Perhaps that was for the best, she thought. She was afraid to think what he'd do if he found out.

There was a knock at the door, and before Davis could open it, Dalton Cantrell came in.

"Dalton!" Lucy exclaimed.

Davis scowled. "What are *you* doing here?"

"I come to see my wife." Dalton stood inside the door with his hat in hand. "How you doin', Lucy?" He was soon joined by two other men. Lucy recognized them immediately. They were the men from Webb's front gate. Davis stood up, eyes narrowing as the men approached him.

"What's this about, Dalton?"

"You're under arrest, Davis," Dalton said.

"On what charge?"

One of the men, the tall one, reached into Dave's jacket and produced a small medicine bottle. "Well, look here what I found. Why, if it ain't some moonshine whiskey."

"That ain't mine," Dave snapped, glancing at Lucy.

Indignant, Lucy lifted up from her pillow. "He ain't had a drop of whiskey in years and you know it, Dalton. This is a frame-up."

Davis tried to move but the short, stubby man blocked his path.

"You're coming with us," replied Dalton.

"This is Alamance County," Davis said. "You and your goons don't have no jurisdiction here."

"The sheriff in Burlington seems to think we do." Dalton patted his breast pocket. "He signed these papers to have you shipped back to Eno."

The tall detective pulled a pair of handcuffs from his belt and grabbed Dave's wrist. Davis jerked back his arm and punched the man in the face. The man banked off Lucy's bed and the other one kicked Davis's legs out from under him. Davis was grabbing for the knife in his ankle holster when the tall man leaped forward and clubbed him over the head with the butt of his pistol. Davis's face hit the floor with a wet sounding smack and his eyes glazed over. Lucy screamed. The two detectives propped Davis between them and led him toward the door. A nurse appeared, took one look at the scene, and said, "What are you doing?"

"It's all right, ma'am," Dalton said. The small group of onlookers outside the door stepped back as Dalton took the nurse by the arm and guided her out of the room.

"Dalton!" Lucy yelled, wincing at the stabbing pain in her side. "Don't you hurt him! You hear me? Don't you—"

"Quiet down, Lucy," Dalton said, stepping back into the room.

"What are you doing here, Dalton?"

"My job, Lucy. It don't stop just because my wife's in the hospital."

"Where are you taking Dave? You better not hurt my brother."

"He'll be fine. Just some police business over in Eno County. That's not why I'm here, though. I come to see you."

"Well, you can get out, then. I don't want to talk to you or listen to none of your lectures."

"I ain't here to lecture. I know you're upset. To tell the truth, I don't know how we gonna feed the children now without your salary."

"Don't worry," Lucy said. "I'll find a job."

"Doin' what, Lucy? There's a depression on. What are you gonna find in Eno besides work at the mill?"

Lucy had no answer. Dalton stared out the window. Then without looking at her he said, "I talked to your boss man, Lucy."

"Sumner?"

"Not Sumner. I went to Strudwick and explained things to him. How it was with us and the children and how you didn't mean to spill coffee on Sumner."

"I didn't spill no coffee, Dalton. I threw it at him. He deserved it."

"He knows that and so do I. But you gotta say these things if you want to git along in this world."

"You had no business doin' that, Dalton," Lucy said.

"Feedin' our young'uns is my business."

"You want me to go back over there humblin' myself to Sumner? I cain't do that. He won't never let me live that down."

"Sumner'll do whatever Strudwick tells him," Dalton said. "I talked to Mr. Strudwick about it and he says he'll talk to Mr. Webb. The point is, when this strike mess is all over I think we might be able to get your job back, Lucy."

"Strudwick told you that?"

"All you got to do is sign an oath of allegiance to the mill," said Dalton, brandishing a piece of paper. The President hisself's already got Governor Winant workin' on a settlement, some pledge for the strikers to sign so they can come back to work. Mr. Strudwick spelled it out for me. You can come back to work if you sign it."

"What's it say, Dalton?"

Dalton put his hat back on and stood up as though he had to go.

"Dalton?" Lucy pressed. "What do I have to pledge?"

He looked at her. "That you won't ever mention the word 'union' on the premises again."

"I couldn't do it, Pick. I couldn't promise never to mention any word. The minute somebody says I cain't say somethin', I say it. But especially not that word. Not after what happened with me and Annie Laura. It'd be like spittin' on her grave. It was pure blasphemy, Pick."

"What did you do?"

"I throwed the paper away. I cried myself to sleep that night because I knowed I was takin' food out of the mouths of my babies and probably losin' Dalton, too, but I couldn't bring myself to do it."

"It was a loyalty oath."

"Won't nobody more loyal than me. They were the ones disloyal to me when they run me off. And when they put them men up in those windows."

"Not much has changed, Mama Lucy. Companies today lay off people by the hundreds without thinking twice about it. Loyalty's a one-way street all right."

"Well, I was right upset over it. For hours I just tossed and turned in bed, thinkin' and a-worryin'. Finally I did manage to nod off but . . . well, that was the night of the explosion."

"Of course," I said. "That was September fourteenth, 1934, the Burlington dynamite case. You heard it even in the hospital?"

"It woke me up. The plant won't too far away from the hospital. They tried to say Dave done it. Tried to name him as a conspirator. He'd a-been sent off to prison, too, if he won't a-settin' over in the Eno County jail. Dalton seen to that. Funny how things work sometimes."

The phone rang in the kitchen and I jumped up to grab it. "It's Aunt Florence," I told her. "She wants to come by in the morning."

"I don't want to talk to her," said Mama Lucy. "I don't feel up to company."

"She says she's coming, anyway. To check up on you. Lily and Beth might come, too."

"Ain't they got to work?" she said as I returned to the sofa. But there was no curiosity in her question, only a weary resignation. She tugged at a thread on the sofa and stared out the window at the sun setting behind the trees. "They think I don't know what they're up to," she said. "I know I ain't long for this world but I'll be damned if I'm going to spend the time that's left to me in that Shady Grove hellhole."

I felt like Judas. Here she'd been opening up to me, revealing her most deeply held secrets, and I'd been concealing the fact she was about to be put away. Then I remembered something that I hoped would distract us both.

"Mama Lucy, I almost forgot. I've got a present for you in the truck." Excusing myself, I ran outside, grabbed my sketchbook, and returned to the living room. I sat down on the sofa and opened the pad to the drawing I had done the other morning.

Mama Lucy gasped. "Chicken Bridge. Oh, Pick, it's so pretty."

"I tried to capture it from different angles," I said, showing her the series of sketches then returning to the first, "but this is my favorite."

Mama Lucy stared at the sketch of Chicken Bridge at night. The moon hung over the treetops, shining like a silver dollar and casting its cool glow on the water sparkling below. Jack-o'-lanterns winked like stars along the railing in the distance. She reached out with wrinkled hands and caressed the image with a lover's touch, her expression dreamy yet strangely focused. She traced each pillar of trestling, each arc of the bridge, with her fingers, as if by refamiliarizing herself with the image she could somehow reach back through time to reclaim it.

"It's just like I remember," she said, choking up. "Just like I told you." Then she reached over and hugged me fiercely, as though she'd never again let me go.

"You're right, Mama Lucy," I said when she finally released me. "They're going to put you in the rest home tomorrow."

"I knew it." She stared at the drawing and I watched a hundred emotions play across her face, as though she were reliving everything that had occurred on Chicken Bridge so many years ago.

Then I heard myself say something I never thought I'd say. "Mama Lucy," I said, "I think you should come live with us."

"No!" Cameron said when I broached the subject at home. "Absolutely not."

I had been waiting for just the right time to spring the idea on Cam, although I didn't tell her I had already proposed the idea to Mama Lucy. Wiley was upstairs doing his homework so I forged ahead.

"Just think about it," I said. "She's dying, Cam. It would only be for a few months at most."

"No way," she replied, scraping cold pasta into the trash can and banging down the lid. "I did not move back down here to nurse dying relatives. Let somebody else do it."

"What if I had said that when you asked me if we could take your mother in?"

Cam's expression told me that I was on thin ice. "My mother had cancer, Pick!"

During the weeks leading up to her mother's death Cam had divvied out drugs, changed her mother's sheets, emptied her bedpan, turned her, fed her, bathed her, applied alcohol to her bedsores, to the point of utter exhaustion. She'd been tough throughout the ordeal, never once breaking down. The day her mom died the floodgates opened. She had been out of the room when it happened, she said when she called me at work. In between sobs she asked, "Do you think she was scared, Pick, dying alone? What if she was calling for me?" I had never heard her sound so vulnerable and it made me feel weak and helpless. Then, in a small, shaking voice she asked, "Pick, can you come home now?"

"Right away," I told her.

I had watched my wife's quiet heroism in dealing with her mother's death and her unwarranted guilt in the aftermath and knew now that her resistance to taking in Mama Lucy was fed at least in part by a reluctance to relive her own experience with a dying family member. But as much as I understood that, Cam would not be the one caring for Mama Lucy—I would—and I had ghosts of my own that needed vanquishing.

Cam continued: "Also, she was done with chemo, and we knew she had only a few weeks to live."

"Mama Lucy doesn't have that much longer, either."

"Besides," Cam said, "it was my mother, not your grandmother. Not someone I barely know and whom you've had no use for until just recently. Jesus, Pick, think about *us* for a change. In case you haven't noticed, things haven't been all that great around here lately. Did you know Wiley got in a fight at school? I ran into his teacher at WellSpring. She asked if Wiley showed us the note she sent home. Seems some kid on the playground said his father was a criminal. So Wiley beat the kid up."

"Good," I said, setting a plate in the dishwasher.

"Good?" The look Cam gave me could have curdled milk. "You're proud of that?"

"I'm proud he stands up for himself."

"Oh, like father, like son, huh? You're teaching our son to settle matters with his fists. If he doesn't like what somebody says beat 'im up, is that it?"

"So now I suppose I'm a lousy father, too, right."

"That's not what I said."

"What *are* you saying?" I realized then that we were living in two different worlds. For the first time in our marriage we weren't communicating. We were drifting farther and farther apart, losing touch.

"The only thing you're interested in is your grandmother," she said, lowering her voice and glancing toward the stairwell off the kitchen. "You've been AWOL ever since we moved down here."

"*I've* been AWOL? I'm not the one who moved out of our bedroom. I'm around here all the goddamned time except for the occasional pathetic little jog over to Burlington." I was scrubbing the countertop hard enough to take off the Formica. Cameron stood there, tight-lipped and grim.

"Let me remind you that you're the one who talked me into going to that reunion," I said. " 'It'll be so great if Wiley can get to know his family,' you said. You wanted me to reunite with them in some abstract Hallmark sense but now that I'm really doing it you're jealous. You wanted me to follow you here and be the good little househusband, like those virtuous little bearded eunuchs in Chapel Hill married to all those career women you have decaf lattes with at WellSpring. You should be glad I found something interesting, something that engages me, instead of moving down here and sulking. I may seem preoccupied to you, but—"

"You're beyond preoccupation, Pickard. I love my new job but there's something missing. I was thrilled to move here, thrilled with the job and the challenge of a new home and a new career, but I need to be doing this with a full partner, a committed helpmate, somebody who's interested in me and my work the way I was interested in you and yours when we moved to New York."

"Is there somebody else?" I asked. Cameron looked away. "There is, isn't there?"

"No. Yes. There could be, if I let it."

"It's that WeltanCom jerk Jameson, isn't it?"

"Pick, Roland's a business associate."

"Business associate, my ass!"

"Hey, I saw you at Ruffin's party talking to that . . . Lisa Price. Don't tell me you're not tempted by that little tart."

"She's just a friend, Cam," I protested. And I was trying like hell to keep it that way, I didn't add.

"I'm not stupid, Pick. I see how she looks at you."

"Mom! Dad!" Wiley shouted. He was standing in the kitchen doorway in his underwear, a stricken expression on his face. "Stop fighting!"

"Mommy and Daddy are arguing, Wiley," Cam said. "We're not fighting. Get in the tub. I'll be up in a minute and we'll go over your homework. Go on, up in the tub.

"This is crazy." She swept past me, heading for the dining room. Then, turning to face me, she said, "No, I am not having an affair, but he's made it clear he's interested."

"That's nice of him. Remind me to thank him next time I see him."

"And the scary thing is, the way you've been lately I've actually thought about it." I saw her lower lip begin to tremble and realized she was about to lose it. I saw too that despite her anger, she was terrified. Where, I wondered, had our lives run off track? "I would never do that to Wiley."

"I know that." I took her into my arms and we clung to each other for a long moment. Finally I said, "I've got to do this, Cam. It's here or a rest home and I can't do that to her. I'll take care of her. You won't have to lift a finger. I promise."

She pulled away, a determined look in her eyes. "I said no. I've got the WeltanCom shoots coming up. While I'm gone I have to believe Wiley's got your undivided attention. I can't have you and Mama Lucy holed up in some room swapping bedtime stories."

I grabbed her wrists imploringly. "Cam, we've had these incredible conversations. The stories I'm hearing about my family are amazing. I want to preserve them for Wiley. And I want him to get to know Mama Lucy. He needs to know where he came from."

"You're setting me up, Pick. So everyone will blame me for putting your grandmother in a home."

"I'm not setting anybody up. I'm just trying to do right by her, that's all."

"And trying to guilt-trip me."

"Mom!" Wiley called from upstairs. "When are you coming up?"

"This is my decision, Cam," I said.

"That's right, it's your decision." She glared at me, then headed for the stairs. The last thing she said was, "And I'm telling you, Pick, you're making a huge mistake."

I was sitting in Mama Lucy's kitchen drinking coffee and eating a country ham biscuit when my father and aunts arrived.

"Where's Mother?" my father asked.

"In the bathroom getting ready to go," I replied. They looked at me stunned, their faces inscribed with a mixture of surprise and relief.

"You talked to her about this?" my father said.

"Thank God!" exclaimed Florence.

"But she's not going to Shady Grove," I said. "She's moving in with us."

"Since when?" demanded Florence, irritated not so much at the news as being caught off-guard and not having information she felt entitled to.

"This is all so sudden," my father said.

"We're going to put her in the wing bedroom with her own bathroom and everything. She'll have almost as much room as she has here."

"Are you sure, son?" my father asked. "I mean, she's a handful."

"I'm sure," I said, sounding more convinced than I felt. I led them outside where Lily asked the paramedics to wait while we worked this all out. When she returned she said, "I appreciate what you're trying to do, Pick, but you don't know what it's like being under the same roof with her."

"It's a trial," interjected Beth. "Believe me."

"And she needs constant medical attention," my father added. "How'll you deal with that?"

"Dr. Levin in Chapel Hill agreed to check in on her regularly. Look,"

I said, "it's an experiment. If it doesn't work out then we'll take her over to Shady Grove. She's agreed to go along with my judgment in consultation with Dr. Levin."

Lily looked troubled. "Pick, are you *sure* Cameron's okay with this? This sort of thing can strain a marriage."

"Hell," said Florence, "Mama Lucy practically ruint my first marriage and she wasn't even under the same roof."

"Cameron knows it won't be easy but we're up to the challenge." I glanced at the front window and saw that Mama Lucy had been watching us.

"Well, we'll certainly help out," added Lily. "And chip in, too. Like we would with the rest home. It's gonna be expensive."

"Mama don't eat much no more," said Florence. "I don't think she's gonna last much longer, tell you the truth."

"Whatever," I said, steering the conversation away from morbidity. "We'll deal with it. And it'll be my call. That was part of the agreement."

"If you say so," said Lily.

"Hey, what's she gonna do?" I joked. "It was either this or Shady Grove. The hardest thing for her to give up was her garden. If it was springtime I don't think we could have torn her away. But I promised her we could have one at Oaklawn."

"Well, it's a good thing you got canned or we'd all be up a creek," Florence said in her usual blunt style.

After the aunts were inside and I'd sent the ambulance away I asked my father, "Daddy, can I talk to you for a minute?" We walked over to my truck and surveyed the empty bed.

"I appreciate you taking this on, son," he said. "I know you've had your differences with Mama Lucy."

"Daddy, Mama Lucy told me about Mother."

His eyes were wary. "What do you mean?"

"That Mother committed suicide."

My father blanched and he stammered, "Why in the world did she say that?"

"Did she kill herself?" I asked. His looking away was answer enough. "Daddy, I'm a grown man. Why did you hide that from me?"

"I—I don't know what to say, son. I guess I didn't want you to have to remember your mother that way."

"Mama Lucy said it wasn't the first time. That she'd tried it before."

My father looked as if he were struggling under some great weight.

"There was nothing we could do to stop her. A boy shouldn't have to face something like that about somebody so close to them."

"You had no right to keep that from me, Daddy."

"I'm sorry. I'd hoped you'd never have to find out."

"That's what's wrong with this family. There's too many secrets, and too many assumptions that others can't handle the truth."

"I didn't want you to be hurt, son. Is that so bad?"

"It would have been painful, but at least I would have understood. All these years I've felt guilty for her death, like a murderer, for going along with it and blaming you and Mama Lucy for sending her to that place."

Standing there looking at the old man who had survived so much, a great feeling of sadness and love and regret came over me. I realized my father was still the same little boy who had been farmed out to relatives while his mother recovered in a hospital from a bayonet wound received in the throes of a great social upheaval he wasn't even aware of. He was the teenager who a few years later stormed the beaches of Salerno and Anzio and watched his buddies get blown away and all he could offer was morphine to ease their pain. And though he miraculously survived those carnage-strewn shores he came home to marry a pretty young crippled girl he thought he could care for. But he was no match for the demons she would struggle with all her life and that would leave her a suicide in a mental hospital.

"Daddy, the day we took Mother to the hospital was the worst day of my life," I said, my voice cracking. "I couldn't bear to see Mama Lucy put into a home, too. I couldn't do that to her any more than I could do it to you."

My father looked at me with new understanding. "I'm sorry, son."

"Will you do something for me?" I asked. "After we get Mama Lucy settled in and all, will y'all come spend Thanksgiving with us? You and Tess and all the sisters?"

My father clasped me in an awkward embrace and for a long moment we stood there by the pickup truck. "We'd be proud to."

I felt a surge of relief wash over me. With Cam and Mama Lucy under the same roof I was going to need all the help I could get.

PART IV

THE SECRETS OF ENO

YOU CAN'T GO HOME AGAIN

We moved Mama Lucy into Oaklawn that morning.

"I always wondered what this place looked like inside," she said as I escorted her into the front hallway. She took in the high ceilings and mantelpieces like an awestruck child.

"So what do you think?" I asked.

"I can't believe my grandson owns the house where Spencer Webb lived."

Mama Lucy had packed light: her clothes, her TV set, some photographs, her medicines and Petey, her cockatiel. The wing bedroom, where she would stay, was set off from the main living area of the house and had its own bathroom and a view of the grounds of Oaklawn. "Whooeee! You in high cotton now, ain'tcha, old woman?" I teased. Mama Lucy smiled.

Our son was thrilled with the new addition to our family, especially when he discovered Petey was part of the deal.

"Did you know the Regulators when you were a little girl?" he asked.

I explained Wiley's fascination with the spooky crunching sounds emanating from the attic and his conviction that ghosts haunted Oaklawn because they had been hanged on the property.

"No, I didn't know any Regulators," Mama Lucy replied. "But if there's a ghost around I'll know about it. I know how to keep haints away."

"You do?" Wiley asked, his eyes as big as Ping-Pong balls. "What's a haint?"

"You be good and I'll tell you directly."

Satisfied, Wiley ran off to the kitchen to feed Petey.

"He looks just like you did when you was a boy, Pick," said Mama Lucy. "All eyes and mouth."

Though less exuberant than Wiley about Mama Lucy's presence, Cameron was polite and gracious, and even showed her around the kitchen drawers and cabinets and helped her get situated in the wing. Later, when Cam was tracking down some pillows for our new boarder, I thanked her for being generous to Mama Lucy.

"I've always been nice to your grandmother," she replied coolly. "Why wouldn't I be? She's a guest in our house."

"Well, I appreciate it."

"I'm pretending it's just for a short stay so I can tolerate this. We'll see how I do after the holidays."

Tension arose when Cameron came home from work and found Petey perched on her prized Aubusson chair. "Keep that bird in his cage, Pick," she warned. "I don't want to come back and find cockatiel shit on the new sofa." Mama Lucy capitulated, but insisted on putting Petey's cage out on the side porch every afternoon, ostensibly so Petey could take some air, but also, I suspected, as a gesture of defiance and martyrdom.

Early the next morning Cameron left for New York and Philly to prep for her big shoot. She would be gone almost until Thanksgiving. After walking Wiley to school I returned to find Mama Lucy sitting at the kitchen table staring out the window. "Last night I dreamed that Spencer Webb came to me in this house," she said. "And he was a-standin' there, right in the corner of that room you got me sleepin' in, just as big as life."

"What happened?"

"Nothing. He just stood there lookin' real sad. And all he said was that Bessie was dead."

"Bessie?" I asked. "The colored girl who worked for your family?"

"Uh-huh. That's all he would say, that Bessie had died. It liked to tore me up and I woke up all a-sweatin' an' upset an' I couldn't go back to sleep for a long time."

"But it was just a dream, huh? Not a ghost."

"It was a dream, but I swear"—she seemed haunted by the memory— "I had the same kind of dream about my daddy before he died."

"But you haven't seen Bessie in years."

"She brung me that cake for my birthday, but I never thanked her. I hope nothin's happened."

Guilt and anxiety produced by a vision in a dream wasn't something I knew how to deal with right then. I had trouble enough with real life. "I'm sorry your first night here had to be spoiled by a dream, Mama Lucy," I said and left her to her tea and thoughts.

I had to admit her dream was unsettling, though, and I didn't need any more bad omens. I had already spent half an hour that morning picking up garbage raccoons had strewn all over the yard.

I spent the rest of the morning with the roofers assessing some water damage under one of the gables. When I came in for lunch, Mama Lucy was in her room watching her soaps. I made us soup and sandwiches and we watched TV. She had done some decorating while I was out, and I was pleased to see my drawing of Chicken Bridge taped to her mirror. When I commented, she asked me if I missed drawing.

"Every day."

"If I had a talent like yours I wouldn't let it go to waste." Then she asked me when I was going to get another job. "It ain't right for a woman to support a man."

"Sooner or later." I didn't mention that the only job offers I'd received lately were from a sex-toy manufacturer and a cartoonist friend who drew "Betty Boinks," the buxom parody featuring an impossibly proportioned cartoon vixen, for *Playboy*. He complained that Hefner was driving him crazy editing the way he drew her tits. He said it was good money but that Hef was so obsessive about it he actually sent tissue overlay critiques with red-pencil marks urging her breasts be drawn bigger and more pointy and pert. I graciously declined.

I steered the conversation away from my stellar job prospects.

"Guess where I went today? Panther's Den." That morning, after taking Wiley to school, Russ and I had walked his dog along the New Hope and had stopped at Mama Lucy's old haunt.

"Lord, Pick, you don't mean it." She clicked off the TV with her remote.

"I walked the New Hope Mountain trail and saw the mill village, too. Or what was left of it under the kudzu and underbrush. It's like a lost civilization buried under there—fire hydrants, street markers, fence lines. You were right. Panther's Den is beautiful. It must have been very romantic meeting Spencer Webb up there."

"It was. Until we got caught."

All day long at work in the spool room she had been practicing what to say to Spencer and how to say it. At the end of her shift Lucy waited until the road by the factory was clear of prying eyes, then headed up Dimmock's Creek Road and got far enough around the bend before she slipped off into the woods. As she sat on the rock by the mouth of the cave, watching a snake drop from a tree branch to the ground and slither away, she went over it again, but it still didn't sound right.

Lucy had never known a boy like Spencer Webb. He wasn't at all like the mill village boys she'd grown up with. She could talk to Spencer. He was smart and sensitive like Annie Laura and well-spoken and he seemed interested in what she had to say and he always had something interesting to say himself, which made what she intended to tell him all the more painful.

A few minutes later she heard the whistle from the trail below. She whistled back, indicating the coast was clear. When Spencer appeared, they embraced and kissed each other passionately. Finally, they released each other and settled onto the big rock at the mouth of the cave. Lucy felt sick, wrung out emotionally. She hadn't slept the night before and knew she had dark circles under her eyes and feared that Spencer would always remember their last meeting with her not looking her best. But more importantly, she feared she might be making a big mistake. Spencer started to say something but Lucy touched a finger to his lips. "Spencer," she said. "I've decided to marry Dalton Earl."

Spencer looked as if the breath had been knocked out of him. Lucy looked away, afraid to speak, fearing that if she did, she would take back her words, fearing that she wouldn't. Lucy couldn't bear to look at the hurt on his face, and glanced away. In the near distance, clearly visible through the trees, Chicken Bridge stretched across the New Hope River. Its frame, aglow months ago with grinning jack-o'-lanterns, looked skeletal now and sad.

"But why?" he finally asked. "I know you don't want to. You're too young." Spencer had known about Dalton from the beginning and about the pressure Lucy's parents had put on her to get married, but because of the way she acted with her older suitor and the casual way she talked about it, it had become something of a joke between them. She even used Dalton to tease Spencer and to try to make him jealous.

"My mama and daddy say I have to," she said, fighting back tears. "They say Dalton's a good catch and I'd be a fool to pass up an offer like that." She felt like a fraud using her parents' words against him—words she had scorned when she heard them spoken to her. In fact, she sometimes wondered if her resistance to Dalton was a direct reaction against her parents' enthusiasm. After all, he was nice enough and good looking enough and they said he had money, even if he was as old as Methuselah. Lucy knew deep down that there was no future with Spencer Webb, no chance for a moneyed mill owner's son with a poor linthead girl. Nevertheless she loved him and she didn't want to hurt Spencer and the knowledge that her secret rendezvous with him would have to end devastated her.

"This is ridiculous," argued Spencer. "You're the prettiest girl in Eno. You could have any fellow in town."

"Any fellow, Spencer?"

Spencer looked away.

"We was doomed from the start, Spencer Webb, and both of us knew it."

"I love you, Lucy."

"I love you too." They held each other, afraid to let go.

Lucy, her head on Spencer's shoulder, realized that this might be the last time they were ever alone together. She ran her fingers along the great slab of stone they were sitting on until she felt the crude letters Spencer had carved there months ago—letters the rain and wind and weather had done nothing to diminish: S.W. + L.B.

She always looked for them first thing when she arrived at their secret spot and she sought solace in their permanence now. Panther's Rock was covered with countless such hieroglyphs. From the first, the initials in the rock had been a source of amusement and speculation and there was something wild and reckless in the way Spencer had carved them there, although Lucy doubted anyone would recognize whose they were. He reminded her of Tom Sawyer the way he hung upside down over the ledge, ruining the edge on his Randall knife in the process but engraving the stone forever with evidence of their love. Now the chiseled letters mocked Lucy.

"I brought you something." Spencer removed a book from the back of his trousers and handed it to Lucy. "It's a book of stories." Its cover was coffee-colored burlap with a maroon silhouette of a boy reading a book under a tree. The title on the spine read, *Tales for Young Readers*. Stamped on the inside cover was the legend, *Property of Eno Public Schools*.

"It's my textbook for American Lit. They got some new ones and were going to send these to the colored school. There's some good stories in there I think you'll like."

Lucy thumbed through the pages, weeping at the unfairness of a world that would deny her a future with Spencer Webb. She threw her arms around him and clung to him with a desperation that bordered on panic. When she pulled back, Spencer's face appeared before her as though through a warped windowpane.

The sound of a twig cracking and a girl's hushed giggle snapped Spencer's head around. "Somebody's coming," he said.

But before he and Lucy could untangle themselves, a voice behind them drawled, "Well, now, lookee who's here!" and Jake Satterfield stumbled into the clearing with a dark-haired girl in tow. The girl was a local and known to be wild and loose with the boys. Lucy even heard that before the sheriff put a stop to it she had invited boys behind the West End depot to touch her private parts. She had large bosoms, a bad complexion and irregular teeth. Her name was Connie Mae Locklear but the boys called her Coozie Mae.

"Well if it ain't Lucy Barlow and her boyfriend, Spencer Webb," slurred Jake, clearly drunk. "Why ain't you at the ball game, Lucy, with your little gimp girlfriend Annie Laura Gaskins?"

"What do you want, Satterfield?" demanded Spencer.

Jake steadied himself and scowled at Spencer, his jaw clenching.

"C'mon, Jake," Connie Mae said, "let's get out of here. Leave Mr. Webb's boy alone." She smiled unctuously at Spencer, through her moonshine stupor. She worked first shift in the weave room with Lucy's sister Eunice and was known to flirt with Mr. Sumner and occasionally go into the back room with him.

Jake ignored her. "What y'all doin' up here, Spencie?" He lurched forward, circling them and leering. "Whooee! I bet you carved y'all's names up here on Panther's Rock."

A medicine bottle full of moonshine poked from the back pocket of Jake's trousers. Lucy smelled the alcohol on his breath. Spotting the letters Spencer had chiseled into the stone Jake whooped and called out to Connie Mae to come over.

"C'mere, girl, and lookeheah what I found! S.W. + L.B. Spencer Webb plus Lucy Barlow. I knowed it. They in love. Can you believe that? Now if that ain't the purtiest notion."

"When you gon' carve our names in there, Jakie?" asked Connie Mae grinning coyly, trying to lighten up the charged atmosphere. Jake scowled at her and her smile disappeared.

"So I reckon y'all up here for the same reason I am, huh, Spencie." Jake smirked and pulled the girl to his side. "Git you a little of that West End cooze."

"Get outa here, Satterfield," Spencer said. His voice had an air of authority to it, as though he was not only used to giving orders but also to having them obeyed. "Go home."

"What's this?" Jake lurched forward and snatched the book out of Lucy's hand.

"Give that back!" shouted Lucy.

"I just want to look at it." Jake thumbed through the pages. "Aw, now ain't that sweet. They readin' poems to each other. Love poems, I reckon. Ain't that romantic, Coozie?" Connie Mae flinched at her nickname.

"Give it *back*, Jake," Spencer snapped.

"Who's gonna make me, rich boy?"

Spencer's voice was booming. "Give it back and get the hell outa here!"

"C'mon, Jake, let's go," Connie Mae pleaded. "That's Mr. Webb's boy."

"Shut up, Coozie. I know it's Mr. Webb's boy and the way I figure it"—he leveled his gaze at Spencer—"he ain't in no position to be orderin' me nowhere. Seein' as how his mama and daddy would shit to see their precious Spencie comin' home with a West End girl on his arm." He spat a wad of tobacco onto the ground and wiped his chin with his sleeve "Or are you like your daddy, Spencie? Just come out here to our side a town when the mood hits you?"

In a flash Spencer was up and charging Jake like an enraged bull. The boys collided and the book flew from Jake's hand into the cave. Lucy scrambled after it as Spencer pinned Jake with his knees and pummeled him with his fists. Jake hooked his legs around Spencer's shoulders and tore him off, then scrambled to his feet while a screeching Connie Mae ran to him and tried to pull him back. Jake shoved her away, spat out a mouthful of tobacco and blood, and gave Spencer, who had recovered from the spill and was now circling Jake in a low crouch watching and waiting for an opening, a look that chilled Lucy to the bone. Jake reached into his back pocket and flicked out a long wicked-looking blade.

Lucy screamed. "Look out, Spencer, he's got a knife!"

Connie Mae pleaded, "Leave him alone, Jake. You gonna git us all fired!"

"I don't give a shit if I git laid off workin' for the likes of him," said Jake, his eyes burning into Spencer.

"But your mama needs her job," Connie Mae pleaded.

"Sorry sumbitch thinks he's better'n us."

"Your girlfriend's got a point, Jake," Spencer said. "My daddy's mean as a snake."

"Hell," Jake said, "he might give me a raise if I cut up his boy for bait."

"Yeah, that's right," answered Spencer, "my daddy might not shed too many tears but my mama would, and I can promise you this—he likes her a whole lot better than he likes you."

"You better listen to Connie Mae, Jake," said Lucy, who was more familiar with Jake's capacity for mayhem than Spencer.

"Fuck you, bitch," Jake replied.

"Please," Connie Mae implored, "I can't lose my job. And neither can your people. Please Jake, don't."

Finally, Jake seemed to realize everything that was at stake. He swiped the blood from his mouth, returned the knife to his back pocket, swigged down some moonshine, and allowed Connie Mae to lead him away. Lucy, who hadn't realized she was holding her breath, exhaled a sigh of relief and ran to Spencer. Just then Jake pulled away from Connie Mae and leveled a look of absolute hatred directly at Spencer.

"You gonna regret this, Webb. You gonna be sorry you ever laid a hand on Jake Satterfield."

The next morning I took the truck over to the West End and parked along Dimmock's Creek Road near the wooded area where the old mill village was buried. The sky was overcast and the air was moist but it had not started raining yet, though the absence of morning sunlight made the temperature chilly enough for me to wear a jacket over my sweats. I entered the woods by the overpass where the river trail picked up again and retraced the riverbank route Russ and I had walked the day before, hoping I would remember the spot where the path veered off to Panther's Den. I recognized the fork with no problem and headed up the steep slope.

When I reached the clearing on the bluff with the cave gaping out over the river like a yawning mouth I walked over to the rock I had seen the day before. A used condom lay on the ground like a discarded snake-skin. A number of empty beer cans littered the area. I stepped over the detritus and scoured the rock's surface for markings. Sure enough, it was covered with ancient names and initials like some rural overpass or high school water tower. Although most of the letters were worn away by decades of wear from the elements, there along the front side I saw, faded but still visible, high above the others on the front of the rock facing the river, the large carved initials, S.W. + L. B.

A shiver shot through me as I ran my fingers over them.

"Hello, stranger," said a voice, low and husky and feminine.

Lisa, her figure lithe and buxom in a stylish runner's top and sleek black biking pants, looked up at me from the trail below. The cool temperature caused her breath to hang in vaporous puffs under her radiant smile.

"What are you doing here?" I asked.

"Shouldn't I be asking you that?" She laughed, and jogged up the trail into the clearing until she was standing beside me. "This is my territory, Cantrell. I've walked all over and around New Hope Mountain every morning for years now, rain or shine."

"How did you know it was me up here?"

"I was jogging over the rise by the rock quarry when I saw your truck pull up along Dimmock's Creek Road. I saw you duck into the trees by the river."

"Why didn't you yell at me?"

"Too far away. Besides I wanted to stalk you and see what you were up to. Burying treasure, I hope. Or a body?"

"I'm afraid not. Nothing that glamorous."

"I almost didn't find you. I sometimes walk this trail but I've never been up here on this ridge. Beautiful view, huh?"

"Yeah, look at this," I said, pointing at the letters carved into the rock. "That's my grandmother's initials from when she was a young girl."

"Who's the lucky guy?" Lisa asked. "Your grandfather?"

"No. A boy named Spencer Webb. His family owned the Bellevue mill."

"Any relation to Franklin Webb?"

"Yes, actually. His grandfather."

"How cozy. Eno is a small town. Pretty incestuous, I'd say. That makes you and Franklin kissing cousins, right?" I just smiled while Lisa wandered over to the mouth of the cave and looked around inside. "How did you find out about this place?" she asked, emerging from the shadow of the opening in the rock.

"My grandmother told me about carving initials into this rock when she was a girl. I had to check it out."

"Was this some sort of campground?"

"Actually, it was a Lover's Lane."

"Mmm," said Lisa, suggestively raising her eyebrows and surveying the area again with added interest as if I had told her it was indeed the site of buried treasure or at the very least the signing of the Declaration of Independence.

"Young couples from the mill village would come up here in the early part of the century and court and spark."

"Court and spark, huh?" said Lisa, looking at me seductively. "That's a nice phrase. Sounds so much more modest and evocative than hooking up or sucking face."

"Yeah," I said, ignoring the innuendo and turn of conversation. "It was the only place in the mill village they could get any privacy back then."

"Still seems pretty private to me."

"It was a different time," I said, looking back down at the initials. "I like trying to imagine what it was like back then. Y'know, it really wasn't that long ago."

"This place is pretty charged for you, isn't it?" said Lisa, moving over to inspect the initials in the rock. After a minute, she stood up and gazed out over the vista. "Pick, look," she suddenly exclaimed. "Up there. In the sky."

"Where?"

She pressed closer to me and extended her arm. I turned in the direction she was pointing.

"There. Just beyond that cluster of branches. Look, it's the white hawk. The one that got your dog."

I squinted through the trees into the sunlight breaking through the clouds. There, riding the currents, rising over the mountain, magnificent in its solitude and majesty, was the albino hawk. As I gazed at the raptor I became aware of Lisa's arm around my waist steadying my line of vision and the press of her body against my side. My heart pounded and groin stirred as I lowered my gaze and turned to look levelly into her eyes. She was breathtakingly luscious. It would be so sweet to make love to her right here and now. After all, Cameron was certainly less than amorous toward me lately. And I had not been with another woman in fifteen years. Not since my freewheeling bachelor days had I been around any woman so overtly sensual, so unselfconsciously sexual. I had to admit having a woman like Lisa attracted to me when I had not felt desirable in such a long time had done wonders for my battered ego.

But as my libido soared with the abandon of the great white hawk my conscience remained tethered to the earth. Even if Cameron and I had not been at our best lately I cherished her and did not want to hurt her. Somehow the vulnerability of our marriage and the sheer fragility of my emotional state kept my passions reined in.

"No, Lisa," I said finally, disengaging. "I can't. You're a beautiful woman and I'm really attracted to you, but I just can't do it. I'm sorry. I'll probably kick myself forever but I love Cameron. Things are too shaky right now to risk anything more. There's too much at stake. I'm sorry." I turned my back on Lisa Price and Panther's Rock and headed back down the trail.

I returned home to find contractors making repairs to the slate roof. I had forgotten they were returning and wondered if they had disturbed or frightened Mama Lucy. In the house I scanned the kitchen gallery for signs of her and saw nothing but Petey sitting forlornly in his cage on the counter. The door to her suite was closed and I assumed she was in there reading or watching TV. Then I noticed a note by the phone in the kitchen. Mama Lucy must have taken it down. In her ninety-year-old shaky but still primly legible hand there was a phone number and a message that read, "Pick. Call Marcus Teal, Publisher, *Charlotte Sentinel*."

I called Teal, who said he wanted to meet with me as soon as possible to discuss a cartooning job. Early that Friday before Thanksgiving I drove the two hours over to Charlotte, using the Volvo while Cam was away. The morning was bright and crisp and the traffic manageable. I had no idea what Marcus Teal had in mind, whether he was acting as an agent for somebody else, brokering a deal possibly for some other Gallant newspaper, or inquiring on behalf of the *Sentinel*, which seemed unlikely to me. I didn't ask on the phone because I didn't want to appear too eager, and no matter how skeptical, I was in no position to ignore any opportunity to return to work.

The Charlotte skyline rises incongruously out of the rolling hills and pinetops of the Carolina Piedmont in an eruption of pastel green, the color of money and photosynthesis. It looms and gleams like Oz's Emerald City, a postmodern marvel of turquoise-tinted plate glass gloss and sheen reflecting blue sky, pink clouds, and a sea of pine off the sides of its spires and towers that makes it look like the city itself was created on a computer screen at Disney World and just arrived by E-mail on the border of the Carolinas.

I sat in the chair opposite Teal, looking around the office with its clean glass-topped desk, beige furniture, and modern art on the wall, waiting for him to finish his phone call. He spoke loudly and confidently to his caller, glancing over at me occasionally like he was performing for my benefit, winking with his ice-blue eyes as if we were in on some private joke the person on the line didn't know about. Teal's silver-white hair was as trimly cut as always, framing his tanned chiseled features. He was dressed nattily with a white collar on a blue pinstripe shirt, red tie and matching red galluses, filling out the role of yet another publisher from Central Casting.

"Pick, how the hell are you?" said Teal, flashing his incisors when he got off the phone.

"Fine, I guess."

"Goddammit, Cantrell, we've missed you here in Charlotte." He beamed, reaching over his desk to shake hands and knocking over his coffee cup. "Shit!" He mopped up the mess with paper towels he produced from the bottom drawer. "I've got to admit I was a little miffed at you when you left us, but that's water under the bridge now. The fact is, the paper's gotten duller." He folded his hands, gazed at me earnestly, and settled back into his leather swivel chair. "We don't know how it happened, it just has."

I didn't think it appropriate to tell him that I thought he was the single most responsible person for turning what used to be a lively newspaper, one of the best in the South, into an excruciatingly boring rag. Marcus Teal had come to the *Sentinel* with the mandate from Gallant to make the paper more responsive to the community, which of course meant the "business" community. His Chamber of Commerce–forged columns which criticized stories and questioned the paper's hard-fought editorial positions had alienated the newsroom, undermined morale and driven off talent. He had resisted running the prize-winning brown lung series and postponed it until a group of key staffers threatened to resign if it didn't run. He openly criticized my cartoons and chastised the editorial page editor for running them. When I won the Pulitzer, Teal gave a speech in the newsroom, damning with faint praise the editorial page and the news side for their brown lung series and praising me with faint damns.

"Let me cut to the chase," said Teal, "We want you to come back to work for us."

"Oh?"

"It'll be problematic, of course, but we've given it some thought and we think we might be able to swing it." He grinned and looked out the window at the Charlotte skyline. "Naturally, we won't be able to pay you New York wages. But I would imagine that's not a priority for you at this point in your career."

"Making a living is a priority," I countered.

"The point is, we're all in uncharted waters here."

"What about Rollins?" I asked.

"He'll just have to deal with it," declared Teal, not liking to be reminded of unpleasant wrinkles in his scheme to bring me back. "No law we can't have two cartoonists. After all, you won a Pulitzer Prize for us. I don't think we're in any danger of him repeating that feat." Then Teal looked out the window again and continued contemplatively, "True, you've had your problems."

"How would you handle the scandal?" I asked.

"A brief statement of contrition ought to do it," he said. "Maybe we'll set up some community service, some public penance, that sort of thing. Politicians do it all the time after they screw up. Image rehab to get reelected. Why not political cartoonists? Of course you won't be able to comment on issues of violence in the workplace but we can work around that. We'll take some hits within the media, for sure, but that's manageable."

"You've given this a lot of thought," I said.

"You're a real reader-grabber, Cantrell. Especially among the young readers we're trying to attract. You're worth it." He smiled perfunctorily.

"We just bought a house in Eno."

"What's that? Two hours from here? That's close enough."

This was too much to process. Teal was serious about rehiring me. Maybe I wasn't unemployable as a political cartoonist. My natural guardedness and skepticism were starting to melt away, although I was a little put off by Teal's confidence he could entice me back. But wouldn't Cam be surprised to come home and find her husband employed again? I wasn't crazy about Mark Teal but I had worked for him before. I could do it again.

"And of course, you'll be working with the editorial page editor," Teal continued. "You'll need to get along but he won't try to tell you how to do your job. Our only requirement is that he be comfortable with the comment that runs on his page."

"I don't have any problems with Ron. We worked together for years."

It might actually be fun, I thought, but I wasn't about to commit on the spot.

"Oh, Ron Walters is no longer editorial page editor. Didn't you hear? He decided he missed hard news. He's gone back to Metro. We've got a new man now."

"Who's that?" I asked.

Teal picked up the phone. "Jane, has he showed up yet? Send him in." He put the phone down and said to me, "I asked him to join us. Of course, we've discussed all this and he's really looking forward to working with you. Oh, here he is now." Teal was looking past me toward the door. I turned around and there before me was the *Sentinel*'s new editorial page editor, Tony Weeks.

"Hello, Cantrell," he said.

THE MISSING PIECE

Cameron returned from her trip the night before Thanksgiving and didn't miss a beat shifting into full producer mode. Traditionally, we had spent the holiday in the mountains with her sisters, even when we were living in New York, but this year, because of her work schedule, and because Mama Lucy was encamped at our house, the holiday was turning into something of a Cantrell family gathering and unofficial housewarming for Oaklawn. The numbers had swelled since I invited my father and aunts and I was surprised Cam was willing to take on a houseful of guests between two tightly scheduled shoots. But she seemed to jump at the chance to play hostess for the first time at Oaklawn, especially when I assured her I would handle all the arrangements and my aunts would help prepare the meal. She seemed in good spirits when she got home, if somewhat distracted, and I suspected she welcomed the buffer of guests to keep from facing me one-on-one before she flew out again to Chicago on Monday morning.

Mama Lucy had been keeping mostly to herself, spending most days in her room or rocking on the front porch if the weather was warm, shelling peas, husking corn, or listening to the radio while Wiley went to school and I worked on the house. She had taken a liking to Flappy, who was mending nicely, and would sometimes hold her in her lap, massaging her ears, but only if Petey was in his cage in the kitchen or on the side porch and couldn't see her and get jealous. We usually only talked at mealtimes, but with Thanksgiving approaching and family coming she began fussing and fretting about it, frustrated by her inability to cook and prepare for the holiday as she always had. Although lately with Cameron gone she had taken to sitting at the kitchen table and instructing Wiley and me in the fine art of down-home cooking. With Petey on her shoulder she would bark orders at the two of us as we tried with varying degrees of success to follow her meticulous directions for making iced tea, pork chops, gravy and biscuits, or country-style steak,

Mama Lucy-style. Our efforts were valiant and the results seemed tasty to us, but they never seemed to meet her high standards.

I had worked hard to get the house in shape for our holiday guests and for Cameron's return. True, there were still a few unfinished projects, sawhorses and stacks of wood and bricks covered with plastic lying about, a gaping hole under a gable where the roofers were repairing water damage to a louvered vent, but we had made a lot of progress since September and Oaklawn was beginning to feel like a real home. The kitchen and bathrooms were nearly finished and much of the cabinet work and the new tile floors were done. The walls were painted and most of the rest of the interior's vintage pine floors were freshly polished. It was already beginning to feel like a holiday house, a splendid place for a party.

When my father and his sisters, who had yet to see our new home, arrived on Thanksgiving day they were stunned by Oaklawn's elegance and grandeur. "Are you sure you're a Cantrell?" Florence asked me as I gave her a guided tour of the grounds. Although as children they had lived less than a mile away from Eno's so-called Historic District my father kept saying, "We never knew these houses was over here." Oaklawn was a mansion to them, and it seemed to contradict their sense of my personal fortunes; this was a home for the thriving and prospering, not for someone whose career was on the skids.

A short time later Buzz and Violet arrived, bringing with them the newly sober Wallace Cantrell and his girlfriend. I was glad to see Wallace but he seemed intimidated by the splendor of Oaklawn and he and his girlfriend spent most of their time talking together at the far end of the picnic table where we were to eat. I had invited Sandy Murphy so she could meet Mama Lucy, but before I could introduce them, my aunts buttonholed her and regaled her with stories from their childhood.

The Cantrell girls were extraordinarily close and protective of each other; theirs was the intimacy of foxholes, of soldiers who had seen battle together against a common enemy and survived to tell the tale, and their account of Mama Lucy's many crimes against them left little to the imagination.

They told Sandy how, with no warning at all, Mama Lucy would fly into rages and beat them with hickory switches or clothes hangers until their legs would bleed. Or how, in the war years, if she returned from her job at the furniture factory and found the house even the slightest bit messy she would wake them up in the middle of the night to mop the floors and dust. They told her how as young girls they'd been terrified by Mama Lucy and how they ran away regularly until they were old enough to fend for themselves and finally left home for good.

"If she was dipping snuff, she was in a good mood," explained Lily. "That was the only way we could tell. That's how we monitored her moods. If she had a dip of Strong Dental in her cheek the coast was clear."

"Where was her husband?" asked Sandy incredulously.

"He was off working in Rutherfordton or Hamlet, some other town, trying to make enough money to keep us clothed and fed," explained Lily. "Mama worked in the White Furniture factory in Mebane during those years. They seldom spent time together."

"Nobody blamed Daddy for stayin' gone," said Florence.

Sandy listened to it all like the oral historian she was, with empathy and calm, storing each opinion and anecdote away for recall later, when she would attempt to put together the confusing and often contradictory puzzle pieces—sainted labor movement heroine; abusive mother; defiant wife—that was the woman we all called Mama Lucy.

My aunts had arrived with provisions, platters and trays loaded with gastronomical bounty, and when they finished with Sandy they moved to the kitchen where they bustled about, helping Cameron prepare biscuits and iced tea, turkey and dressing. The men snacked and jawed and watched football and the kids played with the limping Flappy and chased Frisbees and footballs on the lawn.

Later, when it was time to eat, Lily and Beth helped Mama Lucy down the back steps and set her at the head of two long picnic tables we'd placed under an oak tree next to the summer kitchen. The day was crisp and clear, but not cold—perfect for a picnic.

As we ate, I could see Sandy already working hard to reconcile the stories my aunts had told her with the tiny, birdlike creature nibbling her food at the end of the picnic table. When Mama Lucy had trouble cutting her meat my aunts helped her. It was touching to see Lucy's daughters steadying the wrinkled hands that once had beaten them, lavishing on their mother during her final years the loving care and attention she had in many ways denied them during their childhoods.

A few minutes into dinner Buzz surprised me by asking through a mouthful of potato salad, "Pick, what's this about you going to Charlotte?"

"And why didn't you come see us?" Tess said.

"I was just there for a meeting," I mumbled into my corn on the cob, hoping the topic would disappear along with the turkey and dressing on my plate.

Cameron looked at me quizzically. "You didn't tell me you went to Charlotte while I was gone."

"I didn't have a chance."

"What's in Charlotte?" Buzz asked.

"How did you know I went?" I countered, stalling for time.

"Mama Lucy told me," he parried.

I scowled down the table at my grandmother and remembered I had invited a fountain of family gossip into my home.

"I thought ever'body knowed that, Pick," she responded, unintimidated.

"What kind of meeting was it?" asked Cameron.

"Oh, I met with the publisher of the *Sentinel*," I said, trying to play it down.

"Really?" exclaimed my father.

Cameron looked at me questioningly.

"It's nothing, Daddy. He wanted to talk to me about a job, but . . . it's out of the question."

"Why?" Sandy pressed. "I know a lot of people would love to see that."

"The editorial page editor," I answered. "A guy named Tony Weeks."

"He's editor now?" asked Cameron. "How did that happen?"

"Shit floats," I said, forgetting there were kids at the table. Wiley giggled.

"Are you sure you couldn't work something out, son?" implored my father. "Jobs like that don't come around too often."

"I know, Daddy," I said, "but Weeks was a deal-breaker for me."

I could see Cameron stifling her impatience. I knew she favored my taking the job, even if it meant I had to swallow my pride and work for a prick like Tony Weeks. But she was also annoyed that I hadn't told her sooner.

"Besides," I continued, elaborating my defense in anticipation of Cameron's arguments. "It was a setup. The way Marcus Teal and Tony Weeks were colluding gave me the willies. It should have been a tougher decision for them."

"Of course they were laying a trap," Buzz announced, getting up and refilling his glass of iced tea. "They'd like nothing better than to parade the prodigal son, Pick Cantrell, around the newsroom: 'See, this is what happens when you get uppity and run off to the big city.' What a coup. They'd land you back on their pages to liven up their sorry rag and get to punish and humiliate you at the same time."

"Do you really think so?" asked Sandy.

"Absolutely," Buzz said. "And let me guess. They wanted you at a cut rate, too?"

"Naturally."

"Well, you're not exactly in a position to bargain," observed Cameron.

"I'm in a position to say no," I replied. "But, I have to admit it was mighty tempting. Frankly, I was surprised at how tempting."

"I'm sure it was, but you were right not to take it," said Buzz confidently. "They would have tortured you. Don't you worry, cousin. Something's gonna come along for you." I wanted to kiss Buzz Rankin for defending my decision in the face of general family skepticism, and I saw Sandy gazing at him approvingly.

"I hope you're right," I replied, wishing the subject closed.

"Hurry up, Dad," Wiley shouted, tossing the pigskin high in the air. "Let's play football." Then he fired a bullet pass at Buzz, who was returning to the table with his iced tea Buzz snagged the pass one-handed.

"Later, Wiley," I protested. "We haven't finished eating yet."

"You better have cleaned your plate or no dessert, young man," warned Cameron.

"The boy's got an arm like his old man," Buzz said, sitting down. "I swear that kid's gonna have it made when he's a teenager."

"How so?" Cam asked.

"He's athletic for one thing, and good-lookin' like his mama"—he lifted his glass to Cameron, then gestured across the expanse of lawn— "and look at this place. It's the biggest house in town."

"Oh, Daddy, hush," said Violet, punching her father's arm.

"He's gonna be the catch of Eno High," Buzz continued, smiling, putting his arm around his daughter. "All the little redneck girls are gonna want to move into Tara."

"Oh, great," said Cameron, groaning. "We'll have to send him away to boarding school or a monastery. There's already one little girl in his class who has a crush on him. I feel so sorry for her. Her name's Carla. Her mother died and she lives in a trailer with her daddy."

"You better not let her see where he lives," admonished Buzz. "She'll be pregnant before Wiley's sixteen."

Violet rolled her eyes at her father and everyone laughed but I found myself contemplating what Buzz was saying. Until that moment it had never really crossed my mind that my son, by virtue of his living at least by Eno's standards in a state of relative privilege, in the big white house on the hill, would one day be cast in the Spencer Webb role—the scion of a privileged family—and be regarded as the catch of Eno. I glanced down at Mama Lucy, who was surrounded by her daughters, to see if any of this talk had registered on her.

"Mama Lucy," I said, pointing at Sandy, "this is the young lady I told you about who's studied the mill strike. She gave me the pamphlet Dave wrote. The one about the Burlington Dynamite Plot."

"Burlington Dynamite Plot? What's that?" asked Cameron.

"Haven't you told Cam about our illustrious forebears?" asked Buzz, who did not know just then about the vast chasm that now separated me from my wife.

"Not yet," I said. "This is the first family get-together since Sandy gave it to me."

"It was a conspiracy to break the strike Pick's grandmother partici-pated in," Sandy told her, then went on to explain to everyone who had missed our dog and pony show at St. Stephen's about the frame-up Davis Barlow had chronicled so many years ago. Meanwhile I fetched the faded old pamphlet, now encased in a Ziploc bag, from the house and passed it around the table.

"Hey, I didn't know Uncle Davis was a Communist," said Aunt Florence, examining the Labor Defender booklet.

"Dave won't no Communist," barked Mama Lucy. "Who says he was a Communist?"

"How come I never knew Uncle Dave was mixed up in all that, Mama Lucy?" asked Lily.

"Good question," I said, nodding at Sandy.

"Davis was right in the middle of it," Mama Lucy said. "But that don't make him no traitor to his country. He was wounded in the war, y'know."

"World War I," I clarified.

"That's right. And if that don't make you a patriot I don't know what does!" She looked at Florence. "Who said he was a Communist?"

"Nobody *said* he was a Communist, Mama Lucy," I replied. "Florence was just teasing."

"How would we know, anyway?" Lily asked. "He died before any of us was old enough to get to know him."

"All I remember was those snakes of his," said Florence, wrinkling her nose. "How he used to carry 'em around in his pockets when we was little and would ask us if we wanted to see one and liked to scared us to death."

"He collected 'em ever since he was a boy," explained Mama Lucy. "Used to bring home cottonmouths and rattlers and bull snakes."

"I heard he was bit one time by a coral snake," Buzz declared, "the most poisonous snake in North America."

"I didn't think you survived something like that," I said. "What happened?"

"When Davis was young he was bad to drink," Mama Lucy explained. "He give it up in his twenties. But before, he was always mixed up with moonshiners out in the county. He always had a jug on 'im. Anyways, when he was a teenager he come upon the snake when he was out drinkin' and fishin' with some buddies down in Wilmington. Well, he'd never seen one of them before and when he picked it up it sunk its teeth into his thumb and pumped him full of venom. His hand swoll up somethin' awful."

"He shoulda been dead within a coupla minutes," Buzz said. "But he staggered back into town with that snake stuck to his finger. A doctor identified it and they rushed him to the hospital for anti-venom."

"Surviving a coral snake bite," I marveled. "Now that's impressive."

"Davis was one tough son of a bitch," Buzz said.

"We used to tease him that he loved his snakes better'n people." Mama Lucy chuckled at the memory. "And he said he sho 'nuff did, and we asked him why, and he said 'cause you could count on a snake to be a snake."

Cameron was leaning forward listening intently. She was starting to get a whiff of the tales that had drawn me back to my family.

"Davis was quite a character, all right," Mama Lucy said, "but he won't no Communist."

"How did he die?" asked Cameron.

"Accident," Mama Lucy said simply. But, as always, I suspected there was more to the story than that.

*   *   *

The ringing of the telephone pulled Lucy awake. Dalton had not slept well since the strike and was sitting out on the porch of the darkened house smoking a cigarette and listening to a ball game on the radio. He answered the phone in the hallway and Lucy lay there listening to his deep low voice saying "yessir" and "uh-huh" the way he always did when he was talking to Sheriff Roberts. A phone call at that time of night could only be trouble.

Lucy heard him ask, "What kind of accident?" and then say, "Yessir. Chicken Bridge. I'll be along directly."

Several months had passed since the strike ended and Lucy wasn't working. The way the strike died down so quickly after the arrest of the union leaders depressed Lucy. It was like Annie Laura and the others had all died for nothing. Folks just drifted back to work, the ones that were allowed to, with everybody pointing fingers and looking for scapegoats.

The Burlington dynamite defendants were tried in Alamance County Superior Court in Graham on November 28, 1934. Local interest was intense and the courtroom was packed. Lucy couldn't go herself but she read about it in the paper and heard about it from Dave, who was at every session and testified as a character witness for his friends. Lucy didn't know the defendants well but she felt in her bones that the authorities were trying to make an example of them just as they'd made of her when they'd put her on the back of the truck. Most of the evidence was circumstantial, provided by the company dicks from Pennsylvania or based on the testimony of three disreputable locals who had been arrested and charged, then freed for turning state's evidence. But the jury was handpicked by the Burlington sheriff and guaranteed to return a verdict popular with the business community. The trial was over in a week and the defendants found guilty of conspiracy and sentenced to prison. The press called it a triumph for justice and law and order in Alamance County.

Lucy was still moody and depressed over the loss of her friend and her job and would barely speak to Dalton and blamed his brother Bud for Annie Laura's death. Dalton said he was sorry about Annie Laura but defended his brother and told her there was no use dwelling on the past. He quoted scripture about letting the dead bury the dead and said he was relieved Lucy was home now with the children and that they were lucky they had come through this rough time without anything else bad happening to the family. Lucy was still wrapped up in the injustice of it all, but Dalton was just glad the strike was over.

"I got enough trouble staying able-bodied and making a paycheck enough to feed and clothe my children without everybody I know risking their lives going to work every day," Dalton had told her.

"Why do you risk your life goin' to work every day then?" Lucy would say but Dalton usually ignored her. Now he was going back out in the middle of the night to face who-knew-what and Lucy was not about to tell him but she had that bad feeling again—the one she had the morning Annie Laura got shot.

The night was moonless, cold and foggy, and it felt like the dead of winter although it was already mid-March and the perfume of redbuds and dogwoods hung in the air. Just as Dalton was getting ready to drive off Lucy pulled open the passenger side door and piled in. She was dressed in her long johns and nightgown and bundled up in a bedspread.

"What the hell do you think you're doin'?" Dalton demanded.

"Goin' with you."

"No you're not."

"Yes I am," Lucy said.

"Get out. Sheriff says there's been a accident. I gotta git."

"You said somethin' about Chicken Bridge."

"So?"

"So I'm goin', Dalton."

Dalton knew it was useless arguing with Lucy when she got this way and he was already running late. He stared at her for a beat, then backed up the car onto Cornwallis Street and burned rubber for Chicken Bridge.

When they got there Dalton pulled to the shoulder and parked with his headlights partially illuminating the narrow road.

"Stay here," he ordered, stepping out into the predawn dark.

Lucy sat in the car while Dalton placed a railroad flare in the middle of the highway to alert oncoming vehicles of danger. Lucy squinted across the span of the bridge as Dalton paced the blacktop, searching for evidence of a crash. She could tell he was about to give up, when something up ahead caught his eye. He stood there frozen, his back to her, staring into the fog. Lucy opened the car door and gazed hard in the direction Dalton was looking.

They both saw it at the same time.

Just at the edge of the Chevy's headlights where the railing disappeared into darkness Lucy saw a flash of steel. It was the spoke of a tire. As Dalton began walking toward it and then picked up his pace, Lucy thought, *Lord God, it's Davis!*

"Dalton?" she called, almost hesitantly.

"Stay back, Lucy!" Dalton said, turning Davis over and feeling for a pulse. He placed his face close to Davis's and smelled for alcohol. Dave had quit drinking years ago but he checked anyway, partly out of habit from investigating road accidents and partly because he couldn't imagine Davis losing control of his motorcycle like this.

Lucy leaped from the car and sprinted out onto the bridge. The bike was partially wrapped around the bridge trussing. It looked like the rider had tried and failed to leap the railing. A few scraps of metal littered the roadside. Davis's face was covered with blood and barely recognizable, but Lucy knew it was him and she knew he was dead. His bones had been broken in the fall. She could tell by the unnatural way the body lay there and the grotesque manner in which his arm twisted behind his neck like a broken twig. There were tire marks on the pavement and bloodstains where his face and head had skidded over the pavement. Lucy cradled her brother's bloody head in her arms and wept.

"So he ran off the road?" asked Cameron.

"Or was run off," Mama Lucy replied.

"Now, mother, you don't know that for a fact," Lily said.

"Dalton said the sheriff got an anonymous tip about an accident at Chicken Bridge," Mama Lucy stated. "But they never did investigate. Dalton said there was no leads."

"You don't think it was foul play, do you?" Cameron asked.

"All I know is Dave wouldn't a died that way. They said it was reckless driving. But I don't believe it. When they took him to the mortuary for the autopsy Linwood Copeland tole me that Davis had a mark on his neck. Like a burn or somethin'. I'll never forgive Dalton for not followin' up. I begged him to and he wouldn't do it. They was a lot of bad blood between 'em. Especially after Dalton threw Davis in jail on a trumped-up charge."

Mama Lucy seemed drained and out of sorts from telling the story of her brother's death. She put down her napkin and tried to pull herself up from the table.

"Maybe you should go inside and lie down until dessert's ready," Lily said. "Beth and I will walk you back to your room."

Bookended by her two daughters, Mama Lucy made her way up the slope to the house.

"Welcome to Mama Lucyland," I said to Sandy.

"I take it your grandmother and grandfather didn't get on too well," observed Sandy.

"Hatin' Granddaddy was her hobby," said Buzz.

"Things was never the same after your granddaddy come back from Gastonia," my father told me. "I was too young to notice it, but Mother always said that was when things turned sour between 'em. She claims Daddy changed after Gastonia."

"I sure wish he was still alive so we could talk to him about it," I said.

"I talked to him about it," said a voice from down at the end of the table. It was Wallace. He and his girlfriend hadn't participated in the conversation but evidently had soaked up every word. All eyes turned to him.

"You talked to Granddaddy Dalton about Gastonia?" I asked.

"When was that?" asked Buzz.

"He and my grampaw used to take me fishin'," Wallace explained. "That's when we'd talk."

"When was he in Gastonia?" asked Sandy.

"I believe it was 'twenty-nine," Wallace said. "When they had troubles in their mills over there."

"During the Loray strike?" Sandy asked disbelievingly.

"All I know is what Pick's grampaw told me," he replied. "He went to Gastonia to work on a surveying team for the railroad, but that didn't last long. About that time there was some trouble at the mill. The Chief of Police there needed men to help and Dalton signed on."

"Chief Aderholt," said Sandy.

"Yes'm. That was Dalton's first taste of police work and he liked it a sight better than millwork and he liked the chief but he didn't like throwing people out of their houses and the way some of the others used their badges to bully and beat people up. One day at a union rally the police and company men went on a rampage. Dalton went with the chief to strike headquarters to keep an eye on his men."

Sandy looked thunderstruck. "Jesus, Pick, you didn't tell me your grandfather was there when Chief Aderholt was shot!"

"I didn't know until now."

"Some of the strikers were all bloody and bandaged after being beaten by the cops," Wallace continued. "So Dalton said they booed and hissed the police when they pulled up. Armed guards met them inside and asked if they had a search warrant. One of the other deputies said they didn't need a warrant and grabbed the man's gun and another deputy who'd been drinking shoved into the union hall and the chief went in after him to pull him back out and that's when somebody fired. Then others too. Dalton said it sounded like firecrackers. When the dust cleared the chief was lying on the floor."

"He died the next day," Sandy added. "Good Lord, Pick, your grandparents were eyewitnesses to two of the seminal events in our region's history."

"And from both sides of the issues," added Buzz.

"No wonder I'm so conflicted," I said.

Buzz laughed. "And wound up a wild-eyed, pinko, troublemaking political cartoonist."

Cameron, clearly intrigued by the story I had been piecing together since we'd moved back home, asked, "What happened after the police chief died?"

"There was a reign of terror," Sandy said. "The police deputized any man who offered to help. Deputies scoured the countryside for strikers. Fourteen were eventually brought to trial. Soon after Aderholt died an anti-union mob ambushed Ella May Wiggins and ran her and some others off the road. Gunmen fired into the back of the flatbed truck. Ella May was back there. They killed her."

"Granddaddy never mentioned anything about that," Wallace said, "but he did say that he heard her sing once. Said Mama Lucy's voice was prettier, but Ella May could sure stir a crowd."

Suddenly a rasping male voice called to us from the kitchen window. "Yoo-hoo, everybody! Up here in the big house!"

"Who the hell is that?" I said.

"It's my boy, Talbert," said Florence, waving back at him. "I told him and Jerry we was havin' Thanksgiving over here and to drop by if they had time."

"Whooeee!" Talbert whooped as he strode out the kitchen door. "Ain't we fancy." He had a beer in one hand and a turkey leg in the other and was obviously a little loaded. He walked over to us, twanging the *Bonanza* theme song, and set his beer on the table. He swept his eyes over the yard and slapped me on the back. "If this ain't the goddammed Ponderosa you can kiss my ass."

"Why don't you join us for dinner?" Cameron suggested through a clenched smile. I caught her eye and we shared a subtle "Oh, shit" moment. It was almost like bonding.

"Thank you, ma'am," replied Talbert, doffing his Cat hat, "but we already eat."

"Where's your brother?" Florence asked. Just then Jerry appeared from behind the summer kitchen.

"How far back into those woods does your property go?" he asked without acknowledging the guests at the table or exchanging pleasantries. "All the way to the river?"

"Yes," I answered, wondering why he wanted to know.

"Mama Lucy says they's a trail down along the river."

"You talked to her?" I thought they'd just arrived.

Talbert reached across Wallace and dipped his finger in the cranberry sauce. "Yeah, we was in the big house shootin' the shit with her." I could feel Cameron tense at the thought of these two gorillas stomping around her house and she gave me an uneasy glance.

"Well," Talbert said, "I wish we could stay, but . . ." He slapped his forehead. "Aw, shit, I forgot to tell Mama Lucy."

"What?" his mother asked.

"Remember the old nigger come by to give Mama Lucy the cake at the reunion?"

"Bessie Thurwell," I said, bristling at the slur.

"That's the one. Well, I was at Mama Lucy's house pickin' up a lamp, when her niece come by." Talbert stretched out his story, enjoying his time on stage. "Said to tell Mama Lucy somethin'. She didn't know she'd moved."

"Tell her what?" asked Florence.

Talbert grinned triumphantly around a bite of turkey leg. "She's dead," he said.

Talbert and Jerry left after I promised to tell Mama Lucy the news. Call me sensitive but I thought it better if Talbert wasn't the one to to tell Mama Lucy that her girlhood friend had passed away. The afternoon shifted lazily into twilight and all the other guests and family, sated with Thanksgiving calories, started drifting home as well. Cameron was exhausted and, apologizing, retired to her room for a nap. I walked Sandy to her car.

"Thank you for a wonderful day, Pick. I loved meeting your family, and especially Mama Lucy. I wish I'd brought my tape recorder."

"I could tell she liked you," I said. "I'll ask her if you can come back and interview her. I'll bet she would open up to you."

"She seems healthy and strong," Sandy said.

"It comes and goes," I said. "She seems okay one minute and the next . . . who knows?"

"Oh," Sandy said, grabbing a manila envelope from the backseat of her car. "These are for you and Mama Lucy." Inside the envelope were dozens of old depression-era photographs of the New Hope Mountain mill village from Sandy's departmental archives. There were photos of the railroad depot, the mill houses, the front of the old mill at shift change—backdrops and locales I recognized from Mama Lucy's stories. I thanked her and promised to share them with Mama Lucy later that evening.

A few minutes later Buzz and Violet, who'd been inside helping clean up, stopped by to bid farewell. When they left Wallace shuffled over.

After shaking my hand, he said, "I know Mama Lucy don't put much stock in what I have to say . . ."

"Mama Lucy's got her own way of seeing things," I said. "Always has."

". . . but if you want to know more about this, there's a fella living at the old folks' home in Delaney, you might want to talk to."

"You know this guy?"

"Grampaw knew him. Mama Lucy, too."

"Who is it?"

Wallace glanced away and looked back. "Jake Satterfield," he said.

UNTIED THREADS

Later when I checked in on Mama Lucy, I found her sitting on the side of her bed, thumbing through the photographs Sandy had given me. I stood at the bedroom door watching her scrutinize a picture with her magnifying glass. Some she returned to, staring at them as if they contained secrets to be discovered.

"Anything there you remember?" I asked, finally.

"It's been so long. It looks so different from the way it was. But then not."

"Sandy said they were shot in 1937."

"The man who took these musta worked for the company."

"Why's that?"

"There's no people in most of 'em. The ones that's there I know, but they're not the right people. It's like they were took by somebody who didn't know what he was lookin' at. I wish I coulda been with him. I woulda told him what pictures to take."

I sat down beside her. "There's a good shot of the mill hill in there. The part that's grown over now. Are there any of your house?"

"No. But look, right here you could almost see Annie Laura's house but he didn't walk over far enough. Or maybe it was tore down by then. They tore it down not long after she died."

I could tell the photographs were frustrating as much as inspiring Mama Lucy and I felt vaguely guilty for giving them to her. I sat with her while she told me stories about each scene in the photos. Finally, I asked, "Mama Lucy, remember your friend who brought you the birthday cake?"

"Bessie Thurwell."

"I just got word she passed away."

Her face clouded. I thought it might do her some good to talk about it and asked her to tell me about Bessie. Of all the stories she had told me up to that point, the one she told me next surprised me the most.

*　　*　　*

Lucy was standing there near the P.O. window in the back of Khoury's Dry Goods shopping for sugar and flower when Linwood Copeland sidled up and said, "I heard you was gittin' married, Lucy." After blurting out his well-rehearsed opener he said, "Good luck." Then he stepped back, as though expecting her rebuff.

Lucy smiled at him. She knew it was hard for Linwood to say these words because her engagement to the older man represented a personal defeat to the boy who'd had a crush on her since childhood and had tried to buy her box supper at the church auction. But she loved him for his dignity and sportsmanship in the face of disappointment.

Emboldened by her smile Linwood continued awkwardly, "Dalton Cantrell's a good man, and he'll take good care of you and he's lucky to have you."

Before Spencer Webb entered her life she would have been happy to spend all her free time with the awkward boy standing before her, especially since he was working at the funeral home, where he might have a better future than he would in the mill. But that all seemed distant now.

"Thank you, Linwood," she replied. "Mama's real excited about it." Lucy's mama had been on cloud nine since Lucy accepted Dalton's proposal, and was treating Lucy more grown-up lately. Today she'd even left her and Bessie to shop for groceries while she took Icy to a picture show in Durham for her birthday. Lucy's daddy was fishing in the New Hope. With everyone gone it was Lucy and Bessie's responsibility to cook dinner.

Linwood shifted the conversation to the more neutral realm of general gossip. "Did you hear Spencer Webb's been sent away?"

"What?" Lucy hadn't heard a word about it.

"Some say he knocked up a mill village girl," Linwood said. "Probably that Connie Mae Locklear if you ask me. But they say he's been sent away to a boarding school in Virginia."

"I thought he went to Eno High," said Lucy anxiously. "Like his sister."

"Not after this. You know his daddy's not gonna let him git mixed up with no linthead girls."

Lucy, reeling, looked away. She saw Sam Khoury standing at the post office window sorting through the mail. Sam said very little but had always seemed to Lucy like someone who knew more than he let on.

"Lucy Barlow, I have a letter for you," Sam interrupted, handing her an envelope. Linwood took that as his cue and left the store with his sack of flour under his arm. Strangely, the letter Sam gave Lucy bore no postage and no return address. She opened it.

Dear Lucy, [the letter began]

> *By the time you get this I will be in Chatham, Virginia. My father found out about us. Don't ask me how. He may have read my journal, but I suspect it was Jake Satterfield who told Sumner, who told Mr. Strudwick, who told my daddy. It doesn't matter how he found out. He is sending me away to military school.*
>
> *If I don't see you before I go, I am sorry. I told my father you were getting married and we already broke up but he wouldn't believe me. I won't write to you again because I don't want to cause you any trouble in your marriage. Destroy this letter. I asked Sam Khoury to give this to you. If you need to reach me, he can help.*
> *Love always,*
> *Spencer Webb*

"Miss Lucy?" It was Bessie, who had been waiting on the bench out front but had grown impatient and come inside to fetch her. "Miss Lucy? Yo' mama gonna take a switch to us if we don't finish the wash and have supper on the table when they gits home." She stopped when she saw Lucy's face. "What's wrong, Miss Lucy? You look like you seen a ghost."

Lucy folded the letter and slipped it inside her dress pocket.

"Nothin' Bessie," she answered. "You're right. We better get on home."

Bessie was attuned to Lucy's moods and there was little Lucy could hide from her. They were about the same age and had known each other since they were little girls. As children, Lucy and Bessie and Annie Laura, too, used to love to sing and harmonize together. In fact, it was Bessie who taught Lucy and Annie Laura how. Bessie had an uncanny ear for harmonies and taught them new and different ways of listening and singing with minor keys and modulations thrown in that made the gospel standards they sang seem original and haunting. Bessie had a beautiful voice herself and played the piano by ear and they wanted her to accompany them on piano in church, but when Lucy asked her mama at age eleven if Bessie could sing and play with them for Youth Sunday services, her mama said, "Bessie's got her own church, Lucy. Miss Lockhart will accompany you."

Lucy's mood was as dark as a winter storm as the two girls walked home.

"Why you so sad, Miss Lucy?" Bessie asked. Usually, she could cajole and tease Lucy out of her moods and melancholies, but today Lucy just needed to talk.

"Oh, Bessie," cried Lucy. "If I tell you, you cain't tell nobody. Not Eunice nor Icy neither one. I'll get in big trouble if Mama finds out."

She told Bessie the whole story, even though Bessie had heard much of it before. She told her how she had met Spencer when he delivered a special delivery from Dalton and about Halloween and their secret rendezvous at Panther's Den ever since, how she broke up with him to marry Dalton and how Jake Satterfield caught them their last time together and may have snitched and now Spencer was gone.

"Spencer Webb's father sent him away because of me," Lucy said. "Because his boy was seein' a West End girl—a linthead."

Bessie's reaction to the story surprised Lucy. Instead of pumping Lucy for details, Bessie seemed pensive and distracted. Lucy wondered if Bessie disapproved of her in some way.

When they got home Lucy went inside to start supper and Bessie went outside to hang up the wash on the clothesline. Lucy, standing over the kitchen table rolling out biscuit dough, squinted through the windowpanes. Bessie's shoulders were shaking. Lucy rushed outside and grabbed Bessie and turned her around. Bessie's head was bowed and she was holding her stomach and sobbing. Tears rolled down her face.

"What is it, honey?" Lucy asked. "What's the matter? Did I say something that upset you?" Bessie just shook her head.

Just then a voice called, "Anybody home?"

"Back here," Lucy said.

A moment later Annie Laura appeared, carrying a sack of turnip greens. She was on the crutches she sometimes used when her prosthetic limb was giving her trouble. "What's the matter with Bessie?" she asked.

Lucy told Annie Laura about the letter from Spencer Webb and how his father had sent him off to military school. "I told Bessie all about it on the way home from Khoury's," Lucy said, "and now Bessie says she's gonna throw herself off Chicken Bridge."

Annie Laura patted Bessie's back. Bessie liked Annie Laura and trusted her and Lucy hoped her friend's presence might encourage Bessie to open up. "Tell us what's the matter," Annie Laura said. "We can help you."

"I cain't," Bessie whimpered. "I git in trouble."

"Not with us," Annie Laura said. "You know you can tell us anything."

"We won't tell," promised Lucy, raising her hand up in a solemn oath, "Cross my heart and hope to die."

Bessie lowered her gaze as if gathering up her courage and then blurted, "I—I—be wit' chile."

Lucy was shocked. Annie Laura, recovering first, asked, "Who done it, Bessie? Who's the daddy?"

"I—I cain't say," Bessie mumbled. Tears streamed down her face.

"Whoever done it, we can git the sheriff to make him own up to it," Lucy declared.

"No," Bessie begged. "No sheriff! It was my fault. 'Sides, Trouble Woman say she got a root can help me."

Trouble Woman was a white woman who lived in Cabbagetown with the Negroes, and girls pregnant out of wedlock, white and colored, went to her. Rumor was that some had died.

"No Trouble Woman," said Lucy adamantly. "She's dangerous."

"I heard they run her out of South Carolina," Annie Laura said. "She lived down in Pawleys Island 'fore she come to Eno, and when they dug up around her house after she was gone they found tiny bones buried in shallow graves. Some folks think . . ."

Lucy cut her eyes at Annie Laura, who let the subject drop. "Cain't Mother Mary, the midwife, do something about it?" Lucy asked.

"No," Bessie protested. "She'll tell my mama and my mama cain't know."

"You're right." Lucy could imagine the impact on Onnie Lee. It would be worse than if her own mother heard Lucy was pregnant. "She cain't know."

"I be showin' soon." Bessie pressed her dress against her tummy. "Mama thinks I be eatin' too much already. She know soon."

"The father should take some responsibility," Annie Laura snapped. She spun away, turned back. "It was Tommy Ray, the one who works the loading docks at Bellevue, won't it? I'm gonna go down there and give him a piece of my mind."

"No." Bessie grabbed her arm. "It won't him."

"Was it against your will?" Lucy asked.

Bessie whimpered and buried her face in the sheet again. When she looked back Lucy saw the weight of her friend's burden. "Please, Bessie," Lucy urged again. "Who was it?"

Bessie gathered herself and looked them both in the eye. "You cain't tell nobody no matter what. Promise?"

"We promise."

"The father was . . ." A flush of shame rose on Bessie's face and she turned away. "It was Mist' Webb."

Lucy was dumbfounded.

"I didn't want to tell you, Miss Lucy," Bessie sobbed, "knowin' how you feels about his boy."

"She was delivering flowers to the Webbs for her granddaddy," Mama Lucy explained. "Nobody was home but Mr. Webb. He told her to put the flowers in the ice house—I reckon the one right out here," she said pointing toward the window. "And when she did, he cornered her there and raped her. He said that if she told anybody, her mama or daddy or granddaddy, he would punish them for her sins. She had nowhere to turn. She knew deep down nobody would believe her except her family, but they was as helpless as she was."

"She's got to have a operation," said Annie Laura. "That's all there is to it." Bessie was lying down on Lucy's bed while they discussed what to do.

"It costs money," Lucy protested.

"We gotta come up with it then." Annie Laura pulled Lucy away from the bedroom door and whispered, "I'm afraid she's gonna go to Trouble Woman or one of them witch doctors that'll kill her. We gotta help her."

"But how?" Lucy asked. "We can't afford it."

"Maybe she could keep it."

Lucy said, "This ain't a kitten, Annie Laura. She'll throw herself off Chicken Bridge before she'll have this child. Or face her mother with the shame. I know Bessie." Lucy stared out the window at the swing hanging from the sycamore. After a moment, she turned back to Annie Laura. "I know who can help."

"Sam," whispered Lucy, standing at the P.O. window again. "Do you still work for that doctor in Chapel Hill? The one Spencer told me about?" She glanced around the store to make sure no one was listening.

"That's Dr. Ashendorf," Sam said.

"A friend of ours is in trouble," Lucy whispered. "Female trouble."

"Is she sick?"

"Worse," Lucy said.

"Pregnant?"

Lucy looked away.

"This friend," he asked, "It's not you, is it?"

"Lord, no," Lucy laughed. But Sam studied her face anyway, looking for signs of deception. When he saw none, he set aside the mail. "Maybe I can help."

Sam drove them to Chapel Hill in the shiny gray car he borrowed from his brother. Bessie had never ridden in a car before and sat as still as a mouse in the backseat, staring out the window at the passing scenery. Annie Laura sat beside her and held her hand the whole way there.

The mailbox out front of the white clapboard house read, "Ashendorf, MD" in blood-red letters. Sam parked the car.

"I'll go in first," he said to Lucy. "I called ahead and he's expecting us, but he suggested I make sure the coast is clear." After a minute Sam came out and signaled for Bessie. She was scared and nervous and Lucy and Annie Laura walked in with her, one on each side. A nurse met them at the door and she and Sam escorted Bessie into a room. Lucy and Annie Laura sat down in the waiting room, which was really the house's living room. Lucy fretted while Annie Laura read an old *Liberty* magazine. Occasionally Annie Laura would nudge her and show her a picture. After a while Bessie came out, escorted by Sam and the nurse. Sam's coat was over Bessie's shoulders.

Lucy thought Bessie looked sickly and pale but the nurse, who Lucy later learned was the doctor's wife, assured her that the procedure had gone smoothly. Bessie would be fine, she said, but she needed plenty of rest. Lucy and Annie Laura escorted Bessie back to the automobile. Bessie cried all the way back to Eno.

Mama Lucy had come to the end of her tale. She sighed. "It was for the best."

"And she never told anybody who got her pregnant?"

"Not but me and Annie Laura. She was too ashamed. She felt like it was her fault. It near broke my heart."

"And you remained friends over the years?"

"For a time. Once we was grown we saw less of each other. In those days blacks and whites didn't mix like they do today, Pick. She come to work for us when I married Dalton and we still lived in Eno. I lost track of her after the war when she moved off to Atlanta to live with her sister."

"But she sent you a cake for your ninetieth birthday."

"Mm-hmmm," said Mama Lucy, savoring the memory. "Coconut layer."

"So the rich white mill owner was porking the colored help?" said Buzz, shaking his head in amazement. He and Wallace were sitting in the backseat of the Volvo while Sandy rode up front with me. Our destination was Delaney, our quarry, the notorious Jake Satterfield. "No wonder black folks are so pissed off at us."

We were cruising down old Highway 70 toward Delaney, a road I associated with long drives home after emotionally exhausting Sunday dinners at Mama Lucy's. I hadn't been back to Delaney since I left home for college and had never had any desire to return until now. I connected the town with my mother's illness and a general feeling of suffocation, depression, and despair. But I was curious about Jake Satterfield, and having Sandy, another expatriate who shared the experience of growing up there and bore witness to the town's soul-killing capacities, along for the ride was sure to ease my reentry.

Sandy wasn't terribly shocked by Bessie's predicament. "I've heard there's a community of colored Webbs in Eno County that DeWitt sired."

"Mama Lucy claims old man Webb had several black mistresses over the years," I said.

Sandy laughed. "I'll have to ask Franklin if he ever met any of his African-American kinfolks."

"Mama Lucy didn't even know Bessie was still alive," I informed them. "How did Bessie know where to bring that cake?"

"We ran a birthday announcement in the Burlington paper," Buzz said.

"I still can't get over that it was Samuel Khoury who helped your grandmother," said Sandy, repeating his name as if it were George Washington's. "You know he became Mao Tse-tung's personal physician, right? He was the most famous foreigner in China. People all over the country there still speak of him with reverence."

"You're kidding," I said. "You mean, Mama Lucy's Sam Khoury was *that* Samuel Khoury?"

I recalled a *Parade* magazine cover story I had read years before about Mao's Minister of Health, who had eradicated venereal disease and prostitution, and I had been intrigued that he had grown up in a small North Carolina town, but at the time I didn't make the connection to Eno.

Sandy said, "You've really uncovered some dynamite material here, Pick, and I've got a feeling there's even more to come. We're gonna turn you into a bona fide oral historian yet."

We smelled Delaney before we reached the city limits. The aroma of the paper mill infiltrated the ventilation system of the station wagon. The town itself seemed hardly touched or changed by the past few decades except for the proliferation of fast food franchises that dotted the highway leading into town. The lumberyards along the railroads and the old water tower and the bridge across the Neuse River and the inevitable graffiti proclamations with variations on "Seniors Rule" scrawled across the overpass looked just the same. The downtown storefronts had been rearranged and spruced up but the A. C. White department store where my father had worked still dominated the street.

As we passed a brick middle school building not far from my old neighborhood Sandy said, "There it is, Pick, Delaney Junior High. We were pioneers—remember Brenda Carpenter?"

"How could I not?" I said.

It was 1960, six years after the *Brown* decision, three years after Little Rock, when integration came to Delaney Junior High. It came in the form of a little girl with mocha-colored skin and crisp plaid skirts and starched cotton blouses and horn-rimmed glasses. Her name was Brenda Carpenter, and because of the immutable logic of the alphabet the shy, quiet girl sat next to me in Mrs. Peterson's seventh-grade homeroom. I was mortified. Like all pubescent, hormonally challenged thirteen-year-olds my most pressing concern at school was how to get through the day without embarrassing or calling attention to myself. But I could hardly ignore the little bigots in my class, who taunted me at recess and lunch with charges of "nigger lover" and chants like "Pick and Brenda sittin' in a tree, *k-i-s-s-i-n-g*!" Not that I too, at that age and being a product of that time and place, did not share my classmates' primitive views, but my opposition to Brenda had less to do with the color of her skin than with the seating plan that put me so noticeably in her orbit.

Still, but for the teasing I received, the integration of the Delaney County schools passed almost uneventfully, and were it not for one incident in particular the entire social experiment might have faded from my memory altogether.

I don't know what other humiliations Brenda Carpenter suffered that year during her quiet and dignified passage among us, but one situation arose that illustrated the texture of the time and something of the South I know and love.

The school year was drawing to an end and the homeroom class party was fast approaching. Everyone was excited because we had already decided to hold the party at the new state-of-the-art bowling alley next to the shopping center in town. One day, however, when Brenda was absent, Mrs. Peterson announced to the class that we had a problem. "The new bowling alley does not allow Negroes inside," she said. "So if we hold the party there Brenda will not be allowed to attend."

A groan of impatience and discontent arose from my classmates. "So y'all have a choice to make. Have the party at the bowling alley, as planned, in which case Brenda won't be able to come. Or have a picnic at the city park so she can be included. It's your party, so I leave it up to you. Whatever you decide, I'll inform Brenda."

Mrs. Peterson paused to let this new information and circumstance sink in. A charged silence infused the room as my classmates and I eyed each other and considered our decision. Then we voted. The verdict, when all hands were counted, was unanimous. We were going on a picnic.

"Hey," I said, "why didn't we hang out more together in high school? It seems so weird."

"High school is so cliquish," Sandy said. "You were a jock. I was a nerd."

"You don't look like a nerd to me, darlin'," said Buzz.

Sandy blushed.

"You were too mature for me," I said, then told Buzz, "The list of her extracurricular activities took up a whole page in the yearbook: Valedictorian, Class Secretary, Homecoming Court, Most Likely to Succeed—Sandy did everything, made all the big lists."

"Not all," she said.

"Name it," I challenged.

"National Honor Society," she said.

"Impossible!" Buzz exclaimed. "Why?"

"Each year you were tapped in," she said. "Selected in a ceremony in the gym before the whole school. Juniors were eligible and in my junior year I qualified and thought I might get tapped. Parents were notified so they could be there for the ceremony but on Honors Day I sat in the gym and looked around and saw everybody else's mom and dad but my parents weren't there. I cried and cried and couldn't understand why I'd been passed over. To comfort myself I rationalized: Some people weren't invited until they were seniors. Maybe next year, I thought. I was so ambitious.

"My senior year rolled around and before Honors Day my mother warned me, 'Honey, your father and I were not invited again so I want you to prepare yourself.' I was devastated. This was my final year and I knew I'd met every requirement for Honor Society. We were a lower-middle-class family. My father was a fireman and my mother was a homemaker. We lived in a modest neighborhood. My mother went down to the school in her housecoat and slippers and grilled the guidance counselor about the selection rules for the National Honor Society. Why hadn't I been selected? When she came home she told me the four qualities that students were judged on: Duty, honor, leadership, and character. I was mortified. Anyway, that's why I wasn't accepted."

"Because of your mother?" Buzz said.

"Because of my character."

"I don't get it," I said.

"Neither did I at the time." Sandy smiled wanly. "I told you my daddy was a fireman, but he was also an alcoholic. When I was a little girl and he didn't come home on payday I would have to fetch him home from the saloon. It was one of those clichés you read about. Everybody knew it. My daddy was the town drunk. And that's why I was kept out of the National Honor Society. Because of my character." Sandy looked out the window. "I know it's silly," she said, "but I can't help it. To this day it still hurts."

We rode in silence for a while, contemplating the ignorance and cruelty of small towns, and I began to understand the drive and accomplishment of the woman occupying my passenger seat. I glanced in the rearview mirror and saw Buzz, looking almost angry, staring out the window behind her.

The streets I had roamed as a child seemed much narrower than I remembered, the houses smaller and packed together, as if in miniature. As we drove down the block where my mother took me for walks and my father played catch with me I felt a familiar ache, like a wave of nostalgia or panic rolling over me. The trees were larger but the modest ranch-style house my father bought on his A. C. White manager's salary had barely changed since I'd left. Imagining the families moving through those haunted rooms and hallways like intruders who didn't belong, I felt a sudden sadness that surprised me.

I thought of Mama Lucy's revelations about my mother's attempts on her own life in that house and pangs of remorse shot through my soul. But despite the pain it caused me, I was glad I had come back. Returning felt like a completion somehow, the closing of a circle that needed closing.

Neuse County Rest Home was an eyesore of a structure: small, shabby, the color of curdled milk. It looked like the kind of place you wouldn't send even your worst enemy, so it seemed fitting somehow that Mama Lucy's old nemesis had ended up here.

Inside, we met Irene, the staffer Wallace had contacted about Jake, who briefed us on her patient while we signed in at the front desk. When we were done, she escorted us down the corridor.

Jake, she said, didn't get many visitors and kept to himself. His daughter and son-in-law had put him here, but they were both dead now. Jake was now in his nineties and he had done time in prison for murder but he had found the Lord and now spent most of his time reading scriptures and watching TV evangelists. He was half-blind and in poor health, but his mind, she assured us, was as clear as a bell. "A lot of 'em his age"—Irene pointed with her chin toward a group huddled around the TV in the day room—"their wheel is turnin' but the hamster's dead."

We stopped at a room at the end of the hall. The door was ajar.

"Knock, knock, Mr. Jake," Irene warbled, poking her head inside. "Yoo-hoo, Mr. Satterfield, yoo-hoo! You got company."

We entered a small, dimly lit room, with peeling wallpaper and an unmade bed. There was a lamp on a bedstand littered with medicine bottles, and a folding chair with towels and clothes piled on it. A dime-store print of the baptism of Jesus in the Jordan River like you might see adorning a baptismal pool in some rural church hung on the wall over the bed and a door opened on a small bathroom. The sliding glass door opening onto a patio was half-covered with a flower-print curtain and served as the main source of light in the room. An empty wheelchair occupied one corner and an obsolete model television set another. Across from the TV in a rocking chair sat the room's sole occupant.

Jake Satterfield was now a bent, shriveled old man with thick white hair and a craggy, scarred face, no teeth and cataracted eyes that stared blankly in front of him. He stirred, unsteadily, when we entered, lifting his stubbled chin in the direction of the sound at his door, straining to apprehend who was visiting his sad little lair. He couldn't have been much older than Mama Lucy but he showed his age and seemed defeated by it in a way my grandma never had. It was hard for me to imagine this pathetic figure as the imposing, swaggering bully, the swinish mill village thug that had haunted my grandmother's youth. If he had done all the things Mama Lucy claimed, he had paid a price for them. His sins showed in every molecule of his ravaged being, like living proof that there is indeed justice on this Earth.

Wallace reintroduced himself, then introduced Sandy, Buzz, and me. Jake nodded and gave us a tight, gummy smile. His teeth floated forlornly in a glass by the bed like an abandoned biology specimen. He was grasping a battered King James Bible in his gnarled, arthritic hands, anchoring it in his lap.

Wallace proffered a brown paper bag. "I brought you some Hershey bars with some Red Man if you're still chewing tobacco like you used to."

Jake's face brightened. "Doctor says I cain't chew no more, but he ain't said I cain't eat chocolate yet."

"Mr. Satterfield, you don't know me," I ventured, "but I'm the grandson of Bud's brother, Dalton Cantrell. You may remember my grandmother. Her maiden name was Barlow. Lucy Barlow."

Jake gave no indication that he recognized the name. Sandy shrugged and told him about the oral history project she was working on. "We heard you were in the National Guard back in the thirties during a labor strike in the cotton mills and we were wondering if you might tell us a little bit about what that was like."

I saw something flicker behind Jake's cataracts. "That's right," he said. "I was in the guard. What'd you like to know?"

We talked with Jake Satterfield for hours that day. We asked him about his life, growing up in Eno, serving in the guard with Wallace's grandfather Bud. We circled around, testing the waters, wanting to establish trust and rapport before we ventured into more dicey territory. As we talked Jake opened up. It was as if he had been waiting all his life for someone to ask him questions about his personal journey and once he started talking you couldn't shut him up. The years fell away and his memory revved into high gear. What was it about these mean ones? I wondered. They seemed to be fueled by their bile, to feed on it. While less vitriolic souls stifled their rage, became guilt-ridden and developed symptoms and diseases and dropped like flies, these belligerent assholes turned their anger outward onto the world. While others suffered, they survived.

As Jake spoke, his late-life piety and thin mantle of maturity fell away and he changed before our eyes. His swagger and strut was evident in the way he talked and boasted. Although he no longer had the strength and physical power to back it up, you could see it in his demeanor. The brute emerged. And even though he quoted scripture liberally and illustrated his observations with Biblical parables and references, I could tell that for Jake Satterfield the way of the pagan and the barbarian remained his true religion. His heart and allegiance belonged not with the crucified Christ but with the rabble in the crowd shouting for Barabbas, the Judases bought for thirty pieces of silver, the agents of Caesar impaling Him with spears and gambling for His clothes.

But who could blame Jake for trying to make peace with his Maker after the life he'd lived? After all, hadn't the aged Tolstoy turned to religion after a lifetime of profligacy? Or more recently, Malcolm Muggeridge? Wasn't that a time-honored way of facing the end, instead of raging against the dying of the light? Was I more skeptical just because the believer was a sorry redneck peckerwood? Was his conversion experience any less legitimate than that of a Russian count or British wit just because he chewed tobacco and spoke with a southern drawl?

After a while we slipped into an easy rapport and our talk turned to children and Sandy asked about Jake's. He'd been married twice and had offspring with both wives. The first set he lost touch with. The second he was closer to and they'd taken care of him in his dotage until they died.

"Honor thy father and mother," intoned Jake. "That's what the Good Book says." He looked out the window as if contemplating the world's disappointments. "Children today ain't worth nothin'. Drinkin' an' gamblin' an' carryin' on. Gittin' into trouble."

"Mr. Satterfield, did you ever get into any trouble?" Buzz asked.

"No, sir, never did." Jake's hands were crossed at the wrist. Glancing down, he started rubbing a long scar that ran across his palm from fingers to wrist. And as if the scar reminded him of a long-ago transgression, like a cheat sheet answer scribbled on his hand, he muttered, "Except for that time I killed my wife."

I glanced at Sandy, unsure if we'd heard correctly. "I got in some trouble with the po-lice that time." He told us about the argument he and his wife had and how she'd nearly cut off his hand with an ax. He'd grabbed his shotgun from the shed, stuck it in the window, and blown her head off. If he'd done it when she cut him it would have been self-defense, a crime of passion, and he would have gotten off with manslaughter, but because he left the house and returned with his gun the crime was considered premeditated. Jake was convicted of second degree murder. It was hard to imagine this shriveled little man ever menacing anyone, but the scar on his hand offered eloquent testimony otherwise.

"Served twenty year for that . . . with time off for good behavior."

"Yeah," Wallace said. "I remember Grandpaw and me come to see you right after you got out."

Sitting there listening to the off-handed way he acknowledged the killing of a wife and a goodly portion of his own life doing hard time, I marveled at the ability of some human beings to inflict and endure hardship and keep on keeping on as if twenty years' incarceration were nothing more than a drop in the bucket and the irretrievable loss of that time an unfortunate miscue, its wastefulness as common as a cold.

Later on we asked him about his role in the Eno massacre. At first he feigned forgetfulness, but as Sandy described the event and its place and significance in the history of the uprising, Jake's pride kicked in and he began owning up to his participation in the episode. In his halting and self-serving way he described what it had looked and felt like behind those second-story battlements on the day of the killings. When I finally told him that my grandmother, Lucy Barlow Cantrell, was still alive and believed to this day that her husband's brother, Bud Cantrell, shot her best friend, Annie Laura Gaskins, Jake seemed taken aback and brought to himself in some elemental way.

"The day I stabbed her in Burlington, I told her he done it," he said.

I relayed what Mama Lucy had told me about Annie Laura's death, highlighting the conflict with Bud's version. He seemed troubled by the direction the conversation had taken, and his face betrayed his internal struggle. Hadn't he paid his dues to society in prison? I imagined him thinking. Hadn't the statute of limitations run out on these ancient grievances?

Finally I asked him point-blank: "Who shot Annie Laura, Jake? Was it Bud Cantrell?"

Jake looked out the window. "Your grandpaw was a good man," he said to Wallace, "The best friend I ever had although I didn't deserve him, the way I done him."

"Who shot her, Jake?" I asked. "Who shot Annie Laura Gaskins?"

Jake hung his head. Sandy kneeled before him and took his hand. "It's all right. You can tell us. Nothing's going to happen to you now."

Jake's shoulders began to shake. He dragged a leathery hand over his quivering face and snorted loudly as if bucking himself up. His whole frame seemed to collapse inward upon itself.

He sobbed. "I loved that girl. She was the only one I ever loved. But she didn't care nothin' 'bout me. I might as well a been a pile o' donkey shit as far as she was concerned. And I hated Lucy Barlow for what she done to me." He looked at me with haunted, cataract-covered eyes. "I hated her for how she turned Annie Laura against me. I knowed it. She thought she was better'n us, too, takin' up with Spencer Webb like that. She thought her shit didn't stink, but I showed her. I . . . I was aimin' to shoot her that day, but then . . . then . . ."

Wallace leaned forward. "Who shot her, Jake?"

"Bud shoulda followed orders," Jake muttered. "That's why he was up there."

"Did he shoot Annie Laura, Mr. Satterfield?" Sandy asked.

"It was Dalton's fault."

I was hearing confirmation of my worst fears. Wallace grew agitated. "Grampaw said he didn't shoot nobody, Jake."

"It was Dalton's fault," Jake insisted. "She'da been alive if it won't for him. I loved that girl. Bud shouldn'ta done what he done."

"He's lying," Wallace blurted. Buzz quieted him with a hand on his shoulder.

"I'm sorry, Annie Laura!" Jake wailed. A frightened-looking Nurse Irene appeared at the door. Taking in the scene she said, "I'm going to have to ask you folks to leave now. Mr. Satterfield can't take a lot of stimulation."

After a backward glance at Jake and a quick apology to his nurse, we headed for the car. I didn't know what I had expected from our trip to Delaney, but I was surprised at such an outpouring of emotion from Jake Satterfield. Yet the mystery as to who shot Annie Laura Gaskins still remained.

MAMA LUCY AND
THE NIGHT VISITORS

Cameron was due back from Chicago on Friday, the day of the annual children's Christmas pageant at St. Stephen's. She had called home every night during the two weeks she'd been away with reports on how the shoot was going but mainly to talk to Wiley and to read him his bedtime story. This was the longest she had ever been away since we were married and certainly since Wiley was born, and her guilt was almost palpable. I longed to talk to her—I missed her—but our conversations were hurried and breezy and not conducive to the kind of heart-to-heart we desperately needed.

Although it was a mild December day in North Carolina, it was snowing in Chicago. Cameron called mid-morning from O'Hare to tell me that her noon flight had been delayed and she didn't know when she'd be home. Wiley, who had been practicing his solo verse from "We Three Kings" all week long and was looking forward to Cam seeing him in the pageant, was heartbroken. When I told Mama Lucy, who had already helped him create his Wise Man costume from one of her terry-cloth bathrobes and a kaffia-style headdress from a dishtowel, she said, "If his mama can't be there, at least I can."

Mama Lucy, decked out in hand-picked finery, was the Belle of Eno once again that night, and I took great pleasure in taking snapshots of Wiley escorting her up the handicapped ramp of St. Stephen's. The little chapel glowed with candles and poinsettias and the carillon pealed with carols as the late afternoon shadows lengthened and proud parents and parishioners crowded into the tiny nave to watch their offspring reenact the Christmas story.

Russ, who was backstage overseeing lighting and costumes, spotted us in our pew and came out to greet Mama Lucy. After pouring the full wattage of his charm on her and dazzling her with his flattery and attentions, he turned to me and said, "Did you see that the *Sun* fired their publisher?"

"Bob Garvis was fired?" My heart leapt like a fawn.

"And just before Christmas. Can you believe that? See, Pick"—he gave me a wicked wink—"there is a God."

"What happened?"

"The corporate bosses got rid of him. He was charging off all his budget overruns to the New York operation. Two security guards showed up at his office and escorted him out of the building. Well, I gotta get backstage and get ready to emcee this puppy. I'm the voice of the Archangel Gabriel. Nice to see you, Mrs. Cantrell. Merry Christmas, Pick."

I sat there basking like a chestnut by an open fire.

A lifelong Southern Baptist, Mama Lucy had never been inside an Episcopal church before and was taking in all the Anglican finery, pomp, and ceremony. I looked at the rapidly filling pews and caught a glimpse of Lisa slipping into a row in the rear. I glanced into the balcony at the children gathering there, and spotted Wiley and the other two Magi standing among a group of adorable little girls dressed in angel wings and halos. The young woman sitting behind me holding a baby regarded the panorama with tear-filled eyes. "Isn't this the best?" she whispered. "I came to all their rehearsals. It's for moments like these that you become a parent." I smiled and wondered if Mama Lucy, the mother of six, had memories like these.

The service was a simple staging of the Christmas story from the Gospels. The arrival of the Wise Men kicked off Wiley's big moment. I looked over at Mama Lucy as the first few notes of "We Three Kings" bellowed out of the mammoth pipe organ behind the Nativity scene. She was gazing at her great-grandson with unvarnished affection. Seeing such unmitigated warmth pour out of her moved me deeply. When it came Wiley's turn to sing, Mama Lucy squeezed my hand and smiled. Wiley looked out on the audience, knees knocking, bottle of frankincense trembling, eyes wide. But when he opened his mouth he nailed every note, singing with a confidence, a sweetness, a clarity I didn't know he possessed. By the time we left I was bursting with pride.

It was dark when we pulled up in front of Oaklawn, and the onset of winter was evident in the crispness of the air. As I turned off the engine Wiley shouted, "Dad, look! On the porch!"

Looking up, I saw through the boxwoods under the pale porch light a large furry animal scurrying around the side porch. It didn't look like a dog. In fact, there seemed to be two of them and one was up on its hind legs trying to climb the rattan sofa. I leaped out of the car and shouted "Hey!" at the top of my lungs and started sprinting toward the house as two dark forms scampered down the steps and disappeared into the darkness.

"Raccoons," I muttered, then called back, "Wiley, you stay here with Mama Lucy!" I hurried around the steps and found both garbage cans spilled over onto the lawn. "Goddamned raccoons!"

A deep foreboding rose within me when I ascended the steps and saw Petey's cage turned over on its side, the cage door wide open. Mama Lucy's pet cockatiel lay bloody and lifeless in the crook of the sofa. Blood splatters painted the plastic seat cushions, dripped in rivulets onto the freshly painted porch, and puddled at the base of the table. Small claw and paw prints cut a gruesome corridor across the porch and down the steps—evidence of our night visitors' vicious handiwork. I wondered what in the hell I was going to tell Mama Lucy.

"Dad!" shouted Wiley. "What is it?"

"Raccoons!" I said. "Stay there! They could be rabid!" I scurried down the steps and back to the car to appease Wiley and Mama Lucy.

"What is it, Pick?" asked my grandmother.

"Raccoons turned the garbage over again and . . ." I didn't have the heart to tell her, so I lied like a coward: "Wiley, there's coffee grounds all over and I don't want you tracking them into the house before your mother gets home." I escorted them up the front porch stairs, and asked in a nonchalant voice, "Are you hungry, Mama Lucy? I'll make us some bacon and eggs after I clean up."

"No, I'm tired," she said. "You and Wiley go ahead. I'm gonna go on to bed so you and Cameron can visit when she gets in."

Reeling from the disturbing homecoming, I sent Wiley upstairs for a bath and checked the answering machine. Cameron had left a message while we were out. Her flight was tentatively scheduled to leave at five-thirty so she might be late. Linda would drop her off at home. Good, I thought. I had time to clean up. I went out to the side porch and started scrubbing, wondering how I would break it to Mama Lucy in the morning that her beloved cockatiel was dead.

*   *   *

I was in the kitchen frying bacon and scrambling some eggs. Wiley was at the counter sipping a glass of milk and playing with his X-Men action figures, waiting for me to finish up and serve him. Flappy barked from the breakfast room off the side porch.

"Wiley, go get Flappy," I shouted over the sizzle of the eggs. "She's gonna wake up Mama Lucy."

"I think she has to go outside and pee, Dad."

"Let her out, then, but keep an eye on her. Call me if those raccoons show up." I was nervous about letting Wiley onto the side porch so soon after I had cleaned up, second-guessing the thoroughness of my job in the pale porchlight. I hoped he wouldn't remember that we had set the cockatiel's cage outside and ask where it was. In fact, I had stowed Petey's cage in the basement and hastily buried the bird in a plastic baggie, scouring the porch as best I could before I came back inside. Except for some pinpoints of blood spattered on the cushions that I would have to attend to in daylight I hoped there was no sign of carnage. I still dreaded the reckoning in the morning, though.

Flappy barked again. I set down the bacon and raised the kitchen window. Wiley was standing at the edge of the porch, facing into the darkness and calling to the dog to come. "What's the matter with Flappy?" I asked.

"She's barking at the ice house, Daddy."

"Don't move," I said. "I'll come out and check." Visions of Flappy being torn apart again and Cameron's imminent arrival loomed. I turned off the stove and dashed out of the kitchen to the door that opened onto the side porch. "Wiley!" I called. "Wiley! Where are you?"

No answer.

As I rounded the corner a blast of cold night air hit me, filling the room with a brisk chill. A dark, hulking figure blocked the doorway. His elbow was cocked to the side and it took me a second to realize there was something under his arm. I heard a muffled cry and realized that the thatch of blond hair attached to the man's side was my son's head. He had Wiley in a headlock, and Flappy was mewling and struggling against my boy's chest. I froze. There in the man's other hand, pointing straight at me, was a .45-caliber pistol.

"Ding-dong," the man said. "Avon calling."

"Who are you?" I demanded. My eyes moved back and forth between the .45 in the man's hand and my son's terrified face. The man stepped inside, under the light, and for the first time I was able to make out his features. He had a broken nose and dark leathery skin and narrow close-set eyes that made his prominent cheekbones stick out like tumors. He was bigger than I was and had a red, white, and blue skull tattooed on one forearm over the words "Born to Raise Hell" and a scar on the other. He had no eyebrows or eyelashes, to speak of, and under his doo-rag I guessed his head was shaved. In one ear he wore a silver stud. The other lobe dangled in two distinct flaps.

He ordered me to keep my hands over my head and move back into the kitchen as he dragged Wiley along beside him. Flappy was growling deep in her throat but Wiley was petting her and working hard to keep her calm so as not to anger his captor.

The man sniffed. "Just in time for supper. Lucky me."

"Who are you?" I demanded. "What do you want?"

"I'll ask the questions, asshole," he said and shoved me into the corner by the refrigerator. Then, looking around the kitchen impatiently, he asked, "What time is it?"

"Seven-fifteen." I indicated the clock on the stove. My answer seemed to agitate him.

"Where the hell is that dumbass?" he said to no one in particular, then turned back to me. "Why don't you rustle me up some of them eggs and bacon, Mister?" Flappy barked and the intruder jerked Wiley. "I'm gonna stomp that mutt flat if you can't keep it quiet."

"Leave him alone," I said.

He looked at me contemptuously. "Fix me a plate, douche bag." I glared at him. "Now!" He shoved me toward the stove. As I spooned the eggs onto a plate he asked, "Where's the old lady?"

"My wife's out of town."

"I know that. I meant the other one. Grandma."

"Asleep," I said, wondering where he got his information.

"Good. She better stay that way. Now open these windows while I eat. And little man"—he gave Wiley another jerk—"that dog barks again, it's dead."

Wiley's lip trembled and tears ran down his face but he made no noise.

"What do you want?" I asked. "Is it money? Take what you want, just leave the boy alone."

He looked at me as if my words were a revelation. "Yeah, good idea. Give me your wallet. Open it up and slide the money over here on the counter."

I took out the sixty-odd dollars I had in my billfold. "What the hell is this?" he complained, snatching the wad off the counter. "You call this dough?" He shushed us. "What was that? Did you hear that?" I listened but I heard nothing.

The phone rang. I hoped it wasn't Cameron saying she was on her way home. It rang again.

"Don't answer it," the man said.

After four rings the answering machine picked up.

"Pick," the caller said. "It's Russ. Thanks for bringing your grandmother to the pageant and tell Wiley he was dynamite. Listen, I just heard on the news that a convict escaped from the Eno County jail this afternoon and killed somebody. A real bad actor, already up on two murder counts. They haven't caught him yet and they think he headed for Asheville, but he may still be in the area. Police say to keep doors locked and report any suspicious strangers in the area, okay? 'Bye."

"Now ain't that considerate," the man said. " 'He's probably halfway to Asheville by now.' " He muttered under his breath, "Dumb fucks." He shushed us again and his eyes darted around the room in a paranoid fashion. "What's that sound?"

"I don't hear anything."

"That," he said, looking toward the ceiling. "There it goes again. Crunching sound. You don't hear that?"

"I don't know what it is," I answered blankly as the distinct grinding noise we had put up with for weeks echoed overhead. "Squirrels probably."

"That ain't no squirrel," he declared.

The crunching stopped. He cocked his ear, listening again, then moved to the open windows and stared into the woods behind the house. Suddenly, leaning into the open window, he let out a high warbling whistle, like a birdcall.

"What are you doing?" I asked.

He listened. Whistled again.

"You're going to wake Mama Lucy."

"I hear she sleeps like a log," he said, staring into the darkness. Then we heard it, faintly at first, then more distinctly: the sound of an owl answering the calls of our unwanted guest. The man whistled, lower this time and more sustained. The hoot owl answered. *Shit*, I thought. *Reinforcements.*

"Up here!" the man rasped through the open window.

"What the hell are you doing up there, Raiford?" a drawling voice called from the yard below.

"Shut up and git your ass in here," the thug snapped. "What took you so long?"

"It took us forever to find the landing in the dark and I got lost in the woods. Goddammit, I told you to wait in the shed, Bobby. Not in the house. Are they home?" It was then that I recognized the voice. I moved to the window so my cousin could see me.

"Shitfire!" Talbert said when he spotted me. "I thought you were gonna stay in the yard, Raiford."

"Talbert Bailey," I said. "I should have known. Is this guy a friend of yours?"

"Shut your face, asswipe," snarled the convict next to me. "Tal, use that side door. And keep it down. The old lady's asleep." He turned to me, pushed me into a chair with the butt of his pistol. "Stay here. Try anything your son's dead." He disappeared into the breakfast room and I heard the squeak of the screen door opening and some angry whispers outside. I considered going for the phone and calling 911 but he returned too soon, Talbert trailing behind him, head down, Cat hat hooding his eyes and a worried grin glued to his face.

"I know what you're thinkin', Pick," he said, "but this won't supposed to go this way."

"You were casing the joint at Thanksgiving for your friend here," I said. "Your mama's gonna be real proud of you."

"This don't concern you," he said. "We just needed a place to hook up. If dumbass here had stayed outside you never woulda knowed it."

"The mutt come barkin' at me out there," Raiford said. "What was I s'posed to do? Let 'im bring the whole Eno Police Department down on me?"

"What's done is done," said Talbert. "Come on, let's go. Jerry's waitin' at the river."

I was slowly putting together what had happened. Our house had been drafted as part of Talbert's plan to help his convict buddy escape— sort of a safe house for him to hide out in until Talbert and Jerry could pick him up by canoe and paddle him to freedom. What was in it for Talbert and Jerry was unclear, but I had heard from Russ that the all-too-frequent jail escapees were always picked up heading west. I guess this one thought he could outfox the authorities by heading east.

"No, uh-uh," said Raiford. "Are you crazy? This un'll call the police and they'll be all over us."

"That's why I told you to stay put."

Bobby Raiford looked at me. "Why don't I just shoot 'im?"

"Nobody's shootin' nobody," Talbert insisted. "Just tie 'em up. Leave 'em in the ice house."

"What about the old lady?" Raiford asked.

"She'll be out like a light 'til mornin'. She won't know where they went. By the time the police find 'em we'll be long gone."

"We need some cord."

"In the pantry," Talbert said.

Their thoroughness surprised me, and I wondered what else they'd scoped out on Thanksgiving day.

"Shit, Raiford," said Talbert, considering the complications we presented and the magnitude of the task before him. "Why did you git them involved?"

"You worry too much, Tal." Raiford munched a slice of bacon and pinched Talbert's butt.

"Not here," Talbert said, glancing worriedly at me. Jesus, I thought, he must have been playing house with this dude at Central Prison.

"I didn't want family involved," said Talbert.

"Look, that ain't my problem." Raiford shoveled cold eggs onto his toast and into his maw in one swoop. "You afraid they'll rat you out, you take it up with them," he said, nodding at me. "I tell you one thing, if it was my family I could keep 'em quiet. Hell, I'm the one who planned this whole thing and carried it off. Besides, they ain't lookin' for you, Tal, they lookin' for me."

"Sooner or later they'll come after you, Talbert," I said. "Accomplice to murder."

He looked at me with a puzzled expression on his face. Wiley crouched in the corner, holding Flappy and keeping his head down.

"Sounds like your friend popped somebody at the courthouse today," I continued.

Talbert shot Raiford a worried look.

"Shit happens," the convict said. "But you shoulda seen it, bubba. Except for that chump I had to cut, it went off like a dream. I ask the deputy if I can take a shit right before we go into the courtroom. He says okay, removes the cuffs but he's gotta wait outside. You were right—that shitter is a damn tiny room. Not big enough for more than one. I seen Velma slinkin' around outside on the steps when we come in. She looked good, too. All short skirt an' high heels, an' I hear her start flirtin' with Deputy Dawg like we told her to, askin' him for a cigarette and all. He's comin' all over hisself puttin' the moves on her and I climb up and find the clothes in the ceilin' panel jus' like you left 'em, bro', jus' like we planned it."

Talbert was caught up in the story now and had forgotten about his concern over the casualty. "I had a helluva time sawin' that grate yesterday and puttin' it back just right. Velma come with me to stand guard outside and keep folks out for nearly an hour sayin' somebody was sick in there."

"Yeah, well she blew it this mornin'," complained Raiford. "She all tied up with the deputy an' let some asshole court clerk started poundin' on the door makin' a racket just when I had the window removed. I cracked the door open, said I was usin' the facilities and to come back later. He all huffy, sayin' there ain't no more facilities an' to hurry my ass up. He drawin' attention so I acts like I'm goin' out an' I pulls him in and split his gullet with a shiv. I reckon they find him there later after I got away. By that time though, I'm gone to Oaklawn." He beamed at me, perversely proud of his escape.

"Damn," said Talbert, finally grasping his complicity.

I was sitting on the floor along the back windows thinking how close by the sheriff's department and jailhouse we were but a lot of good that did me. If only I could send up a flare. Wiley was sniffling in the corner a few feet away. Suddenly Raiford threw down his fork, strode over to Wiley and backhanded him across the face, drawing blood with the ring on his finger. "Shut up, you little shit!"

"You son of a bitch," I shouted, springing up, but he whirled around and the gun barrel gaped before me like a deep dark tunnel. I heard a click as Raiford drew back the hammer.

"One more step and you eat it, asshole," said Raiford. "Today won't the first time I took care of somebody standin' in my way. And it won't be the last."

"Raiford, don't," said Talbert. "No more trouble." I suppose he was trying to figure out how he was going to explain this to his mama, anyway, and didn't need a dead cousin complicating it. But I had gotten on Raiford's radar and he wasn't going to let me off that easy.

"You wanna get a piece of the action, Talbert, you gotta do what you gotta do," he said, staring at me malevolently. "This is a big stash I got waitin' for me. You been sayin' you wanna play with the big boys. Well, show me what you got. Let me see you take care of your cousin. You got that revolver on you, don't you?"

"Yeah, but—"

"Git rid of him."

Suddenly there was a sound again from the attic—the mysterious crunching sound we had heard before.

"What the hell was that?" asked Talbert. "Sounds like it come from upstairs."

Raiford eyed the ceiling as if the roof was about to fall in. "I thought you said the wife was out of town."

"She's supposed to be," Talbert said. Raiford motioned for silence. I heard the stove clock tick, then the crunching sound again.

"Is it the old lady?" Raiford asked Talbert.

"Naw, she's in yonder," Talbert said, pointing toward the wing bed-room. "Who's up there, Pick?"

"Ghosts," I said.

Raiford pressed his gun to my temple. "Don't fuck with me, wise-ass, or I'll turn *you* into a ghost."

"They hung six men on that oak tree outside the window there in Colonial times," I said. "They say it's the ghosts of the Regulators we hear up there."

"Bullshit!" declared Raiford.

"It may be bullshit to you," I said, "but this is the fourth time I've heard that noise this month." The grinding sound started up again.

"Somebody's up there and it ain't no ghosts," said Raiford, raising his eyes again to the ceiling. "Talbert, you stay here and tie up the boy." He grabbed my arm and shoved me toward the living room door and steered me to the stairwell off the hallway, with the gun band jammed against my spine. "I'll go up and check it out with wise-ass here."

I led the way to the attic landing. A loud cracking sound stopped us in our tracks.

"If you got somebody up here you're dead," Raiford said and shoved me toward the attic door. I had oiled the hinges only a week before and it swung open without a squeak. The full moon shone through an opening under the gable, reflecting off the plastic tarp the roofers had hung when they ripped away a section of siding to repair the water damage around the vent. I could tell by the frigid temperature that the tarp was at least partially blown down. When we entered the attic the crunching sound stopped. The sudden silence was ominous. I scanned the gloom at the far end of the crawlspace and when my vision adjusted I thought I saw a pair of glowing red eyes peering at us through the corner opening. My heart thumped in my chest as I fumbled along the door for the light switch. What I saw when I switched it on, I saw only for an instant, but the image remains with me to this day, etched in my memory like initials carved into stone.

There in the moonlight was the white hawk, its majestic form standing over a pile of tiny bones, regarding us warily with its fierce red eyes and the bloody remains of a mangled rabbit dangling from its enormous beak. Startled by the light and our sudden appearance, the great predator dropped the rodent. Then letting loose a piercing nightmare screech, it pummeled its wings against the eaves, and with feathers flying and screaming like a demon, tore through the plastic tarp and took to the sky like a nocturnal Icarus, bursting the bonds of Oaklawn into the dazzling moonlight.

"Jesus fucking Christ, what was that?" Raiford staggered back, recoiling in fright and self-protection. I seized the moment and slammed my elbow into his solar plexus. The gun clattered to the floorboards. I kicked it away and was on him like a madman, pummeling him with my fists. He was strong as a bull, the result, no doubt, of regular prison workouts, and my punches slowed him down but never quite laid him low. Then finally I gained purchase and, straddling his chest, was on top of him and about to cold-cock him with a lamp base I had grabbed in the fray when I heard a familiar voice say, "Put it down, Pickard." Talbert was standing in the doorway with a gun in his hand. I dropped the lamp base and let Raiford up.

"What the hell took you so long?" demanded Raiford, staggering to his feet, holding his head and nursing a cut on his lip.

"What was it?" Talbert asked.

"A goddamned eagle or somethin'." Raiford was breathing heavily and holding his jaw.

"Can we go now?"

"Where's the kid?"

"Tied up in the kitchen." Talbert eyed me suspiciously as Raiford shoved me past him and back down to the landing. "Let's tie this one up and get outa here."

We passed through the living room. Raiford spotted the fireplace implements beneath the mantel and grabbed a poker. He pushed me through the door into the kitchen. "Take the kid out to that ice house. I'll take care of this 'un so's he don't cause us no more problems."

"Let him be, man." Talbert threw Wiley over his shoulder like a sack of potatoes. "Just tie 'im up and let's get outa here."

Raiford slammed the poker down on my left knee. Bones and cartilage exploded. I screamed and crumpled to the floor.

"Don't tell me what to do, Talbert," spat Raiford.

"Jesus, Bobby, why'd you do that for?"

"Insurance. That was the knee he hurt in college, won't it? The one you told me about?" I whimpered. Never in my life had I felt such excruciating pain. Wiley squirmed and bucked on Talbert's shoulder, his eyes wide with fear.

"You promised not to hurt 'em," Talbert pleaded.

"Go, goddammit!" shouted Raiford, his veins sticking out at his temple, his face twisted with rage. Talbert turned toward the door with Wiley over his shoulder.

I cried out, "Leave the boy alone!"

They disappeared out the side door and Bobby Raiford pivoted back to me with a sneer on his face. He bent down and lashed my hands together with the cord Talbert had used to truss Wiley.

"You love that boy, don't you, Mr. Quarterback?"

"Leave him alone, you bastard."

"Did you see his face when his daddy got whupped and he couldn't do nothin' to help him?" He shoved his face in close to mine. He smelled of bacon grease and body odor. A blob of yellow egg clung to the corner of his mouth. He jerked the knot tight around my wrists, securing my hands behind my back. "Now, what kind of daddy is that?" He looked toward the door, talking to himself as much as to me. "Your cousin don't know me too well. He ain't as bright as you an' me, now is he?"

Then he stood and spun around and there was something unhinged in his manner, as if my present helplessness and the gratuitous brutality he had meted out had ignited something in him that he liked a little too much. He saw the vulnerability in me and homed in on it. "I'm thinkin' we take that boy of yours along for insurance," he teased. "Show him how a real man treats his boy."

I arched my back and tried to confront him but my injury pulled me down like some malign gravity. My knee flared with pain. Raiford towered over me, holding his gun in one hand and the fireplace poker in the other, watching me with an amused smirk. "I don't understand why your cousin don't want me to pop you." He bounced the poker off my knee, sending another jolt of pain knifing up my thigh. A wave of nausea rushed over me and I shrieked through gritted teeth.

"Talbert don't have any more use for you than I do," Raiford continued, enjoying his advantage. "And now that that leg's gone out on you, Mr.Quarterback, you ain't no use to nobody neither, are you?"

"Fuck you," I said, doubled over on the floor, tears of frustration and fury cutting down my cheeks.

"You're like a lame horse. Why don't I demonstrate for Talbert what happens to lame horses." I heard the sound of his pistol cocking just above my head. "What do you say, Mr. Quarterback? Think it's time we put you down?"

Then I heard another sound, one that neither I nor Bobby Raiford expected.

"Drop the gun, mister," a voice called from the end of the kitchen gallery. It was the loud, cantankerous, demanding voice of a little old lady, a voice I had heard and resented all my life, full of piss and vinegar, cracked with age but now clear as a bell. I looked up and saw Mama Lucy in her nightgown and curlers standing in the doorway to the wing off her bedroom. She had a snub-nosed .38 in her hands and it was leveled squarely at Bobby Raiford. He stood motionless, looking down at me with his gun still pointed at my head, then looked back up at her.

"I said drop it." Mama Lucy fired two rapid shots into the unfinished wall above his head.

"Jesus Christ, lady." Raiford dropped his pistol on the floor beside me. "Give me a minute."

"I'm ninety years old. I ain't got a minute. Now you kick that Nazi-stopper on down here to me and keep your hands up."

"Did we wake you, Mama Lucy?" I asked, wondering where she had gotten her gun, which looked suspiciously similar to the one she used to threaten her daughter's boyfriends with. I wondered how she had managed to sneak it past me when I moved her in.

"I woke up worried about Petey bird and remembered we put him outside," she said, "and then I heard talkin', and I thought it was Cameron got home. Then I overheered this 'un and heered a scream." She poked the gun at Raiford and said, "Now kick it on down here."

Bobby Raiford appraised the tiny woman standing before him, then kicked the pistol, sending it spinning across the newly tiled floor in her direction. I could hear his gears turning. He'd taken guns away from cons twice her size and there was no reason he couldn't disarm a feeble old woman. I could tell he was about to turn on the charm and I worried about Mama Lucy's susceptibility and frailty but I also knew she could handle that gun and it wouldn't be the first time a man had underestimated her. Raiford stepped toward her. She fired. Tile shards sprayed across his shoes.

She leveled the gun at Bobby Raiford's gonads. "You take one more step, sonny boy, and you ain't gonna be singin' bass in the glee club no more." Raiford froze. "Now you untie my grandson and make it snappy. Pick, did you remember to bring Petey inside when we got home?" asked Mama Lucy, returning to the business at hand while she waited for Raiford to complete his task. Before I could answer I heard the muffled catching sound of the storm door closing. And so did Raiford, who smirked at me and whispered, "Maybe that's Petey."

"Mama Lucy, look out!" I shouted but it was too late.

"Freeze!" A gun poked through the doorway, pointing at Mama Lucy. Talbert stepped into the kitchen gallery, creating a deadly triangle between himself, Mama Lucy, and Raiford.

"Drop the gun, Mama Lucy," he said. "Drop it. You heard me."

"No, sir," she answered, still leveling the .38 at Bobby Raiford's private parts.

"Put it down, Mama Lucy," Talbert demanded.

"Nuh-uh."

"Goddammit, Mama Lucy, drop the gun! Don't make me hurt you now!"

"You gonna have to shoot me, Talbert." Lucy's eyes were pinned to Raiford. "What you doin' ain't right."

"Shoot her," said Raiford, feeling the dynamics of the situation shifting back into his control.

"Drop it, Mama Lucy," said Talbert, a trace of panic fraying his voice. "I swear, don't make me do it."

"Shoot her, Talbert," Raiford said.

"Don't, Talbert," I said.

Talbert pleaded, "Please, Mama Lucy, don't make me do it."

"Do what you gotta do, son. I've lived my life."

"Shoot her, goddammit!" Raiford shouted. "You wanna play with the big boys you gotta have balls. Shoot her!"

"Don't do it, Talbert," I urged.

"Where the hell is Jerry?" Talbert screamed, beads of sweat stippling his forehead. I had forgotten about Talbert's brother and assumed he was down by the river. I felt a sudden jolt of fear as it dawned on me that he might get curious and come looking for them. The situation was already chaotic enough without another loose cannon.

"Fuck Jerry!" Raiford shouted. "Shoot the old bitch!"

"Drop the gun, Mama Lucy," Talbert pleaded. His voice was cracking.

Suddenly a headlight swept across the room and the sound of crunching gravel grew louder as a car pulled up the long drive. I cut my eyes toward the driveway and prayed it wasn't Cameron.

"Jesus Christ!" Bobby screamed as Talbert glanced out the window. "Who the hell is that?"

"Can't tell," said Talbert, rattled and trying to hold his aim on his grandmother.

"C'mon, Talbert," Raiford pleaded. Veins snaked beneath the skin of his forehead, "Shoot the bitch and let's get the hell outa here!"

"Drop the gun, Mama Lucy."

"Do what you gotta do, son," she repeated. "I've lived my life."

Raiford screamed, "Shoot the fucking cunt!"

"Don't!" I shouted.

"Drop it, please, Mama Lucy," Talbert pleaded.

Raiford stepped forward. "Shoot, goddammit. Shoot her! Do I have to do every fucking thing in th—"

As he slipped past me I reached deep down inside for every ounce of strength and willpower I could muster and shot a leg out and tripped Bobby Raiford. Though my wrists were bound and pain shot through my body like bolts of lightning I lurched up and launched myself at him like a missile. Raiford scrambled to his feet and whirled to face me, his pistol aimed at my head.

The blast was quieter than I'd expected. I crumpled to the floor.

Raiford gaped at the wound in his abdomen, then back up at my grandmother. A look of surprise crossed his face when he saw the small puff of smoke rising from the barrel of Talbert's gun.

The second and third bullets ripped through his chest and forehead, splattering bits of his skull and brains on our new walnut cabinetry. Raiford staggered forward, sagging a bit in the knees, then crashed face first into a bowl of doggie treats. Talbert slumped against the wall and slid to the baseboard, his gun clattering to the floor at Mama Lucy's feet.

The next thing I heard was the welcome jingle of keys slapping against wood, then Cameron opened the front door and shouted, "Hello? Wiley! Pickard! I'm home!"

RAIMENTS

Always cool in a crisis, Cameron took matters in hand. First, she called 911, then rushed to the ice house where she found Wiley bound and gagged, his teeth chattering, clutching Flappy to his chest. She brought our son back inside and the three of us, along with Mama Lucy, clung to each other like sailors adrift at sea. I couldn't choke back the tears when Wiley said he was sorry he couldn't protect me from that bad man.

The police arrived and Talbert, having returned to what passed for his senses, told them the whole story and led them down to the landing on the banks of the New Hope. The canoe was still tied up where he'd left it but Jerry was nowhere in sight. The police scoured the area with their flashlights, calling Jerry's name and Talbert made birdcalls until finally they heard muffled cries from somewhere up the terraced embankment. They found Jerry peering up at them from the floor of the old Bennehan ice pit, shivering and terrified. Jerry, worried when Talbert and Raiford failed to make it to the river at the appointed time, had wandered up the path to look for them and tumbled into the pit. The brothers Bailey were arrested for aiding and abetting a murderer and spent the night in the same Eno County jail they had helped Bobby Raiford escape.

The story that ran the following Wednesday in the weekly *News of Eno* explained that Bobby Raiford had been arrested for a series of burglaries in Eno's Historic District and suspicion of murder in an ATM machine robbery at a convenience store in Chapel Hill. He had already spent time in Central State Prison for felonious assault and armed robbery and was awaiting trial for murder when he escaped from the Eno County courthouse just before his hearing that Friday, and killed a clerk from the magistrate's office in the process. His accomplice was one Talbert Bailey, who had served time with Raiford at Central State a few years earlier for grand theft auto. The article did not mention Jerry, who, according to his mother, was irritated that his name was left out.

Talbert, Jerry, and Jerry's girlfriend were held without bond in the county jail to await their hearing just before Christmas. If convicted, they faced twenty years to life.

Mama Lucy seemed more upset over Petey's death than over the killing of an escaped convict right before her eyes. No matter how many times I implicated the raccoons I'd seen on the porch, she associated the cockatiel's death with Raiford and held him alone accountable. She took pride in her part in bringing the murderer of innocent cockatiels to justice. I marveled at Mama Lucy's courage and spunk. My son and I were alive thanks to her incorrigible insistence on possessing a firearm in spite of the authorities' best efforts to disarm her. I only hoped I would possess as much chutzpah at her age.

Her pluck, unfortunately, couldn't do much to restore my damaged knee. Luckily, surgeons at Duke University Medical Center operated on it promptly and successfully and sent me home to recuperate. I crutched around the house, happy to be alive, even if I would be walking with a pronounced limp well into the next summer.

The carnage Cameron witnessed shook her up profoundly, so much so that she handed over postproduction of the WeltanCom commercials to Linda DiCaprio and took a leave of absence from Oleander through the holidays so she could stay home with Wiley and me. One evening, when we were alone for a change, Cameron built a fire in the living room fireplace, poured us some wine, and we talked as we hadn't since moving to Oaklawn.

We spoke of my trip to Delaney and my visit with Jake Satterfield and of what I had learned from the man who stabbed my grandmother sixty years ago. We talked about Wiley and how he was adjusting to his new school and speculated about how the events of the last few months might affect him. We talked about her work and about her shoot in Philadelphia and Chicago and the big New York agency she had finally won over with her professionalism and resourcefulness. We talked into the night, until we had exhausted every subject and we could avoid the topic of us no longer.

"I've missed you, Cam," I said.

"We haven't been happy with each other, have we, Pick?" She stared into the sputtering flames and poured herself the last glass of wine.

"I guess not," I answered.

"Roland Jameson's asked me to marry him."

I would have preferred another poker across my knee than to hear the words I feared she would utter, but I had to know. "Are you in love with him?"

She gazed into the fire a long time, her knees drawn up under her. Finally she said, "I don't know. I like him very much and he seems to be in love with me, but—"

"C'mon, Cam," I said. "Don't tell me you don't know." My vulnerability was making me testy.

"I may be in love with the idea of being loved."

"Does Jameson know this?"

"Don't cross-examine me, Pick. He knows I'm confused."

"And that's okay with him?"

"It'll have to be." Cameron turned and looked hard at me. "I thought I was in love with you, the Pick Cantrell I married. And that I could never love anyone else. I don't know what's happened to that. We've grown so distant over the last few months. We used to talk about everything."

"We're talking now," I said.

"For the first time in months. You know what I mean."

"What do you want to talk about?"

"I once would have said us, but now I don't know. Now it's like we're in different worlds. My enthusiasm for my job seems to grate on you. Maybe I underestimated the toll being out of work would exact."

"Maybe I did, too."

"Tell me, Pick, 'cause I have to know—are you still in love with me?"

Her question took me aback. I thought it was obvious how I felt. "Cam, I love you. I can't imagine living without you. I know I've been an asshole and impossible to live with lately but I want to make it right."

"Seeing Wiley in that ice house the other night nearly devastated me. It was like a metaphor for what I would be doing to him if I left you, if I followed through on what I've been contemplating."

"In other words, you'll endure being married to me for the sake of our son?"

"It's a worthy motivation for the time being, don't you think?"

"I don't need you sacrificing yourself to stay with me," I said. "And I don't think that's what Wiley needs."

"A child needs both parents, Pick. You know that."

"He needs both parents who want to be together."

"He doesn't need perfection. He needs continuity. Even a strained continuity is better than none at all. I don't know where you and I will wind up. I really don't."

I sat there fingering my glass, trying not to show her how distraught I was.

"Pick, I think I understand your fixation with your grandmother now . . . I do."

"Maybe you can explain it to me."

"Isn't it obvious?" she asked. "You're working through something with your mother."

"With Mama Lucy? C'mon."

"We've been married for over fifteen years and it's time we faced some facts. You were saying at Thanksgiving how strange it was that you never knew any of this family history involving your grandmother. But don't you find it odd that I know so very little about your mom? I'm your wife. Everything I know about Mary Alice I learned from someone other than you. You never talked about her. We were already married before I even learned her name. The things we don't talk about, Pick, the things you can't talk about, that's where the answers are for you."

"The things we don't talk about because we don't even know," I mumbled.

"Pardon?"

I was staring into the fire now. "My mother killed herself in the hospital. She was a suicide."

Cam looked stricken. "Oh, Pick," she said. "I'm so sorry." She settled in beside me, pulling her knees up underneath her chin. I told her what Mama Lucy had told me about my mother and she listened with great sympathy and curiosity. It seemed to explain a lot to Cam and emboldened her to tell me more of what she'd had on her mind.

"It hit me when I was in Chicago," she said finally, "that when Lucy stopped being this monster for you, you created one in me. Well, I'm not playing anymore. I understand the pain you've carried with you all your life, the anger and resentment you felt at losing your mother that you turned on Mama Lucy. But you can't put that on us, not on me."

Cameron had spent years in therapy sorting through all her baggage with her own mother and sisters, but I had always been skeptical of our generation's narcissistic navel-gazing. But everything we'd gone through recently had left me exhausted and I now had no stomach for manning the old barricades.

What Cameron was saying rang true and a bouquet of associations bloomed in my mind. Over the years we'd had numerous friends, many of them artists or writers, who married harradins like Mama Lucy, and I was the first to point out to Cameron the unhealthy calculus of those relationships. Was this the sort of thing I was arranging with Cameron?

"So what do we do?" I asked.

"I've got to decide what I want. Up until recently you've been that. Now . . . I don't know."

"I love you, Cameron," I said. "I don't want to lose you." My effort to woo and win back my wife was vanishing up the chimney with the woodsmoke.

Cameron seemed unsettled by my declaration. "I don't know where I'll land with all this," she said. "I need some time. Right now you're going to have to accept my ambivalence. For Wiley's sake. I'll stay put for the time being and see where things go. If that's okay with you."

"I'm not going anywhere," I said.

I stared into the dying embers of the fire.

Cameron and I stayed up late Christmas Eve putting out Santa's gifts for Wiley, assembling his bike and drum kit and telescope, and on Christmas morning I woke up first and started a fire, turned on the Christmas tree lights and carols on the FM station, and put on a pot of coffee. Although I moved slowly, I got around pretty well on my crutches, a talent I had mastered in college after my first knee injury. I roused Cameron and Mama Lucy and we all watched Wiley open his gifts. Cameron videotaped the whole thing. Mama Lucy sat on the sofa amid all the wrapping paper and boxes and gifts. Cameron gave her a new housecoat and slippers and we both got her a new cinnamon-colored cockatiel whom Wiley named "Re-Petey." Cameron gave me a brand-new drafting table and a sleekly comfortable swivel chair which she set up in the summer kitchen where she had hidden them.

I gave her a coffee table book on the historic homes and architecture of the state with a picture of Oaklawn in it, a new minicam, and an elegant Ralph Lauren cocktail dress. When we dated she had loved when I picked out clothes for her and I had not done it in years. We went through these motions with as much holiday cheer as we could muster but in the back of our minds we both wondered if this would be our last Christmas together.

In the days leading up to Christmas I had worked furiously on the drawing of the old Bellevue mill I had started after Thanksgiving. I gave it to Mama Lucy for Christmas to hang up next to the pen-and-ink drawing of Chicken Bridge. To bring the mill alive I had populated the grounds and included some of the other details that were missing from the official photographs, like mill hands hurrying into work and the "dope wagon," as Mama Lucy called it, parked outside along the chain-link fence, the snack cart that sold Coca-Colas to thirsty workers at breaks and shift changes.

"Oh, Pick, this is better than any of those photographs," she said amid sniffles and hugs.

Cameron fixed us eggnog and hot apple cider and whipped up a hearty Christmas breakfast of bacon and eggs. Later some of the family from Burlington and Saxapahaw dropped by to visit Mama Lucy. Dr. Levin stopped in on his way to the clinic in Burlington to relieve "the overworked Goyim on their holiday," and we wished him a happy Hannukah. Sandy dropped off some Christmas cookies and visited with Cameron and Mama Lucy while I watched Wiley ride his new bike around the playground at school.

Later that afternoon when things calmed down and everyone had retired to their rooms for naps I read by the fire. The crunch of tires on gravel and a loud metallic thunk pulled me from my book. I looked out the window and saw Wallace helping an old man out of his car. I recognized the face under the brim of the Atlanta Braves cap immediately. It was Jake Satterfield. With a twinge of anxiety, I hobbled across the room, opened the front door, and raised a tentative hand in holiday greeting.

"Merry Christmas, Wallace," I said, giving him a questioning glance.

"I hope this is okay, Pick," Wallace said. "Jake wanted to pay his respects to Mama Lucy."

I stepped back. "Yeah, sure, come on in." I nodded a greeting to Jake and led them down the hallway to Mama Lucy's room. The door was open, and I leaned in and saw on TV a young Natalie Wood sitting on Kris Kringle's knee, saying, "I don't believe in Santa Claus."

"You've got a visitor, Mama Lucy," I said.

She switched off the TV. "Who is it?"

"It's me, Lucy—Jake Satterfield."

Mama Lucy turned toward him. She didn't say a word.

Jake shuffled across the room and dropped into a chair directly across from her.

"We saw Jake in Delaney, Mama Lucy," I said, fumbling for an explanation. "I meant to tell you but—"

"Hello, Jake," Mama Lucy said. "What are you doin' here?"

"I know I got no call in expectin' you to see me after all that's happened between us," Jake said. "But I was hopin' in the spirit of the day we celebrate the birth of our Lord you'd hear me out. I been right upset since Wallace an' 'em come to Delaney to visit. I got somethin' I need to get off my chest, before it's too late." Jake looked away, then back, and I noticed he was crying.

He blew his nose and looked up at Lucy. For a moment, they seemed to study each other and I wondered at the history they shared and what, even now, might be passing between them. "Lucy," he said. "I'm the one that killed Annie Laura. Not Bud. It was me that done it. I was aimin' at you, Lucy, Lord forgive me, I shouldn'ta been, but I was and I hit Annie Laura and took her life." He broke down. "I loved her, I did. She was the onliest one I ever cared anything about. And I killed her."

Mama Lucy looked at me and I looked at Wallace, but he raised his hand and said, "Why don't you tell her what you told me in the car on the way up here, Jake."

In that first burst of adrenaline when all hell broke loose in the yard Jake emptied his chamber, his last shot felling ol' man Copeland, the weave room hand who caught him cheatin' on the dock sheet that time and got him laid off. Jake was convinced Copeland was the one who snitched to Sumner and got him fired and Jake Satterfield never forgot a slight. He hit Copeland clean in the back of the head and chuckled to himself when he saw the man's head snap back and legs buckle and watched him stagger from the impact and fall to the ground. He was savoring the moment when out of the haze of teargas he saw Copeland's wife bent over him. Then he spotted another woman with a bandanna over her face rushing to the spot where Copeland had fallen. When the figure turned to look up in the direction the shots were fired, the bandanna fell away and Jake realized that the woman there before him was none other than Lucy Barlow. What luck! he thought. And he had a perfect line on her, too! But then he remembered he was out of bullets. And with no more ammo he was gonna miss his opportunity. People were scurrying like mice across the yard through the gas and haze, stopping only long enough to check the wounded. She'd be gone before he reloaded.

Jake turned to Bud in the window next to him and shouted through the noise and confusion. "Shoot, dammit. Shoot!" But the boy had frozen up. He should have known Bud Cantrell wouldn't have the guts to fire on another human being. It was always that way with these so-called sharpshooters. Bagging squirrels was one thing but layin' a man low was a whole different matter. But Jake didn't have time to argue. He pulled his own weapon from the window and knelt down beside Bud and screamed at him to shoot, goddammit, before the opportunity passed away forever. But the more Jake screamed the more Bud seemed to tighten up until finally the boy cried, "I can't! I can't!" and curled up in a ball, cradling his 30.06 in his lap.

The next thing Jake knew, Bud's brother Dalton Earl was on the boy's other side patting him on the back, comforting him, saying, "It's all right, Bud. It's all right."

Furious, Jake snatched Bud's weapon. "If you won't do it, I will," he snarled, and turned back to the window, crouched down, and leveled the rifle.

"I'm gonna git that bitch," he hissed, but just as he spotted her hovering over Copeland's body and was drawing a bead, somebody in a yellow polka-dot scarf stepped forward and blocked his clean shot. Jake adjusted his sight. His callused fingertip caressed the trigger. Just then, Dalton leaped up and dove across Bud and knocked Jake to the floor. The rifle fired and clattered to the floor as the men tumbled into a heap. They both scrambled to the window. Jake had missed Lucy but hit somebody else. Lucy was hovering over another body now, the body of the woman in the yellow polka-dot scarf.

Jake sobbed into his bony arthritic hands as Wallace knelt beside him and looked at the rest of us helplessly. Nobody knew what to say so we said nothing. Jake sniffled and raised his eyes to Lucy. "I was full of hate and spite when I was a boy and I blamed you for a lot of my troubles, but I was sure enough aimin' at you that day, and it was Dalton that knowed it and spoiled my aim. And I was usin' Bud's gun, which is why the coroner showed it was his bullet that killed her. But I never meant to harm Annie Laura. I swear I didn't, but when it happened I held it against you and Dalton and never forgot it. I know the Lord teaches forgiveness," he said, blowing his nose, "but I never could forgive you, Lucy, for not dyin' instead of Annie Laura. I was a hateful man most of my life and I paid the price. I brought much sorrow into the lives of many people and I am truly sorry. The Good Book says you reap what you sow and I reckon I'm livin' proof. It also says the Lord will forgive me, that He even forgive them that put Him to death. It's hard for me to see it, but I reckon if scripture says it, it's so."

Mama Lucy was clearly moved by what she was hearing but before she could respond Jake continued.

"I had to say it and say it to you. I will carry the blood of Annie Laura Gaskins on my hands to the end of my days. I don't know how you could ever forgive me but I pray that you can."

"Jake," Mama Lucy said when he had finished, "I-I don't know what to say."

"There's more," Jake said. "I didn't tell Pick this, but his visit got me to thinkin'. . . . I was workin' for Mr. Webb from the time I told Bates Strudwick about you and Spencer. I used to come to this house. He paid me in 'shine mostly, but I was a spy for Strudwick and him all those years. Worked with their detectives during the strike. And after. They was settin' up your brother Davis for the dynamitin' of the mill in Burlington. Gonna send him to prison along with the others. But Spencer got wind of it and tipped off Dalton, who arrested Dave that night. They hated Davis and was mad as hell when he got off and mad at Dalton for interferin' with their plans for him. I don't know for a fact, but I think that's why Dalton got laid off by the sheriff after the strike. The sheriff was in on it. The dynamitin'. And they come to me after the strike was settled and the dynamite case was tried to do a job. Them two detectives that worked for Mr. Webb said they was speakin' on his behalf, but when I won't paid after I done it and went to Strudwick to collect my money he said he didn't know what I was talkin' about. They sent me to do it out of spite . . ."

It was a cold day in early April, a few months after the strike. Jake was working again at the Bellevue mill and between that paycheck and his guard duty and the little extra he picked up doing odd jobs he had more pocket change than he'd had since he got laid off for pulling a knife on boss man Sumner on the loading dock. Jake was proud of himself for finally getting some recognition and ingratiating himself to the rich and powerful folks like Webb and Strudwick, though he still resented them and talked about them behind their backs. He knew they depended on folks like him in the dark recesses and shadows of their lives but wouldn't give him the time of day on the main streets of town or invite him into their fine homes for dinner. And he still had one more thing to do for them. The request had come from the company dicks, but Jake knew they didn't shit without running it by Strudwick first. He knew he'd be well-compensated, so he was willing to see it through.

By late November the Burlington dynamite case had been tried and the ones charged had been sentenced. The trial had drawn a lot of attention in the newspapers and on the streets. Dave Barlow knew the accused men and had been raising money and meeting with anyone and everyone who would listen to their cause. After stirring up so much resentment against the mill owners during the strike, many of the company men and their strikebreakers felt that Dave Barlow had gotten off clean. It was Jake's job to bring him to justice.

Jake had kept an eye on old Dave. He knew his habits—that he lived with his mother in Eno but drove his motorcycle every day to Burlington during the trial and visited his sweetheart there every Sunday after church. Usually he stayed for dinner and returned to Eno late Sunday night over the back roads from Burlington through Haw River and Mebane and Efland and crossed the New Hope River outside the West End of Eno at Chicken Bridge.

After fortifying himself with a few drinks at the pool hall, Jake drove out to Chicken Bridge and parked his truck near where the bonfire was built on Halloween to carve the pumpkins by. He walked out in the middle of the empty highway to check visibility. His truck was invisible from the road from both directions. Jake tied the rope between the trussing on both sides of the narrow highway, tested it to make sure it was secure, and then slipped into the trees. His present vantage point offered him a clear view of the entire bridge, from one end to the other. He took another swig from the jar of moonshine and looked up at the stars. The night was dark and moonless. He waited.

Soon he heard the far off drone of a motorcycle. He looked across the river at the stretch of highway that ran down the hill to the bridge. The sound of the engine grew louder. Dave Barlow loved to pop the clutch and wind it out on those long stretches of country highway. Jake had cased the situation for the last three Sundays from different angles and knew exactly how Dave liked to take the bridge. He waited with eager anticipation. A lone headlight soon appeared across the river like a distant star flickering through the trees. The drone increased to a buzz. The buzz became a roar. The light reappeared, blasting like the headlight on a freight train as the motorcycle's tires met the bridge and his quarry bore down on him.

Dave hit the rope at close to forty miles per hour. The rope struck his shoulders, burned up his neck and cartwheeled him through the air. The bike skidded across the blacktop, clanking and screeching and spitting sparks and flame from its tailpipe, then bounced, flipped end over end, caromed off the rails and girders, and entangled itself in the bridge trussing where it ticked and hissed as the engine began to cool. When Jake looked back he saw Dave's mangled body lying in the middle of the road. Jake sprinted past it, cut down and coiled up the evidence and got the hell out of there.

Mama Lucy's head slumped forward and her eyes slid shut. A tiny tear, like a diamond, winked on her lashes and tumbled down her cheek. "I knew it," she said. "I knew it won't no accident."

"I'm sorry, Lucy," said Jake. "If I could take it back I would."

"So that explains the rope burn on his neck," said Lucy. I was amazed at the way she sat there, so composed and stoic, considering this new information with neither rancor nor bitterness, as though she were contemplating a fact of nature—the rising of tides or alignment of planets.

"The sheriff didn't investigate," Jake said. "Dalton tried to get him to. And when he didn't Dalton come after me hisself. But I denied it and he couldn't prove nothin'."

"He knew you did it?"

"He had his suspicions."

"It was after that," said Mama Lucy, "that he was gone looking for work all the time, leavin' me with the young'uns. We never got along after that day."

"Lucy," Jake said, "I could never expect you to forgive me for all I done to you and your family. But I brung you somethin' I thought you should have. With my eyesight gone it ain't no good to me now." Without artifice or fanfare Jake removed a crudely framed picture from a brown-paper sack and handed it to Lucy.

Mama Lucy gasped. "It's me and Annie Laura." The beautifully drawn pencil portrait showed two women standing side by side, their arms around each other's waists. Lucy's dark hair was pulled back in a bun, her luminous eyes gazing out from the page. Next to her was Annie Laura, blond and fresh-faced, with enormous blue eyes. Scrawled across the bottom of the page were the words, *Happy Birthday, Lucy—September 4, 1934. Friends forever*. And on the portrait's lower right-hand corner, the name *Annie Laura Gaskins*.

"Have you ever seen this before, Mama Lucy?" I asked.

"No," she said. "I remember Annie Laura drawin' me but she would never show me what she drawed."

"She was a natural," I said. "It looks just like you."

"Like I used to look," said Lucy wistfully. "She musta drawed it for my twenty-ninth birthday just before she died. She told me she made me a present but I thought it was a dress or a pie or somethin'. She wanted to surprise me but . . ." She swallowed, gazed at the portrait for a long time, then passed it to me. She looked at Jake. "Where did this come from?"

"It's your'n, Lucy. I took it from Annie Laura's house the day after she was shot. All their belongin's from the eviction was still out in the yard. Was nobody around and when I seen the picture layin' next to a chiffarobe I took it."

"Was you at the funeral, Jake?" Lucy asked.

"No, I won't, Lucy. I didn't want to go. Couldn't. But I did visit her grave."

"In the colored cemetery," Lucy clarified.

"I used to take flowers to her grave ever' once in a while, but when I got out of prison and went back somebody had stole the marker."

I thought of Austin Strudwick, and the slate markers embedded in the patio at Sassafras and considered again what a prick the man was.

Mama Lucy stared at the drawing in her hand. After a time she looked up at Jake and said, "Thank you, Jake. Thank you for bringin' me this picture and thank you for tellin' me all that you told. You didn't have to and you did."

Jake Satterfield smiled and his eyes filled with tears of gratitude.

"Pickard," she said, "if it's all right with you could I hang this on the wall with the ones you drew?"

"Sure." I turned to fetch the masking tape and almost bumped into Cameron outside the door. The tears on her cheek told me that she had been standing there listening for quite some time. "Oh, Pick," she said, wiping her eyes before turning away.

The next morning I sat with Mama Lucy while she ate her breakfast. I could tell she needed to talk.

"Pick, at my age it ain't easy to look back and see how much of a fool I been."

I spooned out her grapefruit. "That's not easy at any age. "

"But you got time to make amends, son. I don't. Dalton deserved better than I give him."

"Don't be too hard on yourself, Mama Lucy."

"It was mainly my own hardheadedness. He tried to tell me his side of the story. But I wouldn't hear it. I knowed how I seen it and that was the only way to see it. I reckon after losin' the two people I loved most in the world I was lookin' for somebody to blame. Finally, he just stayed clear of me and I stayed clear of him. We had young'uns and folks didn't git divorced back then like they do nowadays."

"Maybe you loved each other," I suggested. "And that was the only way you knew how to show it."

"Maybe," she said, and I got the idea that Mama Lucy, despite all her accusations and contrary words, had considered this notion before. The thought gave me hope.

"At least you know the truth now," I said. "That's worth something."

"What Dalton had to put up with . . ." She shook her head. "Don't git me wrong. He had his faults. But I see now it won't him I was mad at." She stared at Annie Laura's drawing, smiling wistfully. "I was such a girl. Such a girl."

I left her to her thoughts.

Hobbled by my knee injury, I spent the winter sketching scenes Sandy had requested for a book she was doing on the southern cotton mill culture. I had transformed the summer kitchen into a studio and after a day of location sketching I would return to finish the roughs on my new drafting table by the wood-burning stove. I drew with a passion and pleasure I had not felt in years—pen-and-ink sketches of Lucy and Annie Laura as young girls walking to school, working in the weave room, swimming in the New Hope, singing duets in the Baptist church. I drew a banjo-picking on the front porch of a mill house on New Hope mountain and a mill village baseball team with TWI sewed on their uniforms and a family gathered around a radio at night in their cramped living room listening to the Grand Ole Opry. I drew Mama Lucy and Spencer Webb at Panther's Den, my uncle Dave in his army uniform sitting on his motorcycle, and my grandfather Dalton holding an ax beside a busted-up moonshine still. I captured the scene of the box supper at the church, and the pumpkin carving at Chicken Bridge, and the infant casket that won first place at the county fair. And I tried my best to re-create that terrible day in Eno. I especially enjoyed having Mama

Lucy dictate images to me. As her eyesight failed I became her Seeing-Eye dog. Mama Lucy would describe a scene, then guide my pencil along with her clucks of approval or grimaces of frustration and the image would slowly materialize. One image suggested another, one scene triggered the next, in a chain reaction of remembrance. The moments I cherished most were when she would finally examine my sketch with her magnifying glass, laugh her approval, and say, "That's it, Pick, that's it exactly."

"I don't think Lucy's going to be with us much longer, Pick," Sandy confided a couple of weeks later. All that winter she had been filming interviews with Mama Lucy for her book's companion documentary film project and had just wrapped for the day. "Going over the footage you can see her diminishment week to week. I feel guilty for forcing her to endure all these questions."

"Don't," I said. "I think she wants to get this down. It's what keeps her going. She'll let you know if she's not up to it."

But I was getting worried, too. My grandmother's shortness of breath was more pronounced now and sometimes at night she had to sit up in bed just so she could breathe. She began sleeping with pillows stacked under her head and some mornings I would enter to find the room freezing from a window left open all night. I began to fear that she might die of pneumonia rather than heart failure.

Sometimes I sat with her after lunch, visiting and keeping her company between her naps and my picking up Wiley from school and Cameron returning home. During those short but regular interludes we opened up to each other in ways I'd never believed possible—about our lives, our hopes and dreams, as well as our fears and mistakes and regrets, enjoying an intimacy and vulnerability with each other I doubt many parents and children share, much less grandparents.

Once I showed her a drawing I did of her and granddaddy Dalton as a young couple. They were dressed in their Sunday best, Dalton in a suit and Mama Lucy in a pretty print dress and a sassy hat that made her look like a flapper. The scene was my own fabrication. Granddaddy had his arm around her and the insouciant attitude in their smiles and postures revealed more my wish for them and their lives together than anything reality had ever afforded them.

Mama Lucy lay in bed propped up on pillows and surrounded by her medicines and images hand-drawn from her life. Her breathing was

labored even though she was now receiving oxygen through a nasal can-
nula. She stared at my drawing for a long time and finally said in her feeble, barely audible voice, "Dalton was a handsome man, Pick. You look a
lot like him."

"Do I?" I said. "I don't know. I just hope I do him justice." By then I
was relatively comfortable with the portraits I had drawn of my grandmother as a young woman. I had sketched her so many times at so many
ages and from so many angles that I was uninhibited about showing
them to her, but satisfaction with my grandfather's image still eluded me.

"That's the way he was, Pick," she said, wheezing, "That look around
his eyes, like he wanted to be somewhere else. That was what was so
appealin' and so maddenin' about him."

"I'm glad you like it, Mama Lucy." I gathered up the drawings. "I'm
going back up to Panther's Den to sketch the mountain laurel in bloom
and try to finish that series on the mill village the way it was."

Mama Lucy stared at the drawing in front of her. "You know I won't
be around to see them."

"What do you mean?" I said. "Sure you will." Every now and then she
grew morbid and talked that way, probably because she knew it got
under my skin and she enjoyed my efforts to tease her out of it, but this
time she wasn't playing.

"I ain't got long, son. You know that."

"Don't talk that way, Mama Lucy," I said, but I was getting worried,
too.

"It's okay, Pickard. I'm ready. But I wanted to tell you if I ain't said it
before how much I appreciate all you done for me." I shushed her, but
she continued. "No, you took me in when they was gonna send me away
and I'm mighty grateful to you for that. I feel like we made up for a lot of
hard feelin' over the years."

"It wasn't all that much," I said, looking away. "You saved my life—in
more ways than one."

"Listenin' to an old woman, Pick. Just hearin' me out—that's worth a
lot when you get to be my age," she said. I helped her adjust her nose-
piece. "But I've been studyin' on this, and I got a favor to ask you."

I eased down on the bed next to her. "What's that?"

"I want to be buried in Eno. I already picked out a plot in Burlington
years ago in the cemetery where your mama's buried but I've decided I
don't want to be in Burlington. I want to be buried here where I was

raised, beside Annie Laura." My heart sank. The red tape, I knew, could tie us up for years. But I promised to look into it, anyway.

"And another thing," Mama Lucy said. "I want to be buried in a pine box like Annie Laura."

"But why?"

"I just do," she said. "A pine box is all I need."

"I don't think they make those anymore, Mama Lucy."

Her look was almost coy as she said, "But you could make me one."

"I could, I guess," I admitted. But I wondered: Was this request a product of her rational mind or the whims of a senility that was finally taking hold? And how would I explain it to the family? "What do we do with the Burlington plot?" I asked.

"Maybe I'll let you have that one, Pickard. Leave it to you in my will." I thought I saw a mischievous glimmer in my grandmother's glaucoma-dimmed eyes.

One afternoon when I got home from a lunch date with Cameron—we were courting again, shyly, tentatively, like teenagers—I found all my drawings hanging on the wall of Mama Lucy's bedroom. "Sandy helped me put them up," Mama Lucy said. "They give me comfort."

"It's like a museum of your life," I commented.

"Thanks to you. I guess I don't have to bug you for a drawin' no more." I gazed at the cocoon of art surrounding her, the pen-and-ink renderings surrounding the lovely pencil portrait drawn by Annie Laura, and knew that my grandmother, in her singular and cantankerous way, had coaxed from me something raw and rare and beautiful—something that was uniquely me.

"That was the of best me, Pick," she said, indicating the portrait. "That's what Annie Laura saw. That was before everything happened. Remember what you said to me that time? About Ruth Ann's suicide?" I cringed, remembering how cruel I had been, but Mama Lucy plowed ahead. "That was the worst thing I could have heard. And the truest. I was harder on the girls than the boys. And they was hard on themselves. I wish I'd been a better mama. I knew how to be. But I was a young'un havin' young'uns. I was hurried into parenthood before I had my own girlhood. And I took it out on my own children." She looked as sad as I'd ever seen her, and I didn't know what to say. "I reckon it's hard to mother somebody else when you need motherin' your own self." She forced a smile. "Y'know, when I die there'll be nobody left to remember Annie

Laura. It'll be as if she lived and died for nothin'. Don't let them forget Annie Laura, Pick," she pleaded. "Promise me you won't let them forget."

"I won't, Mama Lucy," I promised. "I won't."

One Saturday morning in April, as Oaklawn blossomed with dogwoods and redbuds and wisteria, we loaded Mama Lucy into the Volvo and all of us—Cameron, Wiley, me, and Mama Lucy—drove to the West End. I wore a suit and tie and Cameron sported a new spring dress and even Wiley grudgingly allowed himself to be outfitted in a necktie and blazer.

"It ain't my birthday," Mama Lucy said, "and I don't like surprises. Tell me where we're goin', Pick."

I ignored her. Soon we pulled up under a giant oak tree. A series of brick steps led up a hill to a fenced-in lot. I helped Mama Lucy out of the car and into the wheelchair. "Do you recognize this place, Mama Lucy?" I asked. She looked around to get her bearings and exclaimed, "Oh, Pick, I ain't been back here since Annie Laura died."

We wheeled Mama Lucy between the oaks and dogwoods. The markers and gravestones were dark and faded with age, some of the graves sunk inches deep into the earth. Many were absent altogether, victims of long-ago thefts and vandalism. Sandy and Buzz watched us from the corner of the old slave cemetery. Under the bows of a giant oak was an old slate marker etched with the legend, *Annie Laura Gaskins*, and newly carved beneath, *born 1905, died 1934*.

We had placed two large bouquets of lilies on either side of the marker. "We wanted a bigger stone," I told Mama Lucy. "But the commission wouldn't allow it, so we replanted the original."

Russ Draper had twisted arms to get this. But not many. Sandy's oral history project had already paved the way. Thanks to her work it seemed everyone in Eno now knew Annie Laura's name. Russ had simply reiterated that to the ever politically correct Ruffin Strudwick and suggested that it would be unseemly not to see the marker of a martyr to the labor movement returned to its rightful place of honor. Twelve weeks later, here we all were.

"How did you know where it went?" Cameron asked.

"Jake told us where it used to be located," I said. "Of course, we're guessing, based on his description, but I think we're pretty close."

"This is right," Mama Lucy confirmed. "I followed the hearse here and stood right under this tree. But I never come back after that. When

Jake said he used to come here I felt so awful, but at the time I just couldn't do it. I couldn't stand it, Pick."

"Well, you're back now," said Buzz, placing his arm around her. "And so is she."

"It's beautiful," said Mama Lucy. "Thank y'all."

We stood under the oak tree as the breeze swayed the grass in the old cemetery and the scent of honeysuckle and wisteria filled our nostrils, and shared the moment with Mama Lucy.

After a time Mama Lucy said, "Don't take this the wrong way. I appreciate what y'all done, I really do. It's just this grave marker's so small. She deserved better."

Cameron and I exchanged a knowing glance. "Well, we'd best be going or we'll be late."

"Late for what?" asked Mama Lucy. "I thought this was why we got dressed up."

"One more stop," I said, and Buzz and I wheeled her back through the bumpy grass to the car.

The road outside the old Bellevue mill was crowded with cars. Reporters and television camera crews and hundreds of onlookers converged on the site that was now the discreet headquarters of Garden of Eden Enterprises. Everyone was here.

Mama Lucy, taking in the milling throng, said, "What on earth is going on?"

Buzz and I rolled her toward the crowd. "Eno's getting another historic marker, Mama Lucy. One that's long overdue. We're going to dedicate it today and we thought you ought to be here."

"What kind of marker?" she asked.

"For the Eno massacre. They're erecting a monument in memory of those who died." Mama Lucy looked at us with an expression of utter confusion on her face.

"Annie Laura's going to get her gravestone," said Cameron. "The one she deserves."

The new memorial, draped in a white silk dropcloth, sat directly in front of the Eden Enterprises building on the spot where some of the strikers had been shot.

We claimed our chairs in the VIP section, not far from where the president of the University of North Carolina stood talking with Dr. Levin and a coterie of distinguished faculty. Sandy waved to a group of her grad students. There were labor leaders from the national offices of the AFL-CIO and UNITE, the successor to the old TWI. Lisa and Nathan Price, who had spruced up the formerly run-down, overgrown side of his property we were now gazing at, shmoozed and mingled and welcomed them all to Eno. Buzz's Tate Mountain Boys provided bluegrass backup for the occasion.

A seemingly endless parade of people—some friends, some strangers—dropped by to greet Mama Lucy.

"It's your day, Mama Lucy," I whispered to her. "Enjoy it."

"I think I will, Pick," she said. "I think I will."

Wiley whispered something to Mama Lucy, and I saw his eyes grow wide as she pointed to a second-story window less than sixty yards away where deputies and guardsmen had opened up on a crowd similar in size to the one that was gathered here today. He looked up at her with awe and newfound respect. Wiley was especially excited and proud of the role he had played in bringing us here. He was so upset when his great-grandmother first told him about her experience that he'd written a letter to the editor of the weekly *News of Eno* asking why, in a town brimming with historic markers, there was no memorial to the men and women who died at the Bellevue mill.

His letter caught the attention of a lot of people. Russ raised the issue at a meeting of the Historic Eno Commission and opened the matter up for debate. Why, he asked, was there a marker to the six Regulators who died for their political rights but not one for the seven textile workers who died for theirs? Didn't these martyrs too deserve to be recognized?

Hear! Hear! many people said. Others could not concur. There was a lot of resistance in Eno, especially from some of the older political leadership. A permanent reminder of a labor dispute turned ugly did not fit into the Chamber of Commerce's image of Eno as a sweet, historic little town. Not surprisingly, Austin Strudwick led the charge of the naysaying brigade. Not only, he said, would the marker be a blight on the town's reputation as a cradle of liberty, but also it would hurt tourism. Naturally, when Ruffin heard his father was against it, he got behind the cause in a big way, holding a fund-raiser at Sassafras and calling upon state and national literary and arts celebrities to help out. But even as donations poured in, red tape created by the town's Byzantine regulations and zoning permits threatened to overwhelm us. Then Lisa Price called me with an interesting question: Did the monument *have* to be on public property?

I was frankly surprised by her interest and grateful to hear from her, and I told her I didn't know. I just assumed that a public monument had to be situated on public lands. After a brief pause, Lisa said, "Let me talk to Nathan . . ."

And that's how Nathan Price, the Dildo King, founder and CEO of Garden of Eden Enterprises and one of the country's leading manufacturers and distributors of sex toys and marital aids, came not only to donate his land but also his money to the building of a monument dedicated to the memory of the men and women who died in the Eno massacre.

"So this must be Lucy Barlow."

The man offered Mama Lucy his hand. "I think you knew my grandfather, Mrs. Cantrell. I'm Franklin Webb, Spencer Webb's grandson."

After a quick squint, Lucy said, "Lord a mercy, if you don't look just like him. He surely was a handsome man."

He smiled. "Also a journal keeper, if you recall."

"He was always scribblin' in that notebook of his when he was a boy."

"Well, he didn't stop when he was a grown-up," Franklin said. "And recently I came across some of his journals in the family archives. You were mentioned in quite a few, as you might imagine."

Mama Lucy blushed.

"Sandy Murphy filled me in on your relationship and I went through some of the volumes from that period. As it turns out you and your family were discussed a good bit. I believe you were being harassed by the county after the strike, am I right?"

Mama Lucy's face darkened. "They were trying to take my children from me. Said I was an unfit mother. Their daddy was gone looking for work. It was true I couldn't afford to feed 'em. But that was a while after the strike. A year or two."

"I want to apologize to you for that. I'm afraid that my great-grandfather, DeWitt Webb, and the mill superintendent, Bates Strudwick, were behind that mess. It was retribution pure and simple. You were being punished for your role in the strike. My grandfather got wind of it and interceded. The county dropped the case, right?"

"Yessir, when I showed up at the courthouse, they tol' me to go home, that the charges had been dropped. I didn't know why. I just thanked the Lord."

"If you'd only known, you could've thanked my grandfather,"

Franklin said. "It was his doing. He was appalled by the massacre and the company's harassment of you, blacklisting you at work, trying to take your children. When he found out his father ordered the firing of your husband and may have had something to do with your brother's death Spencer confronted him. Told him he was in violation of the president's orders prohibiting blacklisting and retaliating against those who went out on strike and if he didn't call off his thugs he would expose his philandering, his assignations with the colored girls from Cabbagetown, and tell everybody about the one girl who had to get an abortion. That was the final straw in their relationship."

"How did he know about them trying to take my children?" asked Mama Lucy.

"It's all here in these papers," said Franklin. "He kept up with you through someone at the town funeral home."

"Linwood Copeland," Lucy gasped.

"That's the one."

"So he knew about Dave's death," I said. "And that Granddaddy Dalton had been let go from the sheriff's office."

Franklin nodded. "He suspected they might go after your grandmother, and when he heard about the court action he made a special trip down from New York. He knew about his father's illicit activities for years but never played his hand."

"But how did he know about Bessie?" asked Mama Lucy.

"From Samuel Khoury," Franklin said. "Sam told Spencer all about it. It's all in the journals. And I must say my grandfather was a very thorough reporter."

He handed me the photocopies. Altogether, the journal pages that referred to members of my family made up quite a volume. They didn't prove the mill owners orchestrated the Burlington Dynamite Plot, but they did mention Spencer Webb's suspicion that something was up the night of the bombing and how his urging Dalton Cantrell to get Lucy's brother out of the way had led to Dave's arrest. Dalton managed to convince the detectives who apprehended Dave that their actions were all part of a master plan to get rid of the union leaders. When they found out Dalton had hoodwinked them, they were furious. That was the beginning of the end for Dalton at the sheriff's office. From the journal entries it was apparent that the alliance between Spencer and Dalton was a tribute to their devotion to Mama Lucy. I made sure over the next few days, as we read through the journals, that she saw the evidence of my grandfather's love and sacrifice in black and white. Dalton had loved my grandmother, no matter how reticently he may have expressed it to her, or how reluctant she had been to accept it.

We sat in folding chairs listening to the Tate Mountain Boys' lilting versions of tunes like "Union Maid" and "Hard Times Cotton Mill Girl" and some other old mill village ballads. Later I escorted Mama Lucy up to the dais. Perched there in the late morning sun, she positively beamed, enjoying her newfound notoriety.

As I returned to my seat I saw Lisa sitting off to the side, looking lovely and serene in a white spring dress. She had told me that she hated politics and felt no sense of civic responsibility whatsoever and didn't even vote, but this was a cause that felt right and just to her, and best of all, eminently doable. She looked to me like someone who was discovering the pleasures of accomplishment in the public arena for the first time in her life—almost as satisfying for her, I imagined, as getting into the Junior League. Nathan, too, was in high cotton that day, serving a good cause, getting his name and picture in the paper, doing his civic duty and mixing with polite society while maintaining his integrity as an inveterate outsider and cheerful pornographer. He looked like the cat who ate the canary.

My people, the Cantrells, my father and his sisters and assorted cousins, huddled together like water buffalo in a thunderstorm, uncertain what to make of this ceremony and Mama Lucy's new celebrity. Wallace sat in the back with his girlfriend, looking wary and sober, but Jake Satterfield, I noted, was not there.

"How you holding up?" asked Russ.

"Fine, so far," I said, indicating the discreet Garden of Eden logo on the side of the factory. "Now if I can just make it through the day without having to explain to Wiley or Lucy what's being produced inside the old Bellevue mill."

"They always said 'union' was a dirty word," he replied with a mischievous grin.

Dr. Levin introduced me to the university president and his wife, then turned to a young Asian woman they had brought along with them.

"Pick, this is Me Li Khoury from Beijing, China. She just enrolled at the University of North Carolina. She's the great-granddaughter of

Samuel Khoury, from right here in Eno." We shook hands and she smiled shyly and rejoined the university president who introduced her to various community leaders and dignitaries.

"My grandmother knew Sam Khoury," I said to Dr. Levin. "She thought very highly of him. He helped a young friend of hers who was in trouble get safe medical help in Chapel Hill."

"From Dr. Ashendorf. Sam Khoury interned for him."

"How did you know that?" I asked.

"Because so did I." Dr. Levin smiled, his gray eyes twinkling.

When the ceremony finally began, Russ introduced Sandy, who gave a brief history of the uprising and thanked everyone who had helped erect the monument to the seven slain strikers and especially thanked Mama Lucy for allowing the oral history project to tape her testimony so that future generations would know what happened here. Franklin Webb spoke movingly of what happened in Eno and how sad it was that it had remained lost to official recognition for so many decades. He sang the praises of people like my grandmother who toiled and sweated and gave up their working lives to put clothes on our backs, and he concluded with an apology to Mama Lucy for her blacklisting and the harassment she suffered at the hands of his ancestor who set loose the violence and bloodshed that brought us there that day. When he asked her if she would like to say anything, she ducked her head and covered her mouth in a characteristic gesture of shyness, and declined. But just before he turned back to the microphone she called him over and whispered something in his ear. He nodded and returned to the podium and said, "Mrs. Cantrell has something she wants me to say on behalf of her friend who died here. It was the last thing Annie Laura Gaskins said to Mrs. Cantrell before she died in her arms, and Mrs. Cantrell has asked me to repeat it here today. It is one word: *Union*."

A great roar rose up from the crowd, echoing Annie Laura's final word on this earth. Mama Lucy wept. Cameron handed her a handkerchief and Buzz wheeled Mama Lucy over to the monument. Franklin Webb presented her with scissors so she could do the honors. The university president held the ribbon. Mama Lucy cut it. Through the thunderous applause we heard Tate Mountain Boys singing Ella May Wiggins's haunting melody, "Mill Mother's Lament." Their high lonesome tenor-rich harmony lifted over the crowd as the drapery fluttered down and the monument was revealed. Tears streamed down Mama

Lucy's cheeks when Franklin Webb read the names of the slain strikers carved on the face of the monument. The last name on the list was Annie Laura Gaskins, followed by this inscription:

IN MEMORY OF THE ENO SEVEN

They sacrificed their lives for the rights and dignity of working people everywhere. These six men and one woman were killed here on this very ground during the General Textile Strike, September 8, 1934. This monument is dedicated to their memory and to their sacrifice, to their families and to all workers. Let their deaths not have been in vain. Let them never be forgotten. They wove in threads and in blood the fabric that covered our shame. Let us fashion the raiments of our gratitude in stone.

EPILOGUE

By late spring Oaklawn was at the height of its astonishing beauty. Dogwoods, redbuds, and azaleas bloomed in breathtaking profusion, like an exclamation point to our decision to move back home. Tensions had thawed considerably between Cameron and me, although we both were still cautious and wary with each other. For the sake of appearances she had moved back into the bedroom when Mama Lucy came to live with us but Cam and I, fearful of exposing ourselves too soon after everything we'd been through, had studiously avoided intimacy. Neither of us really knew where we stood with each other, or if our feelings would be reciprocated. But the signs were there. My affection rose like nectar in a honeysuckle when sometimes in the evenings I would catch a glimpse of Cameron at her desk going over budgets for a shoot, lost in her thoughts and the challenge of her work, or attending to Mama Lucy in the wing bedroom, telling her how pretty she looked while lovingly, meticulously braiding the old woman's hair, and I would stop and stand there and overflow with love and gratitude and wonder at my wife's grace and beauty. At other times, when watching a movie with Wiley she would slip her hand into mine in an unconscious gesture as warm and comfortable as a mitten. But I think the moment we both knew the rough passage was over was in early May when I surprised Cam on her birthday with an oil on canvas portrait of her and Wiley and Flappy siting on Oaklawn's front porch steps. I had painted her beloved pet standing up on her hind legs, with button eyes shining, head cocked sideways in a pose that used to delight Cameron when we first got the puppy. Cam hugged me with a fierce affection, tears in her eyes, and I could feel the walls between us crumbling.

That night lying in bed in the dark Cameron told me that the affair with Roland Jameson was over. That it was over before it started.

"Did you sleep with him?" I asked.

"No."

"Why not?"

"Simple. I don't love him. I love you."

"Thank God."

"I love you so much it hurts," Cam said. "We have a history together, Pick. It's not always been easy, but it's ours and it's what makes us who we are. It just took me a while to get out of the ice house and come inside."

We lay there in silence for a while until finally Cam said, "I'm sorry I was so hard on Mama Lucy." She rolled to her side so she could look at me. "She knew we were having problems, you know. She's very intuitive. Almost spooky sometimes. She told me no matter how hard it was, to stick it out, to stay together. She talked to me about your mom, Pick, and how close you were to her. And how that was going to make it tough for any woman to have a relationship with you. She said Cantrell men had their faults but they were good men. She said, 'Don't make the mistake I did and give up on 'im.' " Then Cameron leaned over and kissed me tenderly on the cheek.

"I'm glad you took her advice," I said. "Even if I didn't."

"That's why we're together," she whispered, and snuggled up against me, moving the warmth of her body into mine.

Mama Lucy's final gift to me would be reconciliation with the woman I adored. That night, as Cameron and I made love, Mama Lucy died in her sleep.

I built Mama Lucy's coffin the following night. As per her instructions, it was made of pine. Early that morning Buzz and I had loaded my chainsaw on the back of the pickup and, towing the portable sawmill behind, drove down the old carriage path to the banks of the New Hope River, where months before a pine tree had been struck by lightning and was standing dead. The wood was dry. We cut an eight-foot length from the heart of the great tree's trunk, rolled it onto the sawmill, and cut the huge wooden cylinder into slabs which we then hauled back to our makeshift shop in the summer kitchen. There we ripped slabs on a table saw into twelve-inch boards and planed a smooth face on top and bottom. Our woodwork would not win us any prizes at the county fair, but that was hardly the point. As we labored, I thought about what a complex and difficult woman Mama Lucy had been and how only in her final days did I get a real sense of her life and all that she had gone through and how it had shaped the woman we all, in our arrogance and ignorance, thought we knew.

We worked on the coffin most of a day and night and I continued to work on it even after Buzz went home, pondering, as I mounted the hinges and completed our task, my grandmother's curious request for a plain pinewood casket. I remembered a story Mama Lucy once told me about her and Annie Laura—about how when they were girls Annie Laura had been ashamed to attend their school party wearing an old worn-out dress. A few weeks before, Lucy, though just as poor, had inherited a beautiful floral-print dress from her older sister and was excited to wear it. Not wanting to show up Annie Laura, however, she had patched together another dress and worn that, instead, to the party. And it hit me just then that perhaps this—this notion of friendship, solidarity, and love for a woman long dead—was behind Mama Lucy's request for a pine burial box. Maybe she wanted to go to the party again just like Annie Laura.

I reached for the pile of nails resting on the velvet drapes I had taken from Mama Lucy's living room and I thought of the painting of the Last Supper that had hung beside those drapes over the living room couch, and of the words from scripture engraved in a plaque on the frame that read, "This Do in Remembrance of Me." When I was a child I had stared at those words, puzzling over their meaning. I had once asked my mother if the word remembrance meant to re-member, in reference to the way we put Christ's broken body back together by re-membering Him in the sacrament of Holy Communion. My mother had smiled at the time but now I thought maybe there was some truth to my childish question. Memory has a way of doing that, of helping us heal ourselves. Mama Lucy helped us re-member Annie Laura, the little girl who lost her leg in a railroad accident, and her life in a labor dispute. By remembering her we put her back together and keep her whole and present. *Union* was the last word Annie Laura Gaskins uttered in Mama Lucy's arms with her dying breath. It was a word charged with political and economic meaning, but maybe it was also a wish she shared with her friend, an expression of their shared yearning for justice, wholeness, completion.

That night as I put the finishing touches on the casket my grandmother herself had requested I offered up a heartfelt prayer that Mama

Lucy and Annie Laura would now have what they had wished for in life—union at last.

At the visitation, while guests milled around the receiving parlor greeting each other and conversing in hushed whispers, I spotted my aunts Lily and Beth standing in the side vestibule staring at Mama Lucy's corpse in the open pine casket.

I slipped up behind them and said, "Don't you want to drive a wooden stake through her heart to make sure she's gone?" They both blanched, then smiled guiltily as if they'd been caught. I could get away with such irreverence because of my recent role as the family do-gooder.

"It don't seem possible she's really gone," said Lily, her eyes puffy and red from weeping. "I was thinkin' how many times I prayed for Mama Lucy to be dead. And now that it's happened she just looks so small and fragile."

"That's why I put the Styrofoam peanuts in there," I said. "To keep her in place."

Beth punched me, then giggled, and we all hugged each other close.

"You're such a Cantrell," said Lily. "Nothing is sacred."

"Mama Lucy's spawn," I said, but she had my number. There was something about death and trauma that brought out the compulsive comedian in me. It was a defense against the pain, and I'd learned to make a living with it.

Still, I had to admit that Lily was right. Gazing at Mama Lucy's corpse, it was hard to imagine the powerful charismatic spirit that had once animated that tiny frame and intimidated her children so much. In life Mama Lucy had always seemed to be more present and alive somehow than we were, and her absence now left a noticeable void. My father could hardly speak. Later that night when the funeral director allowed the family a final look at the body I stood with Tess and my father and I felt my father's shoulders quake as he gazed for the last time at the woman who had brought him into the world.

Mama Lucy was buried in the old slave cemetery next to Annie Laura. She got her wish. I was surprised at the deference the town paid her, but the unanticipated flood of good publicity received from the monument dedication certainly didn't hurt, and the focus on Mama Lucy and her friendship with Annie Laura had elevated my grandmother to minor celebrity status.

The day of the funeral broke bright and clear. A soft breeze suffused the air with pollen and the scent of wisteria and honeysuckle and freshly mown grass. The passing of the mighty matriarch of the Cantrell clan brought out the entire extended family. Russ presided over the graveside service.

The pallbearers were a motley muster of Lucy's male decendants—Buzz and me, my dad and Wallace, and the recently incarcerated Talbert and Jerry. The chastened Bailey boys were out of jail on work-release after serving ninety days of a reduced sentence for their role in the escape and rampage of Bobby Raiford. My testimony on Talbert's behalf and Talbert's contribution to the apprehension of Raiford by shooting him dead had helped in limiting their jail time. At the funeral Talbert bawled like a baby and it occurred to me what a huge role Mama Lucy had played in his life and how odd it must have been for him to see her dead by natural causes when just a short time ago he had been so close to ending her life by other means.

The crowd included many of the people we'd seen at the monument dedication ceremony. Even Odessa Brown, Bessie Thurwell's niece, was there. Later, as I stood up to deliver the eulogy, I saw Jake Satterfield sitting in the back with Wallace. I was deeply moved and had to struggle to hold myself together as I began the eulogy.

"My grandmother taught me something about memory, loyalty, and forgiveness," I said, "and she gave me more than I can ever say. She taught me something about how to live and just as important, how to die, with dignity and humor and grace. I thank her for my sense of humor and my art. And most of all for my fury. I know now that it was her sense of outrage over the injustices done to her and her family and friends that found its way into my cartoons and sought expression in a born troublemaker's political instincts. It was that abiding satirical rage that saw through sham and hypocrisy, the darkest, fiercest part of myself that rose up every day to champion her and people like her, that was the best part of myself and was a gift from Mama Lucy and I pray that it will live on long after she's gone. I don't know if there's snuff in heaven," I said, concluding on a lighter note, "but her pet cockatiel, Petey, better be waiting there for her. If not, I can promise you the Lord's going to hear about it for all eternity."

Accompanied by Buzz on his banjo, we all sang "Just As I Am," Mama

Lucy's favorite hymn. Then while Russ played "Amazing Grace" on his bagpipes we pallbearers carefully lowered the pine box into the earth and we all stood in solemn solicitude before the open grave beneath the sheltering boughs of the mighty oak tree in the corner of the old slave cemetery on that beautiful spring day in Eno. Russ finished the rousing anthem and offered the prayer of benediction. While he prayed I secretly scanned the crowd of bowed heads, closed eyes, and tear-streaked cheeks under the canopy and spilling out onto the field beyond, taking in one last time the human swirl and backwash of my grand-mother's life as her soul passed like a mighty clipper into the silence of eternity. I lowered my eyes to the tiny slate marker, newly cut, with Mama Lucy's name on it, sunk into the freshly turned red clay right next to Annie Laura's. There, beside it, placed discreetly beneath a spray of flowers was a gift from Bessie Thurwell's niece, a foil-wrapped coconut layer cake, just like Bessie used to make. A sudden breeze stirred me, and lifting my eyes to the bright azure sky, I caught a glimpse, floating on the warm spring thermals, frozen timeless in silhouette, of my old friend the solitary white hawk.

Fall rolled around again and painted Oaklawn with its palette of oranges and scarlets and golds. Following the funeral Cameron and I finished renovating the house and in the process somehow became partners again. Recently we seem to have hit our stride and settled into a satisfy-ing and invigorating routine both at home and at work. A few weeks ago, after the first family reunion without Mama Lucy, we returned to New York for a second honeymoon. We stayed at the Plaza Hotel and finally saw the Broadway show we missed on our ill-fated anniversary the year before, when I beat up my publisher. We visited museums and galleries and ate like royalty at restaurants we had only read about in the society pages and gossip columns. Cameron caught up with friends and neigh-bors and shopped on Madison Avenue and in SoHo for antiques to fur-nish Oaklawn, and I met with Will LeGette, a friend of Sandy Murphy's, and the newly appointed editor-in-chief of Perkins Publishing. Will was a tall and courtly North Carolinian with a soft voice, pleasant manner, and genteel bearing—a rare combination of New York street-smart savvy and gracious southerner, pure cashmere—and I liked him immedi-ately. His grandfather had been the editor of the *Charlotte Sentinel* years before I worked there and had covered the strike in Gastonia in 'twenty-nine and was beaten nearly to death by company thugs. Will had seen the drawings I did for Sandy's book, and knew about my fiery grandmother. He was fascinated by the period and wanted to do a book on it and thought I was just the man for the job. The book would be both historical and personal. He wanted me to recount my relationship with Mama Lucy and her role in the uprising of 'thirty-four in drawings, to fashion in word and image a memoir of Mama Lucy's life, and he offered me a generous advance to let him publish it. I liked the idea and told him I'd get back to him. I didn't have to think about it very long. When I called him a week later and accepted the project he was delighted. Cameron marked the occasion by inviting over all my favorite people—Russ, Buzz, Sandy—for an impromptu celebration.

Now that I'm working on the book, Cameron has cut back her hours at Oleander so she can spend more time at home with Wiley and me. Each morning after breakfast I crutch out to my studio in the converted summer kitchen and, situated at the drafting table Cameron gave me for Christmas and surrounded by countless pen-and-ink sketches, I tell the story of Mama Lucy.

My workspace is clean and spare, just as I like it. Tacked to the corkboard above my drawing table is a postcard from Buzz I received yesterday with a D.C. postmark and a picture of the proposed new FDR Memorial on the front. Sandy and Buzz's friendship had blossomed into something more over the summer and she asked him to escort her to a White House ceremony where she was being honored by the president with a National Humanities Medal for her work with the Southern Oral History project.

The president had praised both her work and her character. And in a postscript Buzz announced that he had asked Sandy to marry him and she had accepted. He wanted me to be the best man.

My grandmother had few material possessions but the legacy she left us is rich beyond measure. Her effects were divided among her surviving children and grandchildren. The house went to Buzz. My father and aunts divided the furniture. Talbert and Jerry got her television set and the framed print of the Last Supper. Wallace, who now works for

Nathan Price as a shipping foreman at Eden Enterprises, got the bulk of her savings, which turned out to be considerable. Mama Lucy left me the clock. It now sits on the mantelpiece, ticking away, a metronome of memory reminding me of Mama Lucy and all the things she taught me about her life and mine, the tragic dimension of experience and the terrible inexorability of time.

The clock struck three times, signaling the end of my workday. I added one final touch to my sketch of Mama Lucy and set the page aside. I wound the clock with the old copper key and turned to leave.

Cameron, dressed in biking togs and a T-shirt, stepped inside and said, "Ready?" Recently, partly for fun, partly to rehabilitate my knee, we have been riding bikes in the late afternoons. We approach our outings with eagerness and anticipation. I closed up my studio and changed into my riding gear while Cameron retrieved the bicycles from the ice house.

Our route takes us through town and the West End, where Mama Lucy grew up, and out to the old state highway that winds westward through Eno county toward Alamance and Burlington. We ride for close to two hours. On our return trip we stop at Chicken Bridge and gaze at the glorious fall colors, veins of blood and gold that spill down the hillsides to the banks of the New Hope River. The trees are on fire, their glory flashing and dancing in the swift waters below. We cross the bridge frequently now on our rides through the countryside. It has become a touchstone to us, a welcoming reminder to two weary wanderers that we're almost home. We stand hand in hand in the center of the bridge, taking in the breathtaking panorama. New Hope Mountain rises, sundappled and majestic, in the near distance. Although Panther's Den is not visible from the bridge, I know it's up there. Soon, perhaps this spring when the mountain laurel is in bloom and my knee is stronger, I plan to take Cameron up there. Maybe we will even carve our initials into the rock.

Later that afternoon Wiley and I toss the football on the front lawn while Cameron makes dinner. We eat on the porch, enjoying the languid evening and the comfort of each other's company. After dinner we walk Wiley to school, where his teacher is hosting a birthday party for Carla, the little girl in Wiley's class whose mother died and who lives in a trailer with her father. Her family is dirt poor, and she would have had no party at all if her classmates and teacher hadn't thrown one for her.

After dropping Wiley, Cam and I stroll, hand in hand back through the meadow. We arrive at Oaklawn shortly before sunset. I sit on the porch and a few minutes later Cam comes out carrying a tumbler of ice-cold sweet tea. She uses Mama Lucy's coveted recipe, and she makes the tea perfectly. An emerald green mint sprig from the herb garden beside the old ice house clings to the side of the perspiring glass. We sit side by side in the porch swing on the front porch gallery in the copper-lit September twilight and watch the sun slip behind the trees and the last fireflies of summer rise out of the lawn like dancing spirits.

We rock and sip Mama Lucy's sweet tea and talk about everything that has happened over the past year, about the resilience of our lives and how grateful we are to have weathered our personal storms and seen a better day. We laugh easily, and tease each other, and later, as the harvest moon lifts into the dark limitless sky, Russ's bagpipes and a chorus of katydids serenade us with "Amazing Grace."

"Yknow, Pick, we're really lucky," Cam says. "A lot of couples don't survive what we've been through."

"I know. It's all so fragile."

"That poor little girl lost her mother. She seems like such a sweet kid."

"Yeah, it'll be real sweet when she gets pregnant by our son."

"Pick," Cameron laughs, "they're only eight years old."

"Yeah, but she has her eye on him already," I continue, parodying our concern of last Thanksgiving.

"It is odd, though, isn't it, the way the world works?"

"Yeah, here's Wiley growing up in the big house. Come high school, he's going to be the catch of Eno for all those little linthead girls." I glance over at Cam's lovely profile and see that she's smiling at my little joke. I smile, too, thinking how blessed I am indeed to be married to such a strong woman with such a great sense of humor, yet so fierce in defending the battlements of civilization, who refuses to give up ground so hard won, who frets over such things on behalf of our son who's too young to know all the dangers and snares awaiting him out there, but is lucky enough to have a mother who does.

"Y'know, Pick," Cameron says, sipping her tea and indulging my playfulness. "I hear what you're saying." She sighs and looks out over all that we share together, then turns to me with a look of infinite understanding in her eyes. "But I can't help it. Somewhere deep down inside, there's a part of me now that's pulling for that little linthead girl."

I take her hand and give it a gentle squeeze. "Me, too," I say. "Me, too."

A NOTE ABOUT *THE BRIDGE*

Although a work of fiction, many of the events in *The Bridge* are based on true stories.

There was a massacre of strikers similar to the one depicted in the novel that took place at Honea Path, South Carolina, during the general textile strike of 1934. Twenty people were wounded and six were killed. Sixty years later, a memorial was erected honoring those who died.

My grandmother, Grace Pickard, was bayonetted by a National Guardsman at the Pioneer plant in Burlington, North Carolina, during the uprising of '34. Her sister was put on a wagon and paraded around town by the sheriff.

The Burlington dynamite case was an actual incident that led to the imprisonment of union leaders and became a cause célèbre among students, intellectuals, and humanitarians, including the great North Carolinians Paul Green and Dr. Frank Porter Graham, the historian C. Vann Woodward, then a UNC grad student, and socialist Norman Thomas.

My great-uncle, Walt Pickard, Grace's brother, was a union organizer in Burlington and wrote a pamphlet blasting the frame-up called the "Burlington Dynamite Plot," which was published by the *Labor Defender* in New York and from which I have freely quoted.

I have consulted with Jaquelyn Dowd Hall of the Southern Oral History Program at the University of North Carolina, Chapel Hill, and used her and her colleagues' book, *Like a Family*, as an invaluable resource. The collective amnesia I refer to in the book is documented vividly in the George Stoney and Judith Helfand film *The Uprising of '34*.

The events described in Gastonia 1929, the killing of Sheriff Aderholt and the balladeer Ella May Wiggins actually happened and my grandfather, Robert Earl Marlette, did indeed survey the railroads in Gastonia and worked as a deputy sheriff in Hillsborough, North Carolina, where he met his wife, Gracie, working in the textile mills. I live in Hillsborough today.

And to all the people who ever worked in the cotton mills, whose labor put the clothes on our backs, hose on our feet, and linens in our closets, I salute you.

ACKNOWLEDGMENTS

With deepest gratitude to:

Will Blythe, who first encouraged me to write. Sarah Flynn, first editor, for her compassion and care, and David Prosten, first reader. Esther Newberg, simply the best. David Hirshey, extraordinary editor and first-rate wit. Carolyn Marino, whose keen editorial eye cleared the underbrush and kept me focused. Jeff Kellogg, whose editorial artistry, vision and dogged professionalism keep the spirit of Maxwell Perkins alive. Erica Johanson, Richard Klin, Patti Kelly, Marie Elena Martinez, Christine Caruso, Bob Spizer, Josh Marwell, Eric Svenson, and all the fine folks at HarperCollins. Wendell Minor, fellow artist, with thanks for Chicken Bridge.

Pat Conroy, word-warrior, spellbinder, whose friendship, loyalty, passion, and boundless generosity have sustained and inspired for years. Dr. William and Gloria Blythe, for their wise counsel and kindness. Peter Walsh whose friendship and knowledge were indispensable. Laura Baldwin, for her infinite knowledge of indigenous flora. Jay and Laura Ladd for their friendship and generosity.

Jacquelyn Dowd Hall at the Southern Oral History Program at the University of North Carolina, Chapel Hill and to her colleagues, James Leloudis, Robert Korstad, Mary Murphy, Lu Ann Jones and Christopher B. Daly, for their seminal and indispensible volume, *Like a Family: The Making of a Southern Cotton Mill World*, where I first read my grandmother's name in print. George Stoney and Judy Helfand's film, *The Uprising of '34*, John Salmond's invaluable *Gastonia '29, The Story of the Loray Mill Strike*, and his article in the North Carolina Historical Review, October 1998, "The Burlington Dynamite Plot: The 1934 Textile Strike and Its Aftermath, in Burlington, North Carolina." And Carolyn E. Norris and her article, "The Eno Mill Village," in the *Hillsborough Historical Society Journal*, Vol. 2, No. 1, July 1999 for details of mill life in Hillsborough. Patrick Huber for mill-tune lyrics.

Tim Pyatt, Director of the Southern Historical Collection at the Wilson Library, University of North Carolina at Chapel Hill, Richard Shrader, John White, Rachel Canada, and Amy Davis for mill-tune recordings and Alice Cotton, Harry McKown, and Bob Anthony at the North Carolina Collection. Dick and Meredith Spangler for their stories, and Jim Peacock, Bill Friday, Bill Powell, Larry Koestler, Jim Hevia and

Jim Bryan for their research help. L— stories here and her Hoover Library p—

Michael Chitwood, whose book of p— —spired, and Ron Rash, whose story behind his poem "Accident" was borrowed with permission from his dazzling volume *Eureka Mill*.

The late great Broadway director Mike Ockrent, whose brilliant dramaturgical instincts made me see my story whole for the first time and his amazingly talented wife Susan Stroman, director, choreographer, gracious hostess.

Alice Eakes, sixth grade teacher, who taught me how to diagram sentences and Mr. May, seventh grade teacher, who read *Treasure Island* and *Les Misérables* in class out loud.

Billie Moore Marlette, my mother, who encouraged my art, in loving memory, and Elmer Monroe Marlette, my father, whose life and courage I stand in awe of, and all his sisters, Barbara, Brenda, Dorothy, Beverly, Anne, Virginia, and his brother Earl, Jr.

Robert Earl Marlette, my grandfather, Gracie's husband, and Walt Pickard, my great-uncle, Gracie's brother. Dave Stewart, who first handed me his granddaddy Walt's *Burlington Dynamite Plot* pamphlet. Eunice Dawkins, E.B. Stanfield, Stan Starr, Earl Brogden, John Rokita, Ron Skipper, Teresa Skipper, and all my uncles and aunts and cousins for their stories of Mama Gracie. Gordon, Francis, and all the Sweet Potato and Day-Lily Marlettes. Mike Aldridge and the Bass Mountain Boys for their sweet music. Chris, Peggy, Kristen and Andy Marlette, for his research, Marianne and Terry Neal, Will Kiker, and Marie Marlette. Jack and Pat Hartley, in loving memory. Sandy, Patricia, and Devon Flood, Martha, Reed, Caroline and Lindsey Cole, who went with me to Honea Path. John, Jillian, and Shana Hartley, David, Sharon, Blake, and Lydia Hartley, Meg and Eric Buchanan.

Thanks to Erica Berger for her fabulous photos, and to all those who have patiently listened to me talk about this book over the years: Dr. Vascue and Barbara Brown, Joe Radovanic, Rusty Unger, Katharine Walton, Mark and Kay Ethridge, Bill and Lynne Kovach, Linda Healy, Joe and Victoria Klein, David Apatoff, Nell Minow, Benjamin and Rachel, Patty Marx, Sandra Conroy, John Shelton Reed, Dale Volberg Reed, Ted Teague, M.C. Carpenter, Don Schlitz, Blair Brown, Barbara and Bob Ascher, Anita Finch, Susan Raines, Jim Duffy, Rick Bragg, Alex Jones, Susan Tifft, Helen Whitney, Bill and Jean Anne Leuchtenburg, John and Ann Sanders, Mark and Linda DeCastrique, Bob and Linda Newcomb, Kaye Gibbons, Frank Ward, Susan Cody, John and Grace Jean Roberts, Lanier Laney, Terry Sweeney, Adam Cohen, Judy Goldman, Nancy Tuttle May, Tim and Carol McLaurin, Clyde Edgerton, Janet Peterson, Fetzer Mills, Lucille Dula, Anita Finch, Cynthia Stuart, Dannye Romine Powell, Lew Powell, Bland Simpson, Jake Mills, Ellis Henican, Joe Dolman, Adrian Peracchio, Bill Reel, Claudette Leandro. And hats off to all my *New York Newsday* friends and colleagues.